Purple Honors

A Chronicle of Thyatira

A Chronicle of Thyatira

HEARTBEATS OF COURAGE

Book Three

Purple Honors

A Chronicle of Thyatira

By
David Phillips

Century One Chronicles
Toronto, Ontario, Canada

A Chronicle of Thyatira

.

PURPLE HONORS: A CHRONICLE OF THYATIRA
HEARTBEATS OF COURAGE, BOOK THREE

Canadian Intellectual Property Office CIPO Registration Number:
1152518

Paperback   ISBN 978-1-9994752-4-6
E-Book ISBN 978-1-9994752-5-3

The stories in this book are fictional. Some personages are based on historical fact; these are indicated in the list of characters, but resemblance to persons alive or dead is coincidental and unintended.

For Jennifer, Barry, and David

For those who
have experienced prejudice,
violence, human trafficking,
and great loss
and those who
come alongside with love,
care, and creative compassion
to find the means for helping others
discover their true value as human beings.

Heartbeats of Courage

Book 1: Through the Fire: A Chronicle of Pergamum
AD 89–91

Book 2: Never Enough Gold: A Chronicle of Sardis
AD 91–92

Book 3: Purple Honors: A Chronicle of Thyatira
AD 92–93

Book 4: The Inn of the Open Door: A Chronicle of Philadelphia
AD 93–96

Book 5: Rich Me! A Chronicle of Laodicea
AD 96–97

Book 6: Fortress Shadows: A Chronicle of Smyrna
AD 97–111

Book 7: An Act of Grace: A Chronicle of Ephesus
AD 111

The Songs of Miriam: A Collection of Miriam's Songs

Prologue

The ancient city of Thyatira in Western Turkey, now known as Akhisar, was a rich prize fought over for decades by rulers from the Kingdom of Pergamum to the west and the royalty of Antioch to the east. In the first century, this city, with about one hundred thousand people, was a manufacturing center specializing in metals, clothing, and ceramics. Its products were exported throughout the Roman world. Purple cloth, sold to wealthy Greek and Roman officials, brought riches to the members of a dyers' guild called the Guild of Purple Honors. The city was famous for metal products produced by guilds. Slaves stoked furnaces, and apprentices mixed copper and tin to produce bronze metal cast into various polished and burnished gold-colored products.

There were dozens of other guilds, but cloth weaving, cloth dyeing, and metals were the three that brought the most commercial activity into the city. Though only a few families directly enjoyed the wealth, all citizens, both free and slaves, looked forward to the annual festival days when their guild celebrated its particular patron god or goddess in a city-wide celebration.

This social situation demanded compromise and complicated the lives of early believers in Jesus Christ. They sought to find a balance between their high moral and ethical standards and the ingrained patterns of the society in which they lived.

> To the angel of the church in Thyatira write: These are the words of the Son of God, whose eyes are like blazing fire and whose feet are like burnished bronze. I know your deeds, your love and faith, your service and perseverance, and that you are now doing more than you did at first. Nevertheless, I have this against you…
>
> Revelation 2:18–20

Characters in *Purple Honors*
* Indicates historical figures
Major personages are noted in bold

Emperor
Domitian, 42*, Emperor of the Roman Empire: AD 81–96

Governors
Publius Calvisius Ruso, 42*, Governor of Asia: AD 92–93

Decebalus, 62*, King of Dacia (Romania, Moldova), enemy of Domitian and Rome

In Pergamum
Lydia-Naq Milon, 57, High priestess of the Altar of Zeus

Zoticos-Naq Milon, 43, Chief Librarian in the Library of Pergamum; brother of Lydia

Cassius Flamininus Maro, 42, Commander in the Garrison of Pergamum

Marcos Pompeius, 38, Lawyer; leader of the House of Prayer
Marcella Aculiana, 38, Wife of Marcos
   Florbella Pompeius, 10, Daughter of Marcos and Marcella

Trifane, 26, Mother of Chrysa Grace

In Soma and Olive Grove Farm
Servius Callistratus, 31, Commander in the Garrison of Soma

Anthony Suros, 38, Legionary from Legion XXI, the Predators; married to Miriam

Omerod, 35; **Menandro**, 28; **Sextilius**, 42; **Bellinus**, 28; **Capito**, 30: Five soldiers in Anthony's squad

Farmers – Brothers and wives working at Olive Grove Farm
Nikias, 35, and Penelope, 34, Parents of four children
Nikias's brothers and wives:
   Zeno, 33, and Naian, 31
   Alberto, 29, and Thyra, 30
   Lykaios, 27, and Zenia, 26
   Kozma, 24, and Leta, 25

In Thyatira

Gaius Julius Aurelius Tatianos, 42, Mayor of Thyatira; member of the aristocracy

Fabius Bassos, 39, Benefactor of the city; wealthy businessman; responsible for paying for the Games

Kilan, 40, Assistant to the rabbi in Thyatira

Miriam Bat Johanan, 27, Antipas Ben Shelah's granddaughter; wife of Anthony Suros

Chrysa Grace Suros, 1, Anthony and Miriam's daughter

Jonathan Ben Shelah, 52, Businessman in Thyatira
Rebekah Bat Azgad, 50, Married to Jonathan
Adin Ben Shelah, Eldest son, died in Alexandria
Obed Ben Shelah, Second son, died in Alexandria
Jehiel Ben Shelah, Third son, died in Alexandria
Bani, 23, and **Serah**, 20, Son and daughter-in-law
Gil, 19, and **Danila**, 19, Son and daughter-in-law

Jarib Ben Hagaba, 48, Jonathan's steward
Shiri, 49, Jarib's wife
Jodan, 21, Jarib and Shiri's eldest son
Gedalya, 20, Jarib and Shiri's younger son

Slave

Arte (or Artemedian), 45, A slave from Scythia (Crimea)

Workers in the Guilds

Sibyl Sambathe, 25, Saleswoman in the Guild of Purple Honors; cousin to Lydia of Philippi

Hulda Sambathe, 28, Sister to Sibyl

Melpone, 28, Worker at the Guild of Purple Honors

Adelpha, Dreama, Hesper, Koren, Calandra, Neoma, Celina, and Hypatia: Young women workers in the Guild of Purple Honors

Ateas, 23, and **Arpoxa**, 22, Former Scythian slaves

Saulius, 2, Ateas and Arpoxa's son

In Sardis

Felicior Priscus, 38, Commanding officer at Garrison of Sardis

Diotrephes Milon, 30, Son of Lydia-Naq Milon; Head of the History Department at the Sardis Gymnasium

Alexina, 49, Widow in Sardis who takes in boarders

Diodotus, 40, Manager of the Bank of Hermus

Delbin, 36, Wealthy woman in Sardis; wife of Diodotus

In and near Aizanoi

Diogenes Elpis, 37, Commanding officer at the Garrison of Aizanoi

Fenius, 28, Captured slave; father of seven children

Rebels and Robbers in "The Faithful," a rebel gang

Mithrida, 38, Army deserter; Real name: Flavius Memucan Parshandatha

Sexta, 41, Army deserter; Real name: Sesba Bartacus Sheshbazzar

Craga, 34, Army deserter; Real name: Claudius Carshena Datis

Other rebels:
Taba, Maza, Harpa, Baga, Ota, Arta, Tissa, Tira, and **Spithra**

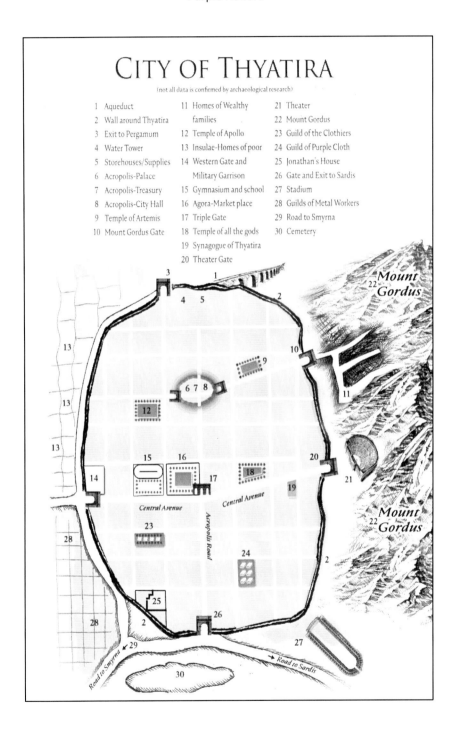

CITY OF THYATIRA

(not all data is confirmed by archaeological research)

1 Aqueduct
2 Wall around Thyatira
3 Exit to Pergamum
4 Water Tower
5 Storehouses/Supplies
6 Acropolis-Palace
7 Acropolis-Treasury
8 Acropolis-City Hall
9 Temple of Artemis
10 Mount Gordus Gate

11 Homes of Wealthy
   families
12 Temple of Apollo
13 Insulae-Homes of poor
14 Western Gate and
   Military Garrison
15 Gymnasium and school
16 Agora-Market place
17 Triple Gate
18 Temple of all the gods
19 Synagogue of Thyatira
20 Theater Gate

21 Theater
22 Mount Gordus
23 Guild of the Clothiers
24 Guild of Purple Cloth
25 Jonathan's House
26 Gate and Exit to Sardis
27 Stadium
28 Guilds of Metal Workers
29 Road to Smyrna
30 Cemetery

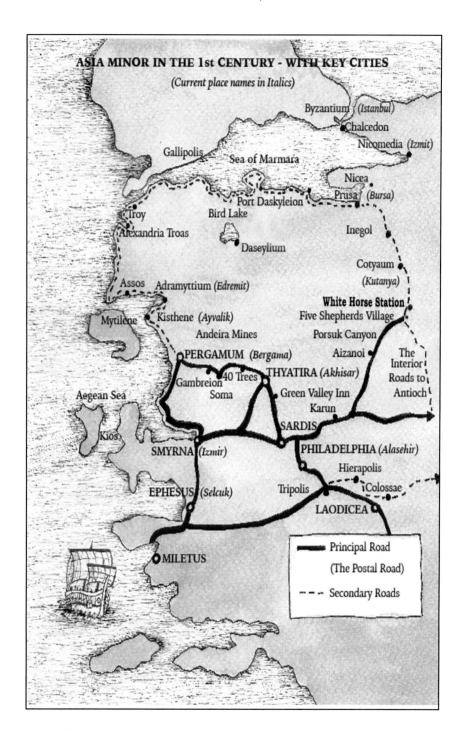

The Ben Shelah family

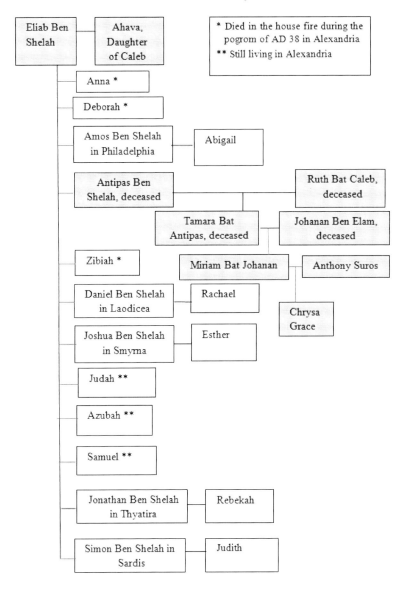

Eliab Ben Shelah — Ahava, Daughter of Caleb

* Died in the house fire during the pogrom of AD 38 in Alexandria
** Still living in Alexandria

Anna *

Deborah *

Amos Ben Shelah in Philadelphia — Abigail

Antipas Ben Shelah, deceased — Ruth Bat Caleb, deceased

Tamara Bat Antipas, deceased — Johanan Ben Elam, deceased

Zibiah *

Miriam Bat Johanan — Anthony Suros

Daniel Ben Shelah in Laodicea — Rachael

Chrysa Grace

Joshua Ben Shelah in Smyrna — Esther

Judah **

Azubah **

Samuel **

Jonathan Ben Shelah in Thyatira — Rebekah

Simon Ben Shelah in Sardis — Judith

Jonathan Ben Shelah and Rebecca Bat Azgad Family in Thyatira

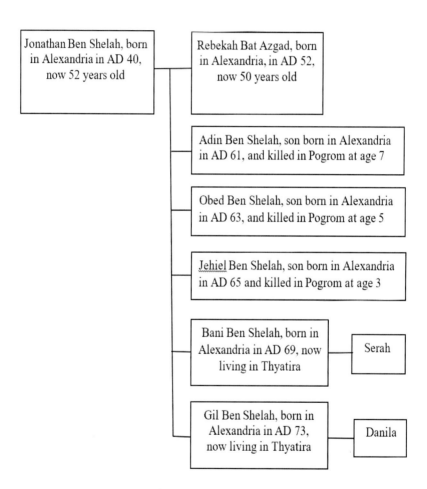

Purple Honors

Part 1
Guilds and Gods

June
AD 92

Chapter 1
An Unwelcome Welcome

THE OFFICE OF COMMANDER SERVIUS CALLISTRATUS, SOMA

Servius Callistratus, the commanding officer of the Garrison of Soma, leaned forward, one hand half forming a fist. Late afternoon shadows darkened the small, stuffy military office where Commander Servius interviewed six road-weary Roman soldiers.

He stared in disbelief as Anthony, the leader, finished telling how the leader of a band of robbers had escaped a year ago.

Servius bent forward as if to better convey his irritation with the newly arrived soldier. A sneer framed his face, expressing his outrage. "Suros, you are supposed to be an experienced scout! But actually, you are disgraced! How shameful!"

The legionary being addressed was Anthony Suros, a veteran of many wars in Upper Germanica. The muscular soldier repeatedly blinked at the harsh words, and he reached his hand up to touch his right cheek. A long scar indicated a harrowing encounter, but Anthony never talked with anyone about how he came to survive that painful encounter.

Red faced and with his eyes blazing, Servius Callistratus turned from the other five soldiers in the room to address Anthony. His tightened jaw expressed disbelief.

"You were leading twenty others, and still you let him get away…running down the mountain into Sardis! That escape showed your complete incompetence! Commander Felicior wrote me saying that there was a problem during the gang's capture, but I did not know it was this bad. I am glad you gave me the details. It will help me to know how to deal with you."

Anthony looked straight ahead. He dropped his hand to his side, and his face was blank. He suspected from this display that Servius, who had a slight build and was shorter than most commanders, felt insecure and needed to impose his will.

"We caught eight of the nine thieves. All were punished, sir."

"But their leader!" Servius stopped to glance at a name on the scroll in his hand. "Taba escaped!"

The tone of the officer's voice conveyed his expectation of strict conformance. The six legionaries could expect no tolerance if they failed in their new assignment in searching for outlaws, smugglers of slaves, and murderers.

Servius pulled a chair away from his desk, sat, and spoke to the five other soldiers: Omerod, Menandro, Sextilius, Bellinus, and Capito. "There must be some reason why Commander Felicior ordered Anthony to be your leader, but I have yet to find it."

He turned back to Anthony. "Suros, what happened to the scouts you trained for the war? Part of Commander Felicior's note to me says that the scouts you trained were surrounded and killed by troops loyal to King Decebalus! You let a criminal escape, and the scouts you trained failed miserably! Do you have anything positive to say for yourself?"

Anthony clenched his hands before answering. "Sir, three days ago, I learned from an army dispatch that the scouts we trained died. They were with five thousand other soldiers. Our army engaged the Dacian army. Unfortunately, Legion XXI, the Predators, is no more. I know that Emperor Domitian is greatly distressed by the news, as we all are."[1]

Anthony knew his reputation was being severely tarnished by Servius's accusation, and a trickle of sweat dripped down his back.

"Inexcusable! And as a reward for your ineptitude, Commander Felicior has named you the leader of a special squad? I really don't understand, but perhaps you will have success this time.

"Two bodies were discovered near Cotyaum, prompting Commander Diogenes Elpis in Aizanoi to believe a gang is operating along the Interior Road. The murdered men were slave merchants, and their slaves disappeared without a trace. The criminals are to be brought to justice. Commander Felicior called the six of you together to work under my direction."

Before answering, Anthony glanced out of the window, where

---

[1] Emperor Domitian sent Legion XXI, the Predators, against Dacia in AD 91 or 92, but it was wiped out. All legionaries were killed in action. Dacia, eventually conquered between AD 101 and 105, was a large kingdom, covering present-day Romania and Moldova and smaller portions of Bulgaria, Serbia, Hungry, Poland, Slovakia, and Ukraine.

the afternoon sunlight cast shadows. He knew that he was not the failure that Commander Servius was suggesting.

Breathing deeply so that he could control his thoughts, he winced. *What I don't know, Commander, is how long this assignment will keep me away from Miriam and my little daughter. I do know that I owe no apologies for my actions.*

Anthony held his head high. "May I give you some relevant details, sir? Here is what we know as we begin our search for the criminals."

"Yes, speak."

"The leader of the gang is named Taba. Before his escape last year, he confided in Little Lion, a young army recruit. Little Lion cleverly wormed his way into their gang and learned that Taba was enlisting more rebels. Commander Felicior believes that they are carrying on an illegal trade in slaves, so he assigned us to find Taba and all those working with him."

Servius spoke rapidly, a bitter note sounding in his words. "There will be no excuse for failing to capture this enemy, Taba!" Examining each member of the squad before him, Servius handed Anthony a scroll.

The commander stood at attention to end the meeting. "Caesar is lord and god!"

The soldiers repeated the words, but when Anthony came to the words "and god," he held his hand to his mouth and coughed.

Servius glared at the legionary with a red scar. He noted that detail. The scarred soldier had not repeated all the words.

A week before, Commander Servius had been slightly drunk in Soma's largest tavern, where he had consumed too much cheap beer. Talking too much, he cursed his bad luck at being assigned to Soma, a small but strategic garrison halfway between Pergamum and Thyatira. The valley narrowed here, so Soma was a crucial point on the road between the coastal cities and the interior.

Servius had boasted, "I'm a capable officer, and I can handle the toughest assignments. It's a shame that nothing challenging could ever happen here in this insignificant place!"

In this squad of six soldiers lay his opportunity for advancement and prestige. His was an insignificant garrison, but he knew his talents were equal to any commander in the larger cities. He longed for greater responsibility.

Servius saw this as an event allowing him to move up. Word had it that Commander Felicior in Sardis was going to be promoted to a southern city within a year, perhaps to Miletus.

Leading a successful operation against bandits on the Postal Road might finally bring the needed recognition of his abilities to headquarters and improve his chance of getting the Sardis assignment. Then, after two years in Sardis, he could be recognized more widely. His persistent dream of an assignment in Rome might be within reach!

Before permitting the six legionaries to leave, Servius wondered if Anthony deliberately did not complete the oath. Was the man with the scar on his face disloyal as well as incompetent?

In his opinion, the squad leader might prove to be a bigger problem than he first thought.

"You are dismissed," he said, and the six members of the newly formed squad left his office.

ON THE ROAD FROM APOLLONIUS TO THYATIRA

While Anthony was encountering hostility from Commander Servius, Miriam, his wife, was riding on the back of a vegetable cart heading for Thyatira. The young woman with a smooth forehead, black hair, and clear olive skin had left Apollonius,[2] the "City of Honey," early in the morning. Nearing Thyatira, the manufacturing city, the cart bounced on a cracked paving stone. She reached out a hand to balance herself and her one-year-old daughter lest they both slip and fall. Her lips quivered, as they often did, whether from either excitement, joy, or anticipation.

It was early-afternoon, many hours since she waved goodbye to her husband. The tantalizing scents of fruits and vegetables filled the wagon between her and the driver. She realized she felt hungry, having spent hours since the early morning breakfast at Apollonius.

Miriam looked again at the vegetables and fruits. Boxes held melons, cherries, almonds, apples, peaches, figs, apricots, and vegetables too: celery, green beans, mint, cabbage, artichokes, lettuce, radishes, spinach, cucumbers, and herbs.

Tears in her eyes indicated sorrow and disappointment. She did not want to be separated again so soon after her marriage from

---

[2] Ancient Apollonius is known today as Ballica, or "Place of Honey." The distance from Ballica to Thyatira, modern Akhisar, is 9 miles (15 km).

Anthony, the soldier she had married. He had been given a new assignment that would cause an extended absence.

Once more, the heavily laden wagon jolted on the uneven paving stones of the Roman road. "It's a rough ride," called the wagon driver as he turned his head to the back of the wagon. "The road to Thyatira always needs repairs! But of course, no one cares enough to do the job. As a result, we all suffer."

The young mother grimaced, holding her one-and-a-half-year-old daughter, Grace, with one hand. Miriam clutched the wagon with the other while the little girl giggled, unaware of danger. "She thinks it's fun, but I'm petrified!" said Miriam to one of the two women riding with her.

Passing Grace to one of the two sisters, Miriam rearranged herself. Happy to have a more comfortable position, her lips relaxed. Taking Grace back on her knee, she strained her head to see how much farther they had to go before arriving in Thyatira.

Jonathan Ben Shelah, Miriam's uncle, lived in Thyatira, and he was expecting her to arrive by mid-afternoon. She tried to relax but could not. With her stomach churning, she mentally composed a letter, wishing she could write it and send it to Anthony.

June 18, in the 11th year of Domitian
From: Miriam
To: Anthony, my beloved husband

I already miss you. One year and two months ago, we were married. Our time in Sardis went by too quickly. Last year you were away so much of the time instructing army recruits at the training camp. Oh, Anthony, I love you so. How will I stand it not knowing where you are? When will I see you again?

The task of keeping Grace safe and happy kept the young women busy. The little girl was passed back and forth between the sisters. The driver was their brother. They came from a family of sharecroppers whose task was to take produce to the farm owner in the city.

Halfway to Thyatira, an enterprising farmer had opened a small roadside stand with simple food for travelers. Miriam had the driver stop so that they could take a break from the heat and the grueling vibration of the wagon. She bought hot flatbread made by the farmer's wife and some soft cheese to share with the driver and his sisters. As they sat in the shade together, one of the sisters asked about Miriam's husband, and she told them he was a soldier.

"Your husband is a soldier! How exciting!" said the older sister.

"What's his assignment?" her sister asked.

"He was recently assigned to a task of keeping people safe on the Postal Road."

The peasant women were satisfied with Miriam's simple reply. She realized that in future conversations, this would be her straightforward answer about Anthony's difficult task.

"Where are you from? You have a different accent."

Miriam answered, "I was born in Alexandria, Egypt, but moved to Judea when I was a small girl. We lived in Jerusalem, but then the Romans attacked the city. Many died there during the Roman siege. My father died as we were fleeing Jerusalem. Soldiers were all around the city. My mother died a year later."

The older sister frowned. "What a sad story! Why are you going to Thyatira?"

"I'll be staying with my uncle and his family."

"Lucky! You are better off than we are. If you are going to be with a family who lives inside the walls, that means the family has lots of money!"

"We are a poor family," added the younger sister, "with endless debts. We will never pay them off. Daddy wants to buy a farm, but how will we ever pay off Fabius Bassos? We owe him lots."

"Who is Fabius Bassos? Why do you owe him?" Miriam asked.

"None of us will ever get rich. Bassos owns most of the farms in our area. During the year, farmers produce vegetables, lemons, oranges, pomegranates, nuts, Egyptian corn, lentils, wheat, oats, grapes, and pears. When they are harvested, all of those will be unloaded at the warehouse owned by Fabius Bassos. From that, we earn barely enough to pay the rent and have what produce we need to live on. There's never any extra money."

"So Bassos doesn't pay a proper wage?" asked Miriam.

"Fabius Bassos paying anyone?" The two sisters and their brother chuckled at the thought. "Landowners like him only want their crop share for the rent. Speaking of which, we need to get back on the road. We must get to the warehouse before it closes."

They could not afford any luxuries, and a tone of sadness ran through their laughter as they continued down the bumpy road.

As they got closer to the city, more and more people trudged alongside the roadway as the wagon passed by. Most waved and yelled, "It's almost festival time!"

The driver and the two young women waved back and called in delight, "Yes, and we'll be there for the big event!"

"In three days, people will commemorate the longest day of the year," the older sister explained. "It's my favorite festival day."

Miriam turned. The city was visible on the horizon now. Ahead, she could just make out the main gate in the city wall.

Chapter 2
Commander Felicior's Squad

THE GARRISON OF SOMA, ASIA MINOR

Looking at each member of the squad before him, Servius handed Anthony a scroll he had prepared. "Here is your commission to begin this operation. Prepare your horses and supplies for a long trip. You will start the day after tomorrow. Expect to travel long distances every day.[3] You will travel 350 miles from here to Prusa then seventy more miles to another garrison beyond that. Every commander along the road must be informed to prioritize the capture of these bandits.

"I'll provide you with documents giving you permission for fresh mounts and supplies in four jurisdictions: from here to Sardis, on to Aizanoi, to Prusa, and then beyond to Port Daskyleion but no farther.[4]

"Sextilius, you have already explained to me that you come from a wealthy family. Your father owns many slaves and is the mayor of Syracuse on the Island of Sicily. You are the most experienced of the six soldiers on this squad, and I can see that you will give good leadership. Commander Felicior notes that you have a good grasp on details and can remember names. You are forty-two years old, coming up for retirement next year, but don't let the

---

[3] Post houses, or relay stations, were located every seven to ten miles on the main roads. Horses traveling at a fast trot managed eight to nine miles an hour. When on urgent assignments, riders covered about 100 miles in a day.

[4] The present highway system in Turkey often matches roads laid down in the Roman Empire. In many cases, modern highways were simply laid over ancient roads. The distances covered in this novel are Soma to Sardis, 66 miles (106 km); Sardis to Aizanoi, 130 miles (206 km); Aizanoi to Prusa, 150 miles (241 km); and from Prusa to Dascylium-on-the-Lake, 69 miles (117 km). Port Daskyleion was a nearby small harbor on the Sea of Marmara.

future take your mind off this assignment! Study the location of every horse relay station. Learn the garrison officers' names from here to Port Daskyleion.

"Bellinus and Capito, this team will need supplies and possibly military equipment. My quartermaster will explain how to account for every denarius spent. He will speak with you at the evening meal. Send me regular reports. I want Taba's ugly face here in the coal-dust mud of Soma, humiliated and pleading for mercy.

"Omerod and Menandro, I read in the report from Commander Felicior that you handled crowd control well in Sardis and can communicate appropriately. You'll work with the other army commanders and relay post officers, providing them with reports."

After their evening meal, Anthony and the five soldiers went to the barracks to talk for a while. All were tired. The dim purple horizon was all that was left of the long June evening.

Anthony stretched. "We'll be getting up for breakfast when the rooster crows in the morning."

He sat down on the edge of his bunk and blew out the lamp. After one more day in Soma, they would be riding for many days to distant Aizanoi and Prusa.

Anthony had become friends with each of them while he was a scout instructor in Sardis. Before stretching out on the bed, he asked, "Sextilius, were you able to return everything to the owners with no complaints? I know you helped Instructor Prosperus return the items stolen by those robbers in Sardis."

Sextilius groaned. "Hmm. It was not easy. That job was a bother; it took a couple weeks to complete. Some families tried to claim what belonged to others! Some claimed that their property had not been found in those caves. But this job? Finding criminals along 350 miles of mostly wilderness? This is looking like the most hopeless assignment I have ever been given!"

Sextilius had three brothers; all were lawyers. He was promised to be the manager of the family's extensive land holdings when he retired in one year. He intended to return home, get married, and begin a family. In the meantime, the challenge of capturing bandits and murderers so close to his retirement worried him.

Anthony stared at the moon through the window, thinking of the next few days. "Everyone says you have an eye for details that others might miss. Yes, we have hundreds of miles to cover but no idea where those slaves disappeared to, so we will be alert to any signs that could point us in the right direction. I can't help but believe these criminals have left some clues."

The only response was a quiet uh-huh and then silence. The other four soldiers had already fallen asleep.

Anthony closed his eyes, trying to sleep to bring an end to his wandering thoughts. Once again, he saw that vegetable cart leaving Apollonius, creaking down the hill toward the narrow bridge. The long line of produce wagons had begun moving toward Thyatira. From the seat at the back of one wagon, holding their daughter, he saw Miriam waving goodbye.

Miriam's lips moved. "Goodbye. We love you!" She was too far away for him to hear her. He turned that moment over in his mind many times.

I already miss you, Miriam. When will I see you again, Grace? I love you both so much.

The road to Thyatira rose slightly near the cemetery, where tall cypress trees punctuated the sky. Legend said that those trees were the pathway for souls to cling to as they climbed into eternity. After going around the corner, Miriam and Grace were out of sight, beyond those slender green trees. That was his last glimpse of them.

Commander Felicior's voice in Sardis, two days ago, came back: *You will not see her again until you have completed this task.*[5]

Anthony tried to stop his mind from skipping from one scene to another. He recalled turning back to the inn where he had placed his well-oiled shield on the stone pavement and where, only moments before, he had embraced Miriam and Grace. He remembered adjusting the red cape that hung from his shoulders to his knees, a Roman legionary's symbol of authority.

He fingered his face, rubbing his finger along the scar. He wanted to talk to Miriam, and he imagined a conversation.

"This ugly scar on my face... Commander Felicior in Sardis overlooked it, and he dismissed some other things that could have annoyed him too. Why did he put me in charge of this squad? He

---

[5] The story of Anthony and Commander Felicior of the Garrison of Sardis is told in *Never Enough Gold: A Chronicle of Sardis.*

demanded, 'Find those bandits!' We really do not know who we are looking for or where they are."

He visualized Miriam once again, seeing her standing in front of him. He mused, "I won't see you and Grace until those thieves have been captured."

He could still see them sitting high over a load of vegetables in a wagon going to Thyatira. That was how they would stay in his memory. He could see Miriam moving one of Grace's hands up and down as if she were waving, saying, "Goodbye, Daddy." Grace's other hand was tucked into a little fist, fitting tightly into her mouth. That was the image he would have of them, and he was going to keep that picture alive in his mind.

"But how did Taba escape? We had him in our hands! And why did Commander Servius take an instant dislike to me?"

Chapter 3
The Slave Traders

A TAVERN NEAR PRUSA, ASIA MINOR (BURSA, TURKEY)

Curses sounded from Craga, a disgraced Roman soldier, as he pulled out a chair. Sitting down with his three friends, he fingered his left leg's damaged muscles, and lines caused by pain creased his forehead. He had chosen this tavern for their meeting because it had outdoor tables overlooking the Marmara Sea. The blue water reflected a cloudless sky.

All four were dressed as Roman soldiers, using armor and weapons stolen when they had deserted the army. The sun had begun to lose its biting heat, and they welcomed the breeze that would soon be cooling them.

"Taba, Maza, and Harpa!" Craga greeted them cheerfully. "So good to see you! How was the sailing from Chalcedon? I had guessed you would be here by yesterday, but the trip is hard to predict with these variable winds. Were there any difficulties with security at Port Chalcedon? No? Me neither. I showed my 'credentials' and quickly got waved through."

During the winter months, Taba had recruited Maza and Harpa, two new criminal gang members, and he described the events. "Chalcedon's authorities only glanced at our papers. Who really wants to march with slaves for days on end? They're happy for older guards like us to be assigned to escort dirty, smelly slaves on their way to Aizanoi."

Craga glanced around once more to assure himself that there were no eavesdroppers. "We have today and tomorrow to discuss my plans. Two days from now, our next 'shipment' should be arriving."

He spoke quietly, and his grin showed he was confident of the coming wealth. Their plan was to be assigned as guards for slave merchants escorting their slaves. They would kill the merchants and then take their stolen "merchandise" to a lucrative market. All this had already been done right under the noses of the authorities.

Craga leaned back, a huge smile revealing several black teeth. He pointed to the nearby mountain rising above the plain. "Isn't

Prusa a wonderful city?[6] We're staying there tonight! Look at that place, the protective home of Zeus rising high above the city![7] Well, men, a chest full of treasures awaits us. In the slave market, male slaves bring in close to 500 denarii. Back in our army days, it took us a year and a half to earn that much! A female slave can sell for many times more if it looks like she will have lots of babies.

"Occasionally, we'll also be handling wild animals to sell to arenas in Asia and Rome. Wild animals will make us a lot of money, but they are troublesome to manage and expensive to feed.

"Eight weeks ago, we conducted two slave merchants who had twenty slaves going south. We sent them to an early death on an isolated section of the road and then took over their 'cargo.' Those slaves never knew what happened. They just thought we were sellers working on behalf of the merchants. Each of those unfortunates ended up in the mines and brought us lots of money.

"Now, let's discuss the plans that involve the three of you and how we shall all become wealthy. Two merchants and a caravan of slaves are going from Prusa to Aizanoi in two days. You will accompany the caravan as a military escort. At the beginning of the trip, the slaves will be conducted by the merchant. He is the owner who starts out with us. But when his slaves are put up for auction in the marketplace, he will be looking at us from the other side of eternity. His merchandise will be ours. No one will ever learn what happened. Even the slaves won't be aware. A few days later, we'll have disappeared."

Laugher flowed smoothly as they dreamed of such easy riches. "The profits, less expenses, are divided by the sum of the sharing members in our 'army.' Mithrida, our general, gets a double share, but then each of us 'soldiers' get one share. Our auxiliaries[8] get a quarter share. If Zeus is pleased with our work, we'll each have

---

[6] Ancient Prusa is today known as Bursa, a large industrial city of about 2,000,000 in western Turkey. In pre-Roman times, Bursa was the capital of Bithynia. It became the first capital of the Ottoman Empire (1535–1563). Today the city is known for its specialized industrial production.

[7] Uludag Mountain, which affords visitors majestic skiing runs, was sometimes known as the home of Zeus, the famous Greek god.

[8] Auxiliaries were the non-soldiers of the Roman army. They performed non-fighting, menial roles, such as cleaning, food preparation, transporting equipment, and, in this case, also tending the slaves being moved.

enough in two years to buy a farm, maybe one or two slaves, and settle down as…"

Maza's eyes bulged with excitement, and he leaned forward in anticipation, completing Craga's sentence: "…as honest owners of lands and properties!"

Craga explained the size of the gang. "For now, our 'army' includes ten soldiers and about twenty auxiliaries, but our forces will grow. The more we have, the more projects we can start. That means more money for us all."

Harpa, the quiet one, had not completely lost his senses, despite several mugs of beer. "We can buy the best farmland in Scythia, far away from Domitian's long reach." He raised his cup again with a "Cheers!" and his three companions responded with gusto.

Several others in the simple tavern heard them laughing loudly and remarked, "Soldiers! Drunk again!"

Craga, rubbing his sore leg with one hand, came back to his main task. "Keep your eyes open for suitable recruits. Remember our code names and how they came to be. If anyone is caught, the others will be protected. Be careful not to draw attention to yourselves. Maza and Harpa, you have new identities: Callistus Flavius and Valerian Atticus. Your former names are known by the army and had to be changed since we are deserters."

Taba nodded his head. "I gave myself the code name Taba in Sardis a year ago, and it has worked well, as expected. Easy to remember. I'm sure I can find the eight men I recruited for our little army in Sardis. I can hardly wait to get back there." As the others laughed with delight, he pondered questions that kept coming to mind.

Last year in Sardis was not a success. It was a disaster. What became of Little Lion, the young man I wanted to join our gang? He probably got caught with the first four men I recruited for our band. I was lucky to escape. The army isn't too gentle with bandits. It was bad judgment on my part to fall into that trap! I'll never tell these guys how I lost everything last year. I escaped only by running down the mountain in the early morning light. I later heard that the other four men I trained were also caught. It was a calamity, but I'll never let something like that happen again.

The sun would soon be setting. Delighted that they had found a way to pass undetected from one Roman garrison to another, they walked an hour to the nearby city of Prusa. Each was certain riches beyond their wildest dreams would fall into their hands. No guards along the Postal Road would bother to question the forged papers of soldiers conducting slaves to market.

Craga, "Callistus," and "Valerian" laughed loudly as they neared the city's main gate. A soldier approached them. "Hail, soldiers! I haven't seen you before. New to Prusa?"

"We are conducting slaves," Craga replied. Using their fictitious army names and presenting the forged documents, he introduced his three companions to the guard, who inspected their credentials.

"Welcome!" said the guard, taking them to the barracks beside the garrison. "You can stay here. There's plenty of room. Every available soldier we had was rushed to Dacia." He paused, not wanting to mention the death of his legionary friends. "Such a sad event! Trained soldiers were killed like flies, just like that!"

He snapped his fingers, cursing the king of Dacia and his army. "How did Emperor Domitian suffer that grievous setback? How could five thousand soldiers spill their blood on barbarian lands?"

"Yes, that's the worst possible news!" said Taba sadly.

His thoughts, however, were of a somewhat different attitude. *If I hadn't deserted four years ago, I would undoubtedly have been one of those who fell on that battlefield. They were my friends at one time. But no longer. They are dead, and I'm alive. And to think that last year I was almost captured in Sardis!*

After the defeat in Dacia, many soldiers from Asia Minor had been reassigned to help maintain security in the area still held by Rome. In provinces bordering Dacia, military outposts were below minimum strength, so army officers were on the lookout for additional legionaries. Thus, they welcomed retired soldiers as guards in cities and as patrols on the Postal Road.

The new recruits to Craga's illegal band were deserters from Dacia who had been disillusioned by the battlefield's lack of leadership. Resentment against the army burned in the hearts of these four men. It was as if embers were waiting to burst into flames. Now each wanted his own riches—the quicker, the better.

Chapter 4
Hidden Stories

THYATIRA, ASIA MINOR

Miriam felt sore and tired. All that bouncing and jostling of the wagon! Such a noisy, rough ride from Apollonius to Thyatira!

The wagon crept toward the city's South Gate as Miriam wrapped her arms around her daughter. Grace's black curls covered her forehead and ran down the back of her neck. She wore a small linen tunic, and her sweet face lay on Miriam's right elbow. As the girl giggled, Miriam squeezed her chubby little cheeks and imitated horse and sheep sounds.

Miriam's tunic was a gift received from her Uncle Simon and Aunt Judith before leaving Sardis. "You'll always be in our hearts," they said as they gave their warm goodbyes two days before.

The young mother knotted her long black braids over her head, lessening the heat on the back of her neck. If the tiny movements around the edges of her lips were accurate indicators, her mind kept shifting from one subject to another.

Outside Thyatira's South Gate, many workshops with short smokestacks on the southwest side of the city were belching out black smoke. The driver explained, "Those are bronze-casting shops. On the northwest side of the city are the homes of the poor."

As they entered the South Gate, she noticed that the city walls were low and narrow compared with those of Pergamum, her home. Miriam wondered what Anthony would say about that and mused, *This city isn't well protected! Even a small, ill-equipped army would win against defenders cowering behind these low walls. No wonder Thyatira didn't help in the wars. How could it keep the Lydian kingdom safe from Persians?*

She felt a little nervous coming into the city as a stranger. She did not know anyone except her uncle. Holding her daughter, Miriam grimaced as the wagon shuddered repeatedly on the uneven stones. *I'm arriving on the back of a grocery wagon, but I'm safe. And so is Grace. Would Grandpa Antipas believe that Anthony would be a leader of a unique army squad? Lord, keep my husband safe!*

Once inside the city, the driver stopped the wagon and pointed down the street immediately to their left. "This is as far as you need to go. Walk down to the end of this side street, and you'll find your Uncle Jonathan's house near the city wall. It's not far to his place. Most anyone down there will know where it is. Everybody knows about his success in ridding this part of the city of mosquitoes. We'll go on to unload the fruits and vegetables in the market area. Everyone there knows and fears Bassos. I'm thankful for your company on the trip, and we enjoyed the picnic!"

Miriam gave the driver a denarius, and his eyes opened wide. "No, that's too much for riding on our wagon! A whole day's wage… I didn't do anything to earn it!"

"You earned it for bringing me here safely," Miriam replied. She gave him another coin, this one worth more. "And this is for two new tunics, one for each of your sisters. Thank you for a ride with no complications along the way, only lots of bumps. I'm happy to be here."

With that, she picked up Grace in one arm and her small bundle of belongings in the other and headed to Uncle Jonathan's.

THE TEMPLE OF ARTEMIS, THYATIRA

The skies over Thyatira were gray from dust and smoke as the afternoon ended. The setting sun was just touching the horizon as the city's twenty most respected leaders gathered to plan the upcoming festival. Lamps burned in the entryway to the Temple of Artemis, where the details for the events on the year's longest day were to be discussed and approved.

Mayor Gaius Aurelius Tatianos, a priest of the Imperial Cult, called the meeting to order. He cleared his throat and thought of his father and mother, who also had been priests in the Imperial Cult. They had offered daily sacrifices to Rome's past emperors. Now, after their deaths, he continued the pattern of that previous generation and received a special honor for fully dedicating his life to the empire, the Imperial Cult, and the Temple of Artemis.

The group laughed together and congratulated themselves on their social status, for the gods favored them. Great honor was theirs. In three days, the festival would confirm how much their efforts were appreciated by ordinary folk. Many would line the streets to show approval during the elaborate processions.

Before the meeting ended, Mayor Tatianos held up his hand to quiet the group so he could address the latest gossip. The scandal was already being discussed on Thyatira's streets.

"Did you hear what happened? Bassos wore a crown yesterday! On an ordinary day, and it wasn't even a religious event! He led a long procession of youth, all walking in pairs, boys with long hair! Many of them carried frankincense in burners in a parade expensive beyond words!"

The people of Thyatira accepted odd behavior, but the antics Bassos encouraged were extreme. City councilors had advised him, "Bassos, tone it down a bit!"

But the wealthy landowner had just laughed at them. Again.

Mayor Tatianos ended, "I don't know what his intent is, but just because he's wealthy does not give him the right to ignore our authority. If he continues to act like a local 'king,' we will have to force the city council to officially punish him in some way. I think some council members are accepting bribes. If this goes much further, they may start paying more attention to his recommendations than ours!"

JONATHAN AND REBEKAH'S HOME, THE CITY OF THYATIRA

"Welcome to our home, my niece!" Jonathan's voice boomed as he came to the door. "When we received the letter that told us you were coming, I said to Rebekah, 'Finally, my niece will be here!' Aunt Rebekah is out shopping but will be home shortly. And who do we have here?"

Miriam could not decide if her uncle meant to speak so loudly in greeting her or if he always talked this way. Thinking back, she remembered him coming to Eliab Ben Shelah's funeral in Pergamum. Eliab, her great-grandfather, had died three years earlier.

Shorter than his brothers, Jonathan Ben Shelah's every word revealed an intense zest for life. People whispered behind his back, wondering how he could be so much more energetic than other fifty-two-year-old men.

"This is Grace, Uncle Jonathan. Anthony and I adopted her in Pergamum after she was abandoned. Anthony won't be coming here because he has an assignment on the Postal Road."

Jonathan chuckled and showed Miriam into his home. "Never mind! Someone must ride beside those caravans, protecting them from flies and bad smells. Rather him than me!"

Miriam was not quite sure how to take his statement, but she did not react. She looked around. Three couches occupied the center of the great room, which was square and decorated with intricately patterned marble floors.

"Endless symbols of eternity," Jonathan stated proudly. "I decided against installing mosaics showing pagan gods, the ones found in almost every home here. Instead, I had artists place interlocking designs to remind me of our home in Alexandria."

Miriam examined the floor, decorated with patterns made of tiny yellow and black stones. Mosaics were arranged with infinite care. Each shape invited the curious eye to find where each design began and ended. Squares and circles decorated the entire room, and other patterns had been laid along the hallway to the kitchen. Others covered his library floor.

"They are beautiful!" she breathed.

Grace struggled, wanting to be put down to walk.

"Twelve different configurations of eternity are spread throughout our house, one for every tribe of Israel!" His hands moved in ever-expanding circles.

A young woman was just coming down from upstairs, and Jonathan waved her over. "Miriam, this is my daughter-in-law Serah, Bani's wife."

"I'm happy to meet you, Miriam," said Serah. "I wish that we could provide you with better weather this time of year. You've arrived when our summer is going to be at its hottest. We have had no refreshing wind for days."

Rebekah, Jonathan's wife, arrived moments later. "My dear niece! Welcome! You must tell me all about your wedding. We heard of you getting married to a Roman! Such a surprise!"

"I'm always happy to talk about Anthony, Aunt Rebekah, but don't expect details about his assignments. I don't understand a thing about the Roman army."

Rebekah's voice turned frosty. "The Roman army! Yes, so many of our family needlessly killed." Rebekah caught herself and added in a slightly forced but warmer tone, "Our evening meal will be ready soon. Everyone will be glad to meet you."

Rebekah took Miriam upstairs to a room with a view of the center of the city. "This room will be cooler for you and the baby in this summer weather. I'll have our slave, Arte, bring up some water, and you can freshen up from your long ride."

Once the water and a large basin and towels were brought to

the room, Miriam was happy to wash off the dust she and Grace had accumulated during the road trip. She laid down on the bed with Grace for a quick nap.

Aunt Rebekah soon called her to come meet with the family and join the evening meal. In the living room, the couches formed a large "U" around the small center table. Three adults could stretch out on a single couch. Rebekah, Jonathan, and Gil, their younger son, occupied the middle one. Miriam sat on the end of the left side couch, holding Grace.

Bani, his wife Serah, and a woman Miriam had not met yet reclined on the third one. Miriam turned to the center couch where her cousin Gil reclined, and he introduced her to the young woman beside Serah.

"Miriam, please meet my bride-to-be, Danila. The first time she came to Thyatira was with her father almost two years ago. I met her when they visited the guild. Her father was here to look at our products, and now he is doing business with our family. We are going to soon be married here!"

Gil turned to Danila. "My dear, this is my cousin Miriam. She married a soldier...."

"I'm pleased to meet you," Miriam said to Danila before Gil could finish his sentence. "Were you born in Thyatira?"

"No, I'm from Laodicea. My mother is a priestess in Hera's temple, and Daddy is a banker."

Miriam strained to keep a straight face. *Gil—his name means joy. A Jewish son is going to marry this pretty young thing, Danila! Her mother is a priestess in a pagan temple! Why is the wedding to be here instead of in Laodicea, where her parents live?*

"When is the wedding going to be?" she asked calmly.

"On July 1, in two weeks! I hope you'll be there!"

Miriam did not want to start off her relationship with her aunt and uncle and her cousins negatively. Searching for something to say and remembering how she had left Pergamum so quickly, she decided to introduce herself to Danila.

"I, too, was married in a home where I hadn't been brought up. It seems that I'm making a habit of arriving suddenly at the homes of my aunts and uncles. Fourteen months ago, Marcos Pompeius, our family lawyer, knew that Pergamum's authorities were plotting against my grandfather, Grandpa Antipas. Now I realize that he attended all the city council meetings.

"That's how Marcos learned Grandpa was facing a dangerous situation. He helped Anthony and me by providing his home for our marriage. The day after the wedding, the mayor of the city came to talk with Marcos. He carried out the legal steps to adopt Grace.

"Next, Marcos set up a little convoy of four wagons leaving Pergamum with Anthony, Grace, and me in the last one. He felt that I might be arrested with Grandpa if we stayed there. We came with another couple, two young people who had been slaves. Several girls from our village and our luggage went in the first three wagons. Marcos told those girls to sing loudly, and of course, he wanted the guards at the Pergamum city gate to be watching them, not us. Those girls were the ones that came to visit you when we left Pergamum."

At the mention of the visit by the girls from Antipas's village last year, everyone talked at once. Gil and Bani had guided the girls around their city for three days. They also had many things to say about their adventures before the group returned to Pergamum.

Miriam sighed and thought, *I'm glad that we have something pleasant to talk about during my first meal at this home, but I'm afraid things will not always be so cordial here.*

After the main course, several kinds of cheese appeared but no meat. There seemed to be no end to the food: slices of apples, peaches, figs, and apricots. Grace reached for a rye cake. She picked the raisins out, one by one, and laughed when others smiled at her.

Miriam asked, "Uncle, how long have you lived in this house?"

Jonathan answered, "When we first came to Thyatira, we lived on the hill, above the city. It was a rented house with a fine view. We were outside the city walls. I opened a shop selling goods that came mostly from Antipas, your grandfather. Then I opened another shop dealing in metal items, mostly bronze from the city foundries. After a lot of haggling, I was finally admitted to the Bronze Casting Guild. We were profitable, and with the extra money I earned, I purchased Olive Grove Farm. That allowed me to provide a broader range of products for sale.

"After several years, I wanted to build a house, so we started looking for land. Nobody wanted this property since it was where dirty water pooled inside the city walls after the rains. Even sentries didn't want to patrol this part of the wall. After a rainstorm, a soggy bog formed here. It was good for growing reeds, frogs, and mosquitoes, but it made this area a useless, smelly swamp. I bought the land from the city council, telling them, 'I'll use techniques I learned in Alexandria and clean it up.' So we dug many trenches and purchased large terracotta pipes."

His voice grew deeper and richer, and his face beamed. "We laid the pipes to drain off the stagnant water and any rainwater that would accumulate. When we finished the project, this property was big enough and solid enough for this house and the large garden."

"I can see that you are proud of your accomplishment."

"Oh, yes. I bought the land for almost nothing, and we've been here for five years. Some people are jealous! However, most are accepting us now. I'm one of only a few strangers to Thyatira to be accepted with civic honors. Some didn't want me living inside the city wall, saying, 'He hasn't been here long enough!'"

Miriam tried to keep any emotional response off her face. *I only asked how long he has lived here, and he gave a long story, telling me all about how he became accepted in the city. Does Uncle Jonathan see himself as better than other newcomers? He is immensely proud.*

It was midnight before Miriam lay down to sleep. Stretched out on the bed, she felt exhausted. *Why won't Commander Felicior let Anthony be with me? A forced separation! How long will it be?*

She hugged her sleeping daughter, whispering, "I won't let anything happen to you, little one! I'll protect you. And above all, God is watching over you. He sheltered you from the first day I took you from the trash dump in Pergamum. You will always have my love."

She ran her hand through Grace's black hair. *I have developed such a deep love for this little girl. She isn't my own through birth, but I love her as if she were. I bless the woman who gave this baby life even if I don't know her and probably never will. God, bless the unknown mother of my daughter, Chrysa Grace.*

She wanted to stay awake, to be comforted with the memory of Anthony's strong arms, his passionate love. Soon she was asleep, tired out from the long wagon ride.

Chapter 5
Olive Grove Farm

THE MILITARY GARRISON IN SOMA

On Thursday morning, a rooster awakened the visiting legionaries at the Soma Garrison. After washing with cold water and shaving, they were ready for a meal.

Menandro was the first to arrive at the breakfast table. It was a long, narrow table with benches on each side that were stored against the wall when not being used. The resident soldiers left space for the six men from Sardis, who would begin their patrol the following day.

Omerod and Anthony were next to join the group. Omerod's family, which went back many generations, came from Carthage in Africa Proconsularis. His ancestors had fought against the Roman army in the Punic Wars.[9] He was the only one of his eight brothers to enlist in the military. His complexion was darker than that of the other five legionaries. As the team's tallest member, he stood out, and some assumed that he was the squad leader. His half-closed black eyes were always moving as if regularly taking in every detail. He was, in fact, a careful observer, and his stories of things he had seen while serving in the army could keep everyone's attention well into the night.

Eventually, the remaining three of Anthony's men arrived. Together they enjoyed a large breakfast of wheat cakes, olives, fresh cheese, and honey.

The Soma soldiers left the table to start their duties. When the team finished their meal, Omerod asked, "Anthony, we've been assigned a huge area to search for these robbers and murderers. Where will we begin?"

---

[9] Carthage in Africa Proconsularis is today known as Tunis, the capital city of Tunisia. Between 264 and 146 BC, three long struggles, known as the Punic Wars, were fought before Rome finally dominated North Africa.

"I've been thinking about the few facts we know. We are going to Karun, and starting from there, we'll break into three groups. We'll all be talking with army officers and collecting any clues from stations and garrisons that will help us get a better picture of what these criminals are doing. Commander Felicior thinks innkeepers in the area would have seen the attackers but would not know they were involved in any crimes.

"Bellinus and Capito, you will search from Karun all the way to where the Postal Road meets the Interior Road.

"You, Omerod and Menandro, search the Interior Road from the Postal Road intersection, past White Horse Station and up to Prusa.

"Sextilius and I will cover the area from Prusa to Port Daskyleion."

"What do you know about these thugs?" Omerod asked.

Anthony began, "Last October, I was training twenty recruits on Mount Tmolus. By accident, we found a cave where stolen goods had been stashed. A small gang had been involved in burglaries, taking items from homes of wealthy families in Sardis. One recruit, Little Lion, contacted the gang and drew them in by pretending to know about 'hidden treasures' buried on the mountain. We set a trap for those five thugs, and in the dim light of an early morning, we captured four of the five. One of them escaped.

"That's what distresses Commander Servius. The gang leader escaped, but Little Lion had learned his name is Taba. From the way Taba commanded the others, we think he probably had been a legionary at some time. He knew a lot about the army. We've been puzzling over this since we learned that Taba answered to a higher-up person named Craga. They have an even higher 'authority,' someone called the 'General.' We know nothing about that person."

Sextilius expressed a concern. "Why was Servius so angry? He said that your tactics weren't well thought out."

Anthony grinned lamely. "He's right to be upset. No one could believe that Taba escaped! Here is how it happened. Little Lion led the gang to several gold rings hidden at the foot of a tree. I had a squad of recruits surrounding the area to capture the gang, and we sprung the trap in the early morning darkness. In the confusion that followed, Taba escaped. That happened before the sun came up, so it was dark. We captured his four partners."

Sextilius returned to the most recent crimes. "That incident happened several months ago and those men were just thieves, but now we are concerned about two merchants who were murdered near Prusa. That's a big step up in the level of violence."

Omerod joined in. "The first question is 'Who killed them?' The two merchants' bodies, badly decomposed, were found off to the side of the Interior Road and down a hill, just above the nearby river. From Cotyaum onward, not a trace of the murderers could be found at any of the next stations."

Sextilius added thoughtfully, "Whoever they are, these killers are well organized." Thinking hard, he rubbed his right wrist with his left hand's fingers. "The bandits struck where there were fewer soldiers to guard caravans and merchandise. These murders happened while Domitian was invading Dacia. Each invading legion had to be at full strength, reducing the number of soldiers providing security here. That fact explains why there were fewer regulars to guard the roads in Asia Minor."

Capito spoke for the first time. "I heard from one soldier that the Interior Road along that stretch has few checkpoints. It's mostly lonely hills and low scrub brush. The Postal Road, going eastward from Smyrna through Sardis and past Aizanoi, joins the Interior Road, which goes north to south.

"The Postal Road has more farms, more traffic, and more villages than the Interior Road, so the robbers might have been caught if they had killed the merchants on the Postal Road. But these criminals did away with the merchants on a less traveled section of the Interior Road. Little chance anyone would have seen them there." He paused. "What animals! Will they do this again?"

Omerod stood up and stretched to his full height. "They got away with it once, and they probably made a lot of money from the slaves. And by Jupiter, I believe they will almost certainly do it again." He then looked at Anthony and smiled. "It does raise a question. Who are we looking for? We know nothing!"

Anthony closed his eyes for a moment, proud of the men he was to lead. *I'm grateful for Commander Felicior's choices. Omerod knows the importance of discipline and doesn't mind long, painful days of riding. He has a strong sense of right and wrong. Menandro appreciates family relationships and knows how to question people. He knows how to get into their minds. Sextilius thinks through difficult issues and refuses to come to quick conclusions. Capito instinctively knows the right way to handle unruly rebels when trouble is brewing. Bellinus says little, but he is like a ship's anchor in a harbor with rough seas, unflappable, and a dependable comrade whose face never shows fear.*

As they stood to leave, Anthony said, "Somewhere, we'll find out who the criminals are, where they hide, and what they are doing when nobody is watching. We must satisfy Commander Servius; he demands the best. I did not get a good start with him. Commander Servius has given us today to prepare for our trip.

"As we get to it, here's something I want you to know. Before Commander Felicior sent us, he told me that he is worried about the situation in Thyatira. Nothing specific. He couldn't put his finger on anything, but it seems that something is amiss there. He said we should keep an eye out for irregularities, but what kind?

"Also, he is worried that these murderers might get past Soma without being detected. To the west, the Mount Tarhala area restricts traffic, so travelers must stay on the east to west road. He wonders if they might use the orchards on the north side of the Postal Road to bypass the checkpoint. I passed Felicior's concerns on to Commander Servius."

Bellinus rarely commented on things, but this was an exception. "Bandits have miles of wilderness along the Postal Road and the Interior Road, all the way to Prusa. So why is Commander Felicior worried about this small, out-of-the-way section near Soma?"

His question brought a chuckle from the others. Anthony answered, "I don't know why, but his instructions were to look carefully around Forty Trees, only eight miles away. I stayed on a farm close by last year at an orchard called Olive Grove Farm, and the owner is my wife's uncle, Jonathan Ben Shelah. The Postal Road runs by Olive Grove. Below the farm, there is a shallow river, the Gelembe River.

"It's possible that the criminals might go along the river if they were attempting to avoid being detected. I'm going to take a quick trip there this morning to look the place over. Commander Servius wants a list of every person living or working on the farms close to the Postal Road. He's thorough and intends to prevent rebels from getting past Soma undetected."

Sextilius stood to stretch and rubbed his wrist again. "Has Commander Felicior given us a deadline? I like to know what is expected of me. Do you remember that I retire next year? I don't want this assignment to hold me back when I should be leaving."

Anthony laughed lightheartedly. "No specific schedule came from Commander Felicior, but Servius wants the assassins captured yesterday! Remember, these attacks took place in the wilderness, on the road south of Prusa. We'll soon be examining that far-off area. The Interior Road stretches out through rugged valleys with no villagers to notice anything amiss. There's a long history of outlaws. Could this be 'sons following in the steps of their fathers,' as the saying goes? Expect surprises, and be ready for violence."

As Anthony saddled his horse, he prayed. *Lord, it's an impossible assignment! Forests, caves, and mountains! So many places where bandits could be hiding! How many rebels are there? How are they organized? Who is their leader? From what we heard, robbers attack caravans without warning. I need help. Teach me your paths, Lord, for in you I have put my trust.*

OLIVE GROVE FARM AT FORTY TREES, ON THE POSTAL ROAD

Arriving at Olive Grove, Anthony scowled. He looked at the sky, worried because black clouds churned overhead. *Strange…farmers would not expect a heavy rain after April.*

For miles around, trees produced olives, which yielded food, oil, medicine, and soap when the fruit was processed. Miriam's Uncle Jonathan occasionally came here to supervise things.

Anthony had reason to trust the five families living at the farm because he and Miriam had stayed there for a while a year ago, before going to Sardis. The farmers were brothers, originally from Stratonike, a small city north of the Gelembe River.

Nikias, the eldest, was in charge, and Penelope, his wife, served tasty food to her visitors. Laughter often rang out as the brothers teased each other.

Anthony asked Nikias to walk with him. "I want to look at the little river at the bottom of the hill. Do you remember when I came with Miriam last year?"

"Of course! You only stayed two nights though! Come back and stay longer!"

"Thank you for letting me take one of your horses to Sardis. You'll never know how important that was for me to quickly see Commander Felicior."

Anthony examined outcroppings of stone ledges running across the creek. The ridges were high enough to effectively block anyone trying to get horses or wagons through the area near the creek. Still, a person going on foot could get across and get past the authorities at Forty Trees.

A few drops fell from the rain clouds, and the men ran back up the hill. Nikias insisted on Anthony stepping inside, even though the rainstorm blew over before they got there. In his home, Nikias walked back and forth across the rough wooden floor, preferring to stand.

"I keep thinking about you and Miriam and your baby. Your wife taught me a song as I took her into Sardis while going through the Royal Cemetery. That was the day after you ran off on my horse!" He chuckled. "Everyone going to Sardis along that road fears the spirits of the dead. In a dark cemetery, unseen forces leave me petrified. Just then, Miriam sang a song, and she wasn't afraid! No one dares to sing a melody there. The Royal Cemetery is for dead kings and powerful spirits. Tall mounds of dirt cover the graves of all the kings and princes of the ancient Lydian kingdom![10]

"Since then, I keep singing her song. I think about Antipas, her grandfather. Like her, I was young when I lost my father."

Nikias sang Miriam's song, happy to be sharing the words.

I grasped Grandpa's hand, tracing small, brown specks,
And then I wound a ribbon 'round his neck.
He told stories of our land. It seemed grand
To trace the veins upon his well-worn hand.

An arrow took Daddy's life. He was gone,
And I was young, not knowing right from wrong.
Grandpa gripped me tight. "God is our delight.
I'm here, close by, my child. No need for fright."

Grandpa lingered on Abraham and Ruth,
Teaching me: "God's promises bring us truth.
I know He cares; a loving home prepares.
He understands our thoughts and hears our prayers."

---

[10] The Royal Cemetery is a national park in Turkey. It is located five miles north of the ruins of Sardis. Extraordinary finds in the tombs give witness to the unparalleled wealth of the kings of the Kingdom of Lydia.

Grandpa hated the sight of iron chains.
He gave slaves freedom, sensed their deepest pains.
Now freed, singers strum with skillful fingers.
Remembering, gratitude still lingers.

"Yeshua's realm is our prize," Grandpa said.
"Our expected king was rejected, led
Away, while some cursed Yeshua to his face.
But when He prayed, he banished shame through grace."

"Those hands," he taught, "were nailed upon a tree.
His lifeblood spilled in love for you and me.
Stronger than the grave, by his grace, we're saved.
His life transforms the timid into brave."

Anthony asked, "Why does her song mean so much to you? Why are you still singing it?"

"For the first time, I could think other thoughts. After taking Miriam and Grace to Sardis, I returned to Thyatira to speak with Rebekah Bat Azgad. She lets me call her 'Aunt Rebekah.' I told her about Miriam's song and learned that she also believes in the Messiah. I thought about that a while, and then I told her, 'I want to learn more. Would you teach me?'"

Anthony leaned forward expectantly. "What happened?"

Nikias paused, remembering the impact of Miriam's song. "I said to Rebekah, 'I want to be free from fear.' She asked, 'What makes you fearful?' and I replied, 'My mother died when I was twelve years old. All my life, I've been petrified when thinking of death. Our father died later, in an accident on the farm. We were poor and had no land. Since then, I've wanted my own farm, a way to help my brothers and their families. I don't want to always be working for someone else.'

"Anthony, sometimes I would wake up in the night covered with sweat. I always avoided cemeteries and funerals. I don't want my wife to die in childbirth. Penelope has given us four little ones, but I was terrified each time she went into labor.

"I explained all this to Aunt Rebekah, and she said, 'Yeshua Messiah came back to life. He was laid in a stone tomb and watched by guards, but he came out, showing he is stronger than death.' That was good news to me."

"And now you're not so afraid of death?"

"I'm not afraid like I used to be. I became a follower of the Way. That's not all," Nikias added, grinning. "I tell everyone else about what I have found. My four brothers and their families don't know what to think about it. Kozma, my youngest brother, doesn't like the people coming here from the little town up the road."

"Why are they coming to Olive Grove?"

"Several families in Forty Trees have been friends for years. We enjoy their friendship, and now they are special in a new way. I have been teaching them what I am learning. Penelope agrees with me, and Jonathan encouraged it too if it didn't affect the farm work. I want them to meet every week, not just once a month. Here's what happens: When I go to Thyatira, Aunt Rebekah teaches me more things from the Matthew story. My friends from Forty Trees come here, and I pass on to them what I learned."

"Great! Oh, Nikias, that reminds me of something you should know. Last year, we left most of Grandfather Antipas's scrolls here. Miriam took a few with us when we left and we read them in Sardis, but most are still here."

"Well, of course! I sealed them in some old olive jars to keep them safe. Would it be all right if I read them?"

"Certainly. Most are copies of the Scriptures that you should be reading for information. Some are notes that Antipas wrote, sort of a diary."

"Would Miriam mind if I read those too?"

"No, I don't think so. But Miriam wouldn't want them being taken away."

"I was thinking that if I could get copies of scrolls to other people, they could be reading those stories themselves. You know, I like going to other farms, only when I have the time though. I've always been interested in other people and other farms. Jonathan really should have animals and crops here too, not just olive trees and madder plants to make dye for the Guild of Purple Honors."

Thin lines again covered Anthony's forehead, but this time it was concern about Nikias going to nearby villages and towns. *Nikias is hungry to learn the Scriptures! He is enthusiastic, generous, and big-hearted. Maybe a little unwise too. He seems restless, and his brothers are not happy with what he's doing. And on a small farm where five brothers must deal with each other every day, this could cause problems.*

48

"Let's talk more about the scrolls another day. You should read and learn from them, but don't loan them to other people. They are too valuable to lose. But first, I have an assignment to complete for the Soma Garrison. My commander wants me to make a list of farmers and families who live along the creek. Nothing to worry about, Nikias. My commander just wants everyone to be safe."

THE MILITARY GARRISON IN SOMA

Shortly after Anthony returned from Forty Trees, Servius called for him to come to his office. "I need a final word with you, Suros."

"Final instructions, sir?"

"No. Commander Felicior sent me a letter. Do you know what it's about?"

"No, sir, no idea."

"He says that you have a mind of your own, that you talk about another kingdom, but in our creed, there is only the Roman Empire, and we are loyal to the emperor. According to his letter, you were found to have instructed recruits about that Jewish Messiah. One of your best scouts became enthralled with this belief. It appears that his last written words were about this other kingdom. Is this true?"

"Yes, sir, I did talk to one recruit, Little Lion. This should not be a problem. I call it 'the kingdom within,' but I have always been loyal to Caesar. Please, let me explain. After discovering the cave where the robbers were hiding stolen treasures, Little Lion asked me how I found it. I explained how I prayed to the Almighty God, who showed me where to take the recruits on our first night in the forest."

Servius looked totally disinterested in Anthony's explanation. "No more long explanations! I demand that you not speak of this 'other kingdom' to Omerod, Menandro, Sextilius, Bellinus, or Capito. The story about the Jewish Messiah is a myth! It should have perished with Jerusalem. That so-called 'kingdom' ceased to exist twenty-two years ago. The legend, as well as Jerusalem, is nothing more than a pile of ashes."

"I understand your orders, sir." But as he said this, Anthony thought, *The kingdom of heaven I learned about from Antipas will never cease to exist. Servius, you need to know about it.*

"Leave early tomorrow." The commander handed Anthony a courier pouch. "These authorizations will provide your squad with fresh mounts at every horse relay station. I demand a quick end to these thieves. I want all of them apprehended and dealt with. Any footpads helping them, the same punishment! And for the man who created this band, I can't imagine a sufficient penalty."

"Yes, sir."

The next morning, they found their horses already saddled. "I want every outlaw captured alive if possible," Commander Servius demanded. "Review your orders."

Anthony summarized their plans. "We'll be in Sardis tonight, getting fresh horses at relay stations, sir. Two nights from now, we should be in Karun.[11] Every detachment along the road will hear of this mission.

"Bellinus and Capito are to stay in Karun to search garrison records for relevant details as well as to explore the Postal Road to Aizanoi. They will then search the Postal Road from Aizanoi to where it meets the Interior Road. That's only a few miles south of White Horse Station. That effort should take five days. They will then collect their findings and continue to Prusa.

"Four of us will go on from Karun. If the weather holds, we'll be in Aizanoi the next night before continuing on. Omerod and Menandro will start searching at the White Horse Station, talking with officers and stations on the Interior Road through Cotyaum[12] to Prusa. The bodies were discovered on that stretch of road north of Cotyaum.

"After Sextilius and I get to Prusa, we will continue to Dascylium-on-the-Lake.[13] I talked to some of the older soldiers here, Commander, and discovered that several thieves' gangs lived there in ancient times. Perhaps 'families of bandits will come back to life,' as the Phrygian proverb goes! After leaving there and stopping at Port Daskyleion, we'll move on to Prusa to meet the

---

[11] Karun is now Usak, a modern city. The Karun Treasure, an incredible find of 310 Lydian gold and silver objects buried in the grave of a wealthy woman, is preserved in the Usak Museum.

[12] Cotyaum, modern Kutahya, is an important center for the production of ceramics. The city was an important stopping point on the Interior Road from the Black Sea to Mesopotamia.

[13] Ancient Dascylium-on-the-Lake is in the Turkish village of Ergili, on the southeastern corner of Lake Kush Golu. The area around the lake is protected and known as Bird Lake National Park. Millions of birds stop at this lake on their annual migratory routes.

others and compare our findings. We'll write a report and rest before returning here."

Prepared for any kind of danger, they wore full military gear. Anthony rode at the front with Sextilius. The others followed, two abreast. The six horses trotted at a fast canter; they would mount fresh horses every hour.

Around them, a narrow valley spread to the north. Soon steep cliffs on the left sloped gracefully to the fertile land. The green leaves of the olive trees sparkled in the sunlight. They passed long caravans coming to Thyatira. Camels plodded along under heavy burdens, their long necks bobbing with every step, a stubborn gait that never changed. Horses and donkeys carried many loads of merchandise.

Anthony caught himself praying, just as he had when facing difficult situations in Sardis. *Lord, go before us. We are like children; we don't know what to do unless you show us how to protect these roads from evil men. How will you direct me? Both Felicior and Servius prohibited me from saying anything about the Messiah.*

The roads seem secure. Merchants and guards travel together, yet a menace hides somewhere. "I lift my eyes to the hills. Where does my help come from? My help comes from the Lord, the maker of heaven and earth. He will not let your foot slip—he who watches over you will not slumber; indeed, he who watches over Israel will neither slumber nor sleep."[14]

They mounted fresh horses, first at Forty Trees and then at another relay station closer to Thyatira. An hour later, they arrived at Green Valley Inn, where Anthony had stayed on his way to Sardis a year before. After a noon meal, they sped off across the Gordus Plain to the next relay station, Marmara Village.

Auxiliary personnel, accustomed to many regulars arriving and leaving, were ready at each relay station with fresh mounts.

Over a year ago, I went to Sardis, fearful that I would be forced to return to Pergamum. Two hours ago, we passed by Thyatira. We'll soon be near where Miriam sang her song along the Royal Cemetery, the one that moved Nikias so much. I wanted to stop at Thyatira to see Miriam and Grace, but we couldn't even go into the city. I had to pass by. When will I see them again?

---

[14] Psalm 121:1–4

By midafternoon, they were in Sardis, talking with Commander Felicior. "Tell me what you have planned," he said, leading them to his office.

After learning their plans, he said, "I have other news. Commander Diogenes Elpis in Aizanoi named the two murdered merchants. Relatives identified the clothing. Nothing valuable was left on the bodies, but that's hardly a surprise."

His words then echoed those of Commander Servius early that morning. "I want to know who did this, and I want them all in chains."

ON THE INTERIOR ROAD FROM PRUSA TO COTYAUM

Taba and Maza, dressed as Roman soldiers, were guarding slaves being transported in two wagons. They looked back at their captives and then glanced at each other and winked. Each caged wagon carried ten slaves and was pulled by two horses. Harpa rode behind to make sure that no one made a desperate move, either attacking another slave or attempting a getaway. Taba leaned forward and whispered in his horse's ear.

On the first wagon, a slave merchant sat beside the driver. They chatted about sailing from the Black Sea, coming through the Bosporus, and, yesterday, arriving at Port Daskyleion on Marmara Sea's southern shores.

The little caravan descended the gentle green slopes on which Prusa was built and began their trip going east and then southward along the Interior Road.

Maza asked, "When do we get rid of this slave merchant?"

Taba looked behind to make sure that he could not be heard, but he did not need to worry. The sound of slaves bellowing and cursing was louder than the constant clip-clop of horses' hooves and wheels rolling along the roadway's cut stones.

"Today we'll travel normally, and then tonight we'll arrive at an inn and be joined by another 'merchant,' who is actually one of our men. He'll take a seat on the second wagon tomorrow morning. By the time we arrive in Cotyaum, this slave merchant will have 'disappeared' and will no longer be concerned with what happened to his slaves."

They winked again, eager to carry out Craga's plan.

Chapter 6
Uncovering the Past

JONATHAN AND REBEKAH'S HOME, THE CITY OF THYATIRA

Miriam awoke with birds twittering close by. She had slept well in Jonathan's house. Moving slowly, she tried not to disturb Grace, but the baby was soon awake.

She carried her daughter downstairs to the washroom and toilets at the back of the house. Water came in through clay pipes. She took a cold bath using a pitcher to douse herself and washed with sweet-scented olive soap from Olive Grove.

Once upstairs, she put on a clean cotton tunic. Her long, wet black hair was done up in thick braids to keep her neck cool during the summer heat. Even though it was still early, the heat of the morning made her skin feel prickly. She thought, *The heat yesterday made breathing difficult. What must it be like for slaves laboring in the metal shops I passed as I came into the city?*

Miriam returned downstairs carrying Grace just as the breakfast meal was being brought from the kitchen. The rest of the family had already gathered and were reclining.

"Miriam, come and tell us more about your life," Rebekah said, patting the couch beside her. "Jonathan knows most of it already from visiting with your grandfather in the past." There was something about the way she asked, winsome and inviting, not haughty and overconfident like Jonathan.

"Well, I'm twenty-seven years old. I was born in Alexandria, Egypt, and at three months, I left Africa on one of my great-grandfather's trading ships.

"My earliest memories come from a small farm near Bethlehem. We moved there from Alexandria when I was four months old. Five years later, we had moved into Jerusalem for safety, but then we suffered through the siege by the Roman army.

"When we escaped from the city through a small service gate, Daddy was hit by an arrow shot by our guards behind us on the city wall. He died in Mommy's arms, but she was struck at the same time and died a year later in Antioch.

"I grew up in Pergamum with my great-grandfather, Eliab, and great-grandmother, Ahava. We came to Asia Minor when I was six. Grandpa Antipas brought me up, but his steward took care of me for several years. I married Anthony on my birthday in Pergamum fourteen months ago. The next day, we adopted Chrysa Grace."

The family listened intently to every word. Serah knew almost nothing about Miriam. "Who and where is Anthony?"

"I met my husband when he was an instructor at the Sardis garrison. Right now, he's on a special assignment for the army."

"Oh, you must be lonely for him! But how exciting!"

"Yes, I'm lonely for him already. This will be our first time being separated for many months."

Gil was Jonathan's youngest son and, like Jonathan, a practical and to-the-point businessman. "Did Uncle Antipas encourage you to marry this soldier? Did he not believe that legionaries are our enemies?"

Miriam looked around the table before answering. *He is not subtle with his words, so I must remember that.*

She said, "I'll tell you all about our marriage someday but first about Anthony. He was born into a Roman family, and his father fought against Jerusalem. You'll be surprised when you meet my husband. I hope that will be soon!

"About your question, Gil, many things happened in the last three years. Before we were married, Anthony learned about Yeshua Messiah and how to listen to God's voice. For now, I must be separated from him due to his work. However, I'm pleased to be at this table with all of you."

Uncle Jonathan clapped his hands to signal the rest of the household to gather for a prayer. Jarib Ben Nakoda, Jonathan's steward, came in from outside, and he was joined by Gedalya, one of Jarib's sons. A male slave was behind Jarib.

Jonathan stood at his place, and everyone stood to end the meal. "Welcome to another day! This is a time of blessing, and we look forward to a week of service and perseverance. We must pray today for Miriam's husband...."

His loud voice echoed through the house as he quoted a passage he loved. "Rescue me, O Lord, from evil men, protect me from men of violence, who devise evil plans in their hearts and stir up war every day. Keep me from the hands of the wicked; protect me from men of violence who plan to trip my feet. O Lord, I say to you, 'You are my God.' Hear my cry for mercy. Do not grant the wicked their desires, O Lord; do not let their plans succeed, or they will become proud."[15]

Miriam looked at Grace, who was trying to stand up and had just fallen. *Is Uncle Jonathan praying against Anthony, against Romans in general, or against the bad men Anthony is looking for?*

Grandpa Antipas never had slaves. Instead, he freed them and then made them paid servants; he gave them a place to live. And in Sardis, too, Uncle Simon has no slaves.

However, here in Thyatira, Uncle Jonathan has a house slave! I must learn what Uncle Jonathan believes. And coming back to his prayer just now, did he imply that 'Anthony is a man of violence' or...?

Although the temperature was starting to rise, Miriam wanted to walk outside for a while. She placed a little straw hat on Grace's head to protect her from the sun and started to leave, but Jonathan's slave stopped her at the door. He was an older man with hardly any whiskers or beard, and his hair was the color of stubble after harvest.

"Are you really Antipas's granddaughter?" he asked in a whisper.

"Yes, I am."

"I was there at his death more than a year ago."

Miriam's heart started to beat wildly, and her mouth felt dry.

"I'm so sorry for you. I was at both trials, when they took him to the theater and a few days later to the amphitheater."

"What was your name at that time?"

"I belonged to Artemidoros, so my name became Artemidian, meaning his slave. Jonathan Ben Shelah bought me at the slave market a year ago. I thought he would change my name to Jonathan-ian, 'belonging to Jonathan,' but he calls me Arte."

"Are you from the Black Sea area? I can tell by your complexion that you didn't come from a family close by."

"Yes, I was born into an important household in Scythia. Our family is named Koloksai, after the founder of our nation. My father, a city councilor, hoped I would be a great man. I was a free man, but one day, thirty years ago, people invaded my village. I was fifteen

---

[15] From Psalm 140:1–8

at that time."[16]

Miriam blinked several times. *Cruelty and much devastation took place when you were captured, Arte. Probably others were taken from your village as well.*

"What shall I call you, Artemidian or Koloksai?"

"When just the two of us are talking, say 'Koloksai.' Otherwise, it's Arte."

Her voice caught in her throat as she gasped. "All right, Koloksai. How did you come to witness my grandfather's death?"

Grace was anxious to stand on the floor and walk. Stumbling to a chair, she tried to hush the child, but she wiggled in Miriam's hands.

"My master, Artemidoros, a merchant in Pergamum, bought me at the slave auction. I became a 'schoolmaster' for his son until the boy came of age. I accompanied him to both of Antipas's trials."

"And what happened?"

"At his first trial, your grandfather was brought to the Roman theater. He appeared on the stage area dressed in a white linen tunic. Night was falling as several priests and priestesses stepped onto the platform, representing the seven temples in Pergamum. They accused him: 'You're an atheist!' They demanded that Antipas declare, 'Caesar is lord and god,' but he outsmarted them. He addressed their questions to explain Yeshua Messiah. There were more than 15,000 people who heard his stories."[17]

"And at the second trial, why did they kill Grandpa?"

"That took place three nights later. They led Antipas to the amphitheater. It's much larger, and it was packed full of people, not a space left. He paid his taxes but refused to say the oath of loyalty to the emperor. They killed him for two reasons. First, he refused to accept their gods and goddesses, their religion. Then he repudiated the emperor, refusing to say the words, 'lord and god.'

---

[16]Scythia was a kingdom to the north of the Black Sea. At its greatest extent, about 200 BC, it reached south to Iran and north into today's Russia, including almost all of Ukraine, and west into Moldova and Romania. Roman governments considered Scythia to be the home of barbarians. From Scythia came a wide variety of commodities: wheat, animal furs, pottery, metals, timber, and slaves.

[17] Antipas's trial is recounted in the first volume: *Through the Fire: A Chronicle of Pergamum, Heartbeats of Courage, Book One.*

Artemidoros explained that his refusal violated the Law of Majestas.[18] The authorities immediately sentenced him for not supporting the empire."

Miriam's face was white with horror, her breath coming in spurts. "How did he die?"

Koloksai's eyes filled with tears. "Perhaps you mean, 'What kind of a man was he when he died?' The last words I heard him speak were a blessing upon his persecutors.

"But if you mean, 'How did they kill him?', well, with hands bound behind his back, they took him to the New Temple. It's being built in the center of Pergamum. Only the foundations were complete. I covered my eyes when they started to lower him toward the boiling oil. It was in an enormous cauldron shaped like a hollow bronze bull."

Miriam wiped her eyes, tears flowing freely. She held her breath. *The disgrace! The pain! Oh, Grandpa! What humiliation! The shame you endured! Boiling oil!*

"He refused to accept the demands of the priests, even while suffering great shame. His witness was so strong. Miriam, I've not been the same since."

Koloksai could not stop. "Miss Miriam, people knew that Antipas lived a good life. The old man freed one slave every year from the slave market. Each freedman or woman lived in a house. They gained a future and dignity and had the freedom to come and go in Antipas's community. Everyone commented on your grandfather's generosity. He loaned money, he healed people by his prayers, and he had hired many poor people to work in his workshops.

"I feel things that I don't have the words to express. All of us slaves admired him. We talked among ourselves, wondering why he lived that way. I finally became aware of something: His strength came from his faith in the Messiah. Why would he die like that, dying for what he believed? I'm sure you know this. The community he started remains. The congregation now meets in the home of Marcos, a city lawyer. People whisper among themselves about the

---

[18] The Law of Treason, or *lex maiestatis* in Latin, dealt with crimes against the emperor, the state, or the empire's citizens. Traitors were regarded as having the same legal status as public enemies. Punishment might include banishment or death.

injustice of his death, and this bothers the authorities. Secretly, Antipas is respected for what he stood for."

Miriam had not expected to receive news about her grandfather the day after arriving in Thyatira. What he said cut like a sword, but there was much comfort in Koloksai's words. He had been changed by her grandfather's death.

"I'm sorry, Miss Miriam. I didn't want to make you cry, but it's better you know this. After Antipas was killed, many people joined his group of followers."

She wiped her eyes. "Koloksai, how did you come to Thyatira? You used to work for Artemidoros, and now you are part of Jonathan's household."

"In the amphitheater, at the beginning of Antipas's second trial, my master made a bet: 'I think Antipas will yield to the authorities! He must repeat the oath of loyalty, and he will declare, "Caesar is lord and god." I'll stake 500 denarii on it. No one will dare to disobey the emperor!'

"He lost the gamble. To pay it off, he sold me to a slave merchant, who brought me to the market in Thyatira, and Jonathan Ben Shelah bought me here."

Miriam turned from Arte to pick Grace up. She was crawling on the floor. "I appreciate you being honest while telling me about his death. It hurts to know what happened, but I'm happy to meet you."

The toddler saw her mother's tears and reached out her hand to touch them. "Someday, my little one, you will know pain, life, belief, rejection, blessing, and death. Until then, you are safe in my arms."

Miriam abandoned her walk in the sun and took Grace to the garden, resting in the shadow of a tree, where no one could see her weep.

Chapter 7
Gifts from Fabius Bassos

THE BOULEUTERION, THE CITY COUNCIL, THYATIRA

Fabius Bassos stood proudly, his hands on his hips, while other wealthy men in the city looked on. He was boasting about three expensive gifts he was giving to the public. Gasps of appreciation sounded, each louder than the last.

He described the costly bronze statue to be unveiled in the Temple of Apollo. More exquisite than the statue was the accompanying frieze telling Apollo's story. Then, later in the afternoon, everyone was going to see the new altar he had donated for the Temple of Artemis.

Of course, the honor coming to him today for these gifts created resentment with city officials. Bassos felt three donations allowed him a status that was greater than theirs. No other benefactor had ever distinguished himself this way in a single day. His exaggerated gait suggested that he deserved the accolades being bestowed by the city's young men.

Mayor Aurelius Tatianos was standing opposite him with a dark frown on his face. Far too much adulation was flowing to Bassos, his rival. People knew this growing animosity was polarizing the city's councilors.

Everyone in Aurelius's household had urged him to prevent Bassos from getting a permanently swollen sense of self-importance. Consequently, Aurelius was preparing a trap.

Bassos was talking loudly. "Do you know how many youths I had following me around the city?"

Interrupting Bassos and calling the city council to order, the mayor announced, "Magnificent events will occur next Saturday, the longest day of the year. Our city will receive a new altar at the Temple of Artemis.

"There will also be marvelous additions made to the Temple of Apollo. How can we thank Fabius Bassos enough for these gifts, except to recognize him as our city's most generous benefactor?"

Polite cheers and applause sounded, even from those who resented the benefactor's growing popularity.

Mayor Aurelius concluded the meeting, saying, "Arrive early on Saturday! Be prepared for spectacular celebrations. The whole city will be there. The Guild of Purple Honors commemorates Artemis that evening. Afterward, the Master of the Guild will pour out a generous libation followed by much music and merriment."

THE HOME OF FABIUS BASSOS, MOUNT GORDUS, THYATIRA

Following the meeting, Fabius Bassos strolled to his favorite room in his large house, built above a steep incline. The mountain ledge fell off steeply, giving his family a spectacular view of Thyatira. Several scrolls were held open on small tables. All dealt with expenses involved in his more-than-generous donations to the city.

On one side, overlooking the city, a leather chair waited for him, which he heavily slumped into, covering his face with his hands. *What have I done? That altar for the Temple of Artemis cost far more than I expected. Why did I commit to giving equally generous donations to both temples? Priests! Such treachery! They spent double! Thieves without a conscience! And Mayor Aurelius Tatianos is trying to bankrupt me. He makes fun of me, pretending to appreciate my generosity, all the while forcing me to spend everything I have—and more!*

The cost of the last games was too high! My best gladiators were killed—after I spent so much on purchasing them. Why do gladiators in Ephesus survive these fights while mine didn't? I committed myself to providing entertainment in October, and now I don't have the means to carry it out. One thing I can't afford to lose is my popularity!

HOME OF DELBIN AND DIODOTUS, IN THE CITY OF SARDIS

Diotrephes, a young teacher, sat at a table in Delbin's house. He was Director of the Department of History at the gymnasium in Sardis. His room overlooked a small river, and on the other side was the mighty Temple of Artemis.

For one year, Diotrephes had been a boarder at the home of this wealthy family. Delbin was one of the well-known aristocratic women in Sardis, and Diodotus, her husband, was the wealthiest of the partners governing the Bank of Hermus Valley.

Diotrephes finished his weekly letter to his mother in Pergamum. He could hardly write fast enough, so great was his excitement at what he had learned.

June 19, in the 11ᵗʰ year of Domitian
From: Diotrephes
To: My dear mother, Lydia-Naq

> *If you are well, then I am well.*
>
> *I have been in Sardis for one year. Your assistance in getting my position in the gymnasium is appreciated. Your friends are fine citizens and very highly respected. Delbin is happy to have me continue as a boarder in her house.*
>
> *As you had suggested, I fired that teacher, the stubborn little man by the name of Jace. He opposed my efforts to change the direction of teaching at the gymnasium. Jace was the only teacher who resisted my approach and aims.*
>
> *I continue to be on the lookout for Anthony, Miriam, and Chrysa. I saw the baby for only a moment one evening. My sweet little cousin! However, I lost track of them after I wrote Commander Felicior of the Sardis Garrison. It was a denunciation letter about Anthony. The commander now refuses to tell me where Anthony is. I believe that Commander Felicior will not send him back to Pergamum for a military trial, so now I have a man looking for the legionary with a long scar on his face.*
>
> *I regret to tell you that Sardis is in grief over the recent landslide and deaths. Much debris from the acropolis fell on several houses, and they are completely covered. Everyone implores Artemis to prevent further erosion of the acropolis.*
>
> *I await your news. I hope to hear that you are well.*

Diotrephes wished to communicate complete success. He was convinced Zeus would bless the Naq family. Secretly, he wondered how difficult it was going to be to again try to kidnap Chrysa. The Chief Librarian in Pergamum, Zoticos, his uncle and the baby girl's father, would be thrilled to have his daughter grow up in an aristocratic Pergamum home.[19]

---

[19] The story of Diotrephes attempting to kidnap Chrysa Grace is told in

Chapter 8
The Streets of Thyatira

THE CITY OF THYATIRA

The next day, Bani and Gil wanted to introduce their cousin to the city. "Miriam, we asked Serah to take care of Grace while we show you how to get around Thyatira." They left Jonathan's house as the city was coming alive.

"We live on the southwest side of the city," Bani explained as they left Jonathan's property. He pointed to a broad avenue. "This is Acropolis Road, and it runs all the way north to the Odeon, where the city council meets. Acropolis Road is a joke, of course, because Thyatira doesn't have much of an 'acropolis.' The little hill is hardly taller than an average man. You came from Pergamum. Now, they have a real acropolis! And Sardis, too, where the acropolis has a very steep path to the top! Here, our public buildings barely form a pimple upon the flat land."

Miriam was taking in not only the city but learning more about her cousins. *Bani is twenty-three years old, and Gil is nineteen. Grandfather Antipas hardly ever talked about them. What did he know about them?*

"Over there...look across the road. Those are the buildings where some of the metal guild members carry on their work. If you were allowed inside, you would find it difficult to breathe. The workrooms are smoky, hot, and dirty. Furnaces roar, and rooms overflow with hardworking, sweaty souls.

"Now here we are at the city's major crossroads—north and south, east and west. This is Central Avenue. Ahead of us, on that corner across from us, is the agora. Anything and everything is bought in the marketplace: food, clothing, horses, donkeys, ceramics, knives, candles, and slaves.

"Increased prosperity comes from the growing trade between

Never Enough Gold: A Chronicle of Sardis, Heartbeats of Courage, Book Two.

Alexandria and Thyatira. Egyptians want our broad selection of dyed textiles, and they are a good market for us. Now there, beside the agora, that's the Lecture Hall. It's owned by Bassos. He cherishes each of his many properties in and around Thyatira.[20]

"To the north is the way to the Temple of Dionysius. The gymnasium, that high building, is where boys study, starting at age six and finishing at age sixteen.

"And that huge building to our left is the public bathhouse. The Temple of Demeter is the other important building in this quarter. This is the latest addition, an Egyptian temple because their traders are starting to settle here, and they worship their gods."

Miriam made a mental note. *Bani and Gil know all about the pagan temples and seem to enjoy talking about them.*

She kept most of her thoughts to herself, but she did make a comment about Bassos. "I did hear his name. On my way here, I met a family, a brother and two sisters, working on one of his farms. They were bringing produce to his shop at the agora."

"Yes, we know all about him," Bani said, pointing to a building across the avenue. "Over there, many kinds of cloth are woven in those workshops—cotton, linen, and wool clothing as well as related products that go to other cities."

Bustling, dense traffic filled both avenues. To the west, Miriam saw the gate at the city wall. At the east end, Central Avenue butted up against the base of Mount Gordus. The wide boulevard was divided by a central watercourse. Water flowed from the Eastern Gate to the Western Gate, spilling through one shallow pool before splashing into another slightly lower down. Along the boulevard, green vines crept upward on wooden trellises, and long tendrils spread across the street.

This long stretch of greenery cast a pleasant, welcoming shade, so the avenue was a favorite place for people to gather. Along the watercourse, fountains gushed, and little rainbows formed when

---

[20] Little of historic Thyatira has been or can ever be excavated. The ancient city is known today as Akhisar (White Tower), with a population of about 100,000. Only two city blocks have been unearthed, both in the city center. The ruins include a basilica, the agora or marketplace, and the ancient central archway. The description of the city in this novel is an educated guess based upon the geography and public buildings found in other Greco-Roman towns during the same period.

A Chronicle of Thyatira

breezes caught the spray. Birds, large and small, flew into the pools, splashing and chirping. Flowering shrubs brightened Central Avenue from one end to the other.

The two main arteries met at the Triple Arch, which had been built as a tribute to Rome's victories. Bani explained, "This is our expensive colonnade. It borders on the agora and was built by the Clothiers' Guild…"

Gil finished his brother's sentence: "…the most powerful guild."

A moment later, in a softer voice, Bani added, "They want Father's investments and are asking him to join in with them."

"Really?" Miriam's voice rose slightly. "Investments! Does Uncle Jonathan want to be part of another guild?"

"Oh, yes," Bani bragged, "they want his money, but Father is also deeply associated with the Guild of Purple Honors. Everyone in this city belongs to a guild. There's no other way to live."

Gil continued the tour. "Going east up Central Avenue, toward Mount Gordus, that's the basilica, the civic building. Beyond it is a temple. Across from it…see that building? That's our synagogue, where we'll attend this evening.

"Across from the synagogue, that's the 'Temple of the Gods,' built for minor gods and goddesses. Up there, on the side of Mount Gordus, the theater has space for ten thousand spectators. If more people attend, they must sit on the rocky terrain that forms the mountain's upper slope, just above the seating area. It's extremely uncomfortable up there."

He pointed slightly behind them, to the southeast. "That's the stadium where the Games are held."

Again, Miriam waited, wondering if Bani would comment about participating in any activities at those locations, but nothing more was said.

They returned to the agora, and Bani said, "Now we'll go to Father's shop." Jonathan's sales shop was managed by Elisha, a steward who had spent the previous winter in Sardis. Miriam and Elisha greeted each other and shared several memories.

Leaving the shop, they returned to Acropolis Road and stopped at the Temple of Apollo. Bani said, "The high priest at the Temple of Apollo and the other priest, the one in charge of the Temple of Artemis, are in constant competition.

"Of course," he added quickly, "I see from the expression on your face that you disapprove of my even mentioning Apollo and

Artemis. Yes, we are Jewish and should not be involved in pagan things! Being in business here, though, somewhat requires us to be aware of what is happening at the temples."

Clearly, Bani's enthusiasm was inherited from his father, and Miriam commented, "You know this city well, Cousin Bani. I think you enjoy living here!"

"Yes, I do! Thyatira is one of the seven most important cities in Asia, even though many people poke fun at it. You should have been here two years ago when the Asiarchs had their meeting! Important men came from all the cities of Asia, so many that they couldn't fit in our small acropolis. Most had to wait over there, in the gymnasium portico, while offerings were made to Caesar.

"See how small the acropolis is? The city council members meet in this building. Those are the wealthy men of the city who gather to make decisions. I'd show it to you, but we aren't allowed to go inside."

"Entering the city for the first time, the walls surrounding it seem small and unable to protect the city in a time of war," Miriam remarked.

"Miriam, that's why Thyatira was overrun so often! Seleucid kings backed by elephants coming from the east confronted kings of Pergamum marching from the west! All those soldiers were ready to die in battle. At first, the Seleucid Kingdom gained control but only for a while. Pergamum was much closer, and eventually our city came under the rulers of this region."

Bani pointed west to a distant bluish mountain peak. "The narrow pass at Forty Trees kept enemies at bay. But here, it's a wide-open plain. Nothing could stop the recurring onslaughts. Look around! There's no natural protection at all!"

Miriam strained her eyes, staring at the far-off mountain. *Are you there today, Anthony? You said you would be staying in Soma and visiting Olive Grove Farm. Protect him, Lord. And from what I'm learning, I may need shelter just as much as Anthony!*

"This is the most important of all the temples, off here to the right," said her cousin, entering another boulevard that linked the acropolis and the lower slopes of Mount Gordus.

An ancient temple decorated with red bricks and white marble stood before them. "This is the Temple of Artemis, hundreds of years old and built on top of ancient foundations. Isn't it beautiful? This road leads to the north end of the city. Up there are the homes of the wealthiest families. One of them, Fabius Bassos, donated an ornate altar. Maybe you've heard it's going to be dedicated in the temple tomorrow."

Miriam, overwhelmed by the positive way he talked about temples, gods, and goddesses, groaned, "Please, Bani, I'm not feeling well. Could we go home now?"

THE SYNAGOGUE OF THYATIRA

Miriam and Grace left for Friday evening prayers at the synagogue. Jonathan, Rebekah, Bani, Gil, and Danila led the way, and behind them came Jarib and Shiri, Jonathan's steward and his wife.

The Thyatira synagogue was a small building entered by a side door through a high surrounding stone wall. Immediately inside was the portico, a square area with a sparkling water fountain at the center. Men chatted under a roofed colonnade, and women gathered in one corner. Miriam held back, not wanting to open a conversation with anyone until she knew more of the people.

The sky was growing darker as Jonathan, Bani, and Gil entered the synagogue. They sat on one side with the men, while Rebekah, Serah, and Miriam took seats on the other side of the sanctuary area.

"Danila doesn't worship inside," whispered Rebekah, "so I often stay in the portico with her."

Miriam asked, "How did it come about that..."

"...that she is going to marry our son? Jonathan visited Laodicea a few years back, staying with his brother Daniel. While there, he met Danila's family. Then she met Gil here during a visit to the guild with her father. It's a union of families in more ways than one."

Miriam wondered what that meant, but it was not a time for questions.

After the Friday evening worship, Miriam overheard two women arguing. One said, "Rabbi Hanani told me we must keep followers of the carpenter Yeshua and other groups with strange teachings out of the synagogue."

As she spoke, she chopped the air with her hands, and Miriam imagined her trying to act out what Hanani meant by that action.

The second woman said, "Yes, Rabbi Hanani is at a meeting in Antioch, consulting with other rabbis! False teaching about the Messiah weakens us. Those people claim that they..." They lowered their voices when they saw Miriam listening to their discussion.

JONATHAN AND REBEKAH'S HOME, THE CITY OF THYATIRA

At home during the evening meal, Jonathan's family reclined on couches around the small square table in the living room. Arte served a sumptuous selection of tasty delights.

As they were finishing, Miriam asked, "I overheard two women speaking in the portico about Messiah. Why were they so worked up? And who is Rabbi Hanani?"

For a moment, no one answered. Then Jonathan responded slowly, "An argument has erupted, Miriam. The issue is, how will our elders treat followers of Yeshua Messiah? We are part of the group they are concerned about. Those women are purists; I call them traditionalists. Both women want us excluded from fellowship."

He paused, took another bite, and swallowed before speaking again. "They hold onto their traditions and have strict ideas. Rabbi Hanani left for Antioch last September to talk with other rabbis.

"Not everyone agrees with him though. Some believe all Jews should be able to use the synagogue. They say, 'Folk from Persia, Rome, Jerusalem, Antioch, and Alexandria should all find a home together as we worship Adonai.' Do you understand what I'm talking about?"

"Yes, better than you know," said Miriam, trying to keep a frown off her face.

After supper, Rebekah announced, "You all need to be up early tomorrow. It's going to be a full day!"

"Grace wakes me up early every morning anyway!" Miriam was growing fond of Rebekah, a quiet, resilient person. As she went to bed, she had time to collect her many thoughts. *Grandpa Antipas ran into these same difficulties, and we were all excluded from fellowship. Consequently, his name was removed from the synagogue's Book of Life. After that, the Pergamum civic authorities declared him a "non-Jew."*

The summer evening was hot and muggy, but the thought of her family being expelled sent shivers down her back. She folded her arms over her heart, feeling a sudden chill. *Lord, take care of Anthony, and watch over Uncle Jonathan and his household too.*

Chapter 9
The Longest Day

THE CITY OF THYATIRA

The longest day of the year arrived. Unusual for a summer day, clouds were blowing in from the west. As breakfast was ending, Jonathan beckoned, "Celebrations begin soon at the Temple of Apollo. Let's not be late or else there won't be a good place to stand to watch the procession go by!"

Miriam felt her body freeze. *This is our Sabbath! He can't be going to the Temple of Apollo! No one in our family would compromise the covenant, not in a thousand years!*

As the festival began, those walking in the parade strutted and smiled broadly while talking loudly and enjoying the prospect of being watched by the crowds. The high priest of the Imperial Cult walked at the front of the procession. He was young, and many predicted that he would become a significant figure in the city. Purple ribbons lined his cape, and a gold diadem graced his head, the gold leaves of the laurel sparkling against his black hair. It was a simple crown.

The emperor's worship wove every province together more tightly than the finest cloth from Thyatira's best weavers. Clothing grew old and could be torn apart, but the empire was held together by daily sacrifices across a vast area.

The high priest of the Temple of Apollo came next in the procession, proud to play a part in these special commemorations. Today his place of worship would receive two magnificent additions from Fabius Bassos. Having given generously to two temples, the wealthy benefactor gained the right to walk beside the high priest.

Mayor Aurelius Tatianos walked behind Bassos. This was a religious procession recognizing the benefactor's great generosity. Tatianos grinned. Last night, while tossing and turning, he had hatched a plan to bring Bassos down.

Soon he would undermine the popularity of his rival.

Two years earlier, when the Asiarchs met in Thyatira, Bassos had obtained written permission from the emperor for gladiator fights with sharp weapons. Such a document was needed to authorize any gladiator combat that would result in death. Without this permission, gladiators were indeed roughed up, but they lived to fight another day.

However, Tatianos remembered that Bassos had gladiators who had died during those four memorable days. Well-trained gladiators cost a sum only Bassos could manage. Recently, he had learned that depleted bank accounts were all Bassos had to show for having supported death sports.

But now, he had a scheme to force Bassos to spend even more, far beyond his means. His grin was genuine. After his plan was executed, he, Mayor Tatianos, would be left as the undisputed, most prominent citizen of the city.

Bassos looked over his shoulder and waved at Tatianos. His mind was buzzing. *Having to underwrite the costs of the Games and fights in October and next year in May could bring me close to bankruptcy. I'm perspiring but not because of the heat, which is already noticeable. I was too reckless, too ready to agree to these suggestions to give these gifts to the temples. One day I must put my foot down. Why can't I say no to Mayor Tatianos?*

For their part, the spectators were thrilled to see Bassos walk by. They shouted, intensely appreciative of him. They knew he was determined to make Thyatira better known in Asia, but that took money—lots of it.

The new altar, which was about to be dedicated, was proof of their famous benefactor's efforts.

Gossip traveled fast. Everything seemed to revolve around shame and honor in a city where stories about these adversaries added to the chatter around family dinner tables. Struggles between gladiators lasted only four or five days. However, political rivalries were delicious morsels to be chewed over all year long.

Standing on the top step of the Imperial Temple, the high priest raised his head, stood up straight, squared his shoulders, and, with a booming voice, called out, "Caesar is lord and god!"

Everyone cheered loudly, repeating the phrase. The high priest lifted his hand and suddenly brought it down, signaling for tambourines and harps to be played. Cheering arose.

Colors flowed, with each priest wearing fine linen imported from Egypt. People waved freshly cut branches. The priests of Artemis and Apollo paraded slowly, leading their animal sacrifices. Civic pride overflowed in a swirl of glorious color.

Following Artemis and Apollo's priests came those of other temples: Dionysius, Demeter, and Athena. Devotees followed, shouting the names of their deity.

Above their heads, clouds began to roll in. Priests looked up apprehensively. Rain was unknown at this time of the year!

Miriam stood beside Jonathan and Rebekah as the procession began, feeling aloof and embarrassed to even be a bystander. People were packed tightly beside her, and she felt uncomfortable. Miriam had never been a witness to such an event. Typically, she would be spending a Sabbath morning with family members at home before attending worship.

Behind the priests and priestesses came each guild's officials, and young maidens danced, throwing flowers into the crowd. Clowns and athletes shouted vulgar comments. Miriam felt her breathing becoming difficult.

Just then, Rebekah shook her elbow. "Miriam, see that woman in the front row of the guilds procession? See the one in the blue dress, imitating the actions of some of the leaders?

"That is Sibyl Sambathe. I want to warn you about her. The one next to her is Hulda, her sister. Sibyl is the older of the two women. Hulda has not had good health but many bouts of chest pain and coughs. Did you hear of Lydia, the merchant of purple cloth and dye? She was originally from Thyatira but lived in Philippi, became friends with the Jewish community, and joined Jewish women at prayer beside a little river outside that city.[21] Sibyl and Hulda are related to Lydia, and they were among the first people in the city to follow the Messiah.

"One day Lydia came back to Thyatira and told her family here

---

[21] Lydia, who did originate in Thyatira, is encountered in Acts 16:11–15. Sibyl and Hulda Sambathe are fictional in this novel, as is the story of Lydia's connection with the Guild of Purple Honors.

about the Jewish Messiah; that was almost forty years ago. Many came to her family's house to listen. Lydia had her dye work done at the Guild of Purple Honors. Sibyl and Hulda, related to her on her father's side, were young girls. Hulda was having breathing problems even back then. They heard what Lydia had to say about healing and liked what she taught.

"They still come to the synagogue and also to our home meetings on Sunday, but they also join in activities at the various temples in the city. I wanted to warn you that they are both defensive of their remarkably diverse beliefs. Their opinions are more tolerated than accepted.

"Sibyl believes herself to be a prophetess. That is what her name means. She comes up with prophecies, but fortunately, few believe her predictions. Last Sunday morning at our Way of Truth assembly in our home, Sibyl said, 'On the longest day, a special blessing will pour down on this city.' Everybody thought that was very strange. Nobody thought that she may be referring to rain. Now that it's June 21, don't those look like rain clouds? I've been here for eighteen years, and it's never rained in June."

Miriam looked up and scanned the sky. "I think we are about to get soaked. The clouds are getting darker. Feel that wind!"

A bull had been sacrificed, and blood was sprinkled on the altar of Apollo. A rumor had been circulated that the new frieze to be dedicated today told the entire story of Apollo's life. The decoration was hidden by a white cloth with purple stitched around the edges.

When the ends of the fabric were released by Tatianos and Bassos, the full majesty of the Apollo frieze would be evident. Many priests served Apollo, whose full name in Thyatira inspired awe: Helios Pythios Trimnaios Apollon.[22] His name in the city wove together four nearby cultures: those of Macedonia, Lydia, Phrygia, and Greece.

After a brief speech by a priest, it was time to reveal the frieze. Fabius Bassos and Mayor Tatianos nodded to each other. Each man held one end of the white cloth covering the sculptured frieze. They let go at the same time, and the fabric fluttered to the ground. The

---

[22] Colin J. Hemer, *The Letters to the Seven Churches of Asia,* Eerdmans, Grand Rapids, Michigan, 1989, p. 110. Several of Hemer's historical insights serve as the basis for describing Thyatira in this novel.

slowly falling material was meant to symbolize Apollo's blessings falling from the sky silently and mysteriously.

Expressions of admiration and sounds of wonderment came from the priests and priestesses. People sucked in their breath, holding it for seconds, afraid such beauty might only be a delusion. Apollo's complete story in fourteen scenes[23] was there for all to see. It occupied an entire wall.

The cold white marble told Apollo's story. Bassos beamed, for the impact of his frieze passed all expectations. As they viewed the panels, the most powerful men and women of the city were elated. Some priests laughed. Others wept, grateful for the unbounded generosity of Bassos.

No one could estimate the cost of such a frieze, but Fabius Bassos was not finished yet, for this was to be the most incredible day of his life. He walked to the front of the temple, where a purple cloth covered a statue. Slowly, he tugged it, and then people gasped.

A life-sized statue of a naked Apollo, the god of light, stood before them. Apollo was glorious, shining with a superb amber and fine bronze polish. Only a few of the Guild of Bronzesmiths knew how to produce such a luster.

The statue stood in a central place of the temple. Above the figure was a wide opening in the roof. A single ray of sunlight shot through a parting in the dark clouds and struck the glittering statue. In an instant, Apollo, the god of light, reflected energy and life to those who were privileged to see him thus unveiled. Was there another temple anywhere that could boast of such magnificence?

While the worshippers were still enthralled by the artist's portrayal of their god, Mayor Tatianos took center stage. "Today we are also dedicating the newest coin in the Empire! The industrious men in the Bronzesmiths' Guild have not only poured the bronze for this statue. They have also created a bronze coin that will outlast the one we use every day. Soon it will be found circulating in the farthest reaches of the empire. Every priest and city dignitary present will receive one of these bronze coins. They will say, 'Oh,

---

[23] Every school child in Phrygia and Asia Minor learned these stories. The original frieze, with its Phrygian interpretation of Apollo, is on display at the Museum of Hierapolis, Turkey, near Laodicea. See more, including many Apollo photographs, at https://en.wikipedia.org/wiki/Apollo.

this comes from Thyatira!'

"You will each get one as a gift. Look at it carefully. See, on one side is Apollo's statue, the image you saw unveiled a moment ago. On the reverse side is an infant, Domitian's child, who died nine years ago. His son is seated on a globe, and above his head are the seven stars of the Great Bear constellation. This coin pays homage to our divine emperor. Domitian authorized Thyatira to create a coin honoring these two: Apollo and the 'son of god,' as we call Domitian's son."[24]

A gasp went up from the crowd. When had Thyatira witnessed anything like this? Tatianos declared, "Caesar is lord and god! Behold this image, the son of god."[25]

Everyone shouted back with gratitude, "Caesar is lord and god!" Their Temple of Apollo was now on a par with others in Hierapolis, Laodicea, and Sardis. Of course, it could never compete with the massive, still unfinished Apollo Temple in Didyma. However, Thyatira would now, without a doubt, become more famous, like larger, wealthier cities. Apollo was alive in his statue, and his image was circulating on the brightest coins.

One of the priests leaned over to a young priest in training. "Now even the great Temple of Apollo in Didyma, under construction for hundreds of years, will have to acknowledge the grandeur of our temple."[26]

Bassos, who had made the expensive donation of Apollo's statue and frieze to the city, would never be forgotten. The benefactor had honored Thyatira in a morning's tribute, and in turn, the city would remember him forever. He had earned his place in Thyatira's history.

---

[24] Apollo's Temple in Thyatira has not been discovered, not surprising since less than one percent of the ancient city has been excavated. One possible location of the city's temple may be under a large mosque in the northwest sector. The description of the coin is accurate.

[25] Suetonius and Martial were ancient contemporary writers who mentioned Domitian's requirement that people address him and refer to him as *"dominus et deus,"* or "lord and god." Coins circulating in Asia Minor showed Domitian's infant son's deification at his death in AD 83. These coins showed a child seated on a globe surrounded by seven stars.

[26] The ancient Temple of Apollo in Didyma, on the Aegean seashore, south of Ephesus, was never completed. The temple became famous as a location for "oracles," or prophecies for the future.

Chapter 10
The Storm

THE CITY OF THYATIRA

Across the plains, to the west of Thyatira, torrents of rain fell. Dark clouds were carried eastward by tempestuous winds, and by mid-morning, the sky became gloomy. The unexpected storm quickly brought an unrelenting deluge on the guests at the Temple of Apollo and the spectators on the streets.

The throngs felt the winds sweeping down before the rain struck. Tree branches flailed wildly, and people wondered what the gods were saying. Individuals ran for cover under colonnades, found them already crowded, and then scurried around, searching for shelter elsewhere. Many stood with open arms, rejoicing as rain brought refreshingly chilly air.

Priests, who stayed dry under the protection of the temple roof, put their heads together. One asked, "Is this an omen? A few minutes earlier, sunlight was reflecting on the statue of Apollo."

The high priest's assistant answered with another question. "Is this a blessing from Apollo? Or a curse?"

The youngest priest replied, "Dedicating the Apollo frieze was an unusual event." But then his facial expressions matched his questions. "Did we omit any words we should have said in his honor? What does it mean when the god of light, Apollo, is rained on after the sun has been shining?"

The high priest answered wisely, recalling ancient myths, "Apollo can get angry. Remember how he skinned his opponent alive? You recall the man who said he could play the flute better than Apollo, don't you? A mortal, Marsyas, had dared to propose a music competition with the god, and he was punished for that. No, this is Apollo's gentle side. Oh, look! The smoke over the city is being cleared away, leaving everything clean."

An elderly priest agreed. "Artemis, Apollo's twin sister, accepted our tribute to Apollo. She makes the land fertile, and she fights on our behalf. I think this unexpected rain must mean

Artemis is happy for the honor that her brother has received. After all, she is being honored by Bassos this evening. She will have a new altar."

By the time the downpour passed by, falling off to a light drizzle and then a mist, word went out: "This rain was a gift sent by Artemis and Apollo, blessing our city."

Sibyl, standing in the portico of the temple, turned to everyone close by, smiling broadly. "I told you! I prophesied it! A special blessing is going to pour down on us."

News of her prediction circulated quickly from one person to another. She had not been specific. Sibyl had not said, "Expect massive outbursts of rain on the longest day of the year." Still, the way her prediction could be interpreted brought her credence.

A friend of Sibyl repeated her conviction to anyone who would listen. "Not only are Artemis and Apollo gracing us with unusual rain but they have given the gift of prophecy to one of our own citizens!"

With dancing in the streets and people chanting in the late afternoon, the mid-year festival brought a satisfaction that overwhelmed the community. Unexpected rain had tamed the scorching heat, preparing everyone for a memorable evening.

Freshly slaughtered meat from sacrifices would be cooked and served free at the thermopolium next to the Temple of Artemis. No one minded that all the celebrations were two hours later than planned. The gods had spoken favorably. Tonight, even poor people would eat well after the new altar of Artemis was unveiled.

Sparkling eyes in the children of poor families indicated gratitude. Many would be eating meat for the first time in months. The temple cook-shops always had tables along their narrow sidewalks. On this night, the streets would also overflow with laughter and song.

Miriam had not wanted to go with the family to the second public event of the day: the unveiling of a new altar at the Temple of Artemis. Still, since Bani and Serah talked excitedly, she felt compelled to stay with the family.

Miriam looked at Danila. The younger woman was dressed in a new linen tunic and seemed mesmerized by the events of this memorable day. Danila's eyes sparkled, and her hair flowed in elegant waves.

The family reached the acropolis and turned right onto a street that led to the temple. Before entering the temple area, people were expected to make a contribution. Poor people gave the smallest coin, a *tesserae*, made of lead, by placing it in the box marked "Gifts."

The presentation ceremony was performed with Fabius Bassos and Mayor Tatianos unveiling and dedicating the new altar to the temple. Following the new altar's inauguration, people started moving to line up for the free meal. Close by, at the thermopolium beside the Temple of Artemis, meat had been supplied from the temple sacrifices.

When Jonathan gently tugged Miriam's elbow, pulling her toward the nearby thermopolium, she resisted.

"It's a special night," he urged. "I have to be seen by the guild members. Please, I want you to join me this evening."

She finally gave in, moving reluctantly.

Danila called excitedly, "Miriam, come on! We're not going to eat this meal without you!"

Hearing this, Miriam paused. *What is happening? I have never sat down at a cook-shop serving meat sacrificed to an idol. Should I say, "I can't go"? Or shall I go but not eat? Perhaps I should make an excuse: "I'm sick and lonely for Anthony." And that is undoubtedly true.*

"I'll come with you, but I won't be eating anything tonight."

"That's all right," said Rebekah. "Maybe you are missing Anthony. Is that what it is?"

Miriam nodded and forced herself forward, following her uncle and aunt. They had hardly started walking when she noticed how many people greeted Jonathan.

Unexpectedly, her knees felt wobbly, and she accepted Danila's arm around her shoulders. *Uncle Jonathan did not object to attending the procession this morning, the frieze's dedication, or animal sacrifices taken to the Temple of Artemis. How much influence does Danila have here? There is so much to think about. The daughter of a pagan priestess has come to live in my uncle's home. She has her own room and Gil has his, but the whole family tolerates them living in the same house before their marriage! Danila has a strange hold over Uncle Jonathan...and why does my uncle show no shame?*

Music sounded from every street corner. Groups of thirty to forty people, or more, danced in each cluster. Each circle moved counterclockwise, two steps forward followed by one step backward, their hands held high and then dropping low to the ground. One young man with a loud voice animated the dancers, calling out the song's words and keeping the rhythm. Crowds strengthened with wine, fellowship, and goodwill shouted joyfully.

People stood around the firepits as fat sizzled on hot coals. Black smoke curled up from the orange blaze into the darkening evening sky.

Finally, Jonathan's family found a place to sit down. Tables were rearranged for all ten people, including Miriam. Roasted meat with flatbread was brought, and a server poured the wine. Jonathan seemed to be well known. Other families passed by, with greetings continually being exchanged.

Sibyl came to their table and Danila asked her to sit down, but they were crowded into a small space. Miriam did not want to sit beside Sibyl, so she stood up, offering her place. She whispered in Rebekah's ear, "I can't eat anything. Something is making me uncomfortable."

"Join in the dancing if you want to, or walk around in the crowd," said Rebekah, sympathetic to her niece, who was here without her husband.

Miriam turned to her uncle. "I'm going for a walk. It's less crowded on the road."

Jonathan lowered his voice so only Miriam could hear. "Don't worry about me. I will explain things to you later. Businessmen are compelled to be members of a guild. That is the only way a person can work or participate in this city. The people greeting me are members of two guilds, the Clothiers' Guild and the Guild of Purple Honors. Most of these men are my close business friends."

His explanation finished, he commented loudly on the activities of the festival.

Miriam noted how everyone dressed their best. Women paraded, sauntering while showing off extravagant hairstyles. The cooler air enabled them to let their hair down, which was unusual for this time of the year. Everyone was dancing with a friend or waving to a crowded table.

An involuntary shudder passed through Miriam's shoulders. *Why did I come with Uncle Jonathan? I have never done anything like this on a Sabbath! Today being with my uncle and aunt meant witnessing Apollo and Artemis's festivities from morning until night. Why didn't I attend a Sabbath service at the synagogue, my first Sabbath in this city? Now I feel dirty and ashamed about being in the middle of this festival. This morning, I watched Apollo being honored with a new statue and an expensive frieze. This evening, Artemis received a new altar.*

She left the throng, walking slightly uphill toward Mount Gordus. At the edge of the crowd, a young woman caught her attention. The stranger was looking back every few steps, her hands twisted behind her back.

"Hail, my name is Miriam."

The young woman looked up, surprised. "Hail, my name is Melpone."

"I'm happy to meet you," said Miriam and kept walking.

A thought struck her: *That young woman looks so sad. Or maybe just lonely.*

Chapter 11
Murder on the Highway

ON THE INTERIOR ROAD FROM PRUSA TO COTYAUM

Caged-in wagons moved down the Interior Road as weary slaves sat in the uncomfortably cramped space. In this caravan, there were two separate wagons with ten slaves in each. They were treated like animals, with no choice but to tolerate conditions that served their captor's needs.

A wagon served as a temporary prison. The cages covering the slaves were built of strong timber, making escape impossible.

Three sat on each side, two at the front, and two at the back. Cursing the merchant, the captives fell silent. A whip had left a welt on the strongest man's shoulders, who had complained loudest the previous day.

At night, they slept in dark, dank quarters, unable to escape. Bed bugs left them scratching at sores all day, and sleepless nights brought increased anxiety. Iron fetters around their ankles and chains binding them together made even the most restless sleep almost impossible. They quietly talked of home back in Scythia and groaned, longing for familiar surroundings.

Food was provided in the early morning before the day's journey and at the end of the day, but it was not nutritious. Their cramped cages brought stiff muscles and cramped legs that made walking difficult when they stopped for exercise. The caravan stopped four times each day: once in the morning, once before noon, and twice in the afternoon. Slaves needed the movement and exercise to remain sellable. They would be displayed at the Cotyaum slave market in two days.

After the second afternoon stop, the slaves were back in their cages. The merchant-owner, not suspecting any danger, was led by Maza off the road and down a slight slope "to see something interesting that we found, just over there."

A stretch of road from Inegol, south of Prusa, to Cotyaum curled around countless hills as it rose to the inland plains. Scrub brush filled the valley. During the late afternoon of the fourth day, the unsuspecting slave merchant was killed on this stretch of the road.

His death was quick, and the merchant did not make a sound as he fell. Maza wiped his sword clean and pulled the body into a small cave that Craga had previously found. Stones had been piled close to the entrance in preparation for this moment.

Craga, aware that inadequate precautions were taken during a slave train theft earlier in the summer, had prepared his gang members more carefully this time. On this trip, no bodies would be discovered.

However, one slave was more alert to what had happened and spoke to the others after they had finished their evening meal and were lying down to sleep.

This slave was born in Bilsk, the most prosperous city in Scythia, and he spoke in the Pahlavi language.[27]. "The man sitting beside our driver is new. Since we were captured and placed on the ship, we've had the same slave merchant. I think the man who captured us got murdered when they went off the road back there."

"Shut up, Strong Guy! We can't do anything about it."

"I know that, but I think it means we may be in for rough handling from here on out. The man who joined the caravan this morning is now our slave master. Did you hear how he snarled at us at the evening meal? Our first slave master had a lower tone in his voice. I am telling you that the man who stole us from our homes never came back up the hill. He is still there, somewhere off the road."

"Close your mouth! Do you want to get us whipped again?"

---

[27] Many slaves were taken from Scythia, the area now known as Ukraine and part of Russia, to the Roman Empire. The Pahlavi language was spoken in Central Ukraine. Bilsk was known as a trading city, bringing goods from the Roman empire north. Merchandise was brought to Bilsk from China along a section of the Silk Road. Tanais, Crimea, one of the ports along the Black Sea, exported slaves and other products from the north.

Chapter 12
Jonathan

JONATHAN AND REBEKAH'S HOME

On Saturday night, it took Miriam a long time to get to sleep. Too soon, the rooster in the garden woke the household; it seemed far too early. The sun had just begun to lighten up the eastern sky. Grace was still asleep, so Miriam made her way alone to the darkened bathroom downstairs.

Less than an hour later, people started to arrive at the house. At first, one family came at a time, and then several others came in small groups. Sounds of laughter filled the house, along with men welcoming men and women greeting women.

It was the weekly gathering of the assembly Jonathan called the "Way of Truth."[28] The meeting at dawn on Sunday mornings brought as many as fifteen families together. Only one family was wealthy. Judging from their clothing, the others were much poorer. Miriam looked around as men and women, young and old, free and slaves, sat together on carpets that had been laid on the floor of the large room.

Jonathan began, his deep, full voice echoing in the room. "Welcome, everyone, to the Way of Truth." Everyone stood as he led, chanting the Shema: "Hear, O Israel, the Lord your God is One God."

Miriam was standing between Serah and Danila. Bani and Gil were on the other side of the room.

Her attention drifted from the chant as she thought about Danila and Gil's relationship. *I'm worried about my cousin. Gil is going to get married to the daughter of a pagan priestess. This is so different from my home! In Pergamum, Grandfather Antipas worshiped in the long shed called "The Cave" for years. While we were living in Sardis, Uncle Simon and Aunt Judith had nothing to do with*

---

[28] Jonathan Ben Shelah took this name from 2 Peter 2:2.

worshiping Greek and Roman gods.

I see some of the same people here this morning that I saw last night at the celebration at the Artemis thermopolium. There's that woman, Sibyl, again!

Jonathan spoke: "Adonai, our Lord, promised, 'With deep compassion, I'll bring you back. In a surge of anger, I hid my face from you for a moment, but with everlasting kindness, I'll have compassion on you, says the Lord, your redeemer.'[29] The prophet Isaiah promised comfort to the remnant. Indeed, that includes us. The synagogue leaders instructed me that in our God-fearers meetings for non-Jews, I should read messages from the prophets each time we meet. I am happy to do so. I also will speak about the Messiah.

"My subject today is the remnant, a personal theme. In my family, we are only a fraction of our previous numbers. Alexandria, in Egypt, was our family home long before my father left for Jerusalem. Adonai kept us alive through the siege of the Holy City and eventually brought us to Asia Minor."

Jonathan developed the concept of the remnant using his own family background to explain God's purpose in allowing some to remain alive after so many others were lost. After challenging the people to be thankful for their daily blessings, Jonathan invited each person to come forward. They participated in the Holy Meal, which involved eating a small portion of matzah bread and taking a sip of wine.

"Taking the wine and bread is what our Messiah said we should do to remember the gift of his body as a sacrifice for our sins," Jonathan explained.

As he was finishing, a well-dressed woman stood, ready to speak. Miriam frowned. *How rude! She could hardly wait for Uncle Jonathan to finish. Sibyl and Hulda, her sister! They were together as the procession went by. Hulda looks frail.*

Both Sibyl and Hulda Sambathe were dressed to attract attention, wearing their hair up with many curls. Bright bronze bracelets complemented their necklaces. Like all women, they used nose rings, and several rings graced each hand.

"Yesterday, we celebrated the longest day of the year," declared Sibyl. "A week ago, I promised an unforgettable day. Remember? I

---

[29] Isaiah 54:7–8

said, 'In the morning, there will be a blessing in an unusual manner. In the afternoon, with the sun in our favor, we'll receive bounties.' Tell me, did my words come true?"

Some didn't remember the words she had spoken previously; others knew that she had added several parts to her original comments. She grinned, pleased with the loud applause. She was happy to believe that her prediction had come true.

Breakfast was served. There was hardly enough space for all in the great room, and many stood against the walls to eat. Guests enjoyed barley flatbread and fruit served in wide bowls.

After farewells were said, families started to leave for their workplaces, including several guilds. Mothers were the last visitors as they were taking their small children home. Miriam returned inside, feeling faint from the heat.

A knock sounded outside, and a moment later, Arte called to Miriam, "Do you remember Nikias from Olive Grove Farm? He wants to talk with you."

Miriam's heart leaped at the thought that Nikias had come to see her, and his message thrilled her even more. "Quickly now," he said. "I can't take long. Anthony came to visit me three days ago. He asked me to bring this message to you, and in turn, I'm to take your messages back for when Anthony returns to the farm. He'll be back in Soma every so often."

"When do you think he'll be back?"

"He couldn't say, but it will be more than a month, I'm sure."

"A long time! But you'll be able to act as our go-between?"

"Yes, I'll be in town almost every week to get provisions for the farm and bring products from there."

Miriam did a little dance with Grace. Going around slowly in a circle, Grace responded to her mother's excitement, repeating, "Ba-ba, Ba-ba, Ba-ba."

She took Grace upstairs and opened Anthony's brief letter. She read it out loud to the baby, who did not understand a single word but babbled joyfully at the attention. The message did not say much except that he missed them terribly and that he would be leaving letters at Olive Grove Farm for Nikias to bring to her.

Miriam lay back on the bed, lifting Grace high up. The little girl squealed with delight.

Miriam whispered, "Little one, Danila is getting married. Nine more days and everyone you meet is going to love you to bits. You will be a sweet little girl, won't you? There will be lots of people at the house. I hope there will be no strange noises or crying but smiles and lots of laughs, all right?"

The next day, she asked Uncle Jonathan for papyrus and wrote a letter to Anthony. Grandfather Antipas had insisted that Miriam learn how to manage his shop, which included keeping track of the sales and making a list of the items sold. She had not written many letters before, but now that Nikias could take messages to Anthony, Miriam had a reason to write something other than songs onto papyrus. It took her all morning to finish it.

June 23, in the 11th year of Domitian
From: Miriam
To: My dear husband, Anthony

Peace and grace.

Five days ago, I watched you from where I sat at the back of a grocery wagon. I couldn't stand watching you disappear in the distance. You are always in my thoughts. Three years ago, you stood in the doorway of Grandfather's shop in Pergamum. That day, I caught my breath as I do now, thinking of you. I never dreamed I could grow to love two people so much: you, my husband, and Grace.

She has captivated the family. Aunt Rebekah, the happiest member of the family, is enraptured. You should hear Grace saying, "Ba-ba, Ba-ba, Ba-ba" so sweetly! Everyone says, "Listen! She is calling for her father!'

I want to tell you about the family. They live in a large house that Uncle Jonathan built within the city walls. They planted fruit trees in the garden. The house has two floors: living quarters upstairs and servants' rooms downstairs. The large room is where Uncle Jonathan holds a weekly assembly called the Way of Truth. It's like the God-fearers' assembly in Sardis.

He has a slave! Yes, that's what I said! He is a Scythian named Arte, a wise man, older than most slaves, with two teeth missing. He lived in Pergamum and was present when Grandpa Antipas was condemned to die in the amphitheater. I'm crying as I write this now as I remember our terrible loss.

I have two cousins. Bani is twenty-three years old. His wife, Serah, is a year younger. They don't appreciate people coming for the Way of Truth meeting here on Sunday mornings. I just learned of it this morning, but I don't know why they object. I wish I knew more about what is going on. I'm worried most about my other cousin, Gil. He is nineteen years old and engaged to a young woman, Danila. She is not a Jew and is not a follower of the Messiah. She's from Laodicea, and her mother serves in a temple there.

So much talk about temples! There are so many here in the city. Each one is associated with a guild. I knew a little about guilds but didn't realize that everyone has to somehow be a part of one to have a decent job here in Thyatira.

The city is drab, flat, dusty, and dirty. Smoke from the metal-making furnaces leaves black soot on everything. The streets are narrow. Horses and wagons move slowly, even on Acropolis Road and Central Avenue.

Uncle Jonathan owns a shop where he sells gold rings, bracelets, perfumes, and glass bottles from Grandpa Antipas's workshops in Pergamum. He also sells clothes in another shop. Some come from Sardis and others from Uncle Daniel in Laodicea.

My first impression is that I'm really not going to like it here. I'll tell you more about the guilds, the temples, the city, and the family later. I don't understand all the relationships yet because they are very complex.

Every moment something else reminds me of you. When people asked me about my husband, I say, "He is a legionary." They say, "Where? What assignment is he on?" and I say, "He is on security duty." What more can I say?

I bless you with these words: "Love and faithfulness meet together; righteousness and peace kiss each other. The Lord will indeed give what is good. Righteousness goes before him and prepares the way for his steps."[30]

He'll show you the steps you must take, my beloved.

---

[30] Psalm 85:10, 12–13

Chapter 13
The Postal Road

ON THE POSTAL ROAD FROM SARDIS TO KARUN

On their second day's journey, Anthony's squad rode from Sardis to Karun. The red feathers on his helmet showed him to be the leader. His breastplate fit his broad shoulders well. He looked strong and overpowering on a horse, but it was the scar on his face that set him apart. As a legionary who had served in Legion XXI, the Predators, when sitting with soldiers in the barracks, he held other's attention as he recounted battles in Upper Germanica. However, those events were before a sword came smashing down.

That ugly scar always reminded him of the secrets he kept concealed in his heart. The other five legionaries asked about his fights against the barbarians. However, he had no wish to take Omerod, Menandro, Sextilius, Capito, and Bellinus down that dark tunnel—the day when treachery struck.

Out loud, Anthony said, "I can't talk about it," or "You really don't want to know what happened."

But within himself, there was a running dialogue. *I know it was one of three officers or someone they sent. All I can remember is walking across the bridge over the Neckar River, going down those wooden steps, stepping on the soggy ground, and entering the dark area under the bridge. Guards on that side of the bridge over the Neckar River hadn't seen any barbarians threatening to destroy the structure. Then what happened? I saw a change in the light, a shadow, as someone from behind came at me. I thrust my sword out at him. Everything went black. Later, I regained my senses, and I realized that I had been in a hospital back in Rome for several weeks.*

As they passed through small villages, peasants stopped their work in the fields to watch the six soldiers. At noon they dismounted at a town for a drink of water. Hot rays from the summer sun had both horses and men covered with sweat.

An old man in a village brought them cool water in a large clay pot. "Are you going to the city of Sardis or Aizanoi? Going west or east?" he asked. He was a peasant sharecropper, always in debt to the owner of the land.

"As far as Karun today, and tomorrow, on to Aizanoi," answered Anthony.

"Young men from our families have gone to Aizanoi. They want jobs! It's a city in need of many workers, but they'll come back to this farmland when they get to be old like me. Everything grows here! Vegetables and fruits in abundance. When you retire, come live in my village!"

"Thank you," called Omerod, wiping his mouth and mounting his horse. "You are kind people. Village people like you are hospitable and rarely cause a problem."

Before evening, they arrived in Karun and checked into the garrison's barracks to spend the night. Shortly after they arrived at their bunks, Anthony called out, "Menandro, you're snoring again. I'm surprised you are asleep already."

"Don't wake me up yet! It's not morning!"

Proud of having descended from a long line of lawyers on the coast south of Rome, Menandro's strong jaw projected a steely determination. The sunburned lines in his face came from years of marching in various campaigns. For him, nothing was healthier than riding a horse, whatever the weather.

"Catch all the rest you can get tonight, all of you. It's your last chance before we actually start our task," Anthony added.

"I'm ready for this assignment," Menandro replied in a sleepy voice. "I love danger and take after my father. If he had been in Pompeii when the volcano exploded and buried the city in ash, he would have made sure all the members of our extended clan escaped. But he was away from the city and was the only one of our family who escaped that destruction. My determination to keep citizens safe has been based on that terrible experience."

Anthony called out, "Remember, four of us leave for Aizanoi in the morning. Bellinus and Capito will stay here to start their work. I want all of us to meet in Prusa on the first day of next month!"

But Menandro had already rolled over.

The next day, as they rode toward Aizanoi, having left Bellinus and Capito for their assignment, Anthony watched the other three men he was assigned to lead. He felt proud to have these trustworthy legionaries with him.

Short, two-edged swords hung from their leather belts, and red capes fluttered behind. Their horses stopped at each military checkpoint. They passed several camel trains, one with thirty animals, stretched along the road with plodding merchants taking their products from one city to another.

FROM KARUN TO THE INTERIOR ROAD

Bellinus and Capito were to take five days investigating the terrain from Karun to the end of the Postal Road below White Horse Relay Station.

Six months before, in Sardis, these two soldiers had distinguished themselves by working long hours to rescue families after the recent Acropolis landslide calamity. Despite the threat of a second landslide, they worked tirelessly in pouring rain, recovering several bodies and saving others from the rubble, making them heroes to the citizens. To Felicior, they were the kind of dedicated soldiers needed for this specialized task.

The morning after they arrived, the commander of the Karun garrison insisted on accompanying Bellinus and Capito. He provided three additional regulars for two days to help search through the territory under his direct authority.

During their investigation, they questioned villagers about any recent strangers or unusual activity in the area.

Small hills, none more than one thousand feet high, provided many places for brigands to hide. Higher up and further west, pine forests guarded taller, gentle slopes. Huge mountains faded into others, each a fainter shade of blue. However, they found nothing to indicate that robbers had been in this area. Bellinus and Capito suffered the heat of the day and cramped quarters at night.

Eventually, the Karun commander and his troops were convinced that their area was safe, so they returned to their garrison. Anthony's men continued their journey on to Aizanoi. As they traveled, the two soldiers told each other many exciting parts of their life stories.

Bellinus explained how his ancestors had been involved in minting coins for the city of Sardis. Starting at age seventeen, he stood guard at the mint and the banks close by. At age twenty-four, he trained to become a legionary. Because his family was related to the aristocracy, the mayor of Sardis requested that he be nominated as the head of local security. Now, at age twenty-eight, he looked forward to using all he had learned to search for rebels.

Capito's ancestors owned vineyards close to Sardis, and he had become a soldier in the city. As a young man, he had worked long, hard hours in the fields each summer. Now, at age thirty, with ten years of experience as a legionary, he had gained the confidence of Commander Felicior, who had promoted Capito to the status of an elite soldier.

Bellinus and Capito arrived in Aizanoi on Thursday evening after more conversations with villagers along the way. They spent Friday with the garrison commander, Diogenes Elpis. Together, they reviewed records of caravans passing through this area.

The commander already knew Bellinus and Capito were coming since Anthony, Sextilius, Omerod, and Menandro had talked with him when they passed through while heading toward Cotyaum.

June 27 was a public holiday in Aizanoi. The festivities marked the date when the Kingdom of Pergamum won the city back from the Bithynian army two hundred years earlier.[31]

After breakfast on Saturday morning, Diogenes showed his guests the city, starting at the Temple of Zeus. "I'm a devotee of Cybele myself," he explained. "Zeus occupies the upper floor, but it takes Cybele to uphold the foundation."[32]

Later they admired each of the six remarkable bridges over the winding, tree-lined river; the mosaics in public spaces; and the colonnaded marketplace. Walking through the city, they heard repeated calls for more workmen to build additional houses.

They ate their noon meal at a thermopolium, the cook-shop

---

[31] Aizanoi guarded the border between the Kingdom of Pergamum to the south and the Bithynia Kingdom to the north. Bithynia and Pergamum fought many battles to gain control over this city. The date of June 27 is fictional, but the historical background is correct.

[32] The Temple of Zeus in Aizanoi is built on the foundations of the older Cybele Temple. Cybele was held to be the goddess of the earth. Aizanoi was founded between 2000 and 2500 BC and flourished from the second century to the fourth century AD. The well-preserved temple is of interest to historians, archaeologists, and tourists.

next to the public bathhouse, noting its extensive, lavishly equipped interior facilities and colonnaded forecourt. Once Commander Elpis began speaking, he talked nonstop about grains, wine, and wool.

Sounding like a merchant, he bragged that profits from city commerce had paid for the new pipe system. Aizanoi was bringing hot water from a distant mountain to the south. He appeared more like a businessman who was ready to sell properties than a garrison commander charged with keeping the city secure.

Bellinus whispered to Capito, "The commander knows why we are here, but he refuses to speak about the matter. He should have been an architect, not a military man!"

When asked directly for his opinion on the deaths of two merchants earlier in April and May, Diogenes responded, "I've little time for that. You have to know that I immediately requested a report on the legionaries guarding the caravan and the 'merchants' who replaced those poor fellows left in the ditch. I did some searching for information on those fake merchants and soldiers. It turned out that all used false identity papers.

"Murders, thefts, death, and crime…what's new? Basically, I am shorthanded. The war in Dacia took all my better soldiers, so I cannot get involved in problems out on the roads. I simply do not have the manpower.

"Now, let us talk about something pleasant, like the progress of this magnificent city! I will take you for entertainment tonight. It has to be in the stadium because the theater is undergoing an expansion."

So Saturday evening found Bellinus and Capito enjoying the seats of civic honor at the center of the stadium. Before the evening was over, clowns, musicians, and vulgar comedies brought the repeated expression, "Stop it! I can't take any more laughs!"

With everyone exploding with laugher, Diogenes leaned over. "I cannot tell you not to carry on this inquiry, but from my point of view, Commander Servius is barging in on what should have been my investigation! If Commander Felicior had sent your squad to me, then I would have had sufficient manpower to take care of it." A note of frustration and envy sounded in his words.

"Bellinus," Capito whispered as the last singer took his place on stage, "there's nothing to learn here! The people in this city are full of their magnificent Temple of Zeus and rude jokes. They constantly brag about how grand their theater will be. When they get it connected to this stadium in such an unusual way, it will be a huge complex.[33] But that does nothing for us!"

Capito replied quietly, "Yes, they are secure and proud, and the slaughter of merchants on the Postal Road is nothing to them. The 'new theater' is not all Diogenes cares about though. I'm sure you noticed a hint of professional jealousy in his comment about Commander Servius. The death of merchants on the roads has no effect on their prosperity, and they are undermanned. They just do not care!

"In the morning, let's move on. We'll continue to check out villages and stations between here and the Interior Road. Then we can continue on to Prusa."

There was only one small village and an inn heading northeast from Aizanoi on the Postal Road. All around were shepherds and their flocks in fields that were beginning to turn brown. Shepherds longed for spring rains and green vegetation to return. Bellinus and Capito asked questions and looked over likely hiding places but found nothing of note.

They continued and noted the graceful double curves in the road as they entered Porsuk Canyon. The canyon walls were almost vertical on the north side and very steep on the south.

When they reached the Interior Road, it was nearly noon. Bellinus looked back at the canyon and said, "I'm glad that's over. We've done our part of the search, so let's hurry on to Prusa. We should be able to get there by Monday noon and get some sleep before the Tuesday meeting with Anthony."

THE HOME OF MAYOR AURELIUS TATIANOS, THYATIRA

On the same evening, at the north end of Thyatira, Mayor Aurelius Tatianos received five aristocratic families for an evening banquet. Couches covered with rich purple, red, and yellow tapestries were soon occupied with reclining guests.

"What wonderful mosaics!" one guest remarked. "I want a renovation in our house, but I could never find an artist with such

---

[33] Unlike most Greco-Roman cities, the stadium and theater at Aizanoi were joined together. The theater was slightly higher up the acropolis, bringing the two major entertainment centers together.

an eye for colors. So many tiny colored stones! A work of art! Look at this floor mosaic! Daphne is turning into a laurel tree to protect herself from the lust of Apollo."

The high priest of the Imperial Cult had also been invited to the gathering. His father had lacked inherited wealth but passed on to his son his determination and skill. With all the sacrifices and gifts coming into the Imperial Temple, he would soon be famous.

Alexander, a priest in the Temple of Apollo, was another guest. He knew the traditions of Lydian, Phrygian, and Macedonian cultures and languages, making him uniquely qualified to be a priest. Few were as relaxed with such a variety of sacrifices or religious heritages.

The mayor thanked Bassos for his astonishing generosity to the temple. "People are coming from far and wide to see the frieze."

All the guests were reclining, and Fabius Bassos was unaware that the evening had been planned to flatter his enormous ego. The four other men intended to praise his past donations, thus tricking him into promising more than he could pay for.

The well-known benefactor and his wife were placed on the center couch in the position of honor. Mayor Tatianos held the upper hand because he knew that privately Bassos was worried about his finances and public image.

Slave owners often carried on private conversations in the presence of slaves as they brought food from the kitchen, and slaves tended to gossip with each other in the marketplace. Consequently, Bassos, "The Great Benefactor," could not know that news of his unhappy financial situation had passed so quickly and easily through his majestic villa's stone walls into the mayor's eager ears. Slaves whispered about the privileged information.

Aurelius Tatianos began by announcing, "Welcome, dear friends. A special welcome, too, to Bassos, owner of vineyards, farmlands, slaves, and gladiators! What a delight to have you here this evening!"

The mayor smiled, covering his guile. *But before the night is over, your pride will be in shreds.*

Wine flowed freely, and laughter built in intensity. After the meal and before the evening's entertainment, important matters were discussed.

However, the most urgent was the upcoming Games. The mayor urged, "Please, drink your fill of wine while I talk about the

Games to be held in three weeks and then again next year in May. I want them to be even more splendid than those two years ago."

Bassos kept sipping his wine as if he had not heard about the Games. He was busy thinking about how he would explain his inability to continue with his great beneficence.

He wiped his mouth with the back of his hand and leaned back on his left elbow. "A banquet fit for an emperor!" He smiled, patting his tummy with both hands. His interlaced fingers were intended to show he was at peace.

Tatianos was opening the jaws of the trap and loading it with bait. "A few days ago, we enjoyed the gifts Bassos donated to the city. Thank you, our worthy friend, for your extraordinary generosity. But now it is time to talk of gladiator fights thrilling spectators. If people are content with the authorities in the city, we can expect a more peaceful atmosphere during the winter." The mayor smiled, taking time before continuing.

"However, if discontentment ever settled in, trouble could be stirred up. We have seen what happens. Thousands of families live in squalid conditions in poor housing outside the city walls. Cramped quarters push disgruntled folk onto the streets, and they disrupt our marketplaces and complain boisterously."

Bassos tried to shift the conversation back to the banquet. "Such entertainment you have lined up for us tonight, Aurelius! Music, flutes and harps, food, and wine! Wonderful! This evening is a reminder of what makes Thyatira the best place to live and the reason young men come here looking for jobs!"

Tatianos relished the secret that he had heard. It was amazing how fast news traveled from one household to another when slaves were unhappy with their owners!

He had started slowly, but now was the time to apply pressure. "Ah, yes, you are right to be speaking of young men, and we must be sure they will be happy after the Games."

The mayor intentionally goaded the benefactor's pride, much as a wild animal was pricked for blood before a fight. "Of course, you have relied on my support to provide those magnificent spectacles. And then what happened? Young men talked about the events for weeks. What will they speak about next?"

Bassos was taking the bait and lunged ahead recklessly, carelessly. The extra wine was doing its job. "The next Games should be the best that money can buy!"

Tatianos, who had been waiting for just such an opening, triggered the trap. "Wonderful! So gracious of you to agree, Fabius Bassos! Two days ago, couriers arrived from Caesar granting permission for Games in October and next May. Oh, I might add, our petition was answered. These Games will take place with sharp weapons between contestants. And might I add that we are grateful for your generosity as you continue to underwrite the costs."

Bassos turned an odd shade of gray, and he spoke in brief sentences. "Everything will be ready. Lct people know. The entertainment will be extraordinary, fascinating."

The mayor had prepared a small scroll, and he unrolled it. "Good. Here is the declaration. My servants will proclaim this, and it's dated for tomorrow.

September 19, in the 11th year of Domitian

Authorization has been given for the Games during the week of October 7–11.
The benefactor of Thyatira, Fabius Bassos, once again invites you to attend. The emperor has granted permission for the use of sharp weapons."[34]

Mayor Tatianos well deserved his reputation for being able to manipulate others to achieve his desired goals. A tiny twitch below the benefactor's right eye told Aurelius Tatianos that his devious plan had pierced deeper than sharp weapons in a gladiatorial contest.

Bassos felt sick, and his breathing had almost stopped. He could hardly compose a phrase. More fear than he could remember engulfed him, and an intense shudder shook his shoulders.

At home, as he groaned and moaned, his wife asked, "What happened at the end of the evening? You became so quiet!"

"Tatianos set me up! He wants to ruin me! Bloody fights in this October and next May too? That would mean having to bring

---

[34] Archaeological evidence from inscriptions unearthed in Ephesus indicates that some Games included fights between gladiators. Certain death was not always a part of the spectacle. Generally, games fought with sharp weapons needed Imperial authorization.

gladiators from other cities for both events. I can't even afford them in October!

"What can I do? I'll be the object of public shame. Whatever it takes, I must protect my honor. I must agree at all cost. Tatianos is my antagonist, and I know he is out to destroy me. I'm already in debt. The Games will cause further expenses in October and May.

"And that's not all. Domitian has required that vineyards be plowed up to plant grain, so I'll have reduced income next year from the vineyards![35] What else can I do but make a sacrifice to Apollo and pray for a miracle?"

The next day, as the sun began to warm the air, Fabius Bassos and his wife led a heifer along the street to the Temple of Apollo. People waved and cheered.

Several approached him for a loan, and he responded, "Perhaps! In Apollo's own good time! I shall speak of this later."

Once in the sanctuary, he called on celestial powers to answer his problems. "Help me, Apollo! I cannot bear the possibility of a loss! I must guard my dignity and honor, and I must not disappoint my followers!"

Outwardly, he showed a face free of emotion, but inwardly, his thoughts swirled in a panic. *Above all, I must not appear weak. I must keep the income from wines, grapes, fruit, and fields to pay off my other mounting debts. How can I afford comfort and nice things if I don't control my expenses better?*

"Apollo, will they forgive me if I cancel gladiator fights? I might get by next year in May with gladiator combats without sharp weapons. But that's not so interesting for bloodthirsty young men. My adversary wants sharp weapons! That's more than I can afford.

"Could my cousin, Julius Bassos, in Nicomedia help? Possibly, but first, I would have to ask forgiveness for the financial trick I played on him years ago. Not a good thought right now…

"I can't tell Tatianos that I am no longer able to supply the funds for future Games. Apollo, help me!"

ON THE ROAD FROM PORSUK RIVER TO PRUSA

After leaving Bellinus and Capito back in Karun, Omerod and

---

[35] During a general famine in AD 92, Emperor Domitian issued a "vine edict." It required half of the province's vineyards to be plowed to allow the planting of grain crops.

Menandro had traveled with Anthony and Sextilius to where the Interior Road met the Postal Road from Aizanoi.

They exited the Porsuk Canyon and left the Postal Road. They then merged onto the Interior Road, which ran north and south.

Menandro observed, "I'm glad we didn't have to search Porsuk Canyon! The walls are too steep for the bandits to drop down on the road. Where would they hide? Maybe Bellinus and Capito will find some sign of the gang around Aizanoi or the canyon."

Anthony and Sextilius said their goodbyes to them and quickly headed north toward Dascylium-on-the-Lake.

As instructed, Omerod and Menandro started their task. They briefed each of the station and garrison commanders.

Their assignment would take them along the Interior Road from White Horse Relay Station and through Cotyaum, Inegol, and Prusa.

The first relay station they encountered lay in a pleasant valley. The sun was halfway down the afternoon sky when they came to White Horse Relay Station. It was named after a splendid white horse taken to Ephesus a generation before. The majestic beast had become famous at triumphal marches. This relay station was the largest on this stretch of road.[36]

The officer in charge welcomed them into his office, where they could sit around a table with plenty of space for Menandro to take notes.

Omerod began the questions. "How were the bodies found?"

"A shepherd hunting for herbs noticed a foul smell."

"About the identities of the merchants, did you learn who they were?"

"Yes, the merchants' families identified the deceased by their clothing."

---

[36] Names and locations of postal supply stations mentioned here are based on where the Postal Road and Interior Road are known to have passed. The Royal Road was first used by the Persians. In many places, ruins alongside Turkish highways are remains of old Roman relay stations and caravan inns. In Turkish, these places were called a "caravansary." The restoration of these historic buildings continues in many areas. The best known is a five-star hotel in Kusadasi, the port city near Ephesus. Others are in Cappadocia. A few of these ancient buildings serve as museums; others are banquet halls, clubs, or hotels.

"Do you keep records on each caravan passing through?"

"We list all merchants and travelers, sometimes the animals as well."

"What were the dates?"

"The first slave dealer was killed about April 7, a week before the Festival of Zeus. After staying overnight in Inegol, he was going south on the Interior Road. He was murdered several miles below Inegol. His body was left off the road, down a slope. It had not been buried but was covered with stones and branches because it was impossible to dig a hole in the hard ground. No one could see the place from the road above, but the smell caused a shepherd to examine the area.

"I know there was a second murder on May 8, the same kind of situation, but you'll have to get those details from the garrison in Inegol. I wasn't sent a copy of those records."

Omerod and Menandro arrived next in Cotyaum. They examined the accounts recording the arrivals and departures of caravans transporting slaves, and they left early Friday morning.

Later that morning, they were in the area where the murders had taken place. At the bottom of a small valley, Menandro raised his hand as a signal to stop just before passing over a bridge.

They looked back along the winding road down which they had ridden. Coming down the sloping road, there was no sign of life. Menandro remarked, "It's a desolate area. With the right timing, it would be easy to kill someone and hide the body. No one would ever know about it."

Ten miles later, they reached the village of Inegol. It was surrounded by wilderness, and the small garrison was in disrepair and short of manpower. This was an out-of-the-way place with no reason for people to stay more than just one night.

It was late, so they contacted the officer in charge and got permission to stay in the barracks. The next morning, they spoke with the officer after breakfast.

"I'm sure you compared your records with those in other post stations," Omerod began as they discussed the crime. "We know this: Each merchant and his group of twenty slaves had two soldiers as guards. Tell us about the first murder, the one around April 7."

The officer looked at his register. "About the first caravan going to Aizanoi: Libanius Praesens was the merchant's name. He was from Laodicea, the brother of a well-known banker in that city. Here are the records: 'The deceased was missing his signet ring. Someone used it to assume his identity.'

"We see that a second merchant joined the caravan just before it left here. He claimed to be a merchant going to Aizanoi on business. His name was Spellius Macer, and he told us that he was related to a priestly family in Didyma. It seems quite likely that Spellius Macer assumed the identity of Libanius Praesens after he was murdered. So first a murder and then the theft of an identity, plus the theft of the slaves.

"Commander Diogenes Elpis of the garrison in Aizanoi followed up on the Mercer name and sent us a copy of the information. The family in Didyma, on the Aegean Sea, is well known and is a family of priests in the Temple of Apollo. They said, 'We've never had a Spellius Macer in our family,' so we know that an impostor was involved in the first murder."

Omerod continued his questioning. "What do you know about the second murder, the one that took place four weeks later?"

"That caravan also stayed here overnight. It left on May 8. I remember because the event took place a week after the Festival of Zeus. The merchant, Nicagoras Opramoas, said he was a cousin to a benefactor in Antioch of Syria.

"The same thing happened to him but just a little bit farther along the road. He was killed, and his signet ring was also missing.

"So two merchants were killed in the same location one month apart. Both had their rings taken. In both caravans, after passing the White Horse Relay Station, the false merchants vanished. Libanius Praesens and Nicagoras Opramoas were murdered for the same reason."

"Tell us about the soldiers guarding the two caravans."

"Hmm, the first caravan, according to records on April 7, had two guards. One guard was Callistus Flavius, the son of a noble family in Aleppo, Syria. The other guard was Valerian Atticus, the son of a benefactor in Damascus, and they were leading two wagons. Altogether, as normal, twenty slaves were accompanied by a merchant. Also, there was one wagon with two wild boars."

"And the soldiers guarding the second caravan, were they the same as those in the first?"

"Yes, the same soldiers, Callistus Flavius and Valerian Atticus.

Look here: The records match for May 8. Their names were written down at the Garrison of Prusa and listed as belonging to a cohort in Chalcedon. It is the cohort that specializes in transporting slaves."

"Did they carry normal credentials?"

"Yes. Everything looked to be in order."

"Describe the second caravan."

"The second caravan again transported two wagons with ten slaves in each. Strong cages kept them from escaping. So both caravans, one month apart, had the same two soldiers assigned. Twenty slaves passed through in April and another twenty in May."

Omerod pushed harder. "When was the last time their names appear in the records? Have you looked into that?"

"Yes! And what we found is strange. After arriving in Aizanoi, they vanished and have not been seen since! I sent a message to Chalcedon, and their names weren't registered there."

Further questioning was inconclusive.

On Sunday morning, before leaving Inegol for Prusa, Omerod and Menandro went over the evidence again with the officer. "You stated that the soldier guards were the same persons for both the April and May assaults: Callistus Flavius and Valerian Atticus. Was there anything special about the time of day that the caravans left? Did they leave first, last, before the other caravans or afterward?"

"Oh, that's interesting! Callistus Flavius and Valerian Atticus absolutely demanded to be the first to leave in the morning. They said, 'Our custom is to always be up bright and early.'"

Menandro said, "That would mean they were on the road for a long time going south *before* they met the day's traffic coming north! It would also mean that they had plenty of time to get rid of the real merchants without other traffic following them on the road. These were normal caravans, right?"

"Usually merchants travel with a variety of merchandise, but these had only slaves. However, the first caravan in April also brought wild animals but in a separate wagon."

"A caravan with wagons can move faster?"

"Much faster. It can cover twice the distance in one day compared to those walking. Listen, Sardis was the focus of the slave trade for years as rebuilding public buildings continued. However, Aizanoi is the new center of activity. It is taking over from Sardis. Many more slaves are needed for work on big projects."

As they mounted their horses to take them to Prusa, Omerod and Menandro went over the details. Menandro asked, "What do you make of these names? It's going to take us a long time to unravel this puzzle."

Omerod joked, "Rome will last forever! And if Romans can build such roads through desolate regions of the world, then we should expect criminal minds to be close behind!"

"Very funny! But you are right; this is a shrewd, dangerous gang," said Menandro seriously. "They struck in the same way each time. Two merchants are dead, and scores of slaves have disappeared!" He grunted. "Only one thing stands out. The two murders took place near the middle of the first week of each month. Could this be a pattern?"

Omerod and Menandro continued north from Inegol, following the Interior Road. It wound through forested areas and eventually arrived at Three Corners Relay Station.

The station stood close to a group of empty and decayed ancient Persian palaces, ruined reminders of those who ruled long before the Roman conquerors arrived. After showing their letters of authority and getting a quick drink of water, the fresh horses were prepared, and the men continued their journey.

In the afternoon, the road took them along the tops of successive ridges to Willow Brook Relay Station. The officer there did not have any other information about the merchant caravans. No one at the station had a theory of how the murders had taken place. No one in the next relay stations on the road to Prusa had any more to say about the merchants or the slaves.

It was Sunday evening when they checked into the Prusa Garrison barracks for the night. They would use the next day to assemble their notes in preparation for the meeting with the rest of the team on Tuesday.

Chapter 14
Danila

THE CITY OF THYATIRA

By the end of June, the summer heat in Thyatira threatened anyone walking outside at noon. There was no escape from the sweltering heat.

Miriam struggled with her feelings. One moment she wanted to judge her relatives. The next, she felt shame for not caring enough about her cousin, who talked only about his upcoming marriage.

As a guest and a woman without a home, she looked for a way to help. She spent time talking with Arte, the house slave, who was cleaning pots, jugs, and plates. Everything had to be washed and scrubbed before Gil and Danila's wedding.

One day Miriam went with Jonathan to the Clothier Guild workshop. Unique gowns for the wedding were sewn and almost ready except for some embroidery on collars and sleeves. Miriam asked for permission to help, telling the supervisor about her experience with sewing in Sardis. Jonathan suggested to the guild master that this was a reasonable request since he was purchasing the gowns. Miriam sat down beside another young woman and was delighted to be doing something useful as she began embroidering on a dress.

"Where did you learn that type of stitch?" Jonathan asked, surprise in his voice.

"Remember those one hundred wedding gowns I had you send to Sardis several months ago? Your brother Simon held a wedding a month ago where we used all of them. A friend of mine, Arpoxa, did the embroidery work on them, and she taught me this stitch pattern. She also did a lot of work for Grandpa Antipas in Pergamum."

"Arpoxa. Not a Greek name, is it?"

"No, Uncle Jonathan. Arpoxa was sold as a Scythian slave in Pergamum, and she and her husband later went with us to Sardis."

"Is she another one of the slaves my brother Antipas freed?"

"Yes, she is. Both she and Ateas, her husband." Miriam changed the subject. "Please tell me about Danila."

"She grew up in Laodicea. Her family belongs to the famous Meres clan. Her ancient ancestors were Persian. One of the Persian kings had a brother named Meres, who was influential in this region, and he married a Phrygian. The family prospered and is now a major partner in one of the largest banks in Laodicea. Just think! This young lady is descended from a famous branch of Persian rulers of Laodicea! Their whole family is coming tomorrow for the festivities! It's going to be a great party!"

The Meres family arrived in style on the Sabbath, on the twenty-eighth of June. Beautiful, matching black horses pulled the three wagons, and the procession brought spectators surging onto the streets. Gifts were taken into the house for both the groom and the bride. Miriam counted a dozen people as they dismounted, and she had trouble remembering all their names.

Loud conversations filled the house until dusk, but Miriam longed for quiet. Initially, Grace thrived from the attention, but she became tired of people squeezing her cheeks, brushing their hands over her hair, and making happy faces.

Adults exclaimed, "Oh, such a sweet little girl!"

Excitement grew on Sunday, and by Monday, the women had examined each stitch of their wedding tunics. These were a universal type of garment but with a variety of bodice styles.

Danila's mother showed off her white stola made of expensive fine linen imported from Egypt. It felt like rare silk from the East, far beyond the lands where the Ben Shelah ships traded. Those worn by her cousins and two aunts were made of brightly colored fabrics decorated with differing embroidery patterns.

A seller of cosmetics stopped by the house to ask if the ladies would be interested in seeing his wares, and they were. The women seemed mostly fascinated by two "anti-wrinkle" creams from Egypt. Increasingly popular in Thyatira, the beauty secrets employed the mythology of eternal life to aid in sales. Sweet almond oil and a hint of frankincense were used in one famous cream. Another product from far up the Nile River included shea butter, lotus oil, lavender, and peppermint.

"I like this cream. It smells divine!" declared Danila's mother enthusiastically.

"I've heard that this one keeps you looking younger," replied Rebekah. "Egyptians use it to keep their queens looking young even after they die!"

Danila's mother had a knack for making people laugh. "I'd rather use it before dying, thank you very much. I want the look of eternal life while I'm still alive."

The women responded well to her quick, witty replies. Each commented how fine they looked after applying the expensive creams, and the salesperson left significantly wealthier.

On Tuesday at sundown, everyone left for the wedding at the synagogue. As they walked, music announced to one and all that a marriage parade was on its way. Tambourines and flutes brought people to the edge of the road to watch the bride's family as they passed by.

Because Danila's family was considered pagan, the synagogue sanctuary was closed to them. The elders had at first been adamant that none of the party could even enter the courtyard. Still, after considerable discussion and a generous contribution to pay for cleaning the area afterward, Jonathan persuaded the elders to admit them to the portico.

When the celebration began, Jonathan's big voice filled the courtyard as he read the words of the covenant. He, Danila, and Gil stood under the blue wedding canopy supported by four tall silver poles. He read the blessings given by Moses but said nothing about his son forming an alliance with a woman from a home where the Greek gods were held in high esteem.

"All these blessings will come upon you," he said, quoting the ancient text. "You will be blessed in the city and blessed in the country. The fruit of your womb will be blessed, and the crops of your land and the young of your livestock, the calves of your herds and the lambs of your flocks. Your basket and your kneading trough will be blessed. You will be blessed when you come in and when you go out."[37]

Miriam bristled and sat up straight. *You left off the requirements of the blessing, Uncle Jonathan! Wasn't there a condition in the promises? That passage begins, 'If you fully obey the Lord your God and carefully follow all his commands I give you today, the Lord your*

---

[37] Deuteronomy 28:3–6

God will set you high above all the nations on earth. All these blessings will come upon you and accompany you if you obey the Lord your God."[38]

She examined the guests from Laodicea. Danila's father's slightly too-large head floated on a massive neck. His eyes twinkled, and like his wife, he enjoyed making people laugh. His arms were covered with black hair, and he wore several rings on his fingers. He frequently pointed his index finger at his listeners, and he punctuated his words with sharp gestures.

Danila's mother was petite, just like the bride. Both mother and daughter had curly black hair, and on this day, their curls emphasized their soft, feminine curves. Long gold traces were woven into their hair to form a diadem. Gold glittered whenever either mother or daughter moved. They looked like twins except that twenty years separated their birthdays. Both of Danila's sisters had the same gracious figures and the same curly, waist-length hair.

The wedding left Miriam wondering about Jonathan's dedication to the ideals of their Jewish faith. She wanted to tell Anthony, "Gil is now marrying the daughter of a wealthy family from Laodicea. Of course, everybody sees economic benefits as a sign of the Lord's blessing. Why did the Meres family come to Thyatira as the place of the wedding? Usually the bride's family hosts the wedding, so why didn't Uncle Jonathan and Aunt Rebekah go to Laodicea?

"Of course, marrying you, I also married outside of my Jewish roots, but you chose to come under the covenant, like a branch grafted into an olive tree. Grandpa Antipas believed Isaiah. He wanted foreigners to bind themselves to the Lord, to serve him, to love the name of the Lord, and to worship him. They would keep the Sabbath without desecrating it. They would hold fast to the covenant. 'These I'll bring to my holy mountain and give them joy in my house of prayer; for my house will be called a house of prayer for all nations.'[39] You are a Roman legionary, but you believe in our Messiah and accept our covenant. But the Meres family? I am not

---

[38] Jonathan quoted Deuteronomy 28:3–6; Miriam added Deuteronomy 28:1–2.
[39] Isaiah 56: 6,–7

so sure."

The wedding feast at the Ben Shelah home lasted for hours. Since the dining area was not large enough for everyone, the garden was set up for guests under the fruit trees.

"What a beautiful way to receive your guests!" Danila's father observed. "The shade of fruit trees by day and now, by evening, an enchanting garden with flaming torches!"

Jonathan's household had been busy for days in preparation for the event. That included his steward, Jarib, and his family: Shiri, his wife; Jodan, their older son; and Gedalya, the younger son. All four had risen long before dawn to clean and ready the foods for cooking.

The wedding party took their places at the central table. Gil, Danila, and Bani were on the middle couch. Danila's mother and father and her older brother, to their right, laughed, delighted at the way they were initiating a profitable business relationship.

Jonathan and Rebekah shared a couch with Serah. Danila's sisters were at another table, and many of Thyatira's most influential people had come for the feast. Prominent persons were present from three guilds. Since they could not all fit into the house, most had to be served in the garden.

Miriam stayed in the background, unsure of what might be expected from her. She did not want to be called upon in any way, so she went to the kitchen, where the staff needed help.

"These are the foods of King Solomon, one of our greatest kings. He specialized in weddings and fine foods," Miriam heard Rebekah say to Danila.

As she returned to their table to bring more food, she overheard Jonathan and Danila's father talking. "So you'll deposit my investment money in your partnership account at the Guild of Purple Honors? Tomorrow? Good!

"That means I will be your 'silent partner' in the guild. After taxes are paid, 80 percent of any profit you derive from my portion of the investment will transfer back to me. You may keep the 20 percent for handling the investment."

Miriam pretended to stand as if she were serving, but she strained to hear every word. She looked at another table, but Jonathan had not noticed her listening to his private affairs. It was a critical moment in the conversation.

Jonathan responded, "Two years ago, I began to gain influence in their workshops where purple cloth is dyed. I'm becoming their main source of purple dye stock that I grow out near Forty Trees. I was recently asked to join and invest in the Clothiers' Guild. Also, I'm already a major seller of goods from the Bronzesmiths' Guild. That's why there are friends here from three guilds. With me handling your additional investments with those guilds and keeping you as a silent partner, we both will gain even more leverage in Thyatira."

She had heard enough. Miriam continued to serve food, but her mind was racing. *This is a marriage of financial convenience! Danila is almost like a goodwill offering between families to ensure harmony and make sure these two families stay together. She can do whatever she wants! People will let her because no one will want to upset her. Why would anyone threaten the financial advantages reached between these two fathers?*

Uncle Jonathan has, with this remarkable wedding, "gained leverage." And he is using the money from Meres to gain more power!

Food was served until the guests could eat no more and the time for speeches had come. Jonathan stood, smiled broadly, and waited until all the guests had entered and remained standing. Then he began his long delivery.

"Most of you have lived all your lives in Thyatira. Pax Romana brought progress to this city and helped it to thrive as never before. The guilds! Look how they are growing—new jobs, new houses, and additions to the temples that were made two weeks ago!

"Citizens of Thyatira love their city. You who live in Thyatira are hospitable, welcoming others. Some have come more recently, like our family. Many are descended from families that settled here well before the time of the Romans. I see peace and prosperity. It seems Thyatira has people from every language, tribe, family, and nation!"

He smiled again, and everyone waited for what he would say about the bride. "Hundreds of years ago, foreigners prospered in these regions! Persian princes came and married local women. Look at the Meres family, descended from one of those famous families, and behold! Such beautiful women!"

Cheers went up to acknowledge the physical charm of the women from Laodicea.

"But if you look a little more closely, you'll see the results of three hundred years of investments in banks, businesses, families, and industry. The Meres family is a fine example of people who know how to prosper in this land."

His hands spread out, including each person present.

"The Ben Shelah story is not much different! My wife and I met in Alexandria. My father went to Jerusalem and experienced frightful fighting that resulted in terrible destruction. Today the Ben Shelah family knows the difference between war's bitterness and the sweet results of peace.

"My brothers and I have been in Asia for a generation. You welcomed my family, and Thyatira has been good to us. We've invested in land and built shops. Now the Ben Shelah and Meres families are being joined. A Persian-Phrygian family has joined a Jewish family living in Thyatira! Again, I say, this truly is a city with people from every family, nation, language, people, and religion!"

Cheers of approval rose again.

"This is not just the union of a bride and a groom. This is the union of two families, two large clans. I represent only one part of the Ben Shelah family.

"I'm sure that my brothers here in Asia and my two brothers and sister in Alexandria will be as thrilled as we are. Great blessings will come from the wedding of these two lovely young people here tonight."

Grace was crying, tired, and grumpy. Miriam gathered her in her arms and left to put the child to bed.

On the surface, it had been such a lovely event. But in her mind, she was troubled because of the unexpected information she had overheard. Was this a marriage or a business deal disguised as a Jewish wedding?

Earlier in the evening, a jug had fallen in the kitchen. Its broken pieces showed that the pitcher was made of ordinary red clay painted on the outside with care, a beautiful scene of Greek women reclining at the mouth of a well.

Rocking her child to sleep, Miriam pondered conflicting emotions. *That shattered pot and Uncle Jonathan's business links of convenience seem to be related. I remember receiving items from him for our shops in Pergamum. He sent fine pots, lamps, and bronze utensils as well as clothing. I remember thinking, "I'm so glad I have an uncle who lives in Thyatira, someone who makes such beautiful objects!"*

Lord, help me as I struggle to understand. I want to bless this young couple. They seem to be well suited. She is adorable and beautiful, full of life and fun. She loves parties, and she has been the life of this party! But a marriage of convenience? Perhaps I do not see the truth as it really is.

Miriam rocked Grace, who fussed for a moment and then drifted off to sleep. She sang a lullaby to Grace. Anthony seemed so far away.

Downstairs, the furniture had been moved to the walls, and a circle had formed with people dancing. They turned two steps to the right, twirling around, and taking one step back. Dancers used intricate movements of hands, feet, and heads, bending down and then standing up suddenly. The singing would go on for a long time.

Miriam placed a small oil lamp on a shelf above her bed, where it would give the best light. Remembering that her deepest agonies had often been relieved by transforming them into a song, she reached for a small table, bringing it close to the bed.

Writing the words of a song and setting it to a tune had she heard at the marketplace, she declared, "I am a soldier's wife!"

When wedding guests get up to dance
I cannot sing or sway or prance.
My mind goes in other ways.
Commanders' orders he obeys.
Equipped with helmet, sword, and lance,
Fighting because savagery is rife.
Lonely? Yes, because you see,
I am a soldier's wife!

I buy the bread; I hold my child.
Her tiny fingers grasp my hand.
Fierce robbers are by all reviled
And hide from those who guard the land.
I have no fear of being defiled.
This wedding band will guard my life.
Struggles? Yes, because you see,
I am a soldier's wife!

Innocent men are led astray,
Spiteful men slaughtered like jackals.
Plunderers try to slip away.
Robbers will be bound by iron shackles,
Regretting pouncing on their prey.
No longer will they wield a knife.
Yes, I'm proud because you see,
I am a soldier's wife!

When evening comes, I comb my hair.
I wish you were here with me.
You make us proud, a loving pair.
I dearly want your company.
I can't ever share you with the world.
But when you're gone. I've inner strife.
Honored? Yes, because you see,
I am a soldier's wife!

Chapter 15
Dascylium-on-the-Lake

AT THE TOWN OF DASCYLIUM-ON-THE-LAKE

Anthony and Sextilius arrived in the late afternoon at Dascylium-on-the-Lake. Five days of riding horses at a fast trot and changing one mount for another almost every hour left them tired and sore. Approaching their journey's end, their horses tossed their heads and slowed from a trot to a slow walk.

Bird Lake, a natural paradise, stretched out before them. Dalmatian storks landed in nests in high trees, standing on thin legs and giving morsels to their nesting chicks, soon ready to fly. Scores of smaller birds flew from branch to branch.

Sextilius pointed out herons, spoonbills, and ducks. A falcon dipped out of the sky and rose again; then they watched it falling out of sight behind pine trees. Sparrows darted everywhere, and swallows zipped through the air, snatching a meal of flying insects. Swifts and thrushes abounded. Hundreds of species passed through the surroundings on invisible migration paths.[40]

The lake was a natural haven, a paradise. Waterbirds, fish, water snakes, turtles, and other wildlife abounded. Pigmy cormorants disappeared into the water and then popped up with a fish, tossing their heads around as if to brag about their underwater success.

The two men dismounted, and Commander Quintus Elpis of the Dascylium-on-the-Lake Garrison greeted Anthony and Sextilius. He was a cousin to the commander in Aizanoi. "Hail, soldiers, welcome!" he stated.

---

[40] Bird Lake National Park is visited by two to three million feathered friends each year. Annual migration occurs from April to June and September to November, with more than two hundred fifty species passing through Anatolia. Approximately sixty-five varieties live permanently in this lake region. Restoration of the archaeological ruins of Dascylium is progressing slowly, barely hinting at their former grandeur.

"Hail, sir! We were sent by Commander Servius Callistratus in Soma. Here are our orders. We wish to get whatever information we can about the recent loss of caravans and the murders of two merchants on the Interior Road."

"Of course, but first, you've had a long ride. I must take you to the baths!" Few outside legionaries came to this ancient city, and the officer was pleased to show them around.

Anthony planned for a full day at Dascylium-on-the-Lake. He wondered how much he might learn about the ancient families of any local bandits. After long days of riding horses, the baths were refreshing. First came the *caldarium* with steam rising from the floor then the tepidarium and the massage on his back. Finally, they walked into the *frigidarium,* dipping in cold water. With skin cleansed by olive soap and tired muscles well massaged, they were ready to talk with the officer.

After the evening meal, they walked with the commander up to the terrace overlooking the lake. The sun was setting, and flocks of birds chattered loudly, searching for space to sleep.

Anthony took a deep breath. *How quiet life is here!*

Small, flat-bottomed punts were being pulled onto a beach and turned upside-down. Men making their living by harvesting reeds or fishing had pushed their small boats onto the shore with long poles. For hours, they had cut tall reeds off at the level of the water. Now they were bringing them ashore for drying. In a few days, the reeds would be taken to the bigger cities to be woven into large floor mats for wealthy homes or hats to resist winter rains.

"You came a long way," observed the commander. "Rest a bit. Enjoy our slower pace of life. Watch those men harvesting reeds. That work has kept this place alive for generations."

Yellows turned to orange and then a dull red in the distant sky as the sun hid itself beyond the horizon.

"Now, you had asked about the murders on the highway. I heard about the missing caravans and the bodies found. A month ago, a messenger came through asking about them and any records we might have listing names or other information. Those crooks did not come through our checkpoint, so we can add nothing to the investigation."

Anthony responded, "Well, anyway, it's encouraging that you heard of the murders. We didn't know how much of that information had been circulated. I'm leading a squad to search for the gang responsible. Other soldiers are comparing records elsewhere to see what they can discover. Commander Servius at Soma thought he had an answer: Perhaps ancient families are coming back as present-day villains."

Quintus Elpis chuckled. "And you think you'll get help from humble citizens enlightened by the squawking of millions of birds?"

"Yes, with your permission and encouragement."

"Then get a good rest," responded the commander. "Tomorrow you'll talk with stooped-over merchants with little to sell. They are happy for visitors to come, but mark my words! Nobody will get anyone from these ancient families to talk. I tried. Accept defeat."

"Why?"

"Those who know anything about the past strongly resist our Roman ways. One was heard to say, 'Almost every man in Bithynia was hunted down after King Mithradates VI was killed, but a few got away and came here.' They saved their lives by losing their identity and staying away from danger. Half a dozen families have never forgiven us for making the old Lydian ways die out. Imagine people holding onto the past like that! Really! I understand why Commander Servius sent you here, but he does not know these people! They still fear the authorities." He laughed again. "Good luck with your questions!"

The garrison overlooked the southeastern shore of the lake. Dilapidated public buildings hinted at previous splendor, and small temples hugged the hot baths. On the north side, a small theater overlooked the merchants' shops. Little suggested to them that this once was the capital city of an ancient Lydian kingdom.

At breakfast, Anthony asked the commander many questions. In turn, he passed on the information that they had gained in passing through Karun, Aizanoi, Cotyaum, and Inegol. Sextilius remained silent, and the commander looked at him with a frown.

"You are a fighter, and yet you let Anthony do all the talking! What do you have to add?" Quintus Elpis asked.

Sextilius replied, "Thank you, sir, but he is in charge. I just need to know where we should begin to ask questions of these people."

"Start with the families over there. But be careful! Most older people don't like Rome. And look at you with uniforms! Those won't help a bit!"

Several old men lounged on a run-down porch barely attached

to a stone house. The house boasted a Persian arch over the entryway, built to protect against wind and rain. Bent over from the hips, an elderly woman came out of her home. Preparing a sacrifice, she mumbled the names of ancient Persian gods.

Anthony waited for a few moments. After she completed the sacrificial act of pouring oil on a small, square altar, he spoke to her, explaining why they had come. "Some robberies took place on the Interior Road recently. Do you have any information that might help us discover who murdered two merchants?"

The old woman responded with strange words. "Every season has its colors. In spring, leaves are light green. In summer, they turn dark green, and by the end of summer, the reeds turn yellow, ready for harvesting. In winter, the colors between the clouds are those of birds flying among the branches. Beware of the seasons. And beware of the season that brings bandits."

They waited, respecting the slow movements of the old people.

One incredibly old man spoke. "Do you want to know...about people here? Then you have to know...about Dascylium-on-the-Lake."

Anthony waited before continuing. "Yes, we'd like to know."

Everything seemed ancient, slow, and without purpose, but they both knew these people descended from a much different tradition.

Sextilius wondered how he could endure the snail's pace, but he forced himself to listen. He did his best to follow the disjointed speech coming from this man with no teeth.

"Dascylium-on-the-Lake was important before Romans came ... before Alexander the Great was old enough to walk ... mysteries of beauty ... nature never far away ... people do not dominate ... just birds coming and going ... storks feed little ones."

Another old-timer spoke. "No one would have known about this place if it wasn't for Gyges."

The old man who made this comment may have been the only lucid one in the crowd. He spoke slowly, had no teeth, and was not easy to understand, so it was a good thing his tongue moved slowly.

The sudden mention of the ancient king of Sardis jolted Sextilius. "You mean Gyges, the famous general of the Lydian Kingdom?"

Anthony glanced at Sextilius, asking himself, *What could Gyges possibly have to do with robbers, thugs, and mischief-making? How long will Sextilius chew on this tasteless tidbit?*

The man continued, "Yes. The father of Gyges, the famous fighter, won great battles. This city is named after the father, but everyone remembers Gyges, the son who became famous. All the nations spoke of him and dreaded him. Oh, yes! We still love Gyges."

He kept picking at long white hairs growing out of his ears.

Sextilius almost jumped to his feet, but he forced himself to talk as slowly as the old man who had given this information. He whispered only loudly enough for Anthony to hear, "Gyges lived more than seven hundred fifty years ago! Is he still a hero among these families?"

Anthony pursed his lips and shook his head slowly as if to say, *What a waste of time!*

Sextilius smiled broadly at Anthony and turned back to the old man. "Elder brother, please tell me why this story is important when we are asking about bandits. Take your time, as much as you want. I'm here to learn."

The old man twirled a few hairs in his ears. "Persians overcame Lydian troops, and after the Battle of the Eclipse, Persia ruled the Lydians.[41] Then Alexander came and then the Greeks...the Kingdom of Pergamum, and now Romans control everyone. All have been robbers! Only here, in this paradise, will you find peace. But two Romans have come to disturb us, asking about robbers!"

Sextilius had a definite feeling that these families were hiding something. Maybe they needed an excuse to talk. He whispered again, "Anthony, I think 'old hairy ears' has helpful information and doesn't want to reveal it."

The best approach seemed to agree with the old man's observations. Sextilius acknowledged, "Yes, you are right. Each army carries off what it wants. I understand. Domination by outsiders is much like robbery. Look how many treasures are being taken to Rome. For instance, all the treasures of the Temple in Jerusalem...where are they? In Rome as trophies!"

"Still, elder brother, I have a responsibility to find those who murder and steal. That should make sense to you because even

---

[41] On May 25, 585 BC, a battle was halted because of the eclipse of the sun. Thales of Miletus predicted this eclipse, according to the Greek historian Herodotus. It is an early historical event that correlates with precision to the current calendar.

Gyges kept guards on the roads so merchants could travel safely, didn't he?

"Whoever attacked our merchants this year, in April and May, is repeating the worst part of ancient times. Now, tell me everything you know about the Lydians. And can you speak about the Persians? Why did Persians destroy your ancient hero, King Gyges?"

A distant look came over the old man's face. "Ah, now you are getting to the heart of it all! Persia, far away! Sardis, closer by, linked by the Royal Road to Susa! Famous cities!"

He paused to watch birds flying overhead. "Persian generals, *satraps*, came to Sardis, governing and making people afraid. For two hundred years, one after another, they spread terror, killing anyone who rebelled. The king of Persia controlled everyone with an iron fist. Almost all the satraps met a violent end. Persians fought against Lydians. Hmph, those satraps were the real robbers."

A partially lame man was a nephew to the man who had been speaking. He interrupted, "In my home, we keep those stories alive. My family is descended from a Persian prince, and my grandmother made me learn all their stories. She still believes that Persia will come back, that a Persian army will conquer Rome. I must not say that to the garrison commander or I would be held for 'rebellion.'

"You Romans think you own the world. But I can tell you the name of every satrap. They had trouble keeping order and taking over Lydia. Our family is still loyal to our heritage."

Sextilius kept listening. The attitude of resistance still lived on. Now was the time to dig deeper.

"I want to know everything," he said. "Where did the conflicts take place? Who led the rebellions? Tell me about each satrap. What challenges did each one face? How did they put down robbers and bandits on the highways?"

Anthony raised his eyebrows, unwilling to suffer any more of this chinwag. He sat back and stopped listening. Such blather!

Over their noon meal at the garrison, Anthony said, "I didn't learn anything from that questioning, nothing to help us in our quest. I suppose you didn't learn anything either."

Sextilius leaned back, his hands high above his head. "Scores of names: Persian kings, wise men, officials, generals, governors, and eunuchs. Who cares about Artaxerxes, Carshena, Shethar,

Admatha, Tarshish, Meres, Marsena, or Memucan? All those satraps in Sardis! I learned about Tabalus, Spithradetes, and even famous eunuchs like Biztha, Harbona, Bitha, and Abagtha. I got details about each of those rulers, some humorous tales, and a few interesting insights about how not to govern a land through domination."

He smiled generously, and his eyes were shining with the new knowledge. "Nothing helpful, of course, but at least I made some friends, all old people."[42]

Anthony observed, "Sextilius, I knew you liked old people, but there's one more worthwhile thing I learned about you: your memory for names."

His companion, restless after receiving useless insights into the long-forgotten struggles between Persia and the Kingdom of Lydia, laughed. "What a futile collection of information! These people are experts in astrology. They wanted to know my birthday to relate it to the zodiac signs and tell my future. We came to find information about thieves, but instead, they told me my fortune!"[43]

Sextilius twiddled imaginary hairs growing out of his ears, and they both laughed.

Anthony closed his eyes. *Sextilius: an excellent protector, takes on the complicated work. He counters boredom with quick quips, patient listening, and gentle humor. Even knows how to please lonely old people. If he gets bored in Prusa, I will have him go to the central square and listen to bygone days' stories.*

Anthony said, "You have a habit, and you are doing it right now."

"What?"

"First, you lean back and raise your hands behind you as far as possible. After a few minutes, you rub your wrist with your other hand. I can tell when you are thinking hard."

"And I can tell when you're hungry. Coming in for the noon meal, you were rubbing the scar on your face."

---

[42] Some of these names are found in Esther 1:10–14.

[43] Interest in astrology was widespread in the Roman Empire and beyond. A mathematical system of 360 degrees in a circle, with subsequent applications, was well developed. The sky's division into twelve sections, each under the influence of a different animal, continued through the Middle Ages until modern times.

They chuckled, more aware of their own foibles and knowing it was not only old people who had strange habits.

FROM DASCYLIUM-ON-THE-LAKE TO PORT DASKYLEION ON THE SEA OF MARMARA

The next morning, Anthony and Sextilius mounted their horses and took one last look at the city. "Our visit to the 'Paradise of Birds' was a failure of sorts, but it was interesting."

Travel from Dascylium-on-the-Lake to Port Daskyleion on the Marmara Sea was easy. The land was almost flat, and the road had bridges over two slow-moving, shallow rivers. They made good time as relay stations again provided fresh mounts. Anthony gazed at low hills on both sides of the road as he rode.

The sun sparkled on the distant giant snowy cap of the majestic Mount Olympus near Prusa.

He offered up a prayer. *God, maker of hills and mountains, are you interested in my tasks when you involve yourself in nature? I laughed once when Miriam and I read something Antipas had written in his diary scroll. It was his reaction after I told him I wanted to marry Miriam. He wrote, 'Anthony is not fit to marry my granddaughter.' He could not find the right word to describe me. None were bad enough! But in the end, Antipas agreed to our marriage. Of course, he could not predict how our wedding would turn out.*

I must remember that. Life is full of small, unexpected surprises. My perceptions of people change; time alters how I understand things. Perhaps one day I'll know why we had to come to this remote place. Was it only to talk with old people?

They changed horses at another relay station, a picturesque spot on the shores of Ulubat Lake. The road split after they left the station, and they took the branch heading north. It was late in the morning as they rode down the gentle slopes toward the Sea of Marmara.

At the head of a cove, a steep cliff protected Port Daskyleion. The long bay was initially open to the sea, and the beach's gentle curve gave no protection against winter storms. However, slave laborers had piled massive stones on the seafloor, forming a long breakwater to protect the harbor. Roman engineering had created a port big enough for thirty large ships.

A Roman warship, a *bireme,* with two banks of oars was leaving port. Its single large, square sail and smaller foresail caught the southern breeze and took the ship northward. Two men stood in the back, one on each side. They guided the vessel with two large steering oars.

At the bow, a three-pronged bronze beak protruded above the waves. It was designed explicitly for ramming the side of an enemy ship and sinking it, even though pirates no longer were a menace. Above the bronze beak, two eyes were painted, one on either side, because ships needed the gods' sharp eyesight in open waters. When required, rowers moved in time with the *trieraules*, the flute player who provided the rhythm to the oarsmen below. The captain stood proudly at the stern of the ship, close to his cabin.

A short time later, a small coastal vessel, with a single sail and crew of five men, departed. It would stop at each small port along the coast, delivering cargo and a few passengers.

Anthony pointed to a merchant ship arriving. They watched it draw into the harbor where a dozen ships were tied up to the pier. The steersman guided the vessel toward the dock, and a line was thrown from the stern so the sailors could pull their craft into a narrow space between two other ships. A few minutes later, it was moored by the stern and attached to the wharf. On its deck were fresh fruits and vegetables. About fifty *amphorae* full of wine and oil were lined up, waiting for the merchandise to be transferred to shore.

The two men sat down at one of the small tables provided by an outdoor food vendor. "I enjoyed the travel this morning more than anything so far," sighed Anthony. "Unfortunately, we can't stay for another day, although I would like to."

Sextilius looked around at the scenery. "Yes, I wouldn't mind retiring here, but I already have a job waiting for me in Sicily."

Anthony nodded, understanding, "We'll interview the garrison commander this afternoon, ensure that he is fully informed about the bandit problem, and see if he knows anything helpful. We'll sleep in the barracks tonight and head out to Prusa early in the morning. By tomorrow afternoon, our team will meet at the garrison in Prusa, and we'll be learning what the others have discovered."

THE MILITARY GARRISON IN PRUSA

Late the next afternoon, the team was gathered around a table at the Garrison of Prusa. They had been comparing their long days of searching for any sign of the highwaymen.

The barracks building formed part of a massive gateway and walkway into the city. Other regulars looked up to see what had caused the noisy outburst from the six visiting soldiers.

Bellinus had slammed his hand on the table in disgust, causing others to glance at the squad. "After hundreds of miles, nine days riding, and I don't know how many bedbugs and other creepy-crawly creatures chewing on me every night, what have we learned?"

Capito burst out, "Not a single clue! Nothing that we didn't know before. Look! Even army regulars are mocking us! Did you hear the term the guards are using for us? 'The Wise Patrol Guards.' What a degrading name! We are well trained, but–"

Anthony interrupted. "Yes, we are well trained and we haven't learned anything important yet, but–"

"What are we to do now?" interrupted Omerod.

Anthony observed, "We can't do anything else here. We'll just have to return to Soma and report what little information we found."

Bellinus stated what they all felt. "I don't mind the time spent if we had been riding out to adventure and administering justice. But it will look like we were failures if we have to return and explain to Servius that we haven't got anything to tell him! He'll be furious!"

Chapter 16
Guilds and Gods

THE CITY OF THYATIRA

Bani knew from Miriam's frown that she was getting upset. "Come with me to the city," he urged on Thursday morning. The wedding feast was finally over as the Meres family could not stay past July 3 and had returned to Laodicea. Jonathan's business ventures would be reinforced as new financial resources from Laodicea began to flow into the guild.

Bani was twenty-three years old, made friends easily with his ready smile, and had a gift with words. His father already saw him as an able salesman, and he was being trained to inherit his father's business enterprise. He knew intuitively that relationships with key persons in the guilds meant future success.

"Let me show you two businesses close to our home," he offered. Miriam wanted some fresh air, so she relented and left Grace with Rebekah, glad to be free from the previous days' constant chatter.

Bani explained his father's past successes as they walked toward the city. "No one wanted to build on the wetland where father now has our home. Stagnant water made this area a disgusting swamp. However, remembering how crowded we Jews had been in Alexandria after the pogroms and how we reclaimed some of the land there, Father had an idea.[44] He convinced the city authorities: 'That useless bit of land, let me buy it, and I'll clean it up. You'll have fewer smells, flies, and mosquitoes!' Because of that, he's now considered a 'Friend of the City.'"

Miriam looked at him with a blank expression.

"That's both a unique title and an honor! You are supposed to

---

[44] Pogroms occurred in Alexandria, Egypt, in AD 38 and 68. Jews who had once lived in two of Alexandria's five districts were crowded into only one section after AD 68.

be impressed, my cousin! In this quarter of the city, inside and outside the walls, you will find four powerful guilds. Up there, on our left, close to Central Avenue, is the Potters' Guild. Their patron god is Pan, the goat-man god who played pipes. Every guild is linked to a god, and the potters support Pan's Temple. They celebrate their festival day one day a year.

"The shop of the Tanners' Guild is in this building. And outside that city gate is where the tannery workers labor every day to turn cow and sheep hides into leather. Look at these beautiful belts in this shop! Gorgeous shields, furniture, bridles, and saddles for horses! Every house benefits from the Tanners' Guild. They honor Hercules, the god holding the stick in his left hand and a lion's skin in his right hand. Just imagine—a lion's skin! Tanners' apprentices claim to be the most powerful. At least they make the most potent smells at their tannery. The city requires that their processing shops be outside the city walls." He laughed and pointed past the city's West Gate.

Bani was talking nonstop. "The fabric preparation and dyeing pots at the Guild of Purple Honors, the guild that Father likes the most, create a bad smell, but the tanners' processes are far worse. At gladiator fights, their workers sit together, boisterous and noisy. From the expression on your face, I can see you won't be going to a gladiator fight!"

"And you, my cousin, do you go to those fights?"

He pretended not to hear. "Everyone of importance has to belong to a guild. If you don't, then life becomes very complicated. It's almost impossible to sell your product in the city. This system effectively keeps foreign businesses out of the city."

They walked back from the West Gate along Central Avenue.

"Right in front of us are the bakers' workshops, and over there, to our right, you can see the wool workers. Potters, tanners, bakers, and wool workers...four guilds. That's our corner of the city."

He waited for a camel train to pass by and then carried on. "Everyone needs fresh bread, so the Bakers' Guild is held in high regard. They inspect their members' products at least once a week for weight, taste, and cleanliness. They pay homage to the Three Beauties, the statue of three virgins. In the myth, each one is jealous because of the beauty of the other two women."

They continued walking toward the city center, strolling north along Acropolis Road. "Bani, you said that every guild is linked to a god. Do you seek to know more about these gods, my cousin?"

Bani frowned briefly and then smiled. "No, of course not, but I do have to know the basics about them. It's good business! Now take this workshop, the Clothiers' Guild. It is extremely prosperous. They import cloth from outside Thyatira and also from the Weavers' Guild in the city. They use silk and linen to make special garments for the wealthy and have uniform contracts with the military too. The inscription at the heart of the city corner says they provided funds for the long Central Avenue colonnaded path-way. Here at the center of the city, the Triple Gate was also paid for by the Clothiers' Guild."

As they walked, they examined the workshops of other guilds. All the hard work was done by slaves or poorly paid workers and apprentices.

"What's the benefit to an individual family of belonging to one guild or another?"

Bani explained, "If a family encounters troubles, others in the guild will usually lend support when a family member is sick or if someone dies. If a woman is widowed and her husband was in good standing, then financial support will be provided all her life. In the case of widowhood, the guild also looks after the children of the deceased man. Most of the children will be accepted as apprentices in the shops when they come of age."

They went to another building. "This workshop is part of the Guild of Purple Honors. Before we go in, I need to explain a few things. The slaves here prepare red and purple dyes. Other colors, mostly blues, are prepared in other buildings so there isn't any accidental mixing of colors."

The air inside was overwhelmingly hot and humid. A section of the roof was open, letting in some sunlight and allowing steam from some of the dye pots to escape. Gradually, Miriam's eyes became used to the dim light, and she saw men carrying rolls of woven cloth.

Stacks were neatly piled: linen, wool, and cotton. Two large work areas occupied the center. Large metal tubs on one side were full of purple dye and lighter red dye was in another section, but the liquid in both basins looked black in the dim light. Roots of madder plants had been brought to the guild's workshop from Jonathan's farm to make these dyes.

"All of the cloth to be dyed was processed in another workshop to prepare the threads for dyeing. I won't take you to see that part of the operation. It's very smelly. We have some 'secret' solutions that we dip the cloth in. It's a different solution, and various temperatures are used depending on the material: wool, cotton, or linen. The processing is necessary to help the dye properly bond to the fibers of the cloth. We keep the processes secret because they allow us to have the longest-lasting colors."

"Why did Uncle Jonathan become part of this guild?"

"Father started investing in the Guild of Purple Honors after they asked him to be a partner. He is not a master dyer, but he had become their primary source of the dye material. Previously, high-quality purple came from two ports, Tyre and Sidon. Gradually the availability of the tiny snails used to extract that color became sparser. Obviously, another source was needed."

Once again, Bani jabbered on, and she could not interrupt him or ask another question. "That's when our city became the chief source of the dye material. The guild used to get red dye from Hindustan[45] made from madder root. They had the root type that produced the best deep red colors; it makes excellent purple. It was delivered by way of Egypt. The guild also had developed the best processes for dyeing different types of cloth red and purple using that root. Our guild's dyed fabric will withstand many washings without fading.

"Several years ago, my father was called aside by a family from Alexandria, Egypt. That merchant believed that the source for the dye root, Hindustan, would have delivery problems. Hindustan's supply route used to come through Persia or by boat up the Red Sea to Egypt. Those land routes were increasingly dangerous due to the Arabian boycotts, and soon pirates were also attacking ships in the eastern seas. Rome got rid of pirates in the Mediterranean, but the empire does not stretch all the way to India.

"Father saw that as another business opportunity. Our family in Egypt procured some of the rootstock and seeds, and they secretly sent them to him. He had some spare acreage at Olive Grove that had soil well suited to growing this madder root. He and Nikias were able to start providing for the loss of delivery quantities from Egypt. Father now has the exclusive contract for supplying the dye material to the guild. Since he became a guild

---

[45] Hindustan is an ancient name for the plains of northern India.

member, he sells the madder root only to them, so they are the only good purple dyers in Asia.

"The guild provides natural dye powder to dye sellers in Macedonia and Bithynia, though we still have the best dyeing process here in Thyatira. Much of our dyed fabric goes directly to Rome. Wealthy people who can legally wear it demand purple cloth and do not seem to care about the price."

"My cousin, the goddess of the guild is…"

"The Guild of Purple Honors respects Artemis, and that's why, at the feast the other night, we had to be at that temple to eat meat with the other men in the guild."

Miriam sucked in her breath. *He loves this city, and he can't get enough of the business world: contracts, work done by the people in these workshops, and sales. He yearns for power and prestige, just like Jonathan, his father.*

Bani moved to a different area of the shop. Large copper pots were being heated and stirred. "These vats are where we are actually preparing dye solutions from the madder roots. Yesterday these men mixed in slices of cut-up roots and let them soak overnight. Now the heat is applied to help extract the dye. Those wagons bring charcoal for the fires."

"Where does the charcoal come from?"

"From the forests on the mountains close by. Slaves handle it with their hands, but the soot and dust are not good for the eyes. Some become blind after years of working with charcoal. We use charcoal to minimize the smoke in this room."

They both had enough of the heat and walked back outside the workshop. "What I just showed you is the most exciting part of what's done at this shop. The other end of the room has more vats where they dye cloth for several hours and then put it on racks up on the roof to dry.

"In various places around the city, women will be sewing the dried cloth, making bedspreads and furniture covers. Temple decorations are among the expensive products; only the wealthiest can afford to make such a donation. The purple cloth, the best quality of all, will go to the main Guild of Purple Honors building— that one over there—to be prepared for wide purple sashes or hems on togas. These are the most prized goods of all."

Bani's eyes danced with excitement. "This is why our family is investing here. The emperor, governors, and senators covet the color. Anything with purple shouts aloud to all, 'Look! Glory, power, praise, and honor!'"

Miriam suddenly recognized one of the workers coming out of the building; she carried a bolt of red cloth. "I know her!" she said to Bani. "That's Melpone, the woman who was at the Temple of Artemis."

Melpone was crying, and Miriam said, "Hello! You are Melpone, aren't you?"

The young woman looked up, embarrassed to be caught crying. "How do you know my name? Who are you?"

"I met you near the Temple of Artemis."

"Right, I remember now. You looked sad, and I know I looked sad too."

"Is everything all right?"

"No, everything is not all right," she replied in a hushed voice. Melpone did not look at Miriam as she spoke. "All the talking in the world won't change anything. Thank you though. You are a thoughtful person. You noticed and asked why. I must deliver this and get back to work at the main building."

Miriam called goodbye to her as Melpone left and turned onto the street.

Bani was embarrassed to see a woman crying, and he tried to draw Miriam back to his tour. "I'm happy to live in Thyatira. It's an important city, not like Ephesus, where people mostly work for the governor. Here, it's all commerce, money, sales, and jobs. You can get rich here! Come on, Miriam!"

"Bani, you said guilds have 'patron gods.' Must every guild have a patron god?"

"Oh, yes! People believe in the protection offered by the gods. Of course, our family knows gods don't really exist. But these people? Well, it's their tradition."

Miriam would not be put off. "But their gods are idols!"

"Correct. Everyone in the Guild of Purple Honors holds the goddess Artemis close to their hearts, just as the bronzesmiths honor Apollo."

"Those are the chief gods in the Greek world!"

"Yes, Apollo and Artemis are twins, two children fathered by Zeus. Of course, he had many others. From Hierapolis to Smyrna and from Pergamum to Aphrodisias, you find the twins being honored in every town and city."

Miriam went over his words in her mind: *"For the people in this valley, Apollo and Artemis are two important children of Zeus." What does he believe? That they are real or not?*

Her voice took on a sharp edge. "I've heard mention of many gods in Thyatira: Irene, Hermes, Cybele, Selen, Pan, Juventus, and Hecate—but Bani! You belong to a Jewish family. I know you must work; businessmen have working relationships. Why can't you belong to a guild without participating in the guild's *social* life?"

"Miriam, my dear cousin, you really must consider why things are this way in Thyatira. Look how weak this city was, forever being attacked. First, the Seleucid kings held it as their westernmost defense against the Kingdom of Pergamum. However, those Pergamum kings saw it as their easternmost defense against Syria, so people who lived here two hundred to three hundred years ago were constantly threatened by war. Thyatira is on the main route through the mountains. The eastern Seleucid kings were finally defeated, and Thyatira came under Pergamum's control.

"What else could they do during all those wars but ask their gods for protection? See for yourself. Thyatira has no protection. Its walls are low. However, consider its location and the supply of materials. It's the best place for manufacturing."

They were nearing Jonathan's house now, and Miriam observed, "I saw a woman in the guild, the one who travels to get new orders. Her name is Sibyl. What can you tell me about her?"

"When she and her sister, Hulda, were young, their parents went from one temple to another, searching for a cure for Hulda. One day they came to the synagogue and listened to the worship inside while they sat in the portico. Their cousin, Lydia, had come back from Philippi, and they heard her speaking about healing. Lydia, the saleswoman for purple cloth, believed in praying for the sick. That was when both Sibyl and her parents started praying for the sickly sister, Hulda.

"Hulda felt slightly better the following year, so the sisters attached themselves to our household. Friendship between the Sambathe family and our family enabled the mothers to share similar problems. Mother had lost my three little brothers, and the Sambathe family, for their part, had been concerned for their daughter's health, so they had lots to talk about.

"Shortly after, when Father was beginning to clean this piece of land, Sibyl and Hulda's parents died, leaving the sisters to take care of themselves. Lydia also became ill and died of the same fever.

"I'm sorry to hear that. But how did Sibyl start to think of herself as a prophetess?"

"In an attempt to sound heroic, Sibyl announced, 'Lydia knew almost everyone in Philippi. I've been there only once, but I'm going back to obtain a major order for the guild from soldiers there.'

"Sibyl's second trip to Philippi was successful. She returned feeling triumphant. That was when she began announcing, 'I brought orders for clothing and many household items. The order is just as large as anything Cousin Lydia ever obtained. See! I knew I can look into the future. I knew I would be successful.'"

They were at the door leading into Jonathan's home. "And now, dear cousin, the noon meal is waiting for us, cooked by our faithful Arte. Smile! Cheer up! We are resident aliens! You don't want to be an unfriendly outsider, do you?"

His last comment upset her, but Miriam could not quite understand why she felt wounded. He had intended to show her acceptance by giving her this tour, but his descriptions led her to doubt his integrity.

Later that evening, she imagined all this talk of gods to be as spreading toxin, something like the nasty spider's bite on her foot and ankle last night. Staying in Thyatira was bringing discomfort. She lay down, scratching her ankle where the sting hurt, and for a long time, she thought of venom as she winced, unable to sleep.

At breakfast the next day, the conversation with Rebekah turned to Hulda Sambathe, whom she had heard was feeling worse than usual. She usually had breathing problems, especially after the colorful flowers appeared on bushes and trees. In the past, she stayed inside her house, that being the only solution.

"Hulda was very sick after the festival," announced Rebekah with a frown. "That silly girl! She danced in the summer rain. When everyone else ran for cover, she had to enjoy the rain! Now she has a cough that won't go away."

Miriam was still upset by yesterday's insight into her cousin Bani. She did not want to hear anything more about Hulda and her sister, so she picked up Grace, excused herself, and left the room.

On Friday morning, Miriam tried to calm herself in preparation for the Sabbath. She took Grace to Jonathan's sales shop, where

Grace wanted to touch everything.

The shop was famous for its wide variety of merchandise. The six Ben Shelah brothers had been carrying on commerce in six cities of Asia Minor for many years and had a loyal following. Perfume still came in small, colorful glass bottles from Antipas's workshops, even after his death.

Jonathan sold pottery that included clay lamps, gold rings, and other jewelry. All these came from Simon in Sardis. Valuable black wool coats, cloaks, and blankets were provided by a fourth brother, Daniel, who lived in Laodicea. Amos, who lived in Philadelphia, was a source of select dried fruits and children's clothing, but he had sent word that he was selling his shop to buy an inn.

Papyrus writing sheets and delicate spices from Judah Ben Shelah, who still lived in Alexandria, Egypt, were supplied on ships belonging to Joshua, the brother in Smyrna.

Miriam caught her breath. *Apart from my uncle and his family, I know only a few people here. One is the woman who sews on purple cloth for the guild, and the last time I saw her, she was crying! I must go see her. Perhaps I can help somehow.*

However, she could not find Melpone at the Guild of Purple Honors.

Rebekah had been watching Miriam for days. After the noon meal, Rebekah motioned her to stay at the table after the others left. "Miriam, are you missing Anthony? I've been watching. Each day you seem unhappier, and today you hardly talked to anyone, just Arte. You went out with Grace this morning and returned late for the meal, and you won't even speak to Bani. Can I help in some way?"

Miriam tried not to cry while rocking Grace in her arms, and the little child chattered away, saying nonsense syllables as she learned to speak.

"Can I tell you a story, Aunt Rebekah?"

"Of course, my child, tell me whatever you want to."

"You are truly kind to me, and yes, I'm lonely. For a lot of reasons."

"Why not tell me something happy? Start with how you and Anthony met. I'm sure Antipas must have struggled with Anthony being a Gentile and a legionary."

Miriam heaved a huge sigh. *It's safe to talk about Anthony because he's far away. I'll tell her about our marriage but not about my unease with Uncle Jonathan, Bani, and Sibyl.*

"Yes, that was a struggle for Grandpa. I met Anthony in Pergamum. He was training recruits as scouts for the Pergamum Garrison. I don't know all of his story, but when he was in Legion XXI in Upper Germanica, he was badly wounded in an ambush. A cut on his face left a large scar. He almost died, and then the army granted him a farm in Philippi. He unexpectedly recovered, they allowed him to return to service as an instructor, and he was sent to Pergamum. It was while he was there that he heard Grandpa debating."

"What was Antipas debating? Where?"

"At the Pergamum agora, on two occasions. Priests from Egypt are building a huge temple there, and he was forced into a public debate explaining our faith. Another time he had to debate with the high priestess of Zeus, Lydia-Naq."

"You mean Antipas debated about religion in public? How courageous!"

"Grandpa didn't accept false gods. He wanted to put Yeshua Messiah's teaching into practice. Later he was put out of the synagogue and suffered because of it. Some boycotted his shops, and then his business went down. Then he was reported to the authorities. The synagogue had cast him out, so he was 'no longer a Jew.'[46] The city authorities put him on public trial fifteen months ago, and then they executed him because he would not accept Domitian as being a god.

"It was while things were getting harder for Grandpa that I met Anthony. He was regularly coming to our meetings. Anthony heard my songs and Grandpa's teaching. He already knew a little because his mother had become a believer in Rome when he was a boy. Anthony came to Pergamum and started following our Messiah. He talked to me about my songs and was impressed that Grandpa

---

[46] Since the time of Julius Caesar and Caesar Augustus, Jews were excused from some taxes. Josephus notes that Jewish men did not have to serve in the army because they would not fight on Sabbath days, and they did not have to say the loyalty oath when paying taxes. To administer these regulations, each synagogue kept a roll of membership if the state challenged any person. A series of treaties were signed granting Jews these legally enforced rights. Josephus, 10.1.185–10.26.267

Antipas bought and freed the slaves. Ateas and his wife, Arpoxa, are two of many. He gave them their freedom papers, and they are dear friends of ours now living in Sardis with Uncle Simon.

"In the early afternoons, he would come to the shop where I was working, and one day, I said to myself, 'Oh no! I'm falling in love with him!' Later he proposed to me even though we knew that Grandpa might not accept him."

"Oh, dear! That was hard for your grandfather, just as it was so hard for me to accept Jonathan's decision that Danila would marry our youngest boy, Gil."

Miriam wanted to digress but continued her story: "Grandpa seemed depressed for about five months. During that time, he re-read the covenant and spent hours reading and thinking about my future, but that was also when his business was having trouble.

"He began by thinking, 'God does not want us to marry foreigners,' and how many times have we heard that? However, he read of God working in strange ways. Rahab, a prostitute, and Ruth, an ancestor of King David, were accepted by God, even though they had worshiped other gods before learning about God Almighty.

"But Grandpa still resisted. 'Can Gentiles really be believers?' Then he read about a soldier who talked with Yeshua. He was a centurion who had a servant who was ill. Messiah stated that this centurion had more faith than the faithful in Israel. Later Grandpa read about other Messiah followers in Judea.

"One day after worship, he announced to the congregation that he was going to celebrate our betrothal. It should have been a party, a big event with all of you invited! Then I could have a year to prepare for our wedding!

"Instead, Grandpa said a long prayer. It was in front of all those people, including our lawyer, Marcos, and his wife, Marcella. A few weeks later, Marcos said we should get married right away because things were getting dangerous for Grandpa. The city elders had been stirred up by the high priestess of Zeus. Powerful men were upset. They were ready to bring him to a public trial. He didn't want us close by in case something bad happened to Grandpa."

It was now Rebekah's chance to express her recent disappointments. She was missing parts of her Jewish heritage in Thyatira, and her son had married a Gentile with Phrygian customs. Aunt Rebekah nodded with understanding.

"That was a hard time for you—all your customs left behind

and Antipas killed. You must have dreamed of a real Jewish wedding with days of festivities, relatives present, and all your friends' blessings. I sort of feel that way about what happened in our home last week."

They stayed silent for a while, and then Rebekah asked, "You said you sang songs that touched Anthony's heart. I'm sad that we don't have much Jewish music now."

Miriam was unable to answer as her eyes filled with tears. *I have one real friend in Thyatira.*

Later Rebekah talked to her husband, saying that she had spoken with Miriam and wanted her to feel safe and relaxed in their home. The next day, Jonathan found Miriam sitting in the garden looking somewhat sad. "Rebekah told me you had some concerns about being in Thyatira. Would you tell me your story just as you told it to her? Perhaps I can think of something that will make your stay more enjoyable."

However, different details came out. Miriam did not mention the songs she had composed. The story of Ateas and Arpoxa being ransomed by Antipas was not even mentioned. *I'm not free to be myself with Uncle Jonathan. I just think he has lost the vision of who we are as Jews. I'm afraid to tell him what I think. He is so unlike Grandfather Antipas.*

When Miriam woke up the next morning, she wondered if she was far too hard on her uncle. Tonight would be the start of Tzom Tammuz, the twenty-four hours of fasting.[47] It was forever fixed in the calendar to mark the day when the Babylonian army under Nebuchadnezzar had forced its way through Jerusalem's protective walls.[48]

---

[47] The fast of Tzom Tammuz is on the 17th day of the month known as Tammuz, usually in July. The dates of the event in our months are variable each year depending on the lunar cycle.

[48] Four additional fasts were added to the Jewish calendar after the period of captivity in Babylon: First is the Fast of the Tenth Month, January 15, 588 BC. This day of fasting commemorated the beginning of Nebuchadnezzar's siege of Jerusalem (2 Kings 25:1, Jeremiah 39:1, Ezekiel 24:1–2). Next, the Fast of the Fourth Month, the month of Tammuz, on July 18, 586 BC, reminded Jews of when the wall was breached by Nebuchadnezzar (2 Kings 25:3, Jeremiah 39:2). The Fast of the Fifth

"Why do you Jews start a fast tonight?" asked Danila at the breakfast table. "Why all these special days? Is something important about those long-ago times?"

Jonathan answered, "So many questions from you, my new daughter-in-law! We avoid food because hunger and thirst make us remember our people's anguish during the siege. We remember the bitterness of the destruction of the walls and, later, twenty-one days from now, the destruction of Solomon's Temple. That happened more than six hundred years ago. Our history both comforts us in times of distress and challenges us."

"How can history ever bring comfort?"

"Remembrance is like salve. It's a kind of love. Why did Adonai call us if we were the smallest nation? Why does he allow us to experience great suffering? We always come back to these questions. Days of fasting lend a certain rhythm to the year."

Having begun, he told Danila the entire story about how Nebuchadnezzar's army came against Jerusalem and took many people as captives back to Babylon.

Miriam thought before going to bed, *I'll write to Anthony tonight after Grace goes to sleep. I'll note that on July 9, this Tuesday, Uncle Jonathan made me proud by explaining so much of our Jewish heritage to Danila.*

Miriam, feeling proud of Jonathan, pulled up a small table beside the bed and, using a quill pen, wrote:

July 9, in the 11ᵗʰ year of Domitian

To my darling Anthony.
I feel lonely tonight. A few days ago, I overcame my loneliness by writing you a song, "I Am a Soldier's Wife!" I can't sing it to anyone in the family, at least not yet.
Tonight is the beginning of our Jewish holiday, the Fast of the Fourth Month. Uncle Jonathan explained the meaning

---

Month, July 29, 586 BC, reminded them of the burning of the Temple on the ninth day of Av, nine days after the walls were taken. All the important buildings in Jerusalem were burned (2 Kings 25:8–10). The Fast of the Seventh Month, in September, 586 BC, marked the occasion of the brutal murder of Gedaliah, the puppet governor established by Nebuchadnezzar (2 Kings 25:22–25; Jeremiah 39:14, 40:5 –16, 41:1–18).

of the covenant to Danila. He described King Nebuchadnezzar's attack and how the collapse of the wall led to the Temple's destruction twenty-one days later. She decided to join in our fast. That makes me proud of her too.

Yesterday Jonathan seemed so well integrated into our own customs and history. In contrast, earlier today he paid respects to the Rope Makers' Guild sacred day. How can he be so Jewish one moment and so involved with the regular citizens of Thyatira the next?

Uncle Jonathan and Bani keep explaining, "If you don't belong to a guild, then you can't sell or market your products or open a shop in the marketplace."

I have been caught between being sorry for myself and feeling sorry for Aunt Rebekah. She's charming, and I find it easy to talk to her.

However, I've decided to stop feeling sorry for myself. I want to talk with Melpone, a young woman who works at Jonathan's dyers' guild. She is about my age. She reminds me of Arpoxa. Both women do exquisite embroidery and edges on cloth.

Grace is growing up without her daddy. Come home soon! I hate that man, Commander Felicior. He is keeping you away from me for too long.

Miriam could not write anymore. Thinking of Anthony, Grace, and the Covenant gave her relief. She went to bed and put her head face down on the pillow.

FROM THYATIRA IN ASIA MINOR TO PHILIPPI IN MACEDONIA

On Thursday morning, Sibyl would be leaving in a wagon for Macedonia. She would travel with a camel train to Port Adramyttium on the western coast of Asia Minor. A ship would then take her and a cargo of goods to the Greek port of Neapolis.[49] From there, she had a short trip to her storehouse in Philippi. She

---

[49] Ancient Adramyttium is known today as Edremit in Turkey, on the shores of the Aegean Sea. Neapolis, in Greece, is presently called Kavala and is a well-known port. Adramyttium was home to a ship in which the apostle Paul sailed (Acts 26:2), and Neapolis was the first port into which Paul sailed after receiving the Macedonian vision (Acts 16:11).

expected to sell large amounts of clothing and wares to retired soldiers in that area and deliver previously ordered products. She told everyone, "On my return, the guild will rejoice more than ever."

Togas were carefully packed. Bed covers lined with purple would be sold to Greek senators, and they would flaunt the beautiful products in Rome. Several assistants rode behind her as her wagon left the city. Covers for dining room couches braided with purple, bright red, and blue designs; bed covers woven with purple strands; white curtains with purple trim: legal papers for bankers; customers' addresses; and supplies for the journey—everything had been thought of and planned for.

Sibyl had carefully packed necklaces, rings, and embroidered tunics, all hinting at importance and status. Customers waited in four cities: Philippi, Amphipolis, Thessalonica, and Berea. She was ready for any eventuality. The Guild of Purple Honors she represented was known and trusted in those Greek cities, beginning from when Lydia sold purple items in Philippi.

"I'll return with another substantial contract," Sibyl called out. "I know it! I feel it in my bones." She delivered her latest prophecy.

Along the way, later in the four-week visit, she planned to stop in Amphipolis, a city on the Aegean Sea close to Philippi. She delighted in the view while standing at the top of the hill. From there, she would gaze at the sea and look down on the marshy beach. Sibyl had not told her secret to anyone. At the top of the sandy bluff south of Philippi, she planned to make a personal offering. A powerful potion had been prepared to pour out over the marshy reeds. She would pray for healing. Sibyl had bought the concoction at the Temple of Artemis for her sister, Hulda.

Where the Amphipolis River meets the Aegean Sea...

Waving goodbye as she left the guild office, Sibyl blocked out the sounds of donkeys braying and children shouting. She made another promise while looking straight ahead as her wagon entered the open road behind a caravan of thirty camels at the Northern Gate. *I'll pour a sacrifice of wine in the river to Adonai. Perhaps the Lord will make Hulda better. He is the Lord of rivers, and seas. That place in the wetlands will be the best place to pour my libation, where waters come together. I'll ask God for extraordinary healing. Indeed, he will hear my cry. I know exactly where I'll pour it. I love that place near the cove where that river meets the sea.*

Chapter 17
Greed and Violence

THE CITY OF PRUSA (BURSA, TURKEY)

Craga returned to Prusa to plan the next attack for his ever-increasing phantom army, now being called "The Faithful" by the leaders. Altogether, he had convinced forty malcontents to commit themselves to what he called this "new source of pride and riches."

Taba had found several new recruits by visiting the taverns and gaming houses. Most had fallen idle and were loitering about in Chalcedon, at the mouth of the Bosporus. They left the army with poor reputations or outright desertion. He spent a significant amount of time with each prospect to ensure they had a quick mind and could be trusted as a part of his "army" before inviting them to join.

Taba had instructed his committed recruits to meet with him and Craga in a rented house in Prusa for indoctrination.

"In your first assignment," instructed Taba, speaking to the newly chosen recruits, "we'll simply be soldiers sent to Prusa. We'll act as additional personnel for guarding two merchants with shipments of slaves going from Prusa to Aizanoi. On the way, we'll 'remove' the merchants and replace them with our own men. We did that before and sold the slaves to the mines in Andeira at pure profit.

"We will soon be completely changing to a safer way to make profits. Getting rid of the bodies of slave traders and replacing them with our own men has been risky. Too many relatives of the 'expired' traders asked what happened when their men didn't arrive home.

"We now have a ship for bringing our own captured slaves from north of the Black Sea, and we need help with some difficult situations. Profits will be divided fairly, unlike the Roman army. Also," he added, "I'm certain that the 'General' is about to lay his hands on another ship."

Taba's new "recruits" were once seasoned fighters. Depending on their present abilities, they were to act as regular soldiers or auxiliaries conducting slaves to market. Those designated as soldiers were equipped with military gear: helmets, breastplates, sandals, swords, and shields.

A royal family in Tanais, part of the Bosporan Kingdom[50] above the northeast Black Sea, had provided forged authorizations to transport slaves in return for bribes. These documents included various versions in the event of "The Faithful" coming under suspicion.

Those recruited as auxiliaries were expected to manage the horses, carts, and more mundane support activities. They did not earn as much money, were not part of the planning, and were not required to use weapons.

It was Craga's turn to speak, and he described their organization in detail. "Mithrida, our general, has chosen alternate new identities for you. I have here forged documents that will protect you in any situation if the authorities uncover our plans. They register you as soldiers associated with the fleet based in Perinthius. It is called Classis Perinthius, and it controls all traffic in the Sea of Marmara.[51] If the authorities in Asia Minor look for you in Perinthius, they will come up blank. You don't exist there. If they search in Classis Pontica,[52] the navy based in Trapezus to control

---

[50] The Bosporan Kingdom, with which Mithrida and Craga are associated in this novel, was an ancient state on the Black Sea's northeast coast. It was located on the Crimean Peninsula and the Taman Peninsula (today Ukraine and Russia). It was a client state of Rome and served as a buffer between the Roman Empire, Central Asia, and Eastern Europe's northern lands. Exports included wheat, furs, timber, and slaves. In AD 64, Nero, seeking to gain control over the Bosporan Kingdom, brought it under the Province of Moesia (modern-day Serbia, Macedonia, and Bulgaria to the mouth of the Danube River).

[51] Classis Perinthia was the name of the Roman navy based in Perinthius, the modern Turkish city of Ereglisi. An enclosed harbor protected ships during stormy winter months. This navy controlled the Sea of Marmara, the Bosporus to the north, and the Dardanelles to the south. During this period of history, this body of water was known as Propontus. I use the modern name, Sea of Marmara.

[52] Classis Pontica was the Roman navy based in Trapezus, the modern Turkish city of Trabzon. Josephus writes that this fleet was composed of

the Black Sea, nothing! They won't be able to trace you either way.

"Last year we were unloading our slaves at Adramyttium. We slipped one hundred slaves to the mine untaxed with the slave-market master's paid cooperation. Unfortunately, the harbor authorities count the slaves as they are unloaded at the port. That would create a noticeable count difference that would be troublesome if some tax officials were to investigate the discrepancy. So we won't be sending slaves there by ship anymore."

One recruit, concerned about the risks of belonging to the gang, asked, "What changes are you going to make? Will they reduce the danger of ending up on the wrong side of Roman law?"

"We changed our plans at the beginning of this year. We will now off-load our 'cargo' at the small, out-of-the-way Port Daskyleion. The slave markets are far away, and there isn't an easy way for authorities to compare slave counts for taxing. From April to June, coming off the Sea of Marmara, we successfully transported our first two shipments of slaves through there for sale at Aizanoi."

His audience, passionate about gaining wealth with such ease, followed every word.

Craga rubbed his sore leg as he explained recent events. "Aizanoi needs more help for its massive building program, and it was easy to sell slaves directly to buyers and avoid paying taxes. We may find it profitable to sell more slaves there, even if we have to register them with the slave market and pay taxes.

"Otherwise, if we don't sell through the slave market at Aizanoi, the path is open to the Aegean Sea. We can transport slaves through Aizanoi to the mines at Andeira, even though it means hundreds of extra miles. We'll soon be able to double the number we transport.

Craga pulled out a roll of papyrus on which he had written his ideas. "Now for the details of the next shipment. Ota, I'm putting you in charge. In Legion XXI, you were a clever strategist. Unfortunately, the first caravan coming to Port Daskyleion has two merchants from the Black Sea area with twenty slaves. They are coming in a ship separate from ours but will arrive at the harbor

---

forty warships and three thousand sailors and soldiers. The Romans knew the Black Sea as Pontus Euxeinos, but I use Black Sea for easier identification.

about the same time. Our soldiers will escort them to Aizanoi in two wagons, along with some wild animals. The merchants are not part of 'The Faithful' army, so we'll have to rid ourselves of those slave dealers after passing White Horse Relay Station.

"I learned about a better place in Porsuk Canyon for disposing of bodies. This will be our last time to escort merchants that we will have to eliminate. I don't want the risk of having to cover up any more crimes.

"The 'General' recently captured another twenty-two slaves, and they will be arriving at Port Daskyleion near the same time as the merchants with their twenty slaves. Therefore, the second caravan will transport two wagons with eleven slaves in each, not the standard ten per wagon.

"The two caravans of forty-two total slaves will travel together under our 'protection.' This, my friends, is the road to riches! Afterward, when you arrive in Aizanoi, you will be bringing forty-two slaves to the auction. No one outside of our organization will be aware of it!"

Hearing the plan, his recruits happily slapped each other on the back, imagining huge profits.

"If anything unusual happens, you are to let all four wagons go through to Aizanoi intact, without eliminating the two merchants. If, for example, the military adds their own regular army guards to the convoy, then you are to back off and abandon our plan. We might lose some of the profits, but let us not jeopardize future projects.

"As far as the Roman army is concerned, we are merely military guards sent from the Black Sea division guaranteeing the delivery of slaves. We simply register slaves as coming into a province, taking them to an auction in Aizanoi. If you find that the Roman Army causes no problems along the Interior Road, then you may continue on the Postal Road through Aizanoi and move them to Adramyttium then to the mines! Strong young men bring higher profits there than those sold for domestic or farm work.

"Listen! Never kill a soldier. It would draw unwanted attention. Let them do their work. Any further questions? No? Well, we'll pick fruit from low-hanging branches a week from today.

"Of course, if things go awry, you have your additional forged papers, but only use them as a last resort. They were expensive."

Taba grinned as he leaned back, but a trickle of sweat down his back revealed the pressure he had been under for the last two hours. *I've convinced them all, including Craga! Fortunately, no one knows that I was almost caught last year in Sardis. I am no longer Callistus Flavius. Thankfully, I have a newly forged name since Callistus has become too well known on the Interior Road.*

THE GYMNASIUM IN SARDIS
July 12, in the 11ᵗʰ year of Domitian
From: Diotrephes
To: My mother, Lydia

You nursed me at the feet of Zeus and taught me secrets of the father of the gods. If you are well, I am happy.

I regret to tell you that I still have no leads about Anthony, Miriam, and the baby. Commander Felicior will not give me information about Anthony, and I no longer have "eyes and ears" in the Ben Shelah shop.[53]

I believe, however, that Chrysa will soon be restored to us. It has been six weeks since they were at Simon Ben Shelah's home in Sardis.

I am happy to report that the "God-fearers" assembly in Sardis no longer opposes my plans. I sat with the mayor at the inauguration of the summer festival. My position as "Friend of the Synagogue" gave me special status.

I fired Jace, a teacher (Did I mention this to you? I'm confident that I did.) He and his wife participate with Simon in worship meetings at the Ben Shelah home. They are also doing something to help the scum that lives in the impoverished section of the city. I know Jace and Simon helped Anthony, Miriam, and Chrysa disappear. I want Jace to somehow suffer double for this.

I can't return Chrysa to Uncle Zoticos until I learn where Miriam is, so this is my new concern: to know where they are. Since Anthony is a legionary, this should not be a difficult task.

I pray the blessings of Zeus upon your life.

---

[53] Cleon, Diotrephes's spy in the Sardis Ben Shelah sales shop, was fired in the previous novel, *Never Enough Gold: A Chronicle of Sardis, Heartbeats of Courage, Book Two.*

THE MILITARY GARRISON IN SOMA

In Soma, Commander Servius had listened impatiently to Anthony's report. His face turned deep red when he heard that the bandits had simply disappeared without leaving a trace.

"Each relay station registers the same two soldiers: Callistus Flavius and Valerian Atticus, from Port Daskyleion to Prusa and then on to Aizanoi. The station commanders all agree: Those guards described themselves as retirees trained by the army and brought back into military service. We know that older soldiers are working as guards due to the shortage of young men. Most stronger legionaries were sent to the province of Moesia for the war. But could these two regulars disappear? Bah! I don't believe it."

Becoming increasingly annoyed, Servius slammed a fist on the table. "Impossible! First, in April, Spellius Macer takes the place of merchant Libanius Praesens. Then he evaporates, gone like smoke on a windy night! And in May, Iambichus Damas finishes off merchant Nicagoras Opramoas. And he vanishes! Why can no one track these criminals?"

Servius stood up suddenly. His voice rose as he continued to point out that Commander Felicior's team of six soldiers had nothing substantial to report. He was thinking about his future. *This does not help my future promotion! It's only a matter of time before I'll ask the right question, and then the full picture will begin to emerge. Where did those thieves go?*

"You went all that way and found nothing! Incredible!"

The commander turned sullen and became silent, but he could not leave the squad without further instructions. He carried on, breathing deeply. "Suros, take your team and go to Forty Trees this morning. Ask the commanding officer to again go over the records of caravans and travelers going from Thyatira to Pergamum. Could those bandits go around our checkpoints unnoticed?"

OLIVE GROVE FARM NEAR FORTY TREES

The officer at Forty Trees Check Station was not due to return from Stratonike until midafternoon, so Anthony went alone to Olive Grove, the farm less than a mile off the Postal Road.

Nikias was overjoyed to see him, and Anthony asked, "What

have you been up to?"

"The usual for summer: We are caring for the animals, clearing brush around the olive trees, and checking and weeding out the acreage growing the madder roots. I go to Jonathan's house every ten days or so. We don't get to rest much until winter."

"Anthony, I've wanted to talk to you about these scrolls. Here's a portion of the Scriptures that Rebekah talked about. I told her that some of Antipas's scrolls were stored here, and she said, 'Find one of the two thick scrolls. In it, you'll find comforting words.' Here it is, written by Isaiah. I like these words, and I want my brothers to make copies."

"What! It takes years to learn how to be a scribe!" Anthony's surprise was genuine.

"Couldn't my brothers learn to copy scrolls?"

The idea seemed preposterous. "How would you do that?"

"Wasn't this copy made from another one? Antipas Ben Shelah received this from someone, didn't he? And he taught people to copy scrolls, working just three evenings a week."

"Nikias, what a memory! Yes, I told you that when I left his scrolls here."

"Well, if Antipas taught men to copy it out, why couldn't I do that too?"

"What would you do with extra copies?"

"Rebekah says Yeshua sent his followers to the towns and villages. What if I went with my brothers after harvesting season to villages nearby?"

"You must get permission from Jonathan. You can't neglect your job here."

"But suppose he says yes to my request? Two or three copies could go to nearby villages. Also, I like Miriam's songs. People might want to learn them too."

"Why exactly would you go?"

"To tell them what is in this scroll. There are a few in each village who know how to read."

"Nikias, if you want to use this book at Olive Grove, then you may do that. However, to share it with other people..." He stopped, brought up short by an internal conflict. Nikias wanted to share good news, yet...

"For sure, read it here, but don't take it anywhere else. People can come from farms nearby and from Forty Trees. Be enthusiastic about Miriam's songs, but also be wise."

"What do you mean by 'wise'?"

Anthony paused. *How should I explain potential difficulties?*

"Not everyone will agree with you or be happy hearing of your belief in a Jewish Messiah, but talk to Jonathan. Tell him that Anthony calls those scrolls the 'Legacy of Antipas.' Ask him if he'll permit you and your brothers the time necessary to copy them, only after regular work is over. Tell him that you are copying out scrolls left by his brother, Antipas."

"Thank you. I think that's a good plan," said Nikias.

"I wish I had more time to work with you. However, I have a certain undertaking."

"What is your assignment? What keeps you so busy traveling on the roads?"

"I can't give you any details."

"That's fine with me," Nikias replied. "By the way, here is a pack of three letters from Miriam. She told me to give them to you as soon as I saw you."

Anthony reached quickly to take the letters while waiting for the commanding officer at Forty Trees to return. An hour later, he wrote a letter to Miriam.

July 23, in the 11ᵗʰ year of Domitian
From: Anthony
To: My beloved Miriam

    It has been a month since I started, but my task has not been fulfilled. I returned from my first exploration trip. My commander has complained to our team every day because we returned emptyhanded. I am in Forty Trees for a short while. My morning was spent with Nikias, but he played a trick on me. It wasn't until I was ready to leave that he gave me three letters from you! I could have strangled him! I'm happy, though, to learn of your comings and goings at the Ben Shelah home.

    I can't tell you about my work for reasons you will understand, but I'll let you know about Nikias. You remember his four children, I'm sure. He was always worried about Penelope dying in childbirth, and now she is expecting another baby, her fifth. Remember when he took you to Sardis, and you sang about your grandfather? The song Nikias memorized is one about overcoming the fear of death. Those words touched him deeply, and he wanted to learn about the Messiah from Aunt Rebekah.

You will not believe this. Nikias wants to carry on the task of making additional copies of the scrolls. He told me he will teach his three oldest brothers: Zeno, Alberto, and Lykaios. He wants them to work as scribes! Can you imagine four farmhands trying to copy Isaiah? That might be a humorous sight, but the more I think about Antipas, the more fascinated I am by what motivated him.

Nikias heard Rebekah talk about Isaiah, and she quoted the prophet, 'Don't be afraid.' He told me that he wants to go to villages, speaking to others about what he has learned. He says he is overcoming fear!

The youngest brother, Kozma, is anything but happy. Since this new teaching came into their family, he has complained that Nikias is neglecting their gods. Five brothers live in Olive Grove, all from Stratonike, and now the tension is building!

Waiting here at the military checkpoint is not easy. I don't like waiting for people. Soon I'll be preparing for another trip.

There's something I want to talk about. My grief haunts me because I mourn the loss of my legion last May.

The army led by King Decebalus killed five thousand legionaries, some of them my companions! I only trained forty scouts, but they had become like brothers. Caesar has begun an inquiry to determine the cause of the defeat.[54]

I realized something about my scar. Suppose I had not been wounded beside the Neckar River or had not been sent to Pergamum to train scouts or had not been invited to hear Antipas's story of his survival and escape from Jerusalem. How would I ever have met you? How would I have come to know and love the Messiah? I woke up this

---

[54] When Legion XXI, the Predators, was destroyed in AD 92, more than five thousand legionaries died. Unlike other disasters in the Roman army, the month and day of this calamity are unknown. For these novels, I placed the date on May 30.

morning thanking Adonai for the wound on my face! That was a new sensation: being thankful for pain!

My life is changing. It's been a long time since I thought of revenge against the man who tried to kill me. I used to enjoy sitting with loudmouths. Instead, I want to read Antipas's notes. I gave your grandfather's scroll collection a name, calling it "The Legacy of Antipas." I hope you agree with that name. How wonderful it would be to have time to read all he wrote. The officer has arrived. I must go. I'll seal this, and Nikias will take it to you. You will be mine forever. I miss you so much. —All my love

He sealed his letter, pressing his signet ring into the red wax. After communicating the instructions sent by Commander Servius to the Forty Trees officer about rechecking the recent caravan records between Thyatira and Pergamum, Anthony made a brief detour, took the letter to Nikias, then returned to Soma. He prayed that Penelope and the new baby would be protected and, like a sealed letter, would be safely delivered.

ON THE POSTAL ROAD FROM AIZANOI TO PORSUK CANYON

On the Postal Road, going north from Aizanoi to White Horse Relay Station, two legionaries accompanied eight merchants on their journey to Cotyaum.

It was a two-day journey, and they had spent the night at the inn in the small village of Kirec. Publius and Felix were the guards, and since they frequently traveled this road, they had known these eight merchants for years.

Now, at midmorning, the ten men and more than forty animals were being held back. They were not permitted to move past the first long, graceful curve entering Porsuk Canyon.

A soldier on horseback blocked their way, shouting, "Robbers were spotted at the intersection of the Postal Road and Interior Road!"

A few minutes later, he yelled again, "Caravans and soldiers, stay back! We are clearing the area of robbers! Wait until there is no danger. You soldiers coming north with your caravans, stay at your posts. We have enough fighters to carry out our search. Stay close to your caravans and merchants! This could be a ruse to attack you if you leave the merchandise unattended!"

The merchants going north to their destination in Cotyaum grumbled but were pleased at the implied protection.

Sometime later, the menace had disappeared. "All clear!" shouted the soldier, who rode in full armor. He was followed by two wagons, one carrying an angry caged bear and another with two boars. Several other soldiers followed in a caravan with four wagons, each with ten slaves.

"Six wagons bringing forty slaves, six soldiers, two merchants, one caged bear, and a cage of grunting wild pigs," said Publius. He commented on the animals. "Look at that bear! He's plenty unhappy about being jostled around like that."

"No sign of danger?" asked Felix, speaking to the soldier who had warned about robbers.

"No, it was a false alarm!" answered the guard, riding beside the bear cage.

Publius led the caravan along the smooth curve, bringing them into a small canyon about two miles long. The stone walls of the canyon to the north and the south rose straight up, reaching a height of two hundred feet.

Farmers in two nearby villages owned lush fields and pastureland wedged between the canyon's walls. The slow-moving Porsuk River hugged the Postal Road. It followed the canyon wall, and two miles later, having risen to the top of the cliffs, the Postal Road intersected with the north–south Interior Road.

When the caravan was about halfway through the canyon, Publius, the lead guard, raised his hand and halted the train. Leaping down from his horse, he knelt over an injured man who had dragged himself up the steep embankment to the side of the road. Blood oozed from his legs and thigh.

"Help, leg ... I hurt ... lose blood ... feel faint."

Publius instinctively pulled out his sword, turned around, and looked in all directions, ready for an attack. He shouted to Felix, "No bandits are in sight, but bandits were here! Be careful! This may still be a trap!"

He looked along the river, east and west. He spotted nothing. Above him, a red stone cliff soared high into the blue sky. No one could hide on those steep, smooth walls. He examined the areas beside the road and saw an abandoned building on the far side of a shallow river.

The caravan had stopped and was waiting. Publius shouted at

the merchants, "One of you, get over here and help this man! He looks like a slave."

He ran down the embankment, crossing the river on a rickety wooden bridge. As he approached the building, he saw many footprints.

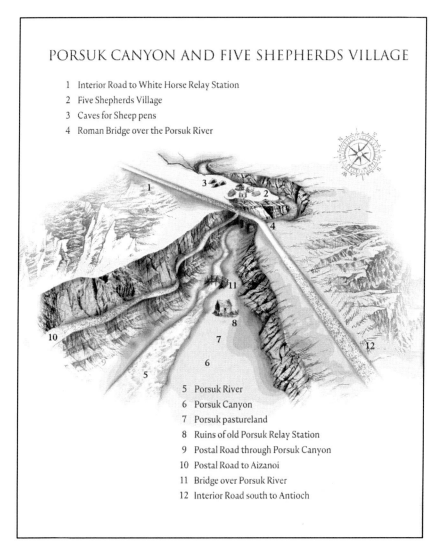

PORSUK CANYON AND FIVE SHEPHERDS VILLAGE

1 Interior Road to White Horse Relay Station
2 Five Shepherds Village
3 Caves for Sheep pens
4 Roman Bridge over the Porsuk River

5 Porsuk River
6 Porsuk Canyon
7 Porsuk pastureland
8 Ruins of old Porsuk Relay Station
9 Postal Road through Porsuk Canyon
10 Postal Road to Aizanoi
11 Bridge over Porsuk River
12 Interior Road south to Antioch

"Felix, come! This place is abandoned, but several people were in here, probably while we were stopped back at the curve in the road."

"Were they the robbers that soldier was talking about?"

Publius halted at the entrance of the crumbling building, his sword at the ready. Glancing around, he exclaimed, "I see blood on the floor and on the ground outside! Lots of it! More than one person was killed here."

The bloodstains began at the room entrance and led to a well on the building's far side. Looking more closely, Publius yelled, "I think there was a fight. Bodies have been thrown in the well."

The merchant on the road yelled down to the soldiers, "We need to get this man to the next station quickly, or he'll die.... He may die anyway." Felix ran back to the roadway with Publius following behind him.

"What happened?" Felix bent over the wounded man, unable to stop the blood flow.

"Cut...my enemy..." He spoke a little Greek, but from his accent, he was Scythian.

Publius pulled his horse over to the bleeding man and yelled, "Help me put him on my horse! It'll be rough on him, but it's the only chance he has. We must get him to White Horse Relay Station! By Jove, what a fight!"

He singled out one of the merchants. "Stay with the caravan and escort it on to White Horse. We will send other soldiers to guard all of you and to examine the bodies in the well. Felix, ride on ahead to White Horse and be prepared for when I get there with this man. I'll have to hold him in front of me so I can't ride as fast as you. We must get to the bottom of this."

By the time Publius arrived at White Horse Relay Station, four miles farther north, the man's life was ebbing away. Felix had a table and bandages prepared to apply a tourniquet to the wounded leg. "Tell me what happened!" the officer in charge demanded in Greek, repeating it in Latin.

"I'm captured ... far away ... north ... sold slaves in Sinop. I come ... the Black Sea." The man struggled to explain what had happened as his strength was almost gone.

"One man is kind ... teach me Greek ... then Chalcedon ... I sold ... simple slave ... not house ... slave for caves ... for mines ... get knife."

"More water! Put more bindings on that wound! We must stop

that flow of the blood! This man knows everything that happened in the canyon! Do not let him die! I want to hear it all!"

The officer was desperate to keep the wounded slave alive, and his regulars were doing their best. "How did it happen? How did you escape? Where did the convoy stay last night?"

"Yes, I ... this morning ... knife off ship from Chalcedon ... under my tunic ... to kill." It was all he could do to breathe. "Ship ... wagon ... many days..."

"Did you hear any names? Who did this to you?"

"Many ... strange names ... Harpa ... Baga ... Ota ... Roman soldier. He ... me with his sword ... he bad man."

"Other names—did you hear any other names?" The moment was dramatic, urgent.

"Soldiers talk ... sometimes ... another caravan too ... Roman names ... sometimes ...Craga... Ota talk to Baga ... about Tira and Spithra."

"Write that down, soldier!" the officer said to an assistant. "Soldiers with odd-sounding names: Harpa, Baga, Ota, Craga, Tira, and Spithra. Not a single Roman name among them, yet the guards were regulars! This slave was with them for days, and he must have heard them talking."

Publius was desperate, and he shouted, "Were you going to kill someone? Were you going to kill Craga and Ota...or other slaves too?"

The dying man closed his eyes, his voice hardly audible. "I want to kill man ... who makes me ... one other slave ... he escape too ... I'm good ... for house slave. I don't want ... mines ... slaves for caves, for the mines. In Sinop learn ... speak Greek." His breathing was slowing. "Leader ... I hear name. They ... afraid in Sinop." He opened his eyes. "Mithrida ... afraid."

They watched him die. The man stopped breathing, and his eyes went blank. He had lost too much blood to survive any longer.

A slave who had no name had given them much information, but little of it made sense. They examined the wounds on his leg and thigh, which had been caused by a two-edged sword.

Publius clenched his fists. "Why leave him wounded? Why would a soldier attack a slave? Who was the attacker? Who was this slave? What happened back there?"

Felix said, "This slave was stabbed in that abandoned building...and he spoke of another slave that escaped. Where is he?

He may be able to tell us what happened. We must go back and examine the building today. Publius, you said you saw bodies in the well?"

"Yeah, I saw bodies down there. I couldn't tell how many. We'll have to pull them out to figure out how they fit into all this."

Bewildered, they looked at one another. Publius summarized the situation. "A dead slave was captured in northern lands. That explains the blond hair and blue eyes. He was shipped to Sinop and trained as a slave to work in a house of Greek-speaking people. But he was being sold for hard labor…'mine,' he said. 'Another slave escaped too,' he said. Two of them escaped. So where is the other one? Or was he recaptured? And who are the bodies in the well?"

The assistant to the officer had examined the records from the previous morning. "No soldiers with names like Harpa, Baga, Ota, Craga, Tira, or Spithra passed through here!"

"Then either this slave was delusional or those soldiers somehow never passed through here before now…or possibly they changed their names," the officer of White Horse Relay Station mused as he looked out the window. "We've got a lot of dead people and plenty of questions with no answers. Nothing about this makes any sense! Send an initial report to Aizanoi immediately. We may know more later after examining the bodies in the well."

THE MILITARY GARRISON IN SOMA

In Soma, Anthony and his soldiers had just begun the evening meal when the door opened suddenly. Commander Servius rushed into the mess room with a strip of paper in his hand. "Listen up! News by carrier pigeon. It's from Aizanoi. It says, 'At noon today, a slave and others were killed close to White Horse Relay Station. Details when you arrive. This message is being sent to other garrisons in the area.'"

Servius shouted, "This is what we've been waiting for!"

The commander did not waste a moment. "Leave tomorrow morning for White Horse! Stop at Sardis and each garrison on the way. Make sure each relay station understands this message. Speak to the officers. Every caravan must be searched, and escorting."

They left early the next day. The tedium they had experienced during their trip a month earlier had suddenly been altered to action.

The outlaws, hungry for wealth, had finally made a mistake.

Chapter 18
Survivors

JONATHAN AND REBEKAH'S HOME, THE CITY OF THYATIRA

"Next week we begin the saddest week of the year," said Jonathan, pushing back from the evening meal. "We will remember, for the twenty-second time, the anniversary of when Jerusalem was destroyed, our sadness, and the futility of standing up to the Roman armies. Titus, what a treacherous 'victor' he was!"

Miriam recalled the day as Antipas kept it. *I'll remember and honor this day the way Grandpa Antipas did. If Uncle Jonathan adds anything—Lydian, Latin, Greek, or Phrygian words or symbols or anything else—I'll ignore him.*

I'm only going to be in Thyatira for a few more days. Anthony and his men will have captured the robbers soon, so I must not get attached to anyone. Uncle Jonathan and Aunt Rebekah, their servants, and Koloksai: these will be the only people I'll spend time with.

"Next Wednesday, we'll do what Jews have done each year since Jerusalem was burned," continued Jonathan, standing up and going to his library. "We'll go to the synagogue in sackcloth and with ashes sprinkled on our heads. May God be merciful to us, his people."

Miriam was content, sure that Anthony would soon take her back to Sardis. Grace was jumping in Miriam's lap when Jonathan said something that left Miriam fearful. "I heard this week that a few Jewish families at the synagogue are not happy with us. Nevertheless, we must sit beside them all day. They, like us, will be in mourning."

"What do you mean, Uncle Jonathan, 'not happy with us'?" asked Miriam.

"At the moment, it means just that. Something is bothering the elders."

The Tish'a B'Av commemoration marked the last day of sacrifices in Jerusalem, when Roman soldiers destroyed Herod's

Temple. Centuries before, on that same day, King Nebuchadnezzar had burned the Temple of Solomon. Remembering the event always brought painful tears.

During the last several days, Miriam had pondered Jeremiah's disconsolate words. She remembered that Adonai had brought some of the most significant promises to his people even on gloomy days.

Non-Jewish visitors to the portico of the synagogue enjoyed learning about Jewish ways. A few wanted more details about what took place during those days of the Roman siege of Jerusalem.

Kilan, the presiding elder, voiced annoyance at the prospect of non-Jews attending this particular service. "No, they should not enter! How can they understand our grief? It's not something to be observed! For me, the strict observance of the Law is mandatory. That means I place a clear separation between our Jewish community in Thyatira and these 'God-fearing' newcomers." The term he used signified his disapproval of physical intrusion by those with a growing interest in Jewish customs.

The Saturday morning service began with the age-old words in Hebrew. "*Baruch Atah Adonai, Eloheynu Melech Haolam.* Blessed are you, O Lord our God, King of the universe."

Miriam sat with the women during the service listening to the men's voices. Grace walked around Miriam's knees, holding one finger of Miriam's hand.

She enjoyed the Shabbat of Prophecy, or Shabbat of Vision as some called it. She longed to talk to Anthony, and if he were here, she would say, "It's easy to remember our past; it comes alive, over and over. Titus, commander of your Roman legions, destroyed our city, and as a reward, he was crowned emperor. Titus died, and now Domitian, his brother, is our emperor.[55]

"Two terrible events in history happened on the same day of the year: Solomon's Temple was destroyed, and then Herod's Temple also went up in flames! Grandpa Antipas found parallels in everything—poetry, prose, psalms, and prayers—but how could Adonai permit our enemies to triumph twice? Why was I one of the few to leave the city and live? Why did you survive that brutal

---

[55] Domitian became emperor on September 14, AD 82. This novel takes place during the eleventh and twelfth years he governed the Roman Empire.

attack, leaving you with a scar? These questions circle in my mind, never stopping."

Monday, July 28, dawned as the hottest day yet. Jonathan said he would eat stale flatbread and only drink a little bit of water, but Rebekah refused all food and drink. She complained, "My dear, where's your passion, your memory, your loyalty? This should be a complete fast!"

Later at the Thyatira Synagogue, the reader for the day pronounced the timeless words of Jeremiah in memory of the great destruction on the twenty-second anniversary of the conquest that made General Titus so famous.

"Hear the word of the Lord. Reform your ways and your actions, and I will let you live in this place. Do not trust in the deceptive words and say, 'This is the temple of the Lord, the temple of the Lord, the temple of the Lord.' If you really change your ways and your actions and deal with each other justly, if you do not oppress the alien, the fatherless, or the widow and do not shed innocent blood in this place and if you do not follow other gods to your own harm, then I'll let you live in this place, in the land I gave your forefathers forever and ever."[56]

Miriam's mind wandered as she pondered the words of the scripture urging her to act. *I'm beginning to accept that I may be in Thyatira for a long time. Anthony is not indicating that his new job will end soon. What if the Ben Shelah family could understand the plight of the unfortunate people in the insulae and actually help them in some way? I could use my time to somehow intercede for the poor in this city like I did in Sardis. I helped create jobs for disabled people there, but the guild system in Thyatira would make that impossible. Indeed, that was something that could be done in Sardis but not here.*

The reader in the synagogue continued reading through the laments. "I'll remember my affliction and my wandering, the bitterness and the gall. I well remember them, and my soul is downcast within me. Yet this I call to mind and therefore I have hope: Because of the Lord's great love we are not consumed, for his compassions never fail. They are new every morning; great is your faithfulness. I say to myself, 'The Lord is my portion; therefore, I will wait for him.' The Lord is good to those whose hope is in him,

---

[56] From Jeremiah 7:2–8

to the one who seeks him; it is good to wait quietly for the salvation of the Lord."[57]

Miriam squirmed as she heard the passages being read. *Our history is full of contradictions! Deep pain and suffering! Punishment for disobedience and violence, yet in Adonai, who brought judgment and discipline, we find our greatest comfort.*

It had been the synagogue's custom to have one family tell their story each year as part of this day's commemoration. Miriam sat straight up and rocked Grace as Jarib and Shiri walked to the front to tell their story.

Jarib began, "My name is Jarib, and I'm Jonathan's steward. Our ancestors were in Egypt and came through the Red Sea. They made it through the dry desert for forty years and through the Jordan River to the Promised Land.

"Much later, our family returned to Egypt, but we almost didn't make it through the pogroms in Alexandria."

Dry humor was appreciated by his audience. Comments that joined history to present predicaments were common.

"Our tribe was one of the favored ones in Israel. Ephraim received a good inheritance. My ancient ancestor was Immer Ben Joshua, owner of a farm in a little village in Ephraim's hill country near Timnath Serah, the home of Joshua, our hero. Every year our ancestors went up to Jerusalem, usually three times during the year: for Passover, Pentecost, and the Festival of Tabernacles.[58]

"When the great division took place with ten tribes separating from Judah, we detested the new beliefs of King Jeroboam, who was leading our nation astray. Generations passed, invaders threatened, and Israel became weaker. An Assyrian army laid siege to Samaria, our capital.

"Our family had no choice but to leave. Assyrian troops took all our food, and we would be either persecuted and enslaved or killed by the Assyrians. So we took refuge by fleeing.[59] My ancestors took their few belongings and moved to Jerusalem, giving up the inheritance of our land. Many other families made the same decision.

"Of course, there was no space for refugees in Jerusalem, so our

---

[57] Lamentations 3:19–26
[58] Deuteronomy 16:1–17
[59] This story is told in 2 Kings 17:1–40

ancestors settled in Gibeon, not far from Jerusalem. We joined the local population, cutting wood and delivering it to the people in the city. After we left our land in Ephraim, we never owned land again. We became workers for other families, and now we are Jonathan's stewards. My cousin, Onias, who lives in Pergamum, was a steward for Antipas, Miriam's grandfather. He is still working there.

"The people often fell away from God. King Hezekiah carried out a long period of purification and reform. Our forefathers were blessed to help in the preparations of cleansing the Temple grounds.[60] But Manasseh, the next king, raised Asherah poles and worshiped the queen of heaven! Then the next king, Josiah, brought another reform, a positive one, destroying all the idols. However, within a few years, the Asherah poles were back up again. Our people loved raisin cakes more than the simple worship of our Creator. Back and forth went the differing sides in a prolonged tussle that did not end well.

"The Babylonians attacked Judah. The first time they besieged Jerusalem, they took the richest and wisest as captives. Later, Jerusalem fell, broken and destroyed. There is a story in our family of an ancestor who stood on a hill refusing to eat or drink until God brought miraculous punishment on Babylon's invading army. They say he died from starvation and a broken heart. He watched Solomon's Temple being burned, and he said he could live no longer. Laments written about his starvation are still quoted today: 'Those nurtured in purple now lie on ash heaps.'"[61]

Jarib's wife, Shiri, took up the story, letting her husband rest while deep emotions stirred his heart. "My husband sometimes can't speak because of the pain of remembering those times. Our ancestors had no future and no hope. A new governor, Gedaliah, was in place; he was killed two months later. Many families decided to walk to Egypt. They were already starving and hungry, and many died while trying to walk that far.[62]

"It was at that time the Ben Shelah family met our ancestors. The Ben Shelah family from Judah had been carrying on trade in

---

[60] The story of King Hezekiah is found in 2 Kings 18:1–30:27. His great Passover festival is recorded in chapter 30. See 2 Chronicles 29:1–32:33.
[61] Lamentations 4:5
[62] The destruction of Jerusalem and the plight of the survivors is found in Jeremiah 39:1–44:28.

shipping between Egypt and Judah. Our family said, 'If you take us with you safely to Egypt, then we'll serve you as stewards.' Our family was saved from murderous Babylonians, and we have worked together for many generations.

"Pogroms in Egypt during these last two generations brought many deaths. You already know how Jonathan's three older sisters were burned to death on the day of Anna's betrothal party when she was eighteen years old. Days later, the Ben Shelah house was nothing but a pile of cold ashes."

Shiri started to weep, and she turned away as Jarib resumed the story. "Shiri was born five years after the first pogrom, and I was born two years after her. We grew up in Alexandria and treasured our location in the city. Occasionally, offensive comments cut us to the quick, but in general, life went well.

"We married in June when I was eighteen years old. The pogrom took place in August, less than three months later. We had saved money for our own house. However, just as we were about to purchase our own property, all the Jewish families moved from two districts into only one. Prices went up. The cost of houses doubled and then tripled. Shortages kept getting worse.

"Years passed, and Jonathan and Rebekah said, 'Let's go to Jerusalem. The Temple built by Herod is completed! Let us serve the Living God there.'[63] What a treasure to return to our ancient roots! We moved to Timnath Serah in the land of our forefathers.

"Jonathan and Rebekah's first three boys, Adin, Obed, and Jehiel, were born in Judah and raised in Ramathaim-Zophim, close to Jerusalem. However, when it was evident that the political situation was increasingly dangerous, Jonathan and his family returned to Egypt. Only a few months later, the second pogrom took place in Alexandria. Jonathan and Rebekah's three little boys were killed in that pogrom, burned by young men who laughed while watching small Jewish children die. They were seven, five, and three years old.

"Ugly words were heard all the time. Was it because we did not have to pay the same taxes they did? At first, some Egyptians boycotted our shops, and even faithful customers stopped coming.

"In the port where I worked for Eliab Ben Shelah, Alexandrian Greeks repeatedly mocked us. We put up with it until we got word

---

[63] Herod's Temple was completed in AD 63.

of the Temple having been burned when Jerusalem fell.[64] Titus commanded four legions and was a great conqueror.

"We wept again after learning that Herod's Temple's treasure was going to be used in Rome to build the Coliseum.[65] And then came the Flavian family, one after the other, three emperors: first the father, Vespasian; then the older brother, Titus; and now the younger brother, Domitian.

"Ships began arriving in Egypt. They came day after day, unloading starving, emaciated Jewish slaves sent from Judea to work the mines in Egypt. Cruel Roman shouts sounded repeatedly. Half-naked, half-dead people stumbled along. Those men and women would never return to Jerusalem.

"Those were the courageous ones, survivors who lived through Jerusalem's siege, but were they better off than the ninety thousand Jewish slaves who were taken to Caesarea Philippi? They died fighting wild animals! I heard about it, and I remember my exact location when the news came. I was standing on the docks beside a ship.

"We could not stay in Alexandria. We received word that Eliab had escaped from the Jerusalem siege with his family, and they were going to Asia. Jonathan said, 'I've no reason to stay here. I'm going to move with my father and older brothers to Pergamum. Will you want to come with us?' We replied, 'Let's go.'

"So we came with our father; sadly, he died several years ago. After a while, the Ben Shelah brothers, all except Antipas, left for other cities. Jonathan chose to make his home in Thyatira.

"You all know Jodan, who was born in Alexandria, just before we moved. He is twenty-one years old, almost twenty-two. He was born with a withered hand, and he works hard but is not always regular in his thinking. He wants me to tell you how much he loves being a part of this congregation. He has a remarkable memory and

---

[64] The gripping history of Jerusalem's destruction is told by Josephus in two books, *The Antiquities of the Jews* and *The Jewish War*. These detail events from AD 50–70, listing names of important persons. In a Jewish civil war, the army of John fought Simon's troops for domination within Jerusalem, while the Romans surrounded the city outside.
[65] Titus became the Field Marshall in AD 69. Jerusalem fell in AD 70. Herod's Temple was burned on the ninth day of Av, the anniversary of the burning of the Temple of Solomon by Nebuchadnezzar 656 years before.

can recollect long passages from Scripture. Perhaps you don't know how well he can remember things since he doesn't talk much.

"Gedalya is our pride and joy, our fifth child, the youngest given to us by the Almighty. He excels in business, does well in mathematics, and will carry on our family name. He is almost twenty now, already a man, almost old enough to take on the tasks carried out by a steward!"

People looked at Gedalya. He really was a fine young man, well built with muscular arms. His face was kind and gentle, and his bright black eyes indicated a vivacious mind. Many took an instant liking to him when meeting him for the first time.

The crowded synagogue was hot and stuffy. The stories linking the two families, the Ben Joshua family and the Ben Shelah family, were shocking. Little innocent children, full of life and vigor, had been killed. Jerusalem had fallen.

After that, no city seemed genuinely safe.

Chapter 19
White Horse Relay Station

WHITE HORSE RELAY STATION ON THE INTERIOR ROAD

As Miriam was listening at Thyatira's synagogue, Anthony and his five companions reached the White Horse Relay Station between Aizanoi and Cotyaum.

"Hail! We are the squad appointed by the commanders of the region. We are back to look into the four men murdered recently along the Postal Road and the Interior Road."

"I remember you, and I'm pleased to have you here again, Anthony Suros. We said you would probably be back to investigate these deaths, so we have been waiting for you. And it's good to see you again, Omerod and Menandro."

"Is your commanding officer in? We require a meeting to go over the details of the recent murders."

A few minutes later, the officer sat with Anthony and the others at a small office table. Anthony said, "Sextilius, I want you to start this debriefing."

Sextilius began, "Have you made written reports regarding the last murder incident in the canyon?"

"Yes. Regarding the caravans, we have clear records. Two caravans traveled together for safety. It was composed of six soldiers, four merchants, forty-two slaves, one bear, and two boars from the Black Sea area. It arrived late in the day, stayed overnight, and left early. Seeing the bear and the wild boars, I assigned Quintus Zosimus, one of my regulars, to the caravan. I was worried about the animals getting loose. So eleven men left in that caravan the next morning, besides the forty-two slaves of course."

"Who was killed first, and who was the last one murdered?"

"The wounded slave was brought here and expired, so he was the last to die. Poor Quintus, his body was thrown in the well on top of the two corpses, those of the merchants."

"Is everything the slave said written down in your report?"

"Yes, we heard the dying man say a few words. It was hard to understand because he spoke Greek very poorly, but we copied down all that he said."

"And of course, you read the later records from the slave market in Aizanoi, where these caravans were headed."

"Yes. That record shows only two merchants were observed in Aizanoi. This agrees because the other two merchants were killed and dumped in the well. Witnesses later said the two men at the agora were inexperienced. However, two of the merchants we talked with the evening before were obviously very familiar with their work. Those were the same men we found murdered in the well."

"Do you think another slave escaped and is still out there?"

"I keep saying that dying slave was not delusional. He specifically said, 'One other slave escaped.' He described what had happened and was not wandering off in his imagination. He spoke only a few words, but that was enough for us to understand a lot of what had taken place. But not all."

Leaning back with his hands high above his head, Sextilius summarized his thoughts. "I'm going to link these four deaths with two previous murders. In the former two highway robberies, the victims were slain and found much later, after the attacks.

"This event is different however. A camel train came later and found the dying slave. Nobody saw anything criminal happen. Legionary Quintus Zosimus was murdered. Why, we do not know. Two merchants are dead, and their merchandise was taken. We know a fight took place in an old building. The crimes were discovered immediately, correct?"

"Yes, that's the way I understand it."

"The camel train coming north was advised to wait because of possible danger. Tell us, sir, about your questioning of persons with the camels."

The commanding officer answered, "I grilled each person until late in the evening: all eight merchants and the two regulars who guarded them. Their answers were consistent and really had nothing new to contribute. I learned that all six soldiers, the two remaining merchants, and the bear and boars had vanished."

Sextilius rubbed his wrist and then placed his face between his hands. "What discrepancies did you find between any witnesses?"

"There were no inconsistencies. Here, let me read my report:

'On July 23, ten caravans left White Horse Station going south. The two caravans we are suspicious about were the first to leave, and they were on their way incredibly early. The other eight left about the expected time. All ten caravans reported in at Aizanoi the same evening. Coming north was a camel train, the one that was stopped before entering the canyon.'"

Sextilius raised his head and leaned forward "Let's go back to the soldiers guarding the forty-two slaves and animals. Were they known to you?"

"I had not seen them previously. The soldiers looked rough and spoke tough. That is what years in the army does to men. They said they had served in the army in Upper Germanica and Moesia."

"So eight other caravans went south that morning, following the two that Quintus was guarding. All eight left about the same time. What did you learn about them?"

"The eight caravans going south were stopped before they could enter the Porsuk Canyon. They could not leave the Interior Road to enter the Postal Road. They were told to wait for a while. The reason given by a soldier on the road who told them to wait was 'There's a threat of robbers.' That was the same message given by the other soldier to the camel train coming north."

"That means the canyon was sealed at both ends. No one could see what was going on. Where were the eight caravans stopped?"

"About a mile before entering the canyon. You've seen the place. It's before you come to the junction of the Postal Road and the Interior Road. There's a small shepherds' village there."

"But why would robbers announce their own presence? Why demand that caravans halt? It would be idiotic to say to other soldiers coming along the road, 'Watch out for robbers!'"

"We have to assume they were excluding other caravans from the area during the murders."

"What questions have you asked as you attempted to learn what happen?"

"I have many. Quintus Zosimus is dead. Why? What did he see? We have no answer to that. And here is a strange thing about that combined double caravan. The first caravan looked normal. Two slave wagons carried ten in each wagon, so that makes twenty slaves. But the second caravan included twenty-two slaves, not twenty, with eleven slaves in each of two wagons. Altogether, that makes forty-two slaves in four wagons.

"If one slave died and another escaped, that would result in two caravans with twenty slaves each for sale. Only forty should have arrived in the city, but forty-two were registered there."

"The records at the slave market in Aizanoi at the end of that day prove that forty-two slaves were sold by two 'inexperienced' slave merchants. We found that forty-two slaves had been sold, which was surprising given that we think two had escaped. Those slaves were ready to be moved out of the city by the buyers. I personally talked to the agora master, who said he thought the two slave merchants were 'inexperienced'; that was his word for them."

"Did anyone question those slaves? What did they see?"

"We tracked them down as they were still being held in Aizanoi by new owners, ready to be moved out to farms. We threatened the slaves, but they refused to say anything. I wanted to torture information out of them, but their new owners rejected the idea and started to complain. None of them would answer any of the questions.

"But they all agreed on one thing: Two slaves escaped from the wagon at the rear and never came back. That is all they will say. The escapees were in the last slave wagon, the fourth. This much is certain: Forty-two slaves were put up for auction and sold well below the going price. Obviously those 'merchants' wanted to get rid of them right away."

This information satisfied Sextilius, and he continued, "Let's get back to the dead slave. Do you think he told the truth?"

"Yes, absolutely. The bodies in the well at the abandoned relay station and blood marks back to the road confirm his story."

Anthony interrupted, "Note this, Sextilius. These thugs probably picked up two more slaves between Porsuk Canyon and Aizanoi, needing to sell forty-two, not forty. They wanted the sell quantity to agree with the White Horse Relay Station count to not bring undue attention. The leader of the caravan believed that the murders would be discovered quickly. He had to do something he had not planned, sell, and disappear quickly!"

Trying to imagine the scene none of them had witnessed, Sextilius stood up suddenly. "I am going to assume that they intended to kill the two merchants but not the two slaves. Your guard, Quintus Zosimus, may have learned something was going on and tried to stop the slaughter, but he was killed. Now, what do we know about the two merchants who were killed?"

The commanding officer answered, "Commander Elpis of the Aizanoi garrison had all three bodies removed from the well for identification. Both merchants had their throats cut, and Quintus died the same way. Then he examined the register in Aizanoi, which showed those two merchants sold the slaves. Their signet ring imprints were affixed to the sale of the slaves. So we are certain the murders were premeditated, and their signet rings were taken intentionally.

"It would make sense that two auxiliaries in the caravan put on the signet rings and sold all forty-two slaves in Aizanoi. All the slaves were men. The average cost was much lower than normal, averaging 450 denarii, not the usual 500."

A knife was on the table. It had been found in the dirt where the slave had crawled onto the road. Sextilius looked at it and asked, "What can you tell us about the dead slave and the knife?"

"We can only guess. One must have cut himself loose as well as the second slave, the one we have not found. Their escape must have been a much unexpected surprise to the gang members."

Everyone started to talk at once, but Sextilius raised his hand to quiet them down. He went to work, thinking out loud. "Let's assume this is the work of the gang that carried out previous attacks. They come and go without being seen, right?"

He received nods of agreement.

"Those strange names. They all end with the same sound. I agree with you, officer. You said, 'The dead slave was not crazy or hallucinating.' Those were not the delusional gasps of a dying man. We are certain two assassinations—the real merchants—were planned. The attacks on Quintus Zosimus and the slave could not have been planned.

"Next, we know these insurgents work together as a gang. That dead slave heard his assailants speaking over time. How long? Perhaps five days. That's where he learned their names."

The commander asked, "Why use such strange names?"

Menandro commented, "Commander Felicior told us on the first day, 'Capture all of them, including Taba. We know he was in Sardis almost a year ago.' Listen, Craga is not just a word. He appears to be the second in command, and those two, Taba and Craga, are part of this gang. Both end with the same sound."

Everyone looked at Menandro, expecting further insights. "With the dying man's garbled description, we have come across several others with that same sound at the end of their name."

Sextilius gave Menandro a strange look. "Yes, something is coming together. In Sardis a year ago, Little Lion witnessed Taba organizing robbers, and four of them were apprehended there. They had stolen treasure from wealthy families. Taba was the one who got away. Put all these names together, and you have something in common—the sound at the end of their names. But that does not help us yet. It's simply another unanswered question.

"However, here's an important detail. What did that dying man say? 'Slaves for caves, for the mines.' This statement has nothing to do with robbing homes like what we saw in Sardis."

He kept on, slowly knitting the pieces together. "This man who died thought he was being taken to the mines or to some form of hard physical labor. Something caused him to try to...what was the word he used? 'Under my tunic ... to kill.' Was that it? Who was he trying to kill? The other slave? Were both escaping together? Were they being sent to Aizanoi, perhaps to work on the massive new theater? Was one going to be sold to a stone quarry? Were both being sent there? Why was he being switched from working in a house to something else? Well, I can't answer any of these questions.

"So let's think about the second slave, the one who apparently escaped. Is he alive? Was he wounded too?"

A shudder crossed his shoulders, and Sextilius walked back and forth across the room. "Let's start with the slaves, not the criminals. Scythians make good slaves. They work hard and look after children well if they are teachers or take on responsibilities in the homes of wealthy men. What is their worst fear? The mines. No one leaves a mine once they enter. They die in accidents, from contaminated air, or in fights. Everyone is treated worse than an animal. A slave never escapes from a mine.

"We don't have to be told that this slave feared the mines. Something gave him a chance to flee. We do not know where the knife came from. The caravan stopped, obviously at a prearranged point, to kill the merchants. Well, I am assuming it was a prearranged point. One slave concealed a knife. He cut his ropes and freed the other one too. How did he get that knife? Why didn't he use it before? Both hoped to get away, but they were in a canyon and could not run away, forward, or backward. We don't know if they were friends or enemies."

The officer broke the silence. "We searched for the second slave for days. No escapee was found."

Sextilius stopped walking. A light began to shine from his eyes and he began talking slowly. "No, I'm wrong. We can't start with the slaves. Let' us go further back. Begin with the names. Taba is the first one we know about, and he was interested in stolen items from households. But if we examine the list, Harpa, Baga, Ota, Craga, Tira, Spithra, and Mithrida... Taba, a Roman soldier with..."

He suddenly realized what he had said, and now his speech was rapid. "A Roman soldier! These men aren't normal bandits or highwaymen dressed up as soldiers. If they were just barbarians, they would be afraid of being caught and never come this far south. I think they were all Roman soldiers, but now they are using fake names.

"Could they be deserters from the army? What would it take for them to be passing themselves off as guards for caravans using false documents? If they are deserters, they would know how to effortlessly pass through each relay station.

"We already know that Taba is a gang member. He is part of a chain of command. The dead slave said that Taba spoke of Craga and talked about a commander over him. That's also what we learned last year. If Taba was a soldier at one time, then we can assume that these so-called 'soldiers' are also fearless, skilled, and dangerous. Friends, they are all part of a well-organized gang."[66]

---

[66] In the second century AD, Apuleius wrote *Metamorphoses,* a theatrical novel of eleven books with a great deal of information about banditry, deserters, and ex-soldiers. The play was famous for decades and is still read. Scholars study this play to understand everyday Roman citizens. In the drama, a friend gives Lucius a magic potion that turns him into a donkey. Before he can drink the second potion to turn himself back into his standard form as a Roman, bandits capture him and force him to carry objects only a donkey could carry. During eleven episodes, he has to tolerate jibes thrown at donkeys. As a donkey and as a Roman citizen, his thoughts contrast vividly with the world of the bandits, whose stolen treasures he must carry. He is forced to bear witness to the deeds, the bravado, and the agony of the bandits. Beyond the hilarity of the situations, *Lucius-turned-ass* illustrated the violence and poverty in which outlaws lived. Deserters from the army had become a growing problem for Italians, whose soldiers occasionally fled the scene of wars against barbarians. The tales, both comic and horrifying, provide vivid examples of

The analysis had taken all afternoon, and a hot evening meal was served. As they ate, Sextilius kept on talking. "Let's assume that these 'soldiers' were legionaries at one time and possibly still are. Rebellious, confident, and operating openly over a wide area in Asia Minor, they will be tough to catch. The dead slave mentioned two cities: Sinop and Chalcedon. Where are those cities? In the north, both in the province of Bithynia and Pontus. If that slave came from north of the Black Sea, which is a logical conclusion considering his straw-colored hair and blue eyes…"

Anthony broke in. "Here's what I think. Taba and the others planned this attack carefully, but something must have gone wrong. I think that the well was meant only for the two merchants."

The White Horse Relay Station commander declared, "I want every part of that abandoned building searched again! We've already examined it, but there may be something that will put us on the outlaws' tracks. If there's another slave in that canyon, I want him found."

He barked at one of the auxiliaries, "First thing tomorrow, ride to Aizanoi! Tell Commander Diogenes Elpis that this is a gang composed of former legionaries masquerading as guards for slave caravans. It's time he took this seriously."

---

impoverished lives.

Chapter 20
Melpone

JONATHAN AND REBEKAH'S HOME

On the day Anthony and Sextilius were pondering the murders near White Horse Station, Miriam's eyes stung, and she wiped a tear away.

She had not heard from Anthony for days, and she wondered what to do. *I don't want to stay here for a long time, but there's always the chance that Anthony is delayed for months. Or even years... I need to start giving more attention to some of the people around me while I'm here.*

She admired Rebekah, whose quiet spirit made it so easy to be open about herself. When others needed attention, her aunt put her immediate tasks aside, no matter how occupied she might be.

The next morning, Miriam said, "Aunt Rebekah, I need to talk with a young woman at the guild, but I can't just barge into the workshop unannounced. Her name is Melpone. Could you help me and ask her if she would mind talking with me? I'll meet with her anytime she says."

Rebekah looked up from her shopping list. "Of course, dear. I'll soon be leaving to shop near there, and I'll drop in and set up a meeting."

Melpone rarely talked with others, but she seemed pleased at Rebekah's bringing Miriam's request to meet. "I live outside the walls, in the *insulae*. I'll meet her at the Three Arches, in the city center. Can she come tomorrow at sundown?"

"Yes, that's fine! She knows where that is."

THE THREE ARCHES, THE CENTER OF THYATIRA

Melpone arrived at the Three Arches, her long black hair done up in a bun to cool her neck. A small, round nose ring made of polished bronze matched her earrings, which hung at the end of long, tiny, interwoven chains. Her earrings were crescent moons curling upward toward two sharp tips, indicating her belief in the moon's mystical powers.

"Where do you want to sit?" Miriam asked.

"Let's go up to the Fountain of Water Nymphs, up there at the foot of the mountain. I sit there by myself sometimes because it's my favorite place. The water ripples down the high marble wall behind the fountain, falling from one little pool to the next. The sound of the splashing water soothes me."

Miriam watched people carrying water to their homes from the fountain.

"Well, you wanted to talk," said Melpone quietly. "Tell me about yourself." She wanted to learn about her new acquaintance before saying anything.

Miriam realized Melpone would probably not say much about her own life. *She's testing me. I'll be honest with her about my struggles, and maybe she'll talk to me about hers.*

Her smile showed she was glad to speak about Anthony. "I'm married to a soldier. We came here recently from Sardis. He is on a special assignment. Don't tell anyone else, all right? No one knows my husband is searching for criminals."

Melpone replied in a hushed whisper, "Your husband is a soldier? How exciting!"

"Exciting, yes, but I'm lonely. I don't know where Anthony is. No one ever knows where robbers will strike next. Since it's such a big secret, Anthony can't tell me a thing! I received one letter from him since I've been here, but all he was free to talk about was the men he is with."

"I see why you feel lonely with him away." It was a simple statement of fact, but Melpone's voice suggested that she knew what it was like to not have her man close by.

"And I wonder how I'll live here in Thyatira. I've been uncomfortable."

"When did you arrive? Are you struggling with the heat?"

"Almost six weeks ago, and yes, I find it very hot."

"You are related to Jonathan and Rebekah, right?"

"Yes, my grandpa and Jonathan were brothers. Altogether there were twelve children. Three girls were killed in Alexandria during a pogrom...burned to death."

"When did the girls die?"

"We still talk about it like it happened yesterday, but it was fifty-four years ago."[67]

"A long time ago! What happened?"

"It was Anna's betrothal day. She had arrived home with her two sisters, Deborah and Zibiah, when a riot broke out."

"How old was Anna?"

"She had just turned eighteen and was ready to marry a year later. Deborah was fifteen, and Zibiah was eleven."

"You said there were others, twelve children altogether."

"Yes, there are several brothers. Much later, my grandfather, Antipas, and my family went to Jerusalem. There were a lot of them who got on the ship from Alexandria. I was only a newborn."

"How old are you?"

Miriam said, "I'm twenty-seven."

"Well, I am too! People talk about your family, saying you lived through the destruction of Jerusalem. They are amazed that you escaped."

The evening passed quickly. Melpone asked probing questions, revealing a keen mind.

Water flowed ceaselessly over the Fountain of Water Nymphs, gurgling and swooshing, lending an atmosphere of well-being. Crowds kept coming to its pool. Five water spirits carved in white marble looked down silently from their marble stands, water continuously pouring out of vessels held on their shoulders. A gentle smile was chiseled into each of their faces.

Women came, drank the water to quench their thirst, and then dipped clay pots into the pool. Then they took full containers of water home, balancing them on their heads.

Melpone looked up to see the sun approaching the horizon. "It's time to go. I must get home now," she said suddenly.

"I hardly got to know you at all, Melpone! Where do you live?"

"You can find me in the second building past the Bronzesmiths' Guild foundry shop outside the city wall. Goodbye."

Irritated at Melpone's sudden departure, Miriam hung her head. *I didn't get to know her at all! She is a good listener, though, and asks many questions. And she does the most delicate embroidery work at the guild. What's her story?*

Two days later, Melpone sent a message from the guild

---

[67] This pogrom in Alexandria, Egypt, took place in AD 38.

workshop to the Ben Shelah home, requesting another meeting to talk with Miriam. Again, they met at the Three Arches as the sun was going down. Miriam greeted her new friend with a traditional greeting. They kissed each other on the cheek, first on the left side and then on the right.

They returned to sit at the Fountain of Water Nymphs because torches lit the area until late in the evening.

"I need to talk to you about my secret," said Melpone quickly. "Did you know that my real name is not Melpone?"

"No! What's your real name?"

"My mother was dying after I was born. She had been a singer in the chorus in the theater. She wanted a boy, but when I was born, she called me Melpomene. Do you know what that means?"

"Of course. It means tragedy."

"Did you look at the frieze around the entrance to the theater? It's the one up on the side of the mountain east of the city."

"No, I haven't been to the theater. What does it show?"

"Nine muses of entertainment, each a beauty. Nine women are standing, each carrying out her performance. Miriam," she said, leaning forward suddenly, "could you be my friend?"

"Yes, I want to be a friend," she said, looking Melpone in the eye and placing a hand on the woman's shoulder.

"Thank you. I was accepted to be in the next play at the theater. I'm in the chorus, singing between the scenes as actors come on and off the stage. But I'm afraid! My mother cursed me by giving me this name, and I hate it!

"I was born to tragedy. My birth killed my mother! I couldn't stand 'Melpomene,' so I shortened it to 'Melpone.' I think no one has ever heard this name before. It makes me feel safe, but then I think, 'It's not the name my mother gave to me!' That makes me afraid. I wake up at night feeling that the gods will judge me for changing my name. I don't know what to do to stop these dreams."

"No, the gods won't judge you!" Miriam did not know if she should challenge her new friend's thinking now or keep on listening. She blinked. *There's much more to Melpone's story.*

Melpone babbled, obviously thinking many things at the same time. "The play is a tragedy, and we'll put it on in six weeks. Tragedy! That's both my name and my life! I've wanted to consult the goddess of fortune, but now I'm afraid to find out what might happen."

Miriam fought the urge to sort out Melpone's problems before she knew what they were. "Tell me more."

"I have two big problems. I was married at eighteen to Phlegon. He was older than me and had been divorced before. My father was against our marriage because Phlegon was a womanizer before he married me. He came to our guild workshop and made friends with a woman there, Sibyl. Did you meet her? She has a loud voice and an opinion on everything. She loves to say what is going to happen in the future."

"Yes, I met her. She is away in Macedonia right now, right?"

"Sibyl supports the guild like no one else. She sells purple cloth like her Aunt Lydia used to, quickly making a profit. More than that, she comes back with additional orders. However, she influences people in bad ways."

A shudder passed across Miriam's shoulders, even though the evening was warm. "What do you mean by 'She influences people in bad ways'?"

"I did not want Phlegon to be with other women, and I told him so. About that time, I started to enjoy your Uncle Jonathan's hospitality when he invited me to attend the meetings in the synagogue portico. Phlegon came with me.

"One day he met Sibyl, who said she was a prophetess, and he asked for advice from her. He told me later, 'That lady can see into my future.' After that, he said, 'Sibyl taught me some mysteries, and I'm going to change my life.' I was heartbroken. I knew there was going to be trouble.

"I was dependent on Phlegon. He didn't stop mistreating me. He beat me a lot."

Melpone wiped a tear away and had a hard time continuing. "He joined Sibyl in dancing at the Artemis temple's social events for the guild, and then he left me for a day at a time...at first. I knew about the sexual immorality that always followed the temple sacrifices. I confronted him and made him promise he wouldn't have relations with women at these temple dances."

There was a long silence. Miriam remembered that Melpone mentioned two problems. *Is she keeping the biggest problem for later in her conversation, or is this the worst thing?*

"He left me with broken promises and kept saying that Sibyl Sambathe taught him secret mysteries. He said these secrets are not being taught at either the synagogue or by Jonathan."

She pointed to the places where he had beaten her. The skin was healed, but a deeper scar remained in her memory.

Melpone stopped talking. She looked at the polished stone slabs making up the pavement surrounding the fountain. Birds twittered and circled over the trees, looking for a perch for the night. Shops were closing, and merchants began heading for home.

As people left their workshops, torches were being lit along Central Road and around the fountain. The summer heat on this Friday night had broken. In three weeks, late August evenings would bring cooler temperatures.

"I loved him, but I couldn't stand the strain in our home. He hit me. I was pregnant, and I lost my second baby." The simple words displayed a wounded spirit still broken.

"I loved him and hated him at the same time. No one has ever listened to me or wanted to know my problems. But I feel very embarrassed telling you about these things. He went to Pergamum...ran away with Ambrosia."

"Who is Ambrosia? I lived in Pergamum, remember? I don't remember ever meeting her there."

"Ambrosia is the daughter of an Egyptian man, a trader from Alexandria. Her mother is a Greek woman from one of the rich families in Pergamum. She is younger than I am and prettier too. I met her one night. Phlegon was staying out late. I went to the Temple of Artemis, and he was dancing with her in front of the altar."

Melpone was distraught. "He says he won't come back! I still love him, and I can't get him out of my mind!"

"Melpone, I'm so sorry about your husband, how he treated you, his unfaithful conduct, and his running away. You must have been heartbroken losing your baby because he mistreated you. Our ancient prophet Jeremiah wrote some words a long time ago. This has been going through my mind. After a terribly painful time, God spoke to his people and said, 'I will add to their number, and they will not be decreased; I will bring them honor, and they will not be disdained. Their children will be as in days of old, and their community will be established before me.'"[68]

"Those are nice words. I wish they could be for me, but..."

As she had done two days before, Melpone suddenly stood up,

---

[68] Jeremiah 30:19–20

kissed Miriam on the cheek, and turned toward home. She sounded cross with herself and muttered, "It's getting late. Why am I telling my life story to a stranger?"

Miriam watched her walk away. Melpone walked across the pavement to a bakery and walked home with a small package of hot flatbread.

JONATHAN AND REBEKAH'S HOME

Jonathan knew that Miriam composed songs. He approached her on Friday with a request for a song about the many Jewish tragedies that happened on Tish'a B'Av, the ninth day of the Jewish month of Av. "We need a lament, a song that grasps the sadness of the events yet leaves the Almighty One fully in charge of the events of human life. Can you compose such a lament so that this Sunday the people at the Way of Truth will understand what we felt during our day of weeping and mourning last week?"

Miriam's face had showed her pain on Tish'a B'Av six days before, and she could not talk about it in the synagogue. Still, the words of Jeremiah had been on her mind since the service. She agreed to the request, and that night, when she could not sleep, Miriam turned over to the other side of the bed and a phrase repeated itself in her mind.

The song came quickly in the silence of the night. *We leave revenge to you. Why was the "city of peace" also a "place of pain and sorrow"? Judgment and mercy—do both really come from the same Lord? How can we believe the Lord is the author of both?*

Now, after Jonathan had led his friends in prayers early on Sunday morning, she was going to express her grief outwardly as a song. Miriam covered her head, pulling her prayer shawl around her neck and shoulders. Grace stayed on Aunt Rebekah's lap as she stood at the front of the group.

As she looked at the Sunday morning worshippers, a wave of compassion flooded over her. These people were unaware of the many who suffered intensely during the sieges on that date. She loved her fallen city, the place she remembered from when she was five years old.

For the exiles, the remnant, she felt a well-spring of love, compassion, and pity. Tenderness flowed from her heart, calming her and taking away her thirst for retaliation. There was no breeze through the house, so the heat in the room was intense. Miriam licked her lips, and her tongue felt thick, her voice cracking with thirst. She would have to sing without musical accompaniment. Usually she would have a flute and a harp or a tambourine, a lyre, and a drum, but today no instruments were used.

"Last Monday was a day of sadness, gloom, and memories of horror," she began. "That is what we recalled at the synagogue: the defeat of our city and the burning of Herod's Temple. However, it also was a day to remember God's faithfulness. Every day he is faithful.

"These words from our Scriptures came back to me: 'I will restore the fortunes of Jacob's tents and have compassion on his dwellings; the city will be rebuilt on her ruins, and the palace will stand in its proper place. From them will come songs of thanksgiving. I will add to their numbers, and they will not be decreased; I will bring them honor, and they will not be disdained. Their children will be as in days of old, and their community will be established before me. So you will be my people, and I will be your God. The fierce anger of the Lord will not turn back until he fully accomplishes the purposes of His heart. In days to come, you will understand this.'[69]

"I'm a newcomer, but most of you already know me. My family was leaving through one of Jerusalem's city wall gates toward the end of the siege when I lost my father. He was shot by archers defending our wall and died instantly. Mother was shot in the leg then too. Several months later, she died in Antioch.

"I used to cry out for vengeance. The men who killed my father were Jewish guards defending our walls. How could I take revenge on our own soldiers? After we escaped, I wanted retaliation against the Roman militias, but it was they who kept us alive after our escape. They supplied my family with food, keeping us from starving. Since learning about Yeshua Messiah, I have learned to leave revenge behind. This has given me a freedom, a peaceful acceptance of grief and mourning that I share with you today. I will now sing a lament. It is called 'We Leave Revenge to You.'"[70]

Her calm voice recalled the day of shame and defeat.

---

[69] Jeremiah 30:18–20, 22, 24
[70] The song is taken from Lamentations chapters 1–3.

You chastised us and sent us far, far away.
Wailing women, return to God and pray!
Jerusalem's people have gone astray.
We intone this lament by night and day.
    "I will destroy my Daughter of Zion.
    My people worshiped the stars, moon, and sun.
    And your reward? Disaster, death, destruction!"
When cast down, Lord, I leave revenge to you.

Danger surrounds us, disaster's roaming.
No food in our homes, people are starving.
Children fall. We know we cannot survive.
Prophets' words will not keep folk alive.
    Were our gates left like that? Undefended?
    Who could bear to see our men tormented?
    Will God's paths, His vengeance, be resented?
Struggling now, Lord, I leave revenge to you.

We had no choice, betrayed by rulers vile.
Bullies taunted. We were sent to trial.
Enemies stood by, looked on, and smiled.
The taste of hate, bitter far more than bile.
    My groans are fading, and to you I call.
    I confess that to pagan gods, we crawled.
    Wounded, no relief. For our thirst, just gall.
Mourning, Lord, I leave my revenge to you.

A laughingstock! Were we still a nation?
All was chaos, a helpless condition!
Pleased, our foes kept up their opposition.
Inside, we cringe, fearing new affliction.
    But we repent! We walked a crooked way.
    Selfishness and sin lured us far away.
    From your loving arms, like lost lambs, we strayed.
Distraught, Lord, I leave all revenge to you.

Before she reached the last stanza, her parched tongue and lips caused her voice to crack. She paused, almost weeping. She remembered her father, limp on the ground with an arrow in his back. Miriam recalled the moment her grandfather took her from her father, running with her in his arms. Then an arrow struck her mother's leg. The scene broke over her once more. She heard those screams again: "Don't turn back!" The remembrance came like a wild wave crashing upon a rock in a violent storm.

The memory caused her voice to break a second time, and she tried to wet her lips. A quiet tremor in her voice was a window into the personal shock and brutality of those terrible moments.

Of course she would want revenge! Her parents had been killed, and days after, those thick city walls had been breached! Disaster, war, devastation, and fire—such destruction! But she was resolutely accepting Adonai's right to bring revenge.

Miriam paused to regain her composure and finished her lament.

> Your covenant brings us great compassion.
> We need your kind and loving exhortation.
> Yearning for your comforting salvation,
> Secure in your love, we find protection.
> > So like the blind seeking the way, we grope.
> > To humble people, you reveal your hope,
> > Confessing sin, we learn that we can cope.
> Forever, Lord, I leave revenge to you.

The room was silent as Miriam sat down. She placed her head between her hands, remembering Jeremiah's promises. They had nurtured her soul when she was hungry for God's promises, for restoration, and for the blessings of the Holy One of Jacob.

Promises burned in her heart. God had not deserted her.

For many years, Miriam had longed for retaliation for the loss of her father and mother. How could she accept that General Titus was rewarded with promotion, glory, and pomp? His victory was the crown, and later he was exalted to emperor. *Yes, I believe in revenge but of a different kind. Our Scriptures say, "It is mine to avenge, I will repay."*[71] *Lord, I do not know the answer to all our troubles. Still, I know that continually taking vengeance and refusing to forgive results in ever more bloodshed and hatred.*

Later, the people in the Way of Truth commented on the day. They could never forget what the fall of Jerusalem meant to those

---

[71] Deuteronomy 32:35, Romans 12:19

Jews who lived through it and why they commemorated it so intensely each year.

THE MILITARY GARRISON IN PRUSA

Anthony was almost too tired to write, but he needed to send a report to Commander Servius. He had supervised a second search for more than two weeks, and it was now more focused. Participants now included guards and patrols in garrisons and relay stations along the Interior Road.

He wanted to give a report that would satisfy Servius, but the findings so far had not led to any conclusions. Menandro had asked pointed questions during interviews, thinking about merchandise, caravans, and soldiers passing through. Sextilius had delved into comparing schedule records from various checkpoints and the resulting sequence of events.

Anthony drew in a long breath. *We still have not confirmed anything, and we are all asking the same question. How can we find these soldiers who took off their uniforms and simply disappeared after passing through Aizanoi?*

The report would not come together in his mind, so he put it off. Instead, while the others were telling stories and playing a game of dice, he wrote a short letter to Miriam.

August 15, in the 11th year of Domitian
From: Anthony
To: Miriam, the love of my life

Each day is demanding. I cannot say how much I miss you. Some days we ride only a short distance to the next relay station. I can't say anything about my work, so I'll have to tell you about the people and the land here.

We haven't discovered anything substantial, but here and there I saw many beautiful things: hot springs, mountains, forests, waterfalls, and, best of all, in the woods and wilderness, a kind of stillness. It's so calm and peaceful, not like my assignment.

I want to be with you again. I miss little Grace so much. Who would have thought I would grow so attached to our adopted little baby girl? Who could believe she would bring so much joy? And three years ago, I never dreamed I would be married to the most wonderful woman.

One thought keeps coming back. I think about scars, mine and other's. Doesn't Messiah bear scars in his hands? Doesn't he understand our humanity in the most profound ways? Is a wound the worst thing to carry? If I am a slave of Yeshua and this is the scar that marks me for life, why should I complain about it?

I realized something. My thinking is changing, growing in strange ways. I never used to have thoughts like these. To think that I would begin to realize that the scars carried by Yeshua Messiah were to my benefit!

Again, I think of you both all the time. I treasure your letters. Write again. Trust Nikias. Don't send messages to me with anyone else. Duty calls, and I have another letter to write tonight. Words can never tell you how I miss you.

He finished. Standing up, a thought pushed him in a new direction. *The wounded slave came from lands north of the Black Sea. His hair was fair. Blue eyes. Just like Ateas! Why didn't I think of this before? Ateas is Scythian. If he had been at White Horse Relay Station, he could have understood what the slave was saying.*

Anthony reached for his pen once more. He rolled up the letter to the commanders, reopened the message for Miriam, and added a paragraph. Ateas would go to Olive Grove Farm, while Arpoxa would stay at Jonathan's house.

August 15, in the 11th year of Domitian
From: Squad leader Anthony Suros
To: Commander Felicior and Commander Servius

If you are well, then I am too.
My formal report is attached to this request.
After questioning many soldiers, we gained important information but not sufficient to come to any conclusions. One slave escaped from the bandits, gravely wounded, almost certainly a Scythian. Before he died, the officers could hardly understand him because he spoke extremely poor Greek. We believe a second slave may also have escaped. Perhaps the other one also came from Scythia.
Here is what we know: The deceased slave was captured

near the Black Sea, taken to Sinop, and taught a little Greek. He was brought to Asia Minor, having passed through Chalcedon. He was initially trained to be a house slave, but we think he was being sold for hard labor in a mine. Before he died, he indicated that he and one other slave escaped from the same wagon. Commander Diogenes Elpis supervised the guards who found three men's bodies in a well at abandoned ruins off the road near White Horse Relay Station. One was a Roman soldier from that station and assigned at the last moment to accompany two caravans heading to Aizanoi. We do not know why that soldier was murdered.

After the forty-two slaves were sold in Aizanoi, the bandit soldiers and two fake merchants disappeared. Unless we learn what happened, this may happen again.

Here is my request: Two Scythian ex-slaves work for Simon Ben Shelah in Sardis. Ateas and his wife, Arpoxa, were freed by Antipas Ben Shelah. Ateas is lame with a broken leg and uses crutches. His wife, Arpoxa, has club feet. I need Ateas with me to help with translation if we find the second slave, the escapee. I request that he be paid as an auxiliary.

I request that Arpoxa be taken to stay at the Ben Shelah home in Thyatira with my wife, Miriam. I also ask that Ateas be taken on to Olive Grove Farm near Forty Trees, where he will be able to learn to again ride with his lame foot while waiting for my return to Soma. We can pick him up from there for our next trip north.

Chapter 21
Ateas and Arpoxa

JONATHAN AND REBEKAH'S HOME

Miriam's heart soared. The hot days of summer were coming to an end, and she had received two letters from Anthony. Grace stood on the floor, walking around the bed, pulling herself up on top, and immediately climbing back onto the floor. She was always moving, singing, and chattering in baby talk.

A papyrus letter from Marcos lay on the bed. He was the Ben Shelah lawyer in Pergamum handling the dispersal of Eliab Ben Shelah's estate. The message confirmed that he was about to send another distribution of the Eliab estate to his heirs.

Since Antipas had died and Miriam was his only heir, she was now receiving Antipas's share twice a year. Miriam had received her first of ten payments in May. She would receive the second payment at the beginning of November and, afterward, every six months for the next four years.

Having read his letter, Miriam lay back, thinking, *I'll give most of the money to Uncle Simon in Sardis to develop those workshops for people from the insulae. He'll pay Jace, the store manager and a teacher of poor children who would not otherwise learn to read and write.[72] In this letter, Marcos says that Great-grandpa Eliab's estate will have been wholly divided among the heirs in ten payments five years from now. After that, all of Grandpa Antipas's houses, businesses, and shops will be registered in my name. Lord, when will I be back in Pergamum? I miss it—my home since I was little.*

She stood up, remembering the struggle to get Uncle Simon to support training poor people in Sardis. They included a couple of blind men. Several suffered from damaged limbs caused by accidents while moving heavy stone blocks at construction sites.

---

[72] The story of Miriam's generosity to poor families is told in *Never Enough Gold: A Chronicle of Sardis, Heartbeats of Courage, Book Two.*

Many poor women were also being helped. All were learning skills: processing wool, simple dyeing, making thread, and weaving cloth. Each one was earning enough to feed her family.

The second letter was from Anthony. Nikias had brought it from Olive Grove when he had come on his weekly trip. She reread her favorite parts:

> *I want to be with you again. I miss little Grace so much. Who would have thought I would grow so attached to our adopted little baby girl? Who could believe she would bring so much joy? And, three years ago, I never dreamed I would be married to the most wonderful woman.*
>
> *Please tell Uncle Jonathan that I am requesting Commander Felicior to ask Ateas and Arpoxa if they would come to Thyatira. I think the military will accept it. I hope there's room for them with you, although Ateas will be taken to Olive Grove to relearn how to ride a horse. I want him with our team on the road as a Scythian translator. Hopefully this will speed up the end of this project.*

She reread the last paragraph several times. *Oh, Anthony! This is good news indeed! I have missed my friends.*

The evening air of the first Sabbath in September was warm and pleasant. Grace behaved well and sat in Miriam's lap at the synagogue without making a fuss. Miriam sat with the other women, ready to leave if Grace became noisy.

As the leader began Sabbath prayers, Grace tried to remove Miriam's prayer shawl from her head. Miriam put it back in place, but little hands grabbed the blue-colored cotton. As Grace attempted to place it in her mouth, Miriam took it away and said a big, silent "No!"

The service began with, "Hear O Israel, the Lord your God is one God."

After worship, everyone gathered in the portico. Sibyl had come in late and stayed outside the sanctuary, ready to talk with people after the service.

"I've just returned from a successful trading trip to Philippi," Sibyl said in a loud voice. It was apparent that she wanted to be noticed. As people gathered, she told them about many orders for purple products.

Heads nodded in agreement, but Miriam frowned. *Why doesn't someone challenge her? How can she participate in the congregation of God-fearers and the Temple of Artemis at the same time? Sibyl has strange beliefs. She is going to lead people astray.*

THE GUILD OF PURPLE HONORS, THYATIRA

On Sunday, the workshop at the guild was buzzing. People crowded around, ready to hear every detail of Sibyl's trip. Before telling about her sales in Philippi, she described the city's spacious theater, the massive acropolis above the city, and houses overlooking the fertile plain.

"I love watching retired soldiers gather at the thermopolia to eat and drink. They talk all day about distant lands. While drinking beer, they compare battles and brag about wars. It's all 'conquests, victory, and glory'! They call Philippi 'Little Rome.'"

She paused so the effect of her words would thrill her audience. "Still, it's better to have them harmoniously living together in Philippi than causing trouble in Rome!"

People laughed nervously, not sure if Sibyl was close to making a "rebellious" remark or not. No one wanted to be accused of rebellion, but they responded well to gossip.

"Retired fighters receive parcels of land around Philippi for their military service. Old warriors, pensions, and comfort for all! And what can we give them? What do they want to buy? Lots!"

Her listeners already knew the answer and were thrilled with the direction she was taking. "Lots of comfort! Colored cushions, pillows, and blankets for beds and decorations for couches!"

The workers cheered.

"I brought an additional order back, beyond all those items wanted by the retirees!" she bragged. "In eight months, Domitian will hold grandiose Games in Rome. Three senators from Macedonia want fine linen garments," she paused, "lined with a fringe of purple to represent their province! I also have orders for special embroidery work for their wives."

Loud, long applause sounded. The work produced in their guild would be admired in Rome! "Now for a tiny bit of gossip! Not a word of this beyond this room! The Senate is powerless to stand up to the emperor. It is a tug-of-war. Domitian wants power, so he promoted some from humble backgrounds. He won't let senators exercise the authority they've enjoyed for generations. At least that's what is being said in Philippi. Yes, thirteen major figures opposing the emperor have been killed at last count. One observer called it all a 'purple struggle'; another said a 'royal fight'!"

Sibyl's unique ability to galvanize opinion gave her a controlling touch: an ability to bring people to her point of view. She had spread gossip about her home province of Asia Minor to anyone who would give her attention in the Philippi agora, where retired legionaries spent their time. And now she brought further orders for goods, promising increased wealth for all at the guild.

"Melpone," Sibyl announced, "here is the biggest order of your life! You will manage this embroidery and complete the work perfectly! Others will produce the other goods. Much of this order will go to senators in Rome!"

JONATHAN AND REBEKAH'S HOME

Miriam arrived home from the guild with mixed feelings. Lying on the bed and gazing at the ceiling, she pondered what she had just heard. *How did Sibyl get all that gossip about Rome? She gained lucrative orders for garments and decorations from senators. She must have had a nonstop social whirl in Philippi!*

Grace was sleeping soundly beside her, and she gently traced the curve of the little girl's arm from her wrist to her elbow. She heard a man call out, "Is this the Ben Shelah residence?" At the same time, a woman's voice called, "Is this where Jonathan Ben Shelah lives?"

"Grace," Miriam whispered, "did you hear that? It sounds like Ateas and Arpoxa are at the door!" She took the sleeping child in her arms and went down the stairs as quickly as it was safe to do.

"Arpoxa! Ateas! Saulius! How did you get here so quickly?"

A soldier helped a very pregnant Arpoxa walk to a couch beside the small, square dining table. Miriam recognized one of the regulars, who, a year ago, had guarded Simon Ben Shelah's gate in Sardis.

"Hail, Mistress Miriam!" He smiled. "Two of us were assigned to bring this family to Thyatira. I think you know them."

"Yes, I know them! Thank you for bringing them here from Sardis! Anthony wrote that he had asked Commander Felicior to request they come to Thyatira."

"Anthony wants Ateas on his team as a translator. We will take

Ateas to Olive Grove Farm. Anthony is to pick him up when he gets back to Soma. Arpoxa and her little boy will stay here. Orders from Commander Felicior!"

Miriam turned to the Scythian family, tears brimming. "This is such a welcome arrival, a hundred times over! I'm so glad you've come!" Miriam bent over and kissed Arpoxa. "Welcome, Ateas! Come here, little Saulius! Uncle Jonathan and Aunt Rebekah are at the guild. My cousins are with them as well. I'm the only one home right now."

The two army men brought Arpoxa's bags into Jonathan's house. "Sorry to break up a family gathering before it begins, Mistress Miriam, but Ateas must now go with us to Olive Grove Farm. Ateas, we will wait for you outside. It will be almost dark by the time we get there. We'll spend the night at the Forty Trees Relay Station and then return to Sardis tomorrow."

"When did you learn you were coming, Arpoxa?" asked Miriam.

"We received a visit from these guards a few days ago saying that Anthony was asking that we pack everything to leave for Thyatira for an unknown length of time. 'An assignment' was all they said. It was hard to leave Sardis, but I wanted to see you again. I thought we would never like it when we arrived a year ago, but now I have good friends there."

"How are you feeling? How are your sore feet?" Miriam asked.

"I'm fine, but I feel so heavy. I always have trouble walking thanks to these crooked feet! With this extra weight, it's painful to walk, almost impossible."

"When are you expecting? Due in just a few months by the look of things!"

"Ateas is so kind and helpful, especially considering that he is also lame." Arpoxa was the talkative one. She had learned Greek more quickly than her young husband. Miriam realized that he still could not express things correctly, in the past...or the future.

"I help Anthony," said Ateas. "He send letter. He say I am translator for him."

"Well, our time is short, Ateas. Quick, tell me about Uncle Simon, Aunt Judith, and my cousins! Tell me about Jace and Kalonice! How are Eugene and Lyris? What is happening at the shop in Sardis? I want to know all about the poor families we visited."

OLIVE GROVE FARM NEAR FORTY TREES

Half an hour later, Ateas hobbled out to the wagon on his crutches, and the three men left: two legionaries from Sardis and a lame man who had been a slave. Through the West Gate, the horses headed north to the intersection and past the insulae, where thousands of poor families lived in small, crowded apartments. Within a few minutes, the wagon was headed for Olive Grove Farm and the Forty Trees Relay Station. They would stop briefly halfway, at one of the main villages. Fresh horses were always ready at military relay stations.

Along the way, olive trees grew everywhere, spreading north, east, and west. To the west were the tall cliffs of Mount Tarhala. To the south, the mountain's steep cliffs tapered off into shallow slopes. Little villages dotted the fertile plain.

"How did you learn Greek?" asked the wagon driver.

"I speak only little Greek. I from north country, Scythia. My people sell me as slave. I break my leg in water well when we are digging. My wife also crippled. We are in slave market in Pergamum. One day in marketplace, we are last slaves be sold. Crippled slaves are for anyone no good. They can't help anything to do. Kind man bought us. Name is Antipas. He is taking us home and giving us freedom. We are not slaves after he bought us."

A few details of his story gradually came out: that he had been born far away, north of the Black Sea. However, he did not tell them that he was trained as an expert horseman as a youth who protected Scythian merchants who went to trade on the Silk Road. He did not mention that he had completed two trips on that long merchant road or that his family lived in a faraway, large, important city.

The wagon driver exclaimed, "Scythians! Nothing but trouble. They can't even learn to speak correctly!"

The other added, "Well, at least this one is trying and can translate for Scythian slaves. Simon Ben Selah in Sardis says he is also particularly good at making gold jewelry. He is lame; that broken leg was never fixed right and never can be. If this is how Squad Leader Suros thinks Ateas will help catch a gang of bandits, then does Rome's future look a lot brighter? Or dimmer?"

Both laughed at the prospect of Ateas capturing highwaymen. How could he help to capture the bandits who had already outwitted the six smartest soldiers from the Garrison of Sardis?

They registered their arrival at the Forty Trees Relay Station. The soldier wrote: "September 7, Sunday; Ateas, a Scythian translator, was taken to Olive Grove Farm from Sardis per Commander Felicior's orders. He is to wait there until Squad Leader Anthony Suros takes him on a special assignment."

THE HOME OF FABIUS BASSOS, THYATIRA

Fabius Bassos rode in his comfortable carriage on the road back to Thyatira. Returning from the annual meeting of the Asiarchs in Philadelphia, he thought of his responsibilities. For five days, he had been caught up in the energy and excitement of being with the province's most important personages. He had shaken hands with the governor and met representatives from each of the eighteen districts comprising the province of Asia Minor. Special attention was given to the representatives of the seven central cities, Thyatira being one of them.

He smiled with pleasure. During the annual meeting, people congratulated him on how successful he had become. He reminisced on the scenes of affection, with wealthy citizens of other cities commenting, "We heard about your generosity! The statue of Apollo! And the frieze telling of his life! And then the new addition in the Temple of Artemis! Congratulations!"

However, no one could perceive his inner turmoil.

Bassos frowned. The indentations on his forehead were much deeper. He hardly noticed the clip-clop of the horses' hooves or the swaying of his carriage. The end of the day found him arriving home, close to the theater on the lower slopes of Mount Gordus.

His mind was churning. *How will I cover my expenses? Being a benefactor has left me nearly penniless! In a few weeks, after providing for the Games in Thyatira, I'll be broke. But the city has high expectations. How can I deny those young men who call for Games with sharp weapons! Why does everyone say, 'Let's get back to what we had two years ago! We want gladiators with sharp, three-pronged pikes and nets against the ones with swords and shields'?*

The raucous shouts of the youth returned to his mind. How much joy and pleasure there had been when he brought out his best fighters! But no one wanted combat without bloody action. Last year, with the use of blunt weapons, was not such a good show.

Bassos scowled, remembering the hefty payments made for a prizefighter. *One combatant, twenty-one years old. Four years of training. He won four fights in the last year of training, but he died of wounds to his shoulder and back. It was only his fifth battle, his first fight with me as his owner. He was too young, too expensive, to die that soon![73] And then my best gladiator died at age thirty. He fought thirty-one fights. Twenty-one victories and nine draws. Then one defeat! That was it. He was dead! I hated to watch that hulk of a man go down like that. Domitian gave me permission for only four days of Games with sharp weapons, and I lost two men in those conflicts.*

Last year, I didn't lose any combatants, but of course, those were fights without sharp weapons. The young men of my city, especially the Clothiers' Guild, are clamoring loudly for violence. Mayor Aurelius Tatianos incites the youth. They demand expensive Games, and then he leans on me to make it happen. Aurelius has become my greatest adversary.

Bassos struggled under the burdens of wealth and debt. As a benefactor, so much was expected from him. This year, he had reached the limits of his purse. Yet he could only remain popular if he provided more expensive entertainment. The muscles in his cheeks were tight. He could not continue the pace without new sources of income.

THE CITY OF THYATIRA

September 14 was the anniversary commemorating the day Emperor Domitian ascended to power. A procession of animals to be sacrificed at the altar of the Imperial Cult made its way through the city, led by virgin priestesses. They stepped intentionally, dancing in carefully choreographed movements as pipes, flutes, tambourines, and drums stirred the citizens. Behind them came a bull, a sheep, and a pig as sacrifices in the emperor's honor.

Bassos led the procession, dressed in an expensive fine linen toga. It was wrapped around his body with one end attached to his tunic. The other end flowed gracefully over his left shoulder, leaving his right arm free. The tunic folds and the toga had been carefully clumped and kept in place with a *fibula*.

---

[73] The sarcophagus of this gladiator was discovered in Ephesus. The Gallery of Gladiators in the Museum of Ephesus concludes that these fighters were professionals. Not all fights ended with death. Some gladiators died at ages 80 or 90, retired and honored for bringing entertainment for many years. These were considered "men of renown."

Thousands marched in the procession on this, the twelfth anniversary of Emperor Domitian coming to the throne. He was being honored this way everywhere in the empire.

Governor Publius Calvisius Ruso was waiting at the temple for the procession to arrive. He was on his way back to Ephesus from the Asiarchs' meeting in Philadelphia and took this opportunity to officiate at the sacrifice.

The procession arrived at the northern end of the broad street. The governor's declaration was echoed by thousands: "Caesar is lord and god! September 14! The beginning of Domitian's twelfth year in power! Caesar is lord and god!"

The city's young men waited, hoping to learn that the next Games would involve sharp weapons. However, by the end of the day, no statement had been given.

Melpone watched the procession go by. She shied away from the scene, fearing the consequences of her work with purple.

Noise like this made her want to put her fingers in her ears. *They are shouting, 'Caesar is lord and god.' A purple sash means that person wields power and authority. I'm told no one can legally wear one unless permission has been given, but the work in purple I'm going to do is not for Caesar.*

They say that Domitian has eyes and ears everywhere. Will the purple sashes I'm going to make for senators cause me trouble? Will he find out that I'm the one who made them for the Macedonian senators? I can't stop worrying about this.

THE MILITARY GARRISON IN PRUSA

In Prusa, the sacrifices celebrating the anniversary of Domitian's reign had been completed earlier in the morning. Now Anthony, Omerod, and Menandro sat together after the noon meal. They sifted through the notes supplied by garrisons, inns, and relay stations. On the other side of the table, Sextilius ran his finger down a list of names while Bellinus and Capito looked on.

"Any more inconsistencies, Sextilius?" Bellinus could not stand this lack of action.

Sextilius shook his head, mumbling, "Don't interrupt me right now."

Comparing records from each of the relay stations between Soma and Prusa was tedious work. Each of the several officers had promised, "We'll make a copy and send that to Prusa." The squad had collected the dozens of records sent, but still not every report had yet been received.

Omerod looked at Anthony, slightly distrustful. "Today was an important day, the twelfth anniversary of Domitian ascending to power. You should have been there! Everyone in the city came. But you stayed here, looking over these records!"

Anthony nodded but did not say anything.

Omerod pushed a little more. "Anthony, there's something about you that's odd. I've never heard you say that phrase as we do, 'Caesar is lord and god.' Why not?"

Anthony searched for an answer that he could live with if this conversation came to light later. "Both commanding officers, Felicior and Servius, have talked to me about it."

All five looked at each other, incredulous.

Menandro burst out, "That's not an answer!"

"Accept it! It's all that I'm going to give you. Now back to real work. After four weeks, what have we discovered? Do we know who took the place of the two merchants between White Horse Relay Station and Aizanoi? It's more important to find if there's an answer in this pile of documents than to attend another ceremony. This is hard work comparing every detail from every station and caravan inn.

"We legionaries are usually proud of what we do. But why can't the military teach their people to write legibly? I need all the time I can get to read this handwriting. It takes forever to compare the names of merchants, the arrival and departure dates, and the lists of animals and merchandise."

Chapter 22
The Price of Honor

JONATHAN AND REBEKAH'S HOME

The most important day of the Jewish calendar had arrived, Rosh Hashanah. The following day, Arte and others prepared Jonathan's banquet, making sure the evening would be a grand celebration with the tastiest vegetables and meat dishes.

Uncle Jonathan hosted six men from the synagogue and their families. The evening throbbed with the voices of women, children, and young people all talking simultaneously. Souvenirs of the event were printed on small strips of linen. They would be kept by the guests: "Welcome to the Ben Shelah home for a banquet on the day after Rosh Hashanah, Thursday, September 18."

Their house looked its best. Glass bottles, white linens, and alabaster jars from Egypt graced small tables along one wall. Carpets from distant provinces, Galatia, and Phrygia softened the floors that were inlaid with intricate geometric patterns pleasing to the eye. Young people gathered around the kitchen door, sampling food before it was served in the great room.

Rebekah and the rest of her family knew the leading men in the synagogue of Thyatira were increasingly uncomfortable with Jonathan. Many years ago, they were happy to have his family attend worship. Jonathan's personal life was now causing them concern.

After the banquet was over, men gathered in the main eating area to talk. Women and small children found seats in the garden, where they enjoyed a soft evening breeze.

Kilan quickly moved the after-dinner discussions beyond polite conversation. It was time to talk about several issues that needed to be aired. "Jonathan, as elders of the synagogue, we find ourselves divided. Four of us are strict in our interpretation of the Law. We take the words of Exodus and Leviticus literally. Others are a bit more lax. However, whatever our personal convictions, we are all concerned by your actions.

"Rabbi Hanani is away in Antioch debating the future of Jewish worship, so this leaves me in a difficult position. I do not want to make decisions that he would object to. However, we think you are not a good influence. It appears to us that you have made financial gain of greater importance than following the Law of Moses."

"Would you like to give me an example?"

"Yes! The marriage of your son to Danila, a Gentile and daughter of a priestess, disturbs us greatly!"

Jonathan knew the confrontation was about this.

Kilan continued his well-rehearsed speech. "The children of Israel in the desert copied the people in Egypt by worshiping a golden calf."

Another synagogue elder added, "That generation died out, but the following generations did the same by worshiping other gods, leading to the sins of Balaam. Punishments followed. We do not want our children to be led astray, and yet you are allowing that very thing in your home."

After he had listened to all they had to say, Jonathan spoke. "You question my ways because I take part in two guilds and now am trading with a third. At first, I started business with the Bronzesmiths' Guild and then became associated with the Guild of Purple Honors. This means that I must associate with citizens in those businesses in Thyatira. Few Jews have acquired such a presence. Even the wealthiest and most influential citizens, those in the Thyatira city council, respect me. They come for advice on business matters. When they discuss city affairs, my opinions are taken into consideration.

"Most of you have been here since your childhood. You recall the problems with water drainage. I hired technicians from Egypt, and they installed a new drainage system. The bad smells disappeared after I installed water channels that improved the city's sanitation. That took years to complete and was awfully expensive.

"When it comes to marriage, I see your eight families, who are related to many other families close by: in Pergamum, Sardis, Philadelphia, and Laodicea. Your children marry those families' offspring, and then you do business with one another. It was not that way for me because I came as a refugee from the pogroms in Egypt. You opened your synagogue to us for worship. Still, you did not open your families, either for marriage or business partnerships.

"You, my friend Kilan, have an unspoken agreement to trade in such a way that it benefits your families. You buy, sell, and loan money to each other and form business arrangements that help a handful of families. Your social life overlaps with your business. You do not attend the theater or other social events. Your only reason for going to the agora is to open your shops. Your young men do not follow the news about the Games. Gladiator fights are not permitted. Together, you are like a guild with many networks.

"However, I'm different. When I came, I decided to become part of the guild system and to be involved in this city's daily life. I deal in purple and bronze, both of which are mentioned in our Scriptures. The work of the potters fascinates me, and I buy from them, sending fine products to my brothers' shops."

The tone of the conversation, which had started amicably, had entered a touchy area. Jonathan wanted the topic to be broader—how a Jew should live in Thyatira.

Kilan rapidly brought the encounter back to a narrower focus. "Jonathan, you told us you were a follower of the carpenter, Yeshua, when you came here. You said, 'He is the promised Jewish Messiah.' We disagreed with you in that matter, but you asked to worship with us, and we said yes.

"Please continue to worship with us. However, I must impose three requirements. Stop openly promoting these ideas of your 'Messiah.' We Jews maintain high standards. We permit Gentiles who are seeking God to worship together with us on the portico. We are not against the meetings you have early every Sunday morning for the same reason. But you are responsible for watching out for spiritual and sexual adultery.

"Secondly, you are a Jew. Therefore, you must restrict your association with the guilds to strictly business. Stay away from the temples that they support.

"Third, keep your family members away from the guilds. Do not let your sons become part of them. Prevent those friendships.

"The time has come for careful observance of Jewish tradition! If you honor your position in our midst as a reader of the Torah, then you must be above mistrust in every way."

Jonathan knew it would be difficult to satisfy the requirements of both the synagogue and the guilds.

Chapter 23
The Weight of Tradition

THE SYNAGOGUE OF THYATIRA

No more lambs would be sacrificed in Jerusalem. Temple worship had come to an end twenty-two years earlier. The men and women attending worship at the synagogue of Thyatira on Saturday, September 27, came with heavy hearts. The Day of Atonement, Yom Kippur, marked their annual day of seeking God's forgiveness by confession of sins. Offerings were brought to the synagogue, and today all members would fast and do no labor.

After the service, Miriam was upset by what Sibyl had said while leaving the synagogue: "We should all be at the Temple of Artemis tomorrow night. I want you there to say prayers for my sister. Hulda has been on a bed of affliction for three months; she suffers in her breathing. This will be a social occasion as we pray for her recuperation."

Miriam commented on this to Jonathan while walking home. "Uncle, why don't you speak with Sibyl about the false power of idols? She shouldn't be attending both the temple services and the Way of Truth."

Jonathan sauntered with his hands clasped behind his back, his preferred style of moving about the city. He thought it made him look more dignified. "Yes, we know that they are idols. We were taught that from childhood. Look at this city. People are void of culture. Why, if I went to the insulae, who would know what I mean if I even mentioned the Law of Moses or anything like that?

"No, Miriam, they must learn about God by watching us. We live among these people as friends, as a 'light in the world.' Who else will teach them about the Almighty? And if we do not go to their social events, how will they know who we are and what we believe? If we reject them, they will leave us."

Miriam was far from satisfied, so she questioned, "But about idols and social events, aren't we supposed to keep our distance from such things? By attending their 'prayers' at these temples, people will learn their myths, but don't we also teach others anything about what we believe? Can't Sibyl be required to make a choice in her beliefs? It's not right that she can try to tell others in the Way of Truth that both are correct."

She wanted to walk faster, but he would not change his pace, and she thought, *His daughter-in-law, Danila, is a pagan in his home. How did he ever permit that?*

"My dear niece, there's a reason. If we do not participate with them at the temples, they will accuse me of rejecting my guild's social life. I told you this before! All guilds are strong, and they control the life of this city. If you do not participate, then you do not build relationships of trust. You lose your honorability and are excluded from business with the guild."

"Uncle Jonathan, I don't accept that! Be a partner in the guild. Invest in business, and encourage the production of quality products. Be friends with the members of the guild, but do not attend functions dedicated to Artemis!"

"Do you fully understand, my child? Refusing to participate in their social activities means they would reject my economic interests. What if I could not buy or sell? What if I didn't have friends or an everyday life? My privileged position was bought with money, time, and sacrifice. It gives me position, honor, and status.

"Now, look at you. Will you not become a rich woman, wealthier than I? That lawyer Marcos has settled things in the Pergamum district court, and you are to inherit Antipas's estate: his land, buildings, houses, shops, and workshops. On his property, there are thirty-eight houses, right?

"Antipas's workshops generate wealth from many items: perfumes, fine glass bottles, clothing, and pottery. What will you do with your money when it starts arriving? You need to be thinking about how you'll invest it."

His question unnerved her, and she had no reply. *Uncle Jonathan is trying to get a response out of me. He's asking me to continue the family business, assuming that I'll cooperate. I'm already using my money to support the workshops in Sardis. One thing I know: I'm not going to invest in his businesses!*

Grandpa made lots of money, and he invested in people. He freed many people, and one of them, Arpoxa, was purchased from a slave market. Will I use some of the money for myself? I'd love to have a home with Anthony close by.

They walked a little farther, approaching Jonathan's home. "We brothers, the Ben Shelah men, always work together. It not only keeps us close as a family but brings tangible wealth. Isn't that a true blessing from God? We receive from one another and increase our wealth and position."

Miriam kept silent. She knew he wanted her to respond, but she was hesitant to talk about her inheritance with her uncle.

Jonathan frowned, coming back to her topic of conversation. "Of course, Miriam, we know idols have no power. They are made of stone or wood and are overlaid with silver. Their stories are myths. These humble people live in a world inherited from Greek writers. They are children needing a schoolmaster. Rome rules them now, so we can only change them slowly."

They were now at the entrance to his property. Miriam asked, "Are you pulling the people up to your level, or are they pulling you down to their level? Uncle Jonathan, I'm worried. I think your sons, Bani and Gil, are becoming believers in Artemis. They do not seem to share your convictions. I think they already half believe what they hear, see, and touch."

Jonathan clenched and opened his fists. He was angered that she would be addressing issues that should only be his concern as head of the house. It seemed ironic that the synagogue leaders were irritating him in the same way.

He realized that he had started to speak too soon about Miriam entering a business partnership. She obviously did not trust him on several levels. He had been thinking of asking her to someday invest in the Bronzesmiths' Guild.

He could see that there was more than a little of his brother's obstinate spirit in her. She had Antipas's convictions and direct speech. Miriam had inherited his brother's stubborn character, and he was worried it would bring her much trouble. As much as he wished, Jonathan could not get his father's dying words out of his mind.

He remembered being back in Pergamum three and a half years before. There was Eliab, his father, on his deathbed. He had been kneeling beside the bed, almost weeping when Eliab gave each of his sons his final blessing. His father's last words to him came back, his "blessing" uttered phrase by phrase, his dying breath punctuated by soft-spoken words.

"Jonathan, as my youngest son...I give you my blessing. You have built where others saw only a wasteland. You invest in burnished bronze...clothe others with purple honors. Greater treasures than these await you...for in the poverty of others you'll find...joys that can't be weighed...on a scale. Restraint will conduct you along the path of wisdom. The fear of the Lord will uplift you, my son."

They had reached the door of the house, and he said, "Please enter first, my dear niece. We'll talk about these things again."

JONATHAN AND REBEKAH'S HOME

The evening was cool at the end of September when Melpone came to visit Miriam. They sat on a small bench under fig trees in the garden. Arpoxa sat on a blanket on the ground nearby, caring for Grace. Saulius, Arpoxa's little boy, jumped and laughed, enjoying the evening breeze. Both young children said nonsense things, sang a bit, and fell on their bottoms from time to time. They were increasingly steady on little legs and feet.

"I told you that I have two problems," said Melpone. "I told you about my name, meaning that I was born a 'tragedy.' That's coming true because now I have a difficult problem. Sibyl brought an unbelievable order from three Senate members: Three identical, purple-edged togas need lots of embroidery. Those senators also want decorations for their houses in Rome: material for couches, curtains, and cushions."

"How could this be a problem? Aren't extra sales good for business?" Miriam didn't understand where the conflict lay.

"I have the job of embroidering the togas. I fear that will be my tragedy, my downfall."

"I don't understand," Miriam replied. "The guild received a good order, and you were chosen, honored with this delicate work. If you need help, ask Arpoxa. She is wonderful with her hands. You should see the things she made in Pergamum."

"Miriam, you don't understand! Nothing is as it first appears. There's gossip coming from Rome. It has to do with the nasty disagreement between the emperor and members of the Senate."

"What does that have to do with you in Thyatira?"

Melpone jaw was tense. "A few senators want to weaken Domitian. I heard that they objected to his increasing influence. That puts them in danger because he has already executed senators and governors for rebellion—thirteen in all!"

"But those men acted in rebellion! You'll only be stitching togas! Asking for a toga isn't considered rebellious!"

Melpone grasped Miriam's wrist. "Domitian gets rid of his enemies one by one. I'm worried. This order for fine purple came from three senators who recently spoke out against him. If anyone in Domitian's palace thinks their use of purple is an affront to his authority..."

"Oh, I see. You are worried that Domitian's counselors would trace these items back to you." Miriam now understood the cause of Melpone's unease, and she frowned.

"Listen, Miriam, several other senators also want purple products. They intend to restore the historical powers of the Senate. Sibyl mentioned a phrase that sums up their disgust at living under a dictator: 'He's drunk with purple honors.' It's the senators' way of saying the emperor has gone too far.

"He doesn't accept 'Pax Romana,' the balance of power that Augustus brought. One man in Philippi voiced a fear. He thinks these senators might wear sashes to increasingly identify themselves with the provinces more than with the empire's authority. Domitian will not allow that. He demands that the empire be recognized above individual provinces! If those three senators are accused of treason, and if someone asks, 'Who made these?'..."

Melpone was an excellent artisan. She embroidered quickly and without error. Her perfect eyesight and the memory needed to count the tiny threads and sew patterns were beyond the scope of most.

Miriam put her arms around the frightened woman. *She is like a wild horse in Cappadocia about to be seized and shown who has the power. Later, people see a horse pulling a cart; the driver snaps his whip loudly behind the creature's ear, and it turns whichever way he wants. Anxiety has almost immobilized her. Is there something else she isn't telling me? Why is she so concerned?*

September had come and gone when Miriam asked Jonathan and Rebekah to listen to her. "Did you know that Melpone lost her baby after Phlegon, her husband, hit her?" Neither Jonathan nor Rebekah knew those personal stories.

"Also," she added, "Melpone has received a special order, and she is alarmed." She explained more, describing the situation between the Senate and the emperor.

Jonathan looked serious. "You are learning quickly, Miriam. Nothing here is what it appears to be. Will the emperor's wrath reach all the way to Melpone? I don't know. I remember ships sailing into port in Alexandria. Nearby, there were placid waters where dangerous rocks lay close to the surface. I'll let you in on a little secret. Deep jealousy exists between the Weavers' Guild and the Guild of Purple Honors. The small but growing Guild of Outer Garments is also jealous. Why? Their work overlaps: All three guilds make clothing. Yet it would be shameful to talk openly about their conflicts.

"No one wants to reveal secrets. Nobody sees those jealousies, but they are as treacherous as jagged rocks just below the waterline. People's lives get destroyed when the craving to control the lives of others starts using jealousy and antagonism."

Miriam wanted him to understand Melpone's emotional state. "Uncle Jonathan, Sibyl told Melpone she has to complete this task. She has no choice. The guild's master will not allow her to refuse the work, and she can't quit and go to another guild."

"My dear niece, you are right. Sibyl accepted the work for the guild. The guild's master assigned her the work because she has the necessary skills. Melpone has no choice."

"Why?"

"Socially, she is one of the weakest persons in the guild. When people become cruel, it is the frailest and most vulnerable that are affected. You see this at work everywhere."

Miriam suddenly gathered that within the guild system lay hidden layers of power, with corresponding clashes. Uncle Jonathan was right. Melpone had no choice. Workers had to support their guild by joining in the activities at their temple and doing everything to help their organization.

She asked, "Does everybody know that there are mean spirits behind nice words? Uncle, how do you manage here when you see feeble people threatened by the more powerful?"

"The guilds accept me! I either supply their needs, buy their goods, or invest in them! They need people like me."

"Let me understand your idea of business," Miriam said. Her lips were tightly drawn together. "Great-grandpa Eliab came with Grandpa Antipas to Pergamum. The other brothers came there from Egypt over the next few years. Subsequently, Uncle Daniel, and then each of you, left Pergamum to set up businesses in different cities. Each brother committed to supporting the others with the products from their workshops, right?"

Jonathan nodded his agreement. "You are going to follow in your grandfather's sandals!" She knew his pleasant tone was meant to draw her in, just as his warm embrace reached clients. He was always attracting more customers to his businesses.

She nodded, understanding more. *Uncle Jonathan always seeks recognition. He relishes being part of what is happening around him. He started off with bronze lamps and then added linen clothing and the olive orchard. Now he's invested in purple. He doesn't mind if a young woman fears for her safety as long as the guild sells to Rome's senators. He describes her as "the weakest" and the "most vulnerable."*

"Uncle Jonathan, does being a follower of Yeshua Messiah make a difference in what you do?"

Her uncle answered quickly and a bit evasively, "I see your Grandfather Antipas in so much of what you do and how you do it. You are direct, as my brother was."

He paused to let the next words sink in. "Of course, Miriam, that brought my brother great trouble."

Her gaze held firm. *Uncle Jonathan! Are you suggesting that the same thing could happen to me?*

Jonathan saw her eyes flicker. He added quickly, "Yes, I'm a follower of Yeshua Messiah, like my brother. In the same way, I have two areas of difficulty. One is with Domitian demanding we declare, 'Caesar is lord and god.' I repeat the phrase even though, as a Jew, I am exempt from saying it. As a guild member, I am forced to, but I do not believe a word of it. The other is the presence of carved images. I do not think a stone statue is anything more than that, a carved figure. Adonai looks on the heart, at our real intentions.

"I find the worship of Artemis repugnant, primitive, and the work of childish beliefs, but to live in Thyatira, you have to walk a fine line. Maybe this is something you did not know. The Potters' Guild actively worked against me. My first five years, I endured ridicule from that guild's neighbors and friends, with tension in our home, especially for Bani. His friends in the gymnasium gave him a hard time. I never let on at home the problems I faced from one official in the Potters' Guild—and still face. I learned to maintain a jolly disposition, praying in my heart. I quoted Scripture in my mind."

Miriam did not know about his former trials. *That's what you did? You prayed all the time, fighting for your survival when you came to Thyatira? Do you still pray like that and quote Scripture in your mind?*

She repeated his statement. "You quoted Scripture?"

"Yes, especially Isaiah; idols have no power.[74] To answer your question directly: I don't know what Yeshua Messiah would have said about living here. What did he ever say about the guild system?"

Rebekah had not said a word, but she sensed that the time would come when Miriam's words would become more relevant in Jonathan's life. "Miriam, I want you to think about these things, and then we must talk about them again. Is that all right with you?"

In the evening, after Grace had been put to sleep, Miriam wrote another letter.

September 30, in the 12th year of Domitian
From: Miriam
To: Anthony, my heart and my life

I miss you so much.

Uncle Jonathan and Aunt Rebekah live in a complicated world. I thought I understood what was happening here, but now I'm unsure what he should do and should not do. I'm learning more about this city.

When I lived in Pergamum, Grandfather was clear about his beliefs. At that time, I only knew Uncle Jonathan from his summer visits to our home. I saw how much he was involved and how much he participated in society.

Until a few days ago, I thought he was too committed to his guilds. My first impressions were that Thyatira would be an easy place to live. Yet I'm just beginning to understand what it costs Uncle Jonathan to be accepted.

Thyatira is as dangerous for Jonathan in some ways as

---

[74] Isaiah 40:19–20

Pergamum was for Grandpa. It's far more treacherous for him here than for Uncle Simon in Sardis. In Sardis, we were expelled from the synagogue. What a mean spirit Diotrephes demonstrated when he got our family expelled! In Sardis, Uncle Simon resisted him by gathering friends in the Ben Shelah home for worship instead of at the synagogue portico.

But Thyatira is different. Everyone here must adopt dishonorable ethics. Unless you belong to a guild, you will always be at the mercy of others. But once you belong to a guild, influential people demand that you comply with their expectations. "Fit into our social life. Recognize our special days: birthdays, anniversaries, and celebrations of gods."

I had two long talks with Uncle Jonathan and am not sure what to make of him. I think he wants me as a business partner, but I will not agree with that. He thinks getting rich and having public acceptance are the most essential things in life.

Aunt Rebekah is easy to talk to and more concerned for each person's well-being in her family, and if it were not for her, I wouldn't know how to live here. I have a new friend. Her name is Melpone, and she sews at the Guild of Purple Honors. Through her, I've just begun to meet other women too.

Nikias brought your last letter. Thank you so much.

THE STREETS OF THYATIRA

On Tuesday night, vintners danced, celebrating the harvest. After summer rains and many hot days, the grapes were ripe. Juice flowed freely in the agora. Winemakers had set up large, portable vats for crushing grapes. Flutes and cymbals played as people sang harvest songs. About ten at a time, dancers stomped their feet in the wooden vats while grapes were dumped in. Juice from the grapes was drained into a second container, a smaller vessel, where the grape seeds and skins sank to the bottom. Pure juice then overflowed into a third container. Afterward, the liquid would be poured into wineskins or specially made pots and allowed to slowly ferment and turn into wine.

Songs about Dionysius, the god of wine, resounded throughout the night and into the early morning hours. Once again, Dionysius delighted them with hope and prosperity.

Purple Honors

Part 2
Friends and Foes

October
AD 92

Chapter 24
Glory, Honor, and Shame

THE MILITARY GARRISON IN SOMA

No further robberies or murders had been reported on the Interior Road. Guards stationed at each relay station and caravan inn checked and doublechecked merchants and their cargo. A methodical hunt was underway to surprise the rebels before they could strike again. Meanwhile, caravan masters complained because the extra security questioning delayed their travels.

Anthony and his team returned to Soma tired and discouraged. Commander Servius was not impressed with their report and visibly showed it. "Think through the information. I do not want more delays, do you hear?"

"Sir, we have examined facts from every possible angle, but we'll keep working at it."

Servius grinned. "Suros, get away for two days. Go to Forty Trees. Take time to think and talk with the officers and patrol guards there. Maybe they are smart enough to figure this out."

Anthony informed his five companions that he would be gone for two days. He quietly wondered why the commander was letting him take a break in his duties. *Is Servius trying to humiliate me? Does he detect a rebellious streak in my words or actions? Is he separating me from the others to make me feel I am losing my command?*

At the Forty Trees Check Station, Anthony dismounted, tied the reins to a hitching post, and learned that the officer was away for a day. "Come back tomorrow, Suros," said a guard.

This provided a convenient time to go to Olive Grove to see how well Ateas was doing in getting ready for the long ride back north with the squad.

At Olive Grove, two sturdy farm wagons were being readied to take the first batch of new olive oil and olive soap to Thyatira. Nikias, hearing Anthony arrive, opened the olive press door. The farmhand and his brothers were working, sweat running down their faces.

Anthony saw Ateas in the dim light sitting beside heavy stones and emptying a fresh batch of olives into the press. The pressed-out olive oil went through three filtering vessels as it was purified. Leta, Kozma's wife, poured filtered oil into *amphora,* tall clay vessels with narrow necks.

"Anthony, you've come back!" Nikias bellowed. "Ateas has been looking for you to come for a week." His brothers greeted Anthony less enthusiastically. Ateas stood on one leg, balancing himself as he reached for his crutches. He placed them under his arm then hobbled toward Anthony as quickly as he could.

"So good to see you again, Nikias and Ateas—all of you!" Anthony said.

The second oldest, Alberto, said, "Now, Anthony, we are going to learn why you asked for a crippled man to come here. Ateas tells us, 'I come to help soldiers!' What nonsense!"

"Oh yes, he has been called here to help the army! I'll tell you what I can about it over a meal."

Later, at the noon meal, Ateas told his story. "One day Commander Felicior come to Uncle Simon's house. Arpoxa and me are all afraid. We never have a visit from such important man. He talk to me, and he is talking to Arpoxa. He say, 'Freedman Ateas! Anthony needs you at Forty Trees.' I thinking, 'Anthony is hiding in a forest. Too bad! Maybe he is lost in forest.'"

They all laughed with Ateas. He had a way of making them feel at ease even though his story was not always easy to understand.

"Then I learn. He say, 'I want you going to Olive Grove for army work.' I learn riding horse again. My wife, Arpoxa, is staying in big city Thyatira. I not happy. I good at ride now, and there is only one thing I can be doing: putting many olives in olive press. I now am saying, 'Commander Felicior is wrong. Anthony does not need me for army. Nikias and his brothers need me for working hard to forget my loneliness.'"

His small audience chortled. His language skills were far from perfect, but his frustration was understandable.

"So I explain to Nikias: Roman army is changing. Greeks are changing. Jews are changing. The whole world is changing! First, one Jew buys me in the slave market. That is unusual and good. Then Roman soldier commander tells me go to Forty Trees. That is first time and mystery. Next a Greek man and his brothers make me into olive maker and farmer. I squeezing oil, making soap, brushing horses. See, I'm happy Scythian now. I like this new Roman Empire.

This is new, happier, and kinder Roman Empire. Maybe one day I even like Domitian Emperor!"

It was so easy to laugh along with the crippled Scythian man, and they roared again.

The brothers asked Anthony about what he was doing for the army. "My job is more complicated than yours, Nikias. I'm supposed to be keeping the security of the Postal Road. It's a big job. Ateas, I wish everyone were as happy as you are. You should say it this way: 'I am happy on a farm; it's safe and easy.' Well, sometimes there are bad men around." He did not want to say too much.

Ateas jumped in. "Oh, I know many about bad people. Before I'm crippled, I have bag of arrows on my back, bow in my hand, and I'm riding and shooting bad men. We have big fight. They are running away from me. Many rides. Many days away from home. People there, half eyes shut. Now, here at Olive Grove, I busy but not happy. My Arpoxa is far away. She is in far big city, and I making olive soap, olive oil, olive food. Everything here olives! Every meal. Most having olives! I thinking I will soon be an olive."

A cat with brown and black patches lay sprawling in the sun, sleeping on its side. Its head was almost upside-down. Anthony wondered how an animal could twist its neck that way.

Clouds were gathering over the mountain, the first in months. The smell of horses and other animals and the harvest of olives spoke of a regular life on an orchard farm. After the noon meal, four brothers stretched out under the shade of a tree for a quick nap before returning to work.

Nikias took Anthony aside. "I looked at the scrolls you left and learned many things. I wanted to do what Antipas did, so I talked to Jonathan and asked him if he could give me some papyrus rolls. He laughed at the idea and then gave me a few so we could learn to do a new job. But Anthony, I found that you were right; copying those scrolls is difficult! We are five brothers; the three doing the work never learned to read or write well."

"So three brothers are working on this? But you are five altogether. What is happening..."

"Kozma, the youngest, doesn't want me to do any of this. He started speaking against me."

"How is the job going, making scrolls, that is?"

"Very slowly. In an entire evening, we write down only fifteen lines or so. Once I got mixed up, and I jumped over a whole part of

Isaiah's writing. They were all angry with me at that moment. We have all made mistakes. It's much harder than I thought."

"Well, none of you trained as scribes!" Anthony declared. "Why did you attempt such difficult work? It's tough to copy a scroll! People take years to learn to do it well."

"We tried again, getting better, but we couldn't show those to anyone. Too many mistakes! We had to start over; three papyrus rolls were wasted! Jonathan said not to worry about it. He gave me more, but this time we started with the book I like better."

"What was that?"

"Mark's book! It's a much shorter book and has lots of stories about Yeshua that are easy to understand." Nikias exclaimed, "I want to be like you, going from place to place, visiting other villages after harvesting is over. I can explain what I have learned to those people."

"What are you going to tell them?" Anthony asked.

"I'm going to say, 'Long ago, it was written that the great king is coming.' Then I'll add, 'The Lord has already come, and I have good news for you. That's why I came to your farm. And I have a scroll to give you that tells all about it.' What do you think of that? Will others appreciate my saying this to them?"

Anthony stared at Nikias, unable to formulate a proper reply.

"Yes, I'm going to tell them the Messiah has come. The people in villages close by have no idea who or what the Messiah is or what he came to do!"

There was something in the enthusiasm pouring out of Nikias that was attractive, but he possessed a dangerous naïveté too. Anthony advised his friend, "I cautioned you before! Yeshua said, 'Two by two.' Always go with one of your brothers, never alone. People might harm you."

"Why would anyone hurt me? This is good news."

Kozma, the youngest brother, joined them and pulled out a three-legged stool, ready to object. "I disagree with you, Nikias. You are bringing confusion. Be satisfied with who you were before Anthony came. Look at our family now. We have become divided. It's shameful to leave the Temple of Zeus! Since Anthony and Miriam were here, you are trying to be someone new. You are not a scribe! You were not trained to be one. Don't try to imitate Anthony, going all over the countryside!"

"I want to learn new things. We never studied as we grew up!

This is all fresh, and I like it!"

"Leave all of this alone!"

Tension filled the air. Anthony also didn't like it and didn't know what to do or how to tell Nikias that many would likely disagree with what the farmer was doing.

Standing up to look down at his brother, Kozma's voice took on an acidic tone. "Anthony, we argue a lot. Nikias wants us to change. I asked him once, 'Who was this Yeshua Messiah?' Do you know what he told me? 'He was a Jewish man who was killed on a cross because of our transgressions.' I stared at my brother and said, 'You've gone crazy! I don't understand a single word of what you just said.' Since then, he hasn't stopped speaking these meaningless words."

Kozma walked to his house and slammed his door.

Saddened by the division, Anthony looked at Nikias. *Things could get much worse. I am, at the most, a guest. Beyond giving a little bit of instruction about copying, there is so little I can do.*

I will instruct Nikias and his three brothers about Messiah. Strictly speaking, Commander Felicior in Sardis and Servius in Soma does not want me talking about Yeshua Messiah to other soldiers. However, teaching farm laborers, well...I am not really disobeying the commander's order.

Anthony instructed the four families and their wives following the evening meal, but the time was too short. They asked questions about lying, gossip, shame and honor, being kind to one another, prayers, and integrity. Anthony felt the thrill of an instructor whose students wanted to learn.

When Anthony left, he thought, *Is there anything I can do to break down the younger brother's resistance?*

JONATHAN AND REBEKAH'S HOME

Yom Kippur had passed, and the first day of the Feast of Tabernacles had arrived. Finding a quiet moment during the afternoon, Miriam asked Rebekah, "What has it been like for you to live in Thyatira?"

Rebekah answered honestly. "We came seventeen years ago, and I have to say that we are still considered to be outsiders in many ways. Jonathan exaggerates a bit when saying he is 'well accepted.' Yes, we've worked hard and contributed to the city. Outwardly, we're successful. Look at this beautiful house, our furniture, and the colorful clothing! And Jonathan fosters relationships almost everywhere."

"I'm interested in your life. What difficulties did you have settling into this city?"

"Jonathan demands my presence at celebrations of the various deities, and…"

"But most of the time, you stay home. Does Uncle Jonathan mind that?"

"Back in Alexandria, as children, we were brought up to confess Adonai as the only God. Quite honestly, I feel pressed between two worlds, but Jonathan shrugs it off. How he loves people! He can meet with people all day—the more, the better—but too many people leave me tired and grumpy. We're different in more ways than one."

"If you don't like being with lots of people, how do you manage with so many here early on Sundays for the Holy Meal?"

"For some reason, those days are different. As you've seen, it's a simple event, nothing elaborate. At the synagogue, everything is formal and predictable. But when people come here for a simple remembrance before the day begins, we sing and confess our faith. We kneel. I love the moment when I take the bread and the wine and whisper, 'I receive your grace.' I don't feel tired at all."

"And the rest of the week?"

"Thyatira is about work over any other consideration. Only by being present at the guild meetings, making the votive libation sacrifices, and supporting the guilds' goals of ever more sales can anyone get ahead. Otherwise, it may mean discrimination, loss of pay, or even the loss of a job. It's like a very tedious and serious game; you must follow the rules. If someone becomes unemployed, it is hard to get another job, and I do not like that. Look at family members who come to the Holy Meal! Few have land or possessions. They do not have a business, capital, or resources of any nature. And all of them have to work in a guild."

Three nights later, Miriam woke in the middle of the night. A protracted nightmare left her in a sweat. In her dream, she was going into a little house made with branches, the playhouse made by her grandfather for the Feast of Tabernacles. She saw herself playing with other children and all of them lay down for an afternoon nap. Then, in her dream, there was a baby beside her.

Instead of developing normally, she saw the baby getting smaller. When she could not find the child, she started to pull branches out of the little house. Then the miniature baby walked away from her. She woke up, looked around the darkened room, and immediately fell back to sleep.

In another dream, she was standing on the edge of a road, a long, straight stretch from Sardis. No one else was on the road—no farm wagons and no merchants. Hearing a sound, she stirred and turned around. From the ground, men were climbing out of a hole. Instinctively, she knew the men were bandits, and she tried to look at their faces but could not identify anyone.

In her dream, she started to run down the road, crying for help. Where was the little baby she was supposed to be caring for? On the long road, she could not see anyone. She called for help: "Anthony, help me!" She woke up in a panic. Grace was crying.

Miriam took the toddler in her arms and rocked Grace, singing softly in her ear. *Why the bad dream? A lost baby and robbers. Those fears. Dear God! Please don't let anything happen to Anthony! Did you let me get married so that the army could take him and have him killed by bandits? Dear Lord, I'm too young to be a widow. And I love Grace, but I also want my own baby, my family. My grandfather is dead, and I feel as if I'm here without security.*

In the morning, she casually asked Rebekah, "Auntie, what do you do when living in Thyatira gets to you?"

Rebekah turned around after putting an oil lamp on the table. "I'm always calmed by remembering the promises: 'Anyone who trusts in him will never be put to shame.'"[75]

"I'll remember that." *It was only a bad dream about losing a baby and not having anyone to help me. "I will not be put to shame." Even with Anthony far away, I'll not be put to shame.*

Arpoxa called to her, and Miriam went back upstairs.

THE HOME OF FABIUS BASSOS

Fabius Bassos hardly slept, tossing from one side to the other. *The shame of failing to fund the Association of Supporters of the Games. I've run out of time. Tomorrow, and then Friday, and two more. Only four days until the Games. There's not enough time to take*

---

[75] Isaiah 28:16, Romans 10:11

care of everything.

Tonight the Association will expect an answer. I'll tell them I'm going to bring fighters from Pergamum, but I won't tell them I shall have to pay for it by taking out a loan. Why did I permit Aurelius Tatianos to make me promise to provide that frieze in the Temple of Apollo? Oh, for a repeat of last year! I was walking in front of countless cheering young men chanting my name. Now, that was glory! But this year, the mayor has twisted things.

Dawn finally came. He walked onto the porch overlooking the city. His house faced west, taking in the entire valley and the vast fertile plain. Far off were the bluish-gray ridges of mountains where the golden rays of the sun outlined distant peaks. To the left, close by along the graceful curve of Mount Gordus, was the dark, empty theater. Last evening, occupying his place of honor at the theater, he hardly noticed the tragedy played out on the stage. His thoughts kept coming back to one thing only.

I can already feel the public shame.

Entering the house, he was on the verge of explaining to his wife what he would do when he heard a man outside the house call, "Is this the home of Fabius Bassos?"

A slave answered the caller. "Yes. Why are you asking?"

The visitor spoke in a low voice. "I need to speak with him."

As a slave went to open the door, Bassos calculated, *I can't be bothered by anyone right now. I'm leaving home to get a loan, and that might take several hours.*

Putting those thoughts aside, he spoke to the visitor wearing a military tunic. Curious because the man carried no other symbol of belonging to the army, he addressed the guest. "Good morning, I'm Fabius Bassos. May I help you?"

"Are you related to Julius Bassos of Nicomedia?"

"Yes, he's a cousin. It's been a few years since we talked."

"I have a business proposal that might be of interest."

Fabius felt pulled apart by internal conflicts. Harsh words spoken at a family meal years ago with Julius, his cousin, still rankled, so how could he ask for a loan from him? And how could he lower himself to ask for a loan at the bank this morning? Those worries faded slightly as he thought, *What brings an unknown man to my house so early? And how does he know about my cousin?*

"Come in. Why do you ask about my cousin?"

Fabius sat down in one of the three large wickerwork

armchairs. Between the chairs was a bronze table topped with polished black marble. Ornate bronze legs bent gracefully to the floor, where they resembled lion paws at rest. A house slave brought a jug of wine, another poured cool water, and a third appeared with bowls filled with pomegranate seeds. The fruit was at its best right now, fresh off the trees.

Speaking loudly, Bassos asked his slaves to leave. "Stay in the kitchen. Prepare a morning meal worthy of a great guest."

He wanted them out of the way. Lowering his voice, he asked, "What is your name? Who are you?"

"My name is Tira. Today I'm dressed as a simple auxiliary. My weapons and armor are elsewhere. I normally serve in a cohort bringing miserable wretches to the slave market."

"Slaves from where?"

"Chalcedon and cities much farther north."

"How far north? Who is your commander?"

"From Scythia. I serve under Commander Craga."

"Never heard of him. What is your purpose?"

"I have access to wild animals in cages. There's one animal in particular, a large bear caught in the mountains of Pontus. I think you'll be interested in it and, perhaps, also young men who can fight." His voice drifted off, and he did not finish his thought.

Fabius caught the drift of the conversation immediately. *A soldier does not get caught up in the business world, because his commanding officer will be upset. This man is not an ordinary legionary. No man in the army would ever buy or sell wild animals...or men. This man, whoever he is, speaks my language!*

"Please continue, Tira."

"I know of a wounded slave. He would look noble fighting a bear. He is not a real fighter. I call him a 'potential gladiator.' He was injured in a mine tunnel, so he is going to die eventually, perhaps sooner rather than later."

"I don't understand."

"This slave was hurt in a mine collapse, and he has only one arm with which to fight. He lost a hand when rocks fell from the ceiling, pinning his hand. Have you ever dreamed of a fight between a bear and a one-armed slave with only a dagger?"

Tira made another outrageous proposal. "Wild boars live in the mountains and are extremely dangerous," said Tira, "especially if several were to spring out of a cage at the same time."

Bassos looked puzzled. "You know of men who would risk their lives fighting wild boars?"

"No one trains for that kind of fight, but handicapped fighters might provide a spectacle. Potential gladiators, that's what I call them. Slaves, as you know, show a lack of respect for authority, but faced with the possibility of a less demanding life, faint hope brings some almost super-human powers. Such an event, when it rises in a man's breast, is like finding precious gems deep underground."

Clearly Tira was speaking of ideas laden with double meanings. He continued on. "We think that we could give them an incentive to quickly learn to fight. They would have the option of being gladiators for a day, with minimal training of course. Just think: A winner could become a house slave after surviving such a fight. The challenge of killing wild animals would be a powerful incentive for two men to fight well, even if tied to each other. Of course, this is simply an idea, nothing more."

"How much money would it take to turn this idea into a reality?"

"I'm sure we could work something out. Money isn't the main concern; it can always be found. Entertainment...now that's another matter. My commander is interested in providing amusement for young men. Perhaps a small payment now. Later, other unusual combinations of men fighting animals. I was a young man once, so I know what it is for youth to long for good entertainment."

"You talk about slaves, other potential gladiators, and wild animals?"

"Yes, from the north. My commander also deals with other merchandise."

Fabius stared, amazed that the gods had answered him so directly. *Tira talks about entertainment. It's as I thought...a rogue army group. He is bold and has no shame in what he is talking about. He's like me. I, too, have no shame in finding a way to put on the Games if it removes me from begging for a loan.*

"How did you know I might be interested in such a proposition?"

"A slave works in the home of the mayor. Perhaps you know the mayor? Information from deep in the house has ways of coming to us. I gather he overheard some conversations that we'll not talk about now. You never know what you will learn while listening carefully in the marketplace."

Bassos worked out how much he could afford. Trained gladiators, whose cost was too expensive, were not an option. Slaves who had been wounded and could not be sold at the slave market would be cheap enough for use at the Games. No loan was needed. He could still be "The Benefactor."

"I'll be back to see you, Fabius Bassos, in two days. I'll come directly to your house very early in the morning. You'll understand that I can't spend much time here. I tend to carefully avoid the garrison. But we'll be talking again. Two visits this week should complete our present arrangement, and then I'll see you again after six months have passed. How does that sound?"

Fabius watched in wonder as the stranger mounted his sleek brown horse. *I made an offering to Artemis, an expensive offering with prayers. She heard my cry for help and will not let me be shamed before this city's men—instead, glory and cheers from the crowds.*

ON THE POSTAL ROAD FROM SOMA TO AIZANOI

Anthony left Soma, having sent the other five ahead with instructions: "Sextilius, Bellinus, and Capito, stay in the Aizanoi barracks. Search in villages between Aizanoi and White Horse Station. And you, Omerod and Menandro, search villages north of White Horse Relay Station and wait at Inegol to meet us there. I'm coming with Ateas but more slowly than before."

Bringing an extra mount from the Forty Trees Relay Station, Anthony rode his horse half a mile off the road to Olive Grove, ready to pick up Ateas. "Your job will be to help with language, Ateas. Whenever we meet Scythians, whatever they are doing, talk with them. I don't mind if the person is a merchant or shepherd, a villager, or a slave."

"Of course. What I ask to talk about?"

"Ask if they heard about slaves being brought from the north in the last two years. If the answer is yes, ask about the legionaries guarding those caravans. You have a good eye for detail, I know. You made exquisite gold rings with Simon in Sardis. Ask about wild animals."

"Anthony, you both kind but not kind. You keep me from wife Arpoxa and little boy in Thyatira!"

"Do you remember what it was like to have Antipas free you at the slave market?"

"Yes, I cry inside because of long day past as horse rider for traders to east people. When I young as horse rider for guarding traders from bad men, I go far. The next year, I am taken to slave market in Pergamum. The worst day of my life."

"Well, continue to use your imagination. Other people also feel abandoned, betrayed, and hopeless. Other slaves, some like you, were part of an illegal operation. I need your assistance to help them."

Anthony took a deep breath. The days that they would be on this road heading north would give him time to help his friend learn proper Greek. "Now, Ateas, while you are helping the Roman army find bandits, I'll help you in a different way. I want you to speak correctly. You need to say, 'I *was* crying inside. I *was* in the slave market. I *was* sad. I *used to be* a horse rider guarding our traders to the eastern people.' All of that happened in the past. Do you understand? Repeat it for me. No, don't look at me like that! Go on. Say it."

Ateas was proud to have a legionary as his teacher. "I *was* crying inside," he repeated. "I *was* in the slave market, and I *was* sad. I *was* a horse rider guarding our traders to the eastern people. There! I much better, right?"

They laughed as they rode past Thyatira on the way to Sardis. Farmers worked and sang as they piled hay onto flat horse-drawn carts. Cows raised their heads, swishing their tails to chase the flies away. Trees were already wrapping themselves in yellow and brown garments. In a few days, those colorful cloaks would fall to the ground, leaving limbs bare until spring.

"Anthony, life in farms is too beautiful. Why robbers coming to beautiful land?"

"That's a good question." Anthony didn't correct the Scythian's poor grammar. *I ask the same question all the time. How does this beautiful land, yielding such bountiful harvests, endure constant ugly acts of crime?*

Chapter 25
Changing Perspectives

THE CITY OF THYATIRA

At the evening meal on Monday, Jonathan announced that he would take his family on an all-day outing the next day.

"Wednesday will be the last day of the Feast of Tabernacles," he declared as the family began their morning meal. "I've arranged for something different. Three wagons will take us up Mount Gordus for a picnic, and we'll come back down before sunset.

"Arte has been instructed to pack up food in the morning for our trip. We can do a bit of cooking there too. We'll need a few carpets and cushions to sit on."

Rebekah understood Jonathan's strategy perfectly well. Bani and Gil might want to attend the bloody fights at the stadium. By taking everyone up the mountain, Jonathan removed their temptation to watch cruel sports. This was one activity in which Jonathan would not participate.

Right after breakfast the next morning, Jonathan wandered around the house, shouting, "Hurry up, everyone! We're leaving in a little while!"

As they left the city, the road was crowded with folk from small villages coming in for the sports and fights. When they turned onto the road going up the mountain, the wagons had the road all to themselves.

Word had gone out saying unusual combats were to take place. A bear was to fight a wounded slave who had lost his hand in an accident. "If he kills the bear, he'll be set free!"

Bassos kept boasting to anyone who would listen. "You'll see wild boars facing two other slaves. Here's a twist: They will walk with three legs. One of each man's legs will be bound together. If the men become entangled, they'll fall down. Here's my promise. If they win the fight, a much better life! If they kill the wild animals, they'll no longer work in the mines but will be house slaves! It's a contest with a better life as the prize!"

Great crowds were in the city from towns and villages all over the Lycos Valley. The spectacle promised thrills. "Entertainment with a new twist!" Bassos bragged.

Victorious gladiators would move up the slaves' social ladder, from the mines to house slaves.

MOUNT GORDUS

The path for Jonathan's horse-drawn wagons lay along the gentle slope of the mountain's southern flank. Miriam held Grace and pointed out the long lines of olive trees, but the child was not interested in anything except pulling her mother's hair.

They passed through a small town called Julia Gordus, one of fifteen within Thyatira's immediate vicinity. Julia Gordus was built hundreds of years before. Its population lived in a unique setting, secure in a little valley covered with olive trees and nestled against small cliffs.

The road climbed higher. Pine and aspen trees gloated in golden glory. Rebekah pointed, saying, "Look, nature honors its forests by dressing them with majestic garments."

A bubbling spring above the cataract ended in a beautiful, cascading waterfall. From there, the water flowed through the town of Julia Gordus. Many smaller villages were located around springs, but this waterfall was different. It was considered a sacred place.

"People always like to hear the sound of water," said Danila, looking up in awe at the rocky lip over which the stream flowed. "I'm happy to spend a day here with my new husband! Gil, I'm glad you aren't going to watch those terrible fights!"

An early autumn rain had fallen during the night, and the dust in the air over Lycos Valley had disappeared. The air was crisp and clean. The valley below appeared as a patchwork of farms.

Bani and Gil laid carpets on the ground. Everyone waded in the creek or climbed rocks. Arte, who had been to Julia Gordus previously, knew the way up the black stones to the cliff above.

Arpoxa could not walk because of her club feet. However, she was thrilled to be part of the event. Three years before, she had been on an adventure like this when Antipas took his whole community upstream in Pergamum for a cookout meal before

Passover. She watched Grace and Saulius, her son, while Miriam and Danila dipped their legs into the refreshing water. A picnic was served, and then they lay down, resting on carpets and watching feathery clouds float by in the blue sky.

"I work in a crowded, stuffy city with a wall surrounding us. This place is so open!" stated Arte. "Look there. You can just see our house! It's tiny, yet when we are inside, we think it's big. Now look at the valley stretching to those distant mountains. Who could imagine that this perspective could change the way we see things?

"Thyatira is small! The city we think is so big is puny. Look! It takes up only a tiny space in the valley. Yet when I'm in my kitchen, I think I'm at the center of the world. Honestly, at times I think I'm the center of everything!"

They all laughed. It sounded strange to hear a slave say these words: "our house" and "my kitchen." It was even more bizarre for an honest confession to come from a man who would forever be a slave. Arte would always be the poorest man in Jonathan's household, but his casual comment showed that even he knew that things were not entirely what they appeared to be.

Later that afternoon, Jonathan announced that it was time to leave to get home before dark, but no one wanted to return.

JONATHAN AND REBEKAH'S HOME

As she woke on the last day of the Feast of Tabernacles, Miriam dressed Grace in clean clothes. One of Anthony's letters, written a month before, lay open where she had laid it the previous night after their return from the waterfalls at Julia Gordus.

Miriam reread the ancient words: "Some trust in chariots and some in horses, but we trust in the name of the Lord our God. They are brought to their knees and fall, but we rise up and stand firm."[76]

Antipas quoted those words two weeks before he was killed. A shadow passed over her face. Antipas had not been delivered from harm.

Why? How long, O God? How long is this going to last? How long until we can return to Pergamum? Are they still hunting for us? Jerusalem lies in ruins. Grandfather was killed a year and a half ago. And yet yesterday, up on the mountain, I didn't even think of him, not even once!

---

[76] Psalm 20:7–8

Singing took a considerable effort. Miriam did not want to switch from rhetorical questions to song. Still, she hummed a possible new tune to use, a reluctant but positive response to the situation. Long ago, she had discovered that when despondency pulled her down, music lifted the gloom.

After breakfast, she asked Rebekah to take care of Grace so she could write a new song. At the top of a sheet of papyrus, she wrote, "What Deep Shame!"

Rebekah watched her niece's face. Miriam was wiping tears from her eyes. Pulling Jonathan aside later, Rebekah whispered, "Miriam has a new song. Ask her to sing it at Sunday's gathering for the Way of Truth."

Later that morning, the family walked to the Thyatira Synagogue for the last service of the weeklong Feast of Tabernacles. When they returned home afterward, Miriam put the finishing touches on her song. She sang it for Jonathan and Rebekah, and he asked her to sing it to the Sunday morning gathering.

THE CITY OF THYATIRA

Saturday morning, Fabius Bassos forced himself to do something he rarely did. He hated the south end of the city, which smelled terrible. Crowded streets sent shivers down his back. But proud of his achievement of having put on one of the most unusual Games Thyatira had ever seen, he was going to receive honors from the mayor. He knew the people who made their living in cramped, dusty, smoky workshops wanted to see their benefactor.

Immediately upon his arrival, Bassos was surrounded by youth. He waved to all. A genuine grin overflowed from his ample jowls as he lumbered through the crowded streets, where people flocked to see him.

"The man who gave us the Games!" one young man yelled, calling his friends.

"Come talk with our benefactor!" Their voices were excited, compelling.

The hot baths, one of the city's largest buildings, served as a principal place for social interaction. Friends met, enjoying massages given by sweating, muscular slaves. Bassos had his own hot baths in his house, so he usually did not go into the city for the afternoon bath. However, having received an invitation from the mayor, Aurelius Tatianos, to meet there, he called out, "Hail, Aurelius!"

"Hail! Here you are, my friend!"

They met at the massive archway entrance that reached higher than any other arch in the city. People often stopped to stare, wondering by what magic the arch's huge stone blocks were held together. On inner walls, painted plaster portrayed idyllic mountain scenes: forests, streams, and waterfalls. Each division revealed a different mountain close to Thyatira with birds soaring endlessly, their feathers captured in magnificent detail. Wild deer stared forever at naked men entering a pool.

After stripping down, they sweltered in the moist heat of the caldarium. Bassos and the mayor exchanged pleasantries with sweat pouring off their brows, arms, shoulders, and chests. "Bassos, you completely surprised me! I congratulate you on the amazing entertainment. Never have I seen young men so enthused. A fight but not what we expected. A brilliant idea to give slaves a short dagger to fight wild animals. How ironic and deceitful! You placed the animals on a level with intelligent slaves!"

"Thank you, Tatianos. It's an honor to hear this compliment from you." Bassos did not know how to take such praise, especially from Aurelius.

"No, I mean it! Where in the world did you find those wild animals? And you didn't tell a soul until only two days before! The idea of two slaves tied together at their ankles with only one dagger while facing wild boars. I've never seen people roar like that, laughing until they ached.

"The fighters turned around, pulling each other to the ground as the two boars came at them from several directions. They hurt each other more than the boars did! And in the end, all dead, men and beasts, after a long fight. The youth have never seen anything like it. Brilliant!"

After they could not stand the heat anymore, they shuffled along to the tepidarium for a massage that included perfumed oils.

Mayor Aurelius Tatianos groaned as the strong fingers of a slave dug into the small of his back, relaxing the muscles and shedding old skin. "The prizes you arranged for the top athletes were wonderful. Where did you ever get such awards? Strange diadems...they looked like something from far away!"

The city's benefactor avoided discussing the topic, suddenly realizing that quietness, while not being real humility, gave him more satisfaction than bragging. *I don't want to talk about the unusual diadems given to those four winners for running, wrestling, jumping, and javelin. I agreed to buy treasures from Dacia but never thought I would be in such a position.*

Later, the refreshing pool, the frigidarium, closed the skin's pores. They would be ready to return home, relaxed and invigorated.

Bassos enjoyed the recognition, but he would not divulge any information. Various combinations of cruelty had been played out at the Games. *My heart swells after each positive comment from Tatianos. Still, I can't say a thing about the entertainment and all the details. I remain concerned about the legality of my transactions. Tira may be wanted by the authorities, and is that why I feel a slight hesitation about what I did? The mayor must not become suspicious!*

I crave his respect, but he must not find out. Not even my wife knows. Those injured slaves died, so they will never tell their secrets. I am ready for more. More glory! More honor!

Bassos would not comment on the Games, so they talked for a while about gossip coming from Rome.

When it was time to leave, Tatianos commented, "Bassos, there's a side to you that I never knew about. It's something I admire. You take praise with real humility. You haven't said a word!

"Oh! I want to thank you for having that sweet Egyptian massage oil delivered to my home. I didn't know it was from you as a gift to smooth things over from the past, but a slave told me he heard of you telling your wife, 'It's time to give Tatianos a nice gift! You know that old expression of Thyatira: Gifts cleanse the stains from soiled friendships.'"

Bassos smiled broadly, but silently he was thanking the goddess Artemis for revealing the brilliant way of transferring false information to others by using his slave's eavesdropping.

THE MILITARY GARRISON IN KARUN

In Karun, Anthony sat on a chair at the officer's table. The wicks were newly cut so that the oil lamps burned brightly. The words in his letter to Miriam poured out quickly.

He closed his eyes, and memories flooded back. The first time he saw Miriam was when she had stood apart from the slave auction in Pergamum. Then he began to see her more frequently while coming to Antipas's gatherings in the Cave. He smiled, remembering his first encounter at the store where she was helping her grandfather.

October 11, in the 12th year of Domitian
From: Anthony
To: My wife, my love, my every breath

Mercy and peace. How I miss you.

Tomorrow Ateas and I will go to the next relay station. Give Arpoxa greetings from Ateas. He is learning Greek, and I am his teacher!

There is another thing. I am worried because Nikias wants to visit several small towns: Gelembe, Yortan, Nakrasa, Attaleia, Prosperity Village, and Chilara.[77] *He'll have to get Jonathan's permission of course.*

Antipas's influence over me is still strong. I encouraged Nikias and his farmhands to copy the scrolls like Antipas did in Pergamum! They initially began with Isaiah but found it too difficult and gave up after a while. Nikias said he was going to start over with Mark's story.

None of the four brothers writes well, and it's hard to read what they write. Funny...almost a case of the blind leading the blind except that they aren't blind about Yeshua anymore. My thought is this: Antipas was my teacher, and now I'm helping Nikias the same way that I was taught.

I feel fear for the future of this family. Kozma will not have anything to do with Yeshua. He is a loyal devotee of Zeus, Artemis, and Apollo.

A second thought disturbs me. Antipas controlled what happened in his village, but I don't have a say in developments at Olive Grove. I'm far away and only visit on rare occasions. Let's trust God to show Nikias the right things to do.

I'll send this letter to Nikias. He'll deliver it to you. You are with me every day, from the first moment I wake up.

---

[77] These were villages and small cities to the north and west of Thyatira. Little, if any, archaeological research has been conducted in these locations.

JONATHAN AND REBEKAH'S HOME

Early Sunday morning, people started to arrive at the Ben Shelah home. The sun was barely above the horizon, moving into a clear, cloudless sky. When they had assembled, Jonathan started the worship by chanting the Shema. That was followed by all saying a confession of faith from Paul's letter to the Philippians.[78]

Jonathan then discussed the remaining teachings, meanings, and history behind the Feast of Tabernacles week that had not been covered in the previous Sunday's gathering. They ended by sharing the Holy Meal.

He then announced that Miriam had a new song, saying, "Often difficult days come, followed by days of happiness. God brought my niece to our house to brighten our home, and she has a song for us. Her words will help us reflect on how we can respond to things that make us feel ashamed."

Calm and peaceful, Miriam held her hands together. "As my uncle said, worries and thoughts of shame come to us, some worse than others. We Jews still count Jerusalem as our spiritual home and how we feel our loss! It has a strong presence in our lives; its loss is experienced by all of us.

"However, it's not only Jews who feel shame. Gentiles, Romans, Africans, Persians, and all others do too, for different reasons. Think of a mother who has a child unable to talk. Or a father who wants his son to walk, but as the years go by, the boy's legs don't develop.

"My crippled friend Arpoxa was sold by her brother to pay off his gambling debts. That's how she was sold into slavery. She's Scythian. We could look down on her, yet she is one of my best friends, and she has taught me many good things.

"Three days ago, shameful things happened in the stadium. Slaves faced wild animals. Outlandish fights took place, contests no one could imagine. In the end, all were dead. Is it possible to confront this kind of shame? That's what my song is about."

She sang the entire song, singing each line twice. Her clear soprano voice left a hush in the room. Then she sang the song again. By the time she had finished, the people were singing it with her. They would remember it in their homes.

---

[78] Philippians 2:6–11

The siege succeeds, much to our pain.
The temple burns; the priests lament.
Sparks fly, doors fall, scrolls roll in flame,
The wealth of ages in this way is spent.
Permanent loss, does it have a name?
Honor is lost at an abysmal cost
While sackcloth and ashes proclaim our shame.

Babylon's houses fill the plain.
Our harps are hung on trees.
All desire to sing is on the wane.
Captors mock, "Sing for us please!"
Our throats are dry, but why complain?
Honor is lost at a terrible cost!
We all feel the harm, all suffer the shame.

My friend is from the north, and yes, she's lame.
Her brother groaned beneath his debts.
If sums weren't paid, he'd be to blame.
His evil mind formed shocking plans.
Sold as a slave! For him, only a game!
Honor was lost, inexcusable cost!
She was his sister! Such a terrible shame!

Caged beasts snarl. "Watch out! They're not tame!"
Young men shout. Snarling creatures fear,
Leaping to the kill. Fighters cry in pain.
Crude swords made dull, spectators cheer!
"Men and beasts are dead." This is their refrain!
Honor was lost at such a ghastly cost!
Who understands the Games' great shame?

Bodies grow old from weakened frames.
And once more, we pray for restoration.
Now, no longer bound by cruel chains,
We've found grace, ending humiliation.
Golgotha's pain fulfilled its aim.
Honor regained at unmeasurable cost!
We are remade. Messiah banished our shame.

She intended to sit down, but she remembered Arte's words at the end of the day at Julia Gordus. His humble words were wedged deep in her heart. He usually saw the house from inside, but upon the mountain, he gained a new perspective.

"I found it difficult to sing this song," she said. "I didn't want to, but Uncle Jonathan said I should share it with you. It's good to get a new point of view.

"I woke up last night and realized that my husband is working hard to keep people safe. I have found it liberating to put my beliefs into the words of a song. My husband is far away, and I love him, even though people may reject me for being married to a Roman. And some know that I'm raising an adopted child. Grace is not my own baby, but I love her as my own child, and I bless Adonai for the gift of this life.

"Shame doesn't have to hold anyone back. It's important to receive God's mercy, grace, and kindness, more than to seek other's favorable opinions. His compassion, love, and acceptance overcome feelings of dishonor. Learning to accept each other has been a healing moment for me during the eight days of Tabernacles. I identified with our forefathers in the desert. Now I realize that I'm fortunate to have new friends in this city."

As the group was leaving the house, many gathered around her. "So good to have you with us, Miriam" was a phrase she heard many times.

"I'm so glad you came to Thyatira," said Melpone, who had been listening to every word, "even if it means being away from your husband. See how selfish I am?"

The two women hugged, tears filling their eyes.

THE MILITARY GARRISON OF AIZANOI

Arriving the next day at Aizanoi, Anthony met two young legionaries born in Pontus and Bithynia province. They sat on the rough wooden bench in the dining room of the relay station's main building.

Anthony greeted them. "Hail! Where are you going? Where have you come from?"

"Earlier this year, we were going to join Legion XXI, the Predators, as engineers," the older one replied. "However, the battle was over before we finished our military training. Almost everyone in the legion perished, and that was a terrible defeat for Domitian. The general was planning to have a bridge built across the Danube River. We are no longer going to work on that project. Instead, a new bridge will be constructed a few miles east of Tarsus."

"The Predators! That was my legion—at least until a butcher reshaped my face."

"A nasty slice," observed the younger engineer. "Where does one get this kind of injury?"

"On patrol. Along the Neckar River. It was an ambush." Anthony leaned back, the event still sharp in his memory. His last nightmare had been more than a year ago, but he often relived that moment in his mind.

I'm slowly being healed, but the memory of the betrayal! I still can't remember my attacker's face, the soldier who walked behind me. I followed all the others going under the bridge. There was only one soldier behind me, the one who attacked me. Who was he? How was it possible that I was struck by one of our own soldiers?

The engineers mentioned the inquiry that Rome's officials were conducting and the investigation into why the defeat in Dacia had occurred.

"How did an entire legion get wiped out?" Anthony asked.

"Our army walked into a trap. Legion XXI was moving toward fortifications guarding the way to King Decebalus. The enemy separated several cohorts from the main force."

Anthony asked, "How could that happen?"

"At this point, from what we've learned, one cohort provided incorrect information. Scouts reported that a march up the valley was safe, but enemy troops were hiding behind a rocky outcrop. Our right flank was outsmarted, causing two tribunes to be separated from one another. Half the legion went ahead in the commotion, thinking it was safer up the valley and that they would regroup there. But around the bend, our 2,500 soldiers were surrounded and forced into another valley with higher cliffs. The other half stayed back. It was attacked and forced back to a narrow section under a volley of arrows. After they were pushed into a forest at the end of that valley, victory was impossible.[79] It was a

---

[79] Unlike other defeats of Roman legions, this battle is rarely described in ancient military history. Details given here are fictitious. I added them for

very clever maneuver on the part of that enemy army. What brings you to Aizanoi?"

"We are assigned to stop a series of robberies along the Postal Road. Our investigation led us to learn more about the main wealthy families in both Bithynia and Pontus. We don't know if any slaves were being trained in their properties before being shipped south. We're still looking but don't have any solid connection yet."

One of the legionaries raised his eyebrows when Anthony mentioned wealthy families in Bithynia. He said, "I know a lot about the five main families, where they live and their cities. The leaders of those families control the province's wealth: Julius Bassos, Varanus Rufus, Dio Coceceianus, Claudius Euonoppus, and the Apameci family. Together they dominate trade between Prusa, Nicaea, Nicomedia, Chalcedon, Sinop, and Trapezus.[80] I also believe that they probably aren't connected with any robberies. They would be too smart to do that."

"Why? You said they control the wealth, which means what?"

"There is great wealth in Pontus and Bithynia. Fertile lands and superb orchards yield plentiful harvests. Tall trees become masts and timber for ships, and there are many wild animals. The province is full of endless resources! Access to every resource that comes out of that province requires paying those families some sort of tribute, under the table and untaxed. They aren't interested in training slaves for further use by others."

Anthony listened carefully. Any new information, coming from anyone, might be useful.

---

continuity to *Never Enough Gold: A Chronicle of Sardis, Heartbeats of Courage, Book Two.*

[80] These five families dominated the social life of Bithynia and Pontus from AD 85–113. They were formally investigated by Pliny the Younger, who published hundreds of letters and mentioned his dealings with these families. Pliny the Younger's correspondence serves as one of the significant sources on Roman economic and legal affairs. The description of his persecution of Christians and their treatment in AD 112–113 is often quoted in history books.

Chapter 26
Conflicting Stories

THE CITY OF THYATIRA

The annual day of worship for Demeter and her daughter, Persephone, took place the next day in Thyatira. The Festival of Thesmophoria belonged exclusively to married women, and they would be away from their homes for a full day. The city pulsed with hushed excitement. All other festivals were dominated by men, but on this day, not a single man would step inside the Temple of Demeter. Women chatted with friends to catch up on events.[81]

The Greek legend related the abduction and rape of Persephone by the cruel god Hades. Her subsequent reappearance on the earth resonated with all. There was a mysterious pull to the story. It explained the reason for summer and winter, spring and fall.

Women did not need to debate who was the most important in a crowd, as men did when a procession was formed. Nor did mothers bring expensive sacrifices demanded by Zeus, Apollo, or Artemis. Theirs was a constant shared sacrifice, the gift of motherhood, of giving endlessly through long hours at night, and the unending and thankless tasks of keeping their homes.

It would be Danila's first time to participate in the Festival of Thesmophoria, and she wanted to learn everything. She knew she would not hear anything about it at the Ben Shelah home, so she decided to try the guild workshops.

"Can I come to the guild with you today?" Danila asked Miriam as an excuse to talk to Sibyl.

"Certainly, Danila. Let's go together."

Miriam went to the workshops looking for Melpone because she had seemed sad the day before, but she had not come to work

---

[81] A more complete description of the festival is found in *Through the Fire: A Chronicle of Pergamum.*

today. The two women looked around the workshop and heard Sibyl, who never tired of describing her trips across the Aegean Sea. She talked loudly in the back room, and women listened to Sibyl.

Sibyl noticed Miriam and Danila. "Are you both coming to the Festival of Thesmophoria? I'd love to sit with both of you and watch the drama unfold."

Miriam sidestepped Sibyl's query with a question of her own. "Sibyl, I've been curious to know your story. You seem to know everything about all the Greek and Roman gods and goddesses. Yet at the same time, you participate in the meetings about Messiah. Will you tell me about how you were brought up?"

"I'd love to tell you my story," said Sibyl, glancing around to see how many others were listening in, "but there isn't much to tell. My parents lived in Rome as children. My father was Jewish, and as an adult, he owned a shop. Mother came from an ancient family in Corinth. She wasn't Jewish but was influenced by followers of the Way. My parents were married at a tense time. Emperor Claudius faced riots, so he expelled Jews from Rome.

"Father left his shop and established himself in Corinth. They barely survived over the next few years, but I was born in Corinth, just as my father's new shop there began to flourish. He received permission to import purple cloth, and that made him wealthy.

"However, while in Corinth, my mother went back to her roots. Our family was split, father on one side, worshiping Adonai, and mother on the other, respecting Greek gods. She especially paid homage to Hera, the goddess of the home. Every day she made an offering, but my father wouldn't have any of it. They quarreled, and one day he left. I vowed to respect both parents and hold onto each one's beliefs. So did Hulda, my younger sister.

"Later, I married a man who was also interested in the Jewish Messiah. We came here, and I became a God-fearing person. Because of my father's association with purple dyes, my family relationship to Lydia in Philippi, and my connections in Corinth, the guild accepted me right away."

"Where is your husband?" Miriam asked.

The smile dropped from her face. "He lives in Pergamum." She said it with a finality that did not invite further questions about him. That part of her life was like a tightly rolled scroll with seals keeping it securely closed.

"You participate in the meetings at Uncle Jonathan's house, and you also go to the synagogue, where you sit in the portico," Miriam said as a matter of fact.

"Yes, I respect both sides of my upbringing. I believe in the Almighty, respecting the Law of Moses, and I enjoy Jonathan Ben Shelah's home meetings too."

"And you know a lot about the Temple of Artemis." Miriam touched on a subject she had been concerned about for weeks.

Her voice took on a slightly cautious tone. "I participate at the Temple of Artemis, but I don't think that a pinch of salt or small offering to Artemis actually means much."

"Do you participate in all forms of religion that you learned in your home? Your father taught you about Moses and David, and you can teach others about Abraham, Joseph, Isaiah, and Nehemiah. Your mother taught you about Demeter and Artemis, and you teach people about Apollo and Zeus. Is that right?"

"Completely! You summarized it well, Miriam! I don't want to exclude any part of who I am or what I was taught. I have different fragments inside. Some are shattered pieces, like shards of a broken pot. Others are like floor mosaics, good memories. I want to keep all the parts alive. I enjoy the tensions and contradictions."

She changed the topic. "Now, Miriam and Danila, will you be coming with me tomorrow to the Festival of Thesmophoria, or am I going to go alone?"

"I'm coming with you!" exclaimed Danila. "It's my first time. I'm a married woman now!"

"Well, I'm not going," said Miriam. "I don't believe Hades rules the underworld. And Danila, how can you go to that temple on our special day, on a Sabbath?"

Sibyl quickly broke in with "Danila, you'll learn the secrets of the underworld!"

Danila was increasingly animated about going to the festival.

Rebekah and Miriam put their heads together and puzzled over how to bridge the growing abyss. Two different worlds of thought were ready to collide under Jonathan's roof.

The next day, Danila left the house early, walking only a short distance. She joined Sibyl and thousands of other women at the Temple of Demeter.

All married women were welcome: rich and poor, slaves and

free. Greek-speaking women sat beside Latin-speaking mothers, and some grandmothers had not been out of the house for weeks until today. Caring for children left little time at the end of the day. On this day, women gathered as equals, as sisters and wives. Shared struggles and concerns bound them together.

Their clothing matched the season. Tunics dipped in light brown dye complimented the women's black hair. Women who had not seen each other all year enthusiastically shouted greetings, followed by a kiss on each cheek.

Everyone arrived with a sense of eagerness and anticipation, bringing a simple sacrifice. Their sacrifices included raisin cakes and date cakes. The high priestesses had purchased wagons full of pomegranates to be given out at the end of the evening. As they entered the temple grounds, they walked to the precinct's west end where a small temple was located. Women bowed as they carefully placed their sacrifices at the base of the Altar of Demeter. Gifts filled the space as more and more women arrived. The festival was a feast, a communion, and a revealing of hidden secrets.

For one brief day, they had left the world of men. The festival would finish with a celebration of torches in the night and erotic dances before leaving for home. During the day, the epic tale of Persephone's abduction would be acted out. Generally, women knew the words of the theatrical play by heart. The day marked the first introduction to the festival's secrets for Danila and other women recently married.

Opportunities for prayers came after offering sacrifices. Danila stood close to Sibyl, and both women bowed low, making their petitions. Danila had not yet experienced the many pains and trials of married life. She had brought her values from Laodicea and had joined the household of the Ben Shelah family. She was fortunate. Her father had said, "In Jonathan, you will find an open-minded merchant."

Danila's prayer was short and innocent. She wanted to be a good wife and a good mother. She loved her new husband and wanted Gil beside her for as long as she lived. She asked for children and intelligence to know how to relate to her mother-in-law because he knew that Rebekah was holding back in her affection.

Sibyl stood beside her and bowed low before the statue. Her prayer was personal, intense, for she carried many inner scars. Her prayer was partly an attempt to get what she wanted and partly a bargain to obtain Demeter's extra powers. She longed for the strength that would make her increasingly admired both in her guild and in her city.

Look in pity and kindness on me. I want a child so much. My husband is in Pergamum. He was so angry at me a year ago and walked out, saying, "You are not giving us children! You have disgraced my family's name!"

Demeter, you understand my grief! Your daughter was raped, and yet she returned from the realm of darkness. Look in kindness on me, and let my husband come back. If it's not a child you want to give me, then at least enable me to speak out, to speak in prophecies.

Heal Hulda from her bed of sickness! I promise to bring my best to you this year.

Don't let me be barren all my life, please, Demeter!

Every woman feared the winter months. Children became sick. Grandmothers, mothers, husbands, and children had already gone before them on their trip to meet Hades.

And none would return.

The beautiful Persephone would return in the spring, bringing back warm weather and the new crops. Her release cost everyone the winter months' darkness each year during her stay in Hades' dwelling place.

The sun was falling; winter was coming. And when she returned in the spring, life would return to the world.

Only women could learn the deep secrets of the Festival of Thesmophoria. Theirs was "hidden knowledge," kept from men, for they knew both the fear of death and the joy of giving life to the world.

Each woman received a pomegranate as a gift before returning home. Demeter promised them life after the coming winter season, and for this reason, their day was unique, unlike any other. Mysteries of day and night, spring and fall, summer and winter, were apparent to all who walked home shrouded in the evening's warm glow of fellowship.

HOME OF DELBIN, IN THE CITY OF SARDIS

Evening shadows fell over Sardis, and Diotrephes was once again writing to Lydia-Naq, his mother in Pergamum. Even if letters were insufficient for fully describing his victories, he was never tired of keeping in touch. After all, he owed her so much.

Diotrephes had met Mayor Tymon and his wife, Adriana. After a meal at their house, he found himself infatuated with their beautiful daughter, Cynthia. Instead of sharing his happy dreams about a future with the lovely young woman, he merely told his mother about the banquet.

Some secret hopes could not be shared yet.

Thinking back on the dinner two weeks earlier, he recalled Mayor Tymon referring to Diotrephes's speeches at the Lecture Hall of Karpos. After the toast, Tymon and Adriana, Cynthia's parents, clapped and cheered. The young lecturer from Pergamum was already making a distinct impression in Sardis.

The night was dark, and his lamp flickered while he prepared his thoughts. Diodotus, the banker, was at a meeting with his friends. Delbin, the matron in the home where he was renting a room, had gone to spend the day at the women's festival. Diotrephes was expecting Delbin to return at any moment.

October 18, in the 12th year of Domitian
From: Diotrephes, in Sardis
To: Mother, Lydia-Naq

Peace to you; if you are well, then I am well.

I was honored by Mayor Tymon for my series of talks at the Lecture Hall of Karpos. I think the mayor and his wife, Adriana, are pleased with my contributions to Sardis. I was given many kind words for recent lectures about our Lydian roots and current Sardian society.

I won't write a lot tonight. Delbin is at the Temple of Demeter, the same experience you are enjoying in Pergamum. She is kind and treats me as the son she lost during an illness in Sardis years ago. He was only a young boy when he died. Delbin serves good meals and supports my work.

I heard of a man with a large mark on his face. He was with a woman and a child boarding a ship to Alexandria Troas, on the Aegean. Here's good news. I may find this is Anthony and Miriam and our little girl, Chrysa. I hope to have our dark-eyed baby in Uncle Zoticos's arms soon. I'll learn if this was Anthony. If not, I'll keep searching.

I am teaching at the gymnasium. The year started off well with former teachers and a new one, who unfortunately does not have my former teacher's mental capacity. However, his instruction in the classroom is satisfactory.

Jace's concepts of his own abilities were too highly developed, and I found the man to be inflexible. He continues to bother me as he has started a school for poor boys. I sense a spirit of competition driving him.

I'll write again next week. Until then, your loving son.

Diotrephes held a stick of sealing wax over the small flame from the lamp. It dripped onto the edge of the scroll, and he carefully sealed the letter with his signet ring.

JONATHAN AND REBEKAH'S HOME

Danila returned home from the Temple of Demeter, now in on the powerful secret mysteries. From the drama, she understood why spring followed winter and why fall came before winter.

The next morning, Jonathan's home was ready for their weekly meeting and for the Holy Meal. After the guests had arrived and were settled, he read the Scriptures and made a few comments. They sang the words of several psalms.

With the Holy Meal over, Sibyl asked to give an announcement. She had done it many times before. Standing at the front of the large family room, she asked for prayers for her sister.

"Hulda always had trouble breathing, usually in the spring. However, this year, she has been continually sick. I'm going to host a special meal, not only for all of you but all the people from the Guild of Purple Honors."

Miriam asked, "When is this going to happen?"

"Next week, on Wednesday, the regular feast day of Artemis."

Jonathan wanted Miriam to stay quiet, but she ignored her uncle's hand gesture. "Many people believe that those statues have real powers. They commune with spirits."

Some people started to murmur, grateful that Miriam was speaking out this way. One person, who agreed with Miriam, had been disappointed in Jonathan for not voicing objections. Under his breath, he said, "This woman urges us to attend pagan temples."

Sibyl said, "No complaints please! All we want is health for those who are sick. I want my sister to be restored. I want you to know I pray to Adonai for Hulda as well. There's a special place, the mouth of a river in Macedonia, where I made a sacrifice for my sister. I know Adonai will heal her."

Nothing more was being said to challenge Sibyl, so Miriam decided to discuss it at the evening meal.

"Seriously, Uncle Jonathan! She thinks Yeshua Messiah is just another deity on the same level as any god worshiped in the city. She legitimizes the belief in many gods. Please, Uncle Jonathan, be careful about the influence she has in your home during the Way of Truth meetings."

Jonathan was surprised when the leaders of the synagogue came to his home the next evening. The warning Miriam had given him still rang in his ears.

Six elders arrived for a serious discussion. Kilan, as in the first visit, led the delegation. "Jonathan, our dear friend, people report to us about continued unacceptable teaching in your home. We warned you previously. We are surprised that you are not as zealous in keeping your home clear of false teaching as you are to keep the products from your guilds free from imperfection."

Kilan waited for a response, but Jonathan was not prepared to speak, so the synagogue leader finished his request. "Please listen to us. While Rabbi Hanani is away in Antioch, we can't make radical changes. He will have to decide after he returns, but we don't know how long that will be. We came to say that you are making it difficult for the other Jewish families in the congregation.

"Decades ago, when our ancestors came here, Jews were just a small community. They agreed with the city council to bring money and trade to the city. However, they would keep themselves separate from the ways of the Gentiles. Everyone agreed.

"Times have changed, and now we older Jews and these new God-fearers share the synagogue portico. We must tell you; we are finding it difficult to accept a violation of our laws. For instance, this Sibyl woman is spreading false teaching, attempting to combine our worship of the Creator with activities from the pagan temples.

"I learned today that Sibyl is trying to get your home assembly to participate in the sacrifices at the Temple of Artemis. Is this true? If so, she is leading believers in the wrong direction, as Jezebel did!"

Uncle Jonathan realized how serious the situation had become.

Queen Jezebel had been Israel's worst enemy! "I certainly don't agree with all that Sibyl says. She prays for the recuperation of sick people, as I do, and she is concerned for the well-being of people."

Unsatisfied with Jonathan's answer, Kilan realized he was being pushed aside. "This woman's concerns accept involvement with the temples, and we want no part of it. Our other issue is that you continue to teach about 'the carpenter' during your group meetings. If you continue to ignore our warnings, you will face sanctions by the elders."

The men continued the discussion with Jonathan and left shortly afterward. They had received no assurances of action by Jonathan. Sadly, they agreed among themselves that a mutually satisfactory resolution might not be found.

OLIVE GROVE FARM AT FORTY TREES

Nikias sat down at Olive Grove Farm with his three brothers to dictate sections of the scroll called Mark. He had returned from Stratonike the previous day, a small city about ten miles away. The four men lit clay lamps in the darkened room of the large house in Olive Grove.

Nikias and his brothers, Zeno, Alberto, and Lykaios, had been talking about farms. Each wanted to be a landowner instead of a sharecropper. Most farmworkers in Asia existed on sharecropping agreements. "Wages are not sufficient for people on farms along the road to Stratonike," Zeno observed. "They will always be in debt."

Nikias placed his copy of Mark's scroll on the table. "Let's stop talking about our debts for a moment. Instead, here's a new assignment. Jonathan gave us new papyrus scrolls! Let's see how much we can get done by the time we make our next visit to Stratonike."

A new sense of *esprit-de-corps* filled the room. Nikias began to dictate, saying a few words at a time. "The beginning…of the gospel …about Yeshua Messiah…the Son of God." Sometimes he had to repeat a phrase or spell out a word.

In his mind, Nikias was making new plans. *My brothers enjoy this immensely. Before, we used to sit around in the evenings, telling the same stories, the same stale jokes, but we'll soon have three copies of Mark's story, one for each of our cousins in Stratonike. After that, I want to go to Gelembe, Yortan, and Nakrasa. We have distant relatives in those villages too.*

JONATHAN AND REBEKAH'S HOME

Miriam went to the guild workshop for the third time in three days. Melpone, as in the previous two days, tried to push Miriam away. "I'm busy with these purple clothes. Let's talk later, Miriam."

"Melpone, you must take a break. I'll come again tomorrow at midday, and we can spend time together."

The next day, Miriam got her to agree to eat together. They sat together at a table under the colonnaded shade of the agora, but suddenly Melpone declared, "I'm not hungry today."

"Eat something! Here, have some freshly picked figs!"

The food was simple, and the opportunity to talk helped Melpone to relax. She spoke of the need for inner peace when she was doing her work. "I don't know why I've always been a person who gets bothered easily. I have such worries about the future, and then I can't concentrate."

Miriam wondered how she could reach across the gulf between her and Melpone. "Could someone work with you? Arpoxa is an excellent seamstress and does embroidery work. I'm sure she would enjoy working with you."

"Yes. I'd like a helper. I'd be willing to share my pay."

"Is something the matter that has you feeling so tense?"

"I've been worrying about lots of things bothering me. You know, I didn't enjoy singing in the theater chorus a month ago. The story seemed too much about killing. I've been in the choir for many years, and I'm tired of singing about all those fights: Hector against Ajax and Agamemnon wishing Nestor dead. Troy's history was tragic; I know that. However, this year, the story was repetitious. I ask myself, 'Will I always sing in the chorus and describe sad things?

"Since you started being my friend, I find myself questioning things. I'm becoming uneasy, restless, and unenthusiastic about my old life. I can't quite describe it in words."

Miriam said, "Tell me more about your name. Why don't you start with that? I didn't quite understand why your mother gave you such a name."

Melpone took several bits of her food and then moved to her seat's edge, her elbows on the table, her hands holding her jaw. "My mother, Zephyra, was a priestess at the Temple of Apollo. She had a particular role, dancing in a play, *The Wedding Feast of Apollo*.

"She thought about the nine Muses while she was pregnant with me. My aunt told me she was so happy to have a baby. She longed to hold me, to have her own little girl. Auntie told me, 'Your mother could only think of all the sweetness a baby could bring.' Mother thought of the Muses because she was a dancer. You don't know much about the Muses, do you?

"Let me tell you," Melpone said. "The Muses were superior spirits. Zeus, the father of the gods, married the Titan goddess Mnemosyne, or Memory. Memory had nine children, all girls, like some homes here! But Mnemosyne's children made too much noise; all spoke at once, getting in each other's way. The noise drove the other gods crazy! To solve the chaos, Zeus gave each daughter her own place in the family.

"Zeus placed them in the care of Apollo, who had them performing for Zeus for his frequent parties. Apollo straightened things out, giving each daughter a distinct gift. The first was Calliope, the author of poetry. She inspired *The Iliad*.

"The second was Clio; her forte was history, and she recited classical stories. Next came Polyhymnia, who specialized in pantomime. In the theater, she inspires stories without using words. Euterpe, the fourth, was the most beautiful; she was the essence of music. She always played the flute, enchanting all the gods on Mount Olympus.

"Fifth, Terpsichore danced all day long. Mother claimed that was her gift. Erato motivated all people with love poetry. Seventh, Melpomene, that's me, told tragic stories, and even the gods cried after listening to her. I'm named for her.

"Thalia, or comedy, came next. She was always laughing and was the most popular. In the theater, people love Thalia more than any other one. The ninth gift was given to Urania. She tells about our future in this world and in the next. People follow her in the stars and in the sky. Through her, they find prosperity."

Melpone paused while a waiter filled the bowl with more figs.

"When we sing or do anything at the temple or at the theater, it has to be with great expression. If we exercise our gift well, we get promoted. We must be beautiful. For example, Urania has to understand astronomy and interpret secrets for individuals, past and present.

"But I'll never be good enough. How can I be? I'm 'Tragedy'! What skills do I have to show others? I don't like making people cry when I'm singing in the chorus." She stopped speaking.

Miriam asked, "I've heard about the nine Muses. How did your mother decide to name you after Melpomene? Can you go over that part again? I want to understand better."

"Yes, my mother was expecting me in the year many people died of the fever. That plague was a real tragedy. Before I was born, Mother wanted to name me 'Euterpe' to honor the special abilities of music. She loved singing and dancing so much.

"However, the fever took her too. Before she died, she said, 'Her name will be Melpomene, Tragedy. My newborn faces a tragedy,' or 'brings a tragedy.' Something like that. Consequently, I live in fear. There's great power in the words people utter. And I have come to experience great misfortune."

Miriam spoke. "I'm so sorry. So sorry you carry this burden."

Melpone looked at her with wonder. "Really, are you sorry?"

A thought came to Miriam. Her uncle, Simon, in Sardis, was given to few words, but what he said often became a blessing. Also, her grandfather, Antipas, had prayed for people. His last words, even as flames rose from the fire that killed him, making it almost impossible to speak, had been of forgiveness and blessing.

Miriam explained, "Here is how I understand where the nine Muses came from. The Creator made the heavens, the earth, animals, and sea creatures. He made the stars too. Each has a name. Isaiah, a great writer in our past, said, 'He brings out the starry host one by one and calls them each by name. Because of his great power and mighty strength, not one of them is missing.'[82]

"Melpone, I bless you in the name of the Creator of our world. He knows your name, and he has a new name for you. It's not the one your mother chose, the one that makes you feel afraid. Adonai has a plan for you, plans for peace, not evil. Before you even call on his name, he has heard your heart's desire. I bless you, Melpone. You are going to live in the light, not in darkness."[83]

Melpone blinked back sudden tears. "I have to return to the workshop," she said, rising slowly, reluctantly. They talked for a few more minutes. She had spent much longer away from the workshop than she intended to.

Miriam wondered. *Something is bothering her. What is it?*

---

[82] Isaiah 40:26
[83] From Jeremiah 29:11

238

Chapter 27
Gaining Insight

ON THE POSTAL ROAD FROM SOMA TO AIZANOI

Anthony and Ateas traveled the Postal Road northward, taking eleven days on the way to Aizanoi. During the trip, Anthony talked with villagers and then made Aizanoi his base for several days.

Backtracking a bit and going south from Aizanoi, they stopped at a minor side road, one they had not explored before. Ateas and several soldiers assigned to him by the Aizanoi garrison rode toward a mountain ridge four miles away.

The rough track led to four small villages. When they entered Dark Night Village, the first village, Anthony asked to see the head man for questioning, and a shepherd went to one of the mud-brick homes to bring him to them.

An old man, bent over from years of standing in the fields watching over his sheep, eventually came out with a puzzled look and stood before them, leaning on his shepherd's staff.

Anthony said, "Thank you for coming out to see us. I'm sorry if this is a disturbance to your village. We are looking for information regarding criminal activity on the Postal Road. We want it to be safe for your people to travel. Did you receive visits from anyone unusual during the last three months, anything remarkable?"

After a brief discussion with one of the other shepherds, the man answered, "Yes, we had a visit from six soldiers about two moons ago. They wanted to leave wild animals here, and they paid us to take care of them."

A small crowd had gathered, and everyone was interested in the conversation. "What kind of wild animals did they leave here?"

"They left a bear in our village. Wild boars were brought in secure cages to other villages."

"What reason did they give for leaving them with you?"

"They said the authorities had to figure out what to do with them, but they were probably going to be sent to Rome."

"Did you see any slaves with them?" Anthony asked.

239

"No slaves. Recently, they came to take the animals and pay us for the work. One said their commander wanted to send animals to Rome for the circus."

"Describe the men. What did they look like?"

"What do soldiers look like? You all look the same! The only different one with you is that man, the one sitting in the wagon. He is from the north. I can tell from his yellow hair and long, thin nose!"

"Did you get any names of these men?"

"Only one name. It was strange but easy to remember: Tira."

Anthony made his way back to the Postal Road. The number, six soldiers, was the same as when Quintus Zosimus was killed and the same as the report from Aizanoi in the evening of July 23. He scratched his scar, thinking. *Tira. Wild animals. "Animals to Rome for the circus" sounds crazy. They would have to ship by sea, and they wouldn't have a representative in Rome. But they must sell them somewhere.*

This was new information. The next day, Anthony sent a short report to be passed on to each post house, telling them to be on the lookout for wild animals being transported.

"The animals were supposedly being sent to Rome, to the circus. These are certainly the marauders we are looking for. We are on their trail."

Two days later, he wrote a short note to Felicior and Servius from Aizanoi.

October 22, in the 12th year of Domitian
From: Anthony Suros, in Aizanoi
To: Commander Felicior, Sardis Garrison, and Commander Servius, Soma Garrison

If you are well, then I am well.
We have evidence that in addition to slaves, the rebels are transporting wild animals. They may have been going to the circus in Rome. Animals provide a high financial return on a daring, dangerous venture. Eight miles south of Aizanoi, we followed a little-used trail off the Postal Road to four small villages. We found that the fake soldiers had stored the animals there.
Sextilius and Menandro are sure that the attackers

transporting wild animals are the same as those carrying slaves earlier this year. Records from Prusa to Aizanoi agree.

Commander Diogenes became agitated when we showed him this proof. He said, "Something must have happened to upset their initial plan. We could not trace them after they left Aizanoi."

The villagers informed us that six soldiers paid them to take care of wild animals: a bear and wild boars. Checking the relay station records on our way to Soma, we discovered that wild animals were transported by soldiers through the relay stations and inns on the way to Sardis. The records indicate that their return to the village to take the animals happened on September 21.

You must see if wild animals appeared in the Games at Sardis or the Games in Thyatira. If not, then the animals may be intended for Rome.

Ships leaving for Rome stopped sailing in late September, so I think the animals are still in the province.

When asked for descriptions, the villagers said, "They were Roman soldiers." Sextilius is probably right with his guess that we are searching for six deserters from the army.

I am traveling slowly with Ateas along the Postal Road and have found only this one spot where they stored their cargo. Still, they may have other places where they have concealed their "treasures." We will continue our search farther off the Postal Road now.

JONATHAN AND REBEKAH'S HOME

While Anthony was writing his letter, Rebekah approached her niece. She realized that Miriam was feeling increasingly distant from Jonathan. "My dear, tell me what you liked most in Sardis when you stayed with Simon and Judith."

"Strange as it may seem, I enjoyed visiting people in their homes." Miriam began to tell details of individuals and families who had become her friends. "I went to the insulae, and the conditions in those crowded homes are terrible! I made up a song for them too, just before I left Sardis."

Rebekah had wanted to visit an old man who came every week to their home on Sunday mornings, and now she had someone who might go with her.

"Well," said Rebekah, "we certainly have those places here also. I know an area to start where we can go safely, but let's go together and see what's there! We should go after the synagogue services on the Sabbath."

On Saturday afternoon, Miriam and Rebekah visited the old man who attended Jonathan's home meetings. They took him food and were surprised to learn he had a wife his age. She was sick in bed. He had never mentioned her, but both showed signs of malnutrition. Their tiny apartment was on the second floor of a poorly constructed building.

"I hope you take care when climbing those dangerous steps," Miriam said with a chuckle.

The old man responded, "Oh, I do! It's not so dangerous now, but in the winter, the rain makes them slippery. The road between the buildings is even worse and smelly besides!"

"And you had children," Rebekah remarked. "You told us so."

"We did, but they died in the last plague—five children between the ages of six and fifteen."

"I'm so sorry to hear that. Do you have a job?"

"I clean the marketplace each day after the sun goes down, collecting scraps of food, and the marketplace owners pay me a small wage, which helps buy the other things we need."

As they left, he said, "I'll break bread and drink the wine at your home, Rebekah, and partake of the Holy Meal until I die. Then, first thing when I get to heaven, I will do the same. I want to break bread and drink wine at the Lamb's marriage supper, the one Jonathan keeps talking about!"

They visited another family where eight people had hardly any food. "They are worse off than the old couple," Miriam said. "Six young children with little to eat. They can't study at the gymnasium, and without some education, they may never get a chance to find an apprenticeship."

One of the men who oversaw production in the guild workshop had mentioned to Rebekah that his house was not cleaned the previous week. The woman that did it for him had not come, and he was concerned for her health. Rebekah knew roughly where the woman lived, and they were able to find her apartment.

The woman was still sick in bed but recovering and in need of food. They brought flatbread and some fruit for her before returning to the Ben Shelah home. Miriam had offered a short prayer of blessing in each of the three houses.

That evening, as she thought about the people they had seen, compassion began to grow in Miriam for Thyatira's poor people. *I'm worried about myself, asking what I should do, but how many live in Thyatira with only bread for today and none for tomorrow? "God, who provides upon the mountain," you provided a ram for Abraham in the time of his major test. Provide for the three homes we visited today.*

Two days later, a young woman was brought to their attention. She came from Philadelphia, southeast of Thyatira. Rebekah heard about her through salesladies in the family shop. "A young woman is expecting a baby. She was talking with the servants who run our shop. 'I don't want to keep my baby!' she said."

Miriam gasped, remembering how Grace had come to her home, an unwanted child placed at the edge of Pergamum's trash heap.

"What do you think should be done, Auntie?"

"Well, she does not want to keep the baby, probably because she has no place to stay and no way to support a baby. Her family pushed her out of their home. They didn't like her running around with a much older man and shouted, 'You can come home after you deliver the baby! But don't come back with that man's child!' She then found out that the man didn't want to marry her."

They talked it over at suppertime. "Uncle Jonathan, what would you think of this idea? Could the young woman expecting the baby help that old couple, you know, the old man who comes here? His wife is sick and needs care. Poor couple, they lost all their children during a plague. Anyway, this young woman could stay there and look after them a bit for the next five months of her pregnancy. We could pay her a little bit for the work she does for them. They would have company and the joy of a younger person in their home. The old woman never gets out at all. What do you think? After the baby is born, she can keep it or let someone adopt it."

"How much do you think that would cost?" he said quietly.

"Well, the Ben Shelah family would only provide her enough money for clothes for winter and for bread, vegetables, and fruit," Miriam suggested.

"Do you think we could afford it, my dear?" His question was directed to Rebekah.

"Oh, yes, Jonathan! And I think the Ben Shelah family will be much richer for helping this young woman!" Rebekah's compassion was like smoldering coals on the hearth at dawn, waiting to be brought back to a flame. She had been touched by Miriam's responsiveness to the poor people they had visited.

Rebekah put her hand on her husband's arm, saying, "The young woman expecting a baby needs support. She made a mistake, a bad decision. The old couple suffered the loss of all their children in the last fever plague. Is anyone older and more faithful at the Way of Truth? You don't seem to lack when it comes to supporting the guild, and we are making good income from your businesses. Olive Grove Farm and the madder root sales to the guild this fall will bring even more. Yes, I think doing this would make the Ben Shelah family richer. We should help this young lady!"

Realizing that she had discovered a strong streak of compassion in her aunt, Miriam decided to speak more openly about her yearning to help unfortunate people. She thought about how much it meant for her daughter to have a loving home. What if Grace had not been found? What if she had died there at the edge of the trash dump? She shuddered, unable to put the thought out of her mind.

Miriam tried to imagine the feelings of a young woman expecting a baby. *What did she think would happen to her when she came from Philadelphia? How did she come to Thyatira? Perhaps on a farm wagon taking goods from one city to another as I did four months ago? A pregnant young woman arrived with no friends to greet her, and at the first opportunity, in Jonathan's shop, she asked for help. She must have spoken with great fear, trying to control herself and afraid of what might happen next.*

On Sunday morning, after the Way of Truth meeting, when the last guest had left their home, Miriam asked for a moment with her uncle and aunt. "May I talk with both of you?"

Jonathan nodded, and Rebekah smiled.

"When I lived in Sardis, I found that Uncle Simon was full of zeal for the Lord, but he didn't know how to put God's love into action. He had a tough time expressing his feelings about God and his duty to others. This struggle caused lots of pain.

"His son-in-law, Ravid, rejected the idea of doing anything for Gentiles. We had many difficult moments until he left to return to Smyrna with his wife. Ravid did not like Uncle Simon keeping non-

Jews in his house. He finally left Sardis when Uncle Simon became openhearted toward the poor.

"Being kind transforms some things, but it does not make life any easier. If anything, it complicates things enormously. The problems of poor people can become ours to willingly solve. That's what happened in Sardis last year.

"I want to know what you think of my idea. Some money is coming to me from my great-grandfather's will. Much of it is being used to support the projects in Sardis. I met poor people there: blind men, people wounded at their jobs, widows, and children."

"Yes, we know you have a tender spot for poor people," Jonathan said with a smile, and Rebekah squeezed his hand.

"Blind people can do some things to earn wages. Lame men and poor families too, if jobs are made available. They learned some skills, and when they started to earn their own money, they were working for Uncle Simon.

"He sold their products at his store and even sent some to you and your brothers, and now he's making more money than he is paying out to support the poor families. Best of all, those families now have a steady income. They want to know about Adonai and why the Ben Shelah family is showing kindness.

"I know this is a long speech, Uncle, but I have to tell you how we accomplished all that in Sardis. We found broken-down workshops, rented them, fixed them up, and found floor looms for weavers. We had help from Jace, a teacher fired by the director of history at the gymnasium. Jace taught for many years, and we put him to work supervising the workshops and teaching the poor children."

Jonathan held up the palm of his hand. "I can see it now. You are planning to rent workshops here! You want me to invest in something new! 'Come and invest in Miriam's Guild, the newest guild in town!' You won't get rich though. Your guild is being created to give away money. All the others exist to make profits."

The remark was humorous, but these few words exposed his worst fears. His humor carried a sharp, unwelcome edge.

She ignored his irony. "I'm not suggesting you do what Uncle Simon did, but I have an idea since you are so sociable. Families need help and are willing to learn a trade if it puts food on the table. I know you think that everyone is supposed to work in a guild.

"Aunt Rebekah and I went out into the insulae and visited three homes. Each family is poor, and there is no way they can earn a proper livelihood. They don't have the skills needed to work in a guild. Somehow they need some way to be trained so that they are eligible for guild work."

Miriam didn't know what it meant when Jonathan had this stern look on his face, so she said, "Tell me, do you want to keep talking about this idea? If you want me to stop, I will."

"Keep going. I want to hear all you have to say." Her genuine concern helped him put aside his previous reservations. He asked questions, and she gave examples of what his brother, Simon, had done in Sardis.

"My child, I like it when you talk like this. Please tell us what brought about these feelings for the poor people."

She answered, "When Melpone told me about her life, a terrible thought came upon me. She says that her name means 'tragedy.' Her father died before she was born. Three days after she was born, her mother died, so she never knew either one. Her brother was killed when repairing the walls of Thyatira. A massive stone fell out of the sling, crushing him.

"Uncle Jonathan, do you think Melpone feels grief the same way that I do? I lost my mother when I was young and grew up without her beside me. Many people carry grief deep inside. They carry a burden of thoughts, fears, and memories that they have never told to anyone. Those burdens paralyze them, and they aren't able to think of anything but their misery."

Aunt Rebekah moved to the end of the couch and beckoned to Miriam. "Come here, my daughter, and sit with me."

Miriam looked at her aunt. Rebekah had tears in her eyes, and her hand on Miriam's wrist was quivering. "I've never heard anyone say things like this before. I knew that you had something of your grandfather in you, but I can see that you have his heart, his determination, and his vision too. Miriam, I'm thankful that God sent you to our home.

"We lost three of our little boys in Alexandria, so I know what you mean when you talk of grief." Her voice quivered. "My Adin was seven years old. Obed was only five, and Jehiel had his third birthday three months before that dreadful pogrom. There's not a day that I don't remember their little faces. Adin would run into the house to show me a frog and come back to show me a different colored stone from the street. I still hold their little sayings and endearing expressions in my heart. We suffered greatly, and we need to comfort others and be comforted."

Rebekah looked at her husband. He placed his hand on Miriam's shoulder. He nodded, and Rebekah took it as a signal to keep talking. "This is your home, my child, for as long as you want. We do not know why Adonai led you to accept a man that we would always have thought of as an enemy. He is a Roman, a soldier, and your husband. But you are like our daughter. This is your home, and he is welcome to come here."

At breakfast the next morning, Miriam relaxed seeing Jonathan and Rebekah's smiles. Rebekah talked more openly than before. "I think we both see something fresh and spontaneous in you, Miriam. We talked about you for a long time when we went to bed last night. We discussed your idea about helping the young woman who has no home, who wants to give up her baby.

"The ways of God are sometimes mysterious. Why did our three lovely boys die at the hands of others in Alexandria? We never worshiped foreign gods. We wanted to go to Jerusalem to have a bigger part in the covenant. Why did those calamities come upon us? Were we disobedient? I've searched my heart for years over these questions."

In the invigorating autumn air blowing through the house, having Jonathan on one side and Rebekah on the other, Miriam felt warmed. Even if she did not agree with so much of Jonathan's associations in the guilds, she felt loved and accepted.

"We'll never know why the Lord permitted our beloved city to be destroyed," Rebekah continued, "or why he let it be destroyed a second time. Perhaps we'll never stop asking. Women and children died. Screams from the Holy City are remembered twenty-two years later. Silent cries for help go up daily in this city, but you have opened a new window. You are helping us to look beyond ourselves. How often do we hear the cries of families for help? But Adonai hears them all the time."

Miriam looked at Rebekah and then at Jonathan. *Has God answered my prayers? Is this the open door that I prayed for?*

"What do you want to do, child? What is your proposal?" asked Jonathan.

"I thought that we could plan small meals on some evenings. Maybe others, not only Melpone, feel 'tragedy' is not just a word used in the theater. What if one of them finds that they are not merely a spectator to a tragedy but a participant?"

Aunt Rebekah's eyes filled with tears, which began to spill over onto her cheeks. "God bless you, my daughter. You are a true daughter of the Ben Shelah family. But here's a warning from an old lady who has seen the death of three sons.

"When you learn the pain of others, it brings more pain yet. Comforting people will mean you also have to be comforted at some point. As God said through the prophet Isaiah, 'Comfort my people.'[84] Yes, bring people here for special meals. One request though. Before they come, let me know!"

After Jonathan and Rebekah informed the household about Miriam's plans to help the poor and pray for the sick in the community, Arte prepared a special evening meal. Jonathan told everyone to come for a family conference.

During the meal, Rebekah and Miriam gently touched on the initial thoughts of what the family might do to encourage the poor and find ways to improve their future.

As the food was being cleared away, Rebekah cleared her throat. "Jonathan, my dear, we don't usually have women praying at a family gathering, but this is one day we need Miriam's prayer for our home."

He stood and asked everyone to form a large circle. Jonathan prayed, "King of the Universe, blessed be your name, for this food is the fruit of the earth you have provided to us. For all your blessings, we praise your name."

Jonathan looked up and addressed the family, "We want to close off the last Sunday evening in October with a prayer. We are concerned about the health of several sick people at the Guild of Purple Honors and Bronzesmiths' Guild. Miriam, please close this time with a prayer for our home."

Miriam stood and pulled her prayer shawl over her head. She gave Grace to Rebekah so that her child would not distract her. Women pulled their prayer shawls tightly around their hair.

She spoke passionately from her heart. "What can I say, O Lord? The Holy City lies in ruins! You saved me there from famine and destruction. But so few of us were saved! Even so, we praise you.

---

[84] Isaiah 40:1

To say even this much is a sacrifice. And here in Thyatira, we are few in number. We are also divided. Some have different beliefs about Yeshua Messiah, while others are against us for being Jews. We are a small flock, and you have told us to be a light to those around us. Strengthen and encourage us to show others who you are by what we do and say each day.

"O God, you are in this city; you know the hearts of the people. You know the sins of their forefathers. Fill the spiritual emptiness. Remove the hurt in their souls. Open the unseeing eyes of people who live from one festival to another, always hoping for satisfaction. Your grace is sufficient for this. You promised that men would see visions and young men would once again have dreams. Open their eyes! May they respond in faith.

"Lord of Hosts, may your word go forth! Let tears soften hearts. Let streams of mercy flow like water! Let people run to these streams and rejoice just as people would when they come to an oasis in the desert! Forgive their sins and bring repentance. Reveal yourself through dreams. Look in mercy on children who are fainting. Heal those whose wounds are not visible. Show us the truth through the honesty of children, not through the false wisdom of men who seek to create their own world.

"Lord, energize us to look beyond our own selfish needs so that we will desire to help others. Show us how to be available for those in need of our love and care so that they will not continue to accept life in failure and darkness. Empower us with your Spirit that we may be effective to lead those who don't know you into your light and into a better life for themselves and their families."

Miriam stopped for a moment. She had never prayed in public like this before. For a moment, she forgot about the others around her. Her prayers had always been whispered in the quietness of her own heart. Sometimes she spoke with a humble family in their home, but now perspiration dripped down her back and heat flowed down her arms. The room was silent.

"I pray this in the name of Yeshua, our Messiah."

Uncle Jonathan wiped his eyes and made a quick exit. Grace started to speak, saying, "Mama, pray, Mama?" Everyone laughed nervously, responding as much to Miriam as to Grace, whose arms were outstretched to her mother.

Jonathan came back a few minutes later. His eyes were red.

She prayed silently for him. Uncle Jonathan showed so few of the qualities she had seen in her grandfather in Pergamum. *Uncle Jonathan doesn't have the conviction I saw in Uncle Simon, but while we were in Sardis, Uncle Simon did change. He became a strong leader. I bless you to understand yourself, Uncle Jonathan.*

Beneath your bubbly exterior, you are anxious and fear rejection. You do anything to keep people from talking against you or rejecting you. You do it even to the point of compromising your faith. Going against your convictions, you still visit temples, participating in their activities, eating at their thermopolia. Oh, I pray that you'll see and understand who you really are!

ON THE INTERIOR ROAD FROM PRUSA TO PORSUK CANYON

Seven days had passed since Anthony had written to Commander Felicior in Sardis and Commander Servius at Soma. Together with Sextilius, Bellinus, and Capito, he and Ateas entered many villages between Aizanoi and Inegol. Still, they found nothing else to help in their search.

Earlier, Anthony had been convinced that fast communication using fresh horses was best. However, that yielded few concrete results, so he had changed his approach, moving slowly and more deliberately. That was how he had learned about the wild animals in the villages.

Anthony wished they could move faster. *I'm too impatient. All my life, I've prided myself on being a good scout. Yet these assailants—I haven't found a single one! Four months later and not a single arrest!*

Anthony still had no answers. He imagined the next report he would write: "Sextilius recreated the criminals' steps from the army records, from when they left Port Daskyleion and through each army checkpoint along the way. Where did they go after selling the forty-two slaves? Is someone forging documents for them? Are there corrupt officials in Aizanoi doing that? If not in Aizanoi, where? Well, we have a starting point. They brought the slaves into the province through that small harbor in Port Daskyleion."

After leaving Aizanoi and riding beside a caravan of camels loaded with merchandise, Anthony and Ateas arrived at the point where the Porsuk River flowed through the canyon. He stood on the road, looking up. Cliffs rose high on either side.

To the west, the landscape opened into a broad valley with open fields and plains. Those distant, partially forested mountains were the source of the Porsuk River.

He turned his head toward the east, looking up to the cliffs' sharp edges. The cliffs gradually closed in, the opposite sides almost touching where the Interior Road met the Postal Road. Ahead was the bridge, where the river curved sharply to the south. That was where the Interior Road crossed the river.

Down here, the bends in the river formed two double "S" shapes, and the Postal Road followed the riverbank exactly.

The three bodies had been dumped into the well at the derelict building. The river collided against steep canyon walls, and there were only two ways out of the canyon—going to the east or to the west. No one could climb the cliffs.

Having ascended from the river valley, Anthony stopped at a tiny village near the intersection. Not far from the road, a shepherd stood on one leg, watching not more than ten sheep. They had passed here before, and the previous searches of the shepherds' houses had not yielded any helpful information.

Smiling, Anthony walked over to the shepherd. "I want to speak to the head man of this village."

"That's my father. I'll get him immediately."

After a while, an older man approached them, his eyes big and round. He kept wiping his hands as if worried.

"I need to talk to you about something special," Anthony said. "What is the name of your village?"

"We call it Five Shepherds' Village."

"Why did you give it this name?"

"This rocky land supports very few sheep. We take our animals to pasture in different directions, and no more than five families can live here. We are poor villagers."

"You have been informed of the robberies along this road, especially the last one about three months ago. Four innocent men were killed, and we are determined to put an end to the gang that did this."

The man squinted. His skin was bronze, darkened by summer days spent standing in the hot sun. Anthony's comments were met with silence. The man's son stood close by with a thin staff in his hand and a blank look on his face.

"Have you seen anything to cause alarm?"

Both men shook their heads.

"Did other groups of soldiers stop here to talk with you?"

Again the negative answer. "Only soldiers asking about the four murders."

"No merchants have visited you?"

The same answer with the shaking of their heads.

"Were you ever asked to let camels, horses, donkeys, or wild animals stay here? Have you seen a man who doesn't speak our language? We are searching for a man who was going to be sold as a slave."

A blank stare met the questions.

"Do you ever take your sheep to pasture along the river over there?" Anthony pointed to the abandoned buildings and the pastureland toward the river's headwaters.

"Yes, of course. We take our sheep down there."

"Did you see anything unusual about three months ago?"

Again the blank face.

"When did your family move here?"

"We came many years ago from Stratonike. We settled here."

Anthony asked a crucial question. "Have you talked with a runaway slave? We believe that he escaped from a caravan. He may know something about the murders."

Another blank stare was all Anthony received.

"Bandits do cruel things to shepherds. If anyone bothers you, let the guards at White Horse Relay Station know."

"Pan is our god. He protects shepherds."

Anthony could tell that the head man was evasive. Still, it would not be useful to accuse him of lying, so he simply asked permission to look around. Ateas waited on his horse beside the road.

Grass grew on the hill in spring, but now it was brown and dry. The shepherds' village occupied a slight incline at the top of the cliffs. It sloped gradually down, and then the precipice fell straight down to Porsuk River almost 200 feet below.

The village was composed of six huts. Low scrub brush grew all around with bushes growing close together. Stones were piled into low fences to prevent the sheep from wandering into the brush or falling over the cliff. A well-worn trail was formed where sheep walked between their pasture and a series of small caves east of the village. The head man explained that in winter, the shepherds kept their sheep in the caves, protecting them from cold winds.

Anthony walked to the cliff and cautiously looked over the edge down to the river. *No one, certainly not a slave, could climb up this steep cliff.* He walked back to the narrow trail and bent down at the first cave. "What a stench!"

"We keep sheep there only in winter. The rest of the year, we use those round sheep pens." The sheep pens, clustered on the hill, were built with low walls of stacked stones. The roof of intertwined branches and thatch was supported by a tall center pole.

Gusts of wind blew through the brush. Anthony looked around, knowing something was missing. Beyond that, only silence. In every other village he had visited, children raced to talk with him. They always reached up to touch his helmet; little fingers traced the smooth curve of his breastplate. Boys would ask to wear his helmet and wanted to hold his sword. *This valley is home only to sheep and shepherds but no children. Where are the women?*

"Where are your children?"

The shepherd maintained his steady, blank look. "They are away with the sheep in another pasture. This is the dry time of the year."

No bandits. No children. No women and no sheep.

Anthony clenched his jaw. "Well, everything looks okay here," he pronounced, knowing that he had to return. "Ateas, let's catch up to the caravan."

"If all is well, why strange look is on your face?" Ateas asked as they were leaving the village.

"I didn't want to alert those men about my suspicions." *They let me look inside each of the six huts. I went into some caves. What a stench! But no indication of that second slave. Something happened to that second slave! Something is not right in that village!*

THE MILITARY GARRISON IN PRUSA

Anthony and his team came together in Prusa. Sextilius summarized their findings to date. "Apparently, not everyone from Legion XXI was killed. There is evidence that one cohort of about fifty men deserted after the victory was won by King Decebalus. The report lists them as 'missing but not killed.'

"I believe some of those men were recruited by Craga, or Taba, or someone else with armor and uniforms. The army's report doesn't declare them to be deserters, just that they are missing. However, in Chalcedon, one soldier reported a rebel approaching him and asking strange questions. The next day, that soldier was found dead."

Anthony rubbed his face, feeling the scar under his right eye. *After discovering those three malcontents and reporting them to my general, I was ambushed and left for dead. Why does my attacker's face still elude me?*

The camp had received a report: "Barbarian fighters have been spotted coming down to the Neckar River from the forest. Someone saw one of them hiding under the bridge." I was sent out with a small group of other scouts to investigate.

Then, as we were inspecting the space under the bridge, I saw the pattern of light changing behind me. I feared a barbarian was coming after me. My head twisted around as a blade cut into the side of my head. I remember thrusting my sword into a man's lower leg. I collapsed. I don't remember anything else.

His nightmare was happening again, but it was midmorning, and he was awake...while talking with friends.

He pulled back instinctively, as if the unknown aggressor were beside him. He turned his face up and away, and he felt his face being torn in two once again. Thoughts tumbled over each other as he tried to bring himself back to the moment. He rubbed his face again, remembering his long, agonizing recovery.

"Are you listening? Look, everyone, he hears bird calls!"

"Give Anthony his due, Sextilius," responded Bellinus. "He's a married man thinking about being back at home. What is her name again, Anthony? Look! He is stroking his face! He's dreaming of being welcomed back into her arms."

Bellinus had a special touch in his humor. The others laughed.

"No, not about my wife, but yes, I'm thinking. Who might the leader of these killers be? It is a large gang, an unusual one. Could anyone in the Predators have become a traitor? If I met them, would I know any of them? After all, I was in Legion XXI."

Capito was beginning to lose his patience. He enjoyed competitions and played strategy games in his leisure time to keep his mind sharp. These long days without results were grinding him down. "Well, Anthony, what did you find? It took you a long time to travel the roads, but you have proved only one thing so far. You can march as slowly as any merchant."

His sarcasm was not lost on the others.

Capito reached for a darker criticism. "It's time for Anthony to describe his travels, enjoying only hills, rivers, and valleys. Has our Scythian man been of any help?"

Anthony sensed discontentment coming over his team. They had nothing to show for their efforts. Both Capito and Omerod had objected strongly to his idea of bringing a Scythian into their small group of experienced soldiers.

"I told you I was going to take a slow trip, traveling with a caravan. I've been along that road several times and explored the villages along the way. I have found only one new possibility.

"I'm convinced the men at Five Shepherds' Village know something. I talked to the head man, but he was noncommittal. He says only a few families live there. And he seemed afraid. Why? Also, there were no women or children! What would cause women and children to leave their families? I'm going to go back there with Ateas to clear up that little mystery."

Menandro was growing weary of only searching through records from horse relay stations. "What will you do? Wring their necks and ask them to spit the aggressors out?"

Decisive action, the death penalty, and justice for victims—those would satisfy Menandro. He added, "If all the people in Pompeii had acted this slowly, no one would have escaped the volcano's deadly ash and embers.[85] I'm for action, and this slow pace is getting to me."

Anthony scratched his head, thinking, *Lord God, please show us what we should do! Insurrectionists are terrorizing this region, and these men are beginning to question my leadership.*

Anthony said calmly, "I feel just as impatient as you do, and I, too, am anxious to get this over with, to bring these attackers to justice. I have an idea. It might work, but it might fail too. Four months ago, I left my wife behind. The day we joined up together, we were at the inn in Apollonius.

"Do you remember Xenophon, that strange innkeeper, the old man who can't hear a thing and who gets everything wrong? He wanted to teach me how to replace wagon wheels, to show me the

---

[85] Pompeii and Herculaneum, two cities in southwestern Italy, were buried under volcanic ash in late summer AD 79. Menandro is an imaginary descendant of one of the families that suffered complete destruction, based on Casa del Menandro, one of hundreds of homes excavated in Pompeii.

weakest part of a wagon axle and how to mend things.

"I want to plan an intentional accident. We would be in a wagon and have it break down close to their village. Ateas and I would 'make' them give us hospitality. I think three weeks from now will be about the right time because bandits won't come out of their hiding places during winter. I want to be at the village long enough for a more thorough search."

Omerod was against part of Anthony's plan. "I think we should all go with you. What if those humble shepherds are not really harmless?"

"You need us!" Omerod dreamed of doing something heroic.

"No, I want to take the Gideon approach. The fewer men, the better."

"Who was Gideon? What kind of nonsense are you talking about? You want fewer soldiers?"

"Gideon was a successful general against invaders long ago, but I'm not going to tell you about him or his strategies."

Anthony's companions wondered if traveling slowly with caravans was beginning to affect his thinking. He was saying strange things, talking about bizarre strategies.

Omerod objected, "Anthony, don't be stubborn! Let the others go to Soma, Sardis, and Karun. They need to work on the remaining checkpoint records. But when you and Ateas go to Porsuk Canyon, Menandro and I want to be with you. No arguments please!"

"All right," agreed Anthony. "I hate to give in to you, but maybe just this once. We'll go there after the caravans have stopped for the winter but before any severe winter storms start. I do not want to get stuck on the Interior Road in a snowstorm.

"Now, I've been thinking. What was the last date of the rebels' activities? September 21. They were picking up their stored wild animals from four villages at that time, and then they disappeared after check station lists showed them heading toward Sardis. Since then, no sign of them. Why haven't we heard of another robbery? I think that since sailing has ended, they have no more source of slaves, and all they can do until next spring is get those animals sold."

Sextilius added another comment. "If they thought this year was successful, they must already be planning to set up more caravans with lots of slaves." No one said anything more.

Chapter 28
The Invitation

JONATHAN AND REBEKAH'S HOME

Jonathan and Rebekah talked late into the evening, discussing plans for hosting meals in their home. The question was about the number of people they would prepare for. Rebekah decided, "We'll serve nine guests."

The next morning, Jonathan sent invitations to several young women at the Purple Guild. Two days later, as the sun was setting below the horizon, the room began to fill with animated voices.

Melpone introduced the young women she worked with one by one. "These are my friends from the guild: Adelpha, Dreama, Hesper, Koren, Calandra, Neoma, Celina, and Hypatia."

Melpone was the only one at the banquet whom Miriam had spent time with, but Jonathan knew their names, although nothing about their personal lives. However, Gil and Danila had shared a festival meal with them at the temple. Miriam soon learned they were interested in music and dance.

Platters of food were placed on small tables, and the guests were invited to fill their bowls. Some reclined on couches. Others enjoyed the meal sitting on chairs. Most had never seen such a wide selection of foods. All wondered why they were being treated so well.

When the meal was over and all the platters and bowls were removed, the women became quiet. Miriam asked about their lives, and they answered nervously. They had all been born in Thyatira, and all expected to be married before twenty years of age.

One of the more outspoken ones, Adelpha, said, "While we are young, we have excellent eyesight, so we do the delicate work: embroidery and sewing purple decorations. It's all for the wealthy. After we get married, we won't be in the workshop for long. We'll have babies, and we are not allowed to bring them to the guild. This is the most exciting time of our lives."

Looking around, Adelpha said, "This home is so different from our place in the insulae. There the apartments are crowded and noisy."

"I've never been in such a wealthy house," exclaimed another.

Adelpha asked Miriam about her life and received a short summary. "I was born in Alexandria and raised near Jerusalem. After our city was besieged, we were saved by fleeing to a city across the Jordan River. My mother died in Antioch of Syria. After that, my grandfather brought me to Pergamum."

Arte cleared away the couches, placing them against the walls. The room now looked as it did every Sunday morning for worship and the Holy Meal. Carpets were rolled out and covered the floor mosaics.

Miriam started with what they all enjoyed. "I know a few Jewish dances; some are popular at harvest time. A widowed woman in our past was called Ruth. She came to Judah from another country with her mother-in-law, Naomi. At harvest time, she found a husband. He was a kind man. No matter that he was older than Ruth, he fell in love with her at first sight. I'll tell the story and teach you the dance for each section of the story. I know you all enjoy love stories."

"Wonderful! A dance based on a love story!"

All approved of the evening's entertainment.

"Let me teach you the music first. This is a little song we teach our children. It's one of the first songs they learn. It helps them learn how to dance. You'll like it too; it's called 'Ruth's Dance.' Now, hold hands with the person next to you then form a circle. Step forward two steps, put your left hand behind your back, twirl around, do this step, and then go back. Repeat it again, stepping forward two steps, and then the third time, rush into the center and swing your hands up high all at once." Danila joined in, glad to take part.

Miriam showed them the dance, and they imitated her. "Here is my cousin, Serah. She and I will sing the song for you. The words are in Hebrew, my ancient tongue. The dance isn't hard, but the words are. Ready everyone?"

"The dance is easy! It's similar to the one at the temple!" cried Koren. They repeated the movements several times but stumbled on the Hebrew words.

"What do the words mean?" asked Melpone.

"The words tell the story of Ruth. The first words come from

Naomi, Ruth's mother-in-law. She says, 'At first, I was bitter. I went to a foreign land, where I lost my husband. Now I have returned to my home. I am a widow, and how will I live?'

"Here's the second part; these are Ruth's words. 'At first, I was bitter. I lived in my homeland, where I lost my husband. Now I have come to a foreign land. I am a widow, and how will I live? Who will marry me?' Some of the words are the same as Naomi's, but these were spoken by Ruth, the daughter-in-law."

They ran through the whole song, which had several stanzas, and they repeated the dance steps many times. When the hour was late, everyone agreed that it was time to go home.

"Oh, that was fun!" said Adelpha. "Can we do this again?"

"Of course," replied Rebekah. "We'll have you come here again. Miriam will teach you another song and another dance."

As all the young women were leaving, Melpone said, "Miriam, come talk to me in the workshop tomorrow. I want to show you something I'm working on!"

THE GUILD OF PURPLE HONORS

Miriam arrived at the workshop with Jonathan. While he talked about accounts, Miriam went to Melpone's work area.

"Hail! Good morning, Melpone. You said you wanted to show me something?"

"Hail! Good morning, Miriam!"

Miriam had not seen Melpone so joyful. "Look. I'm almost finished with this sash! What do you think of it?"

She held up a purple sash laid along the long edge of a toga. A senator would immediately stand out as an exceptionally well-dressed official when it was wound around his bulging torso in far-off Rome.

"It's almost finished, Miriam. After a few gold threads at the top, it will be ready to send to Rome. The other two sashes will be finished next month."

They talked for a while before Melpone returned to her work. As she left the workshop, Miriam wondered about the quiet young woman, Celina.

Miriam had tried to engage her in conversation several times at the dinner party without success. *Celina didn't speak all evening! She danced but didn't say anything, and she is so thin. Does she have enough food at home?*

HOME OF DELBIN, IN THE CITY OF SARDIS

November 1, in the 12th year of Domitian
From: Diotrephes
To: My mother, the princess daughter of Zeus

Peace be with your soul. If you are well, then I am well.
I have news about the possible sighting of Anthony I had mentioned. The ship went to Alexandria Troas, but the man we were watching for returned by caravan via Assos, Adramyttium, Kisthene, Pergamum, and Pitane.[86] He was not Anthony.
I started a new search. Did Anthony go to Philippi? He has a small farm there. I hold you in my thoughts every day.

THE MILITARY GARRISON IN PRUSA

Anthony finished another letter to Miriam. He read it over and realized changes were taking place in his spirit.

November 1, in the 12th year of Domitian
From: Anthony
To: My dearest wife, Miriam

Peace be with your soul; if you are well, then I am well.
The five brothers at Olive Grove are on my mind. They need more understanding of the Way, and my conversations with them have been limited.
This makes me reflect on how we learn from one another. The knowledge your grandfather shared with me was not like the teaching I received in Rome as a young boy in the gymnasium. That knowledge can lead to a sense of self-

---

[86]Alexandria Troas and these other ports faced the Aegean Sea. Adramyttium is now known as Edremit and Kisthene is Ayvalik. Alexandria Troas is only partially excavated. Alexandria Troas fell into decline after the founding of Constantinople. Assos has been well excavated, and it is a popular destination, sometimes called "the honeymoon capital of Turkey." Pitane was a port close to Bergama, the modern name of ancient Pergamum.

importance. But what kind of learning encourages us to humbly listen to the many poor, meek people in all these towns and villages?

Diodorus, the director of the gymnasium in Pergamum, tried to fill me with knowledge from the classical Roman writers. He said, "Read these books, and then you will be a good citizen."

Antipas had a better way to train leaders. His character was strong, and he faced adversity. That made us want to be like him. Your grandfather emphasized "agape love." At that time, I didn't realize how privileged I was to have him as my teacher.

I want to read everything Antipas wrote. I realize now that my army training and Antipas's instruction represent two contrasting concepts of power. The army emphasizes discipline, continuous physical exercise, and submission to authority.

Antipas trained us differently. He said, "Everything starts in your heart, at the core of your character."

Antipas's way of life and teaching showed a great understanding of every aspect of life. But I must stop thinking about that for now. You'll want to know what I'm doing, not thinking. Forgive me. Of course I'm thinking of you all the time. I am safe.

Anthony wanted to tell Miriam about his daily activities, but such a letter would violate his orders, so he had to be content knowing that he would have many stories to tell her in the future. He sealed the letter and put it in his saddlebag.

Nikias was their go-between, and Miriam would receive it after his next return to Soma.

Omerod and Menandro were returning to Soma to report the squad's recent work to Commander Servius. Their task was to identify the time and place when the rebels switched their names, if that was possible. They were looking for clues in the records for any match with all those strange names.

Another assignment was given to Sextilius, Bellinus, and Capito: to search the other five ports along the Sea of Marmara's southern coast. "Perhaps you can find a clue there that we haven't discovered yet," Anthony said.

Anthony went to the Prusa garrison blacksmith and asked for lessons to maintain military wagons, loosen the wheels, and repair broken axles. *I'll take a wagon from White Horse Relay Station. It will help to develop a problem precisely at the entrance to Five Shepherds' Village. They will not be able to refuse us accommodation.*

MELPONE'S HOME

On Sunday, Miriam asked Jonathan why Melpone had not come to work for the previous three days, but he had heard of no reason for the absence. It was not normal for her to be away that long. Perhaps she was ill and could not leave her home. People wanted her to start work on the second sash.

"Danila, would you like to come with me?" Miriam asked, returning home.

"No, I'm expecting a friend this morning. She is coming from Laodicea, and I haven't seen her for such a long time!"

Miriam got no better cooperation at the guild. "Sorry, I can't come with you" was the comment everyone gave. None of the other young women would or wanted to cooperate.

Miriam walked alone through the Western Gate and crossed the road. To the south, chimneys poured black smoke into the sky. Potters and bronzesmiths bustled about their tasks. The sound of hammers hitting metal rang out from many of the workshops.

She enquired about Melpone and got directions to a decrepit three-story building. Walking through the insulae brought back memories of the human "rabbit warrens" in Sardis. Narrow, winding streets went off in every direction.

Inside the city walls, Thyatira was laid out with a planned grid. Outside, however, buildings filled every available space, seemingly without a plan or pattern.

She talked to the owner of the building, who ran a little shop on the ground floor. "Yeah, Melpone lives here. I think she's up there now. Second floor, up those stairs. Her apartment is on the left."

Miriam held Grace, placing one foot above the other. The stairs were narrow, and several dangerous gaps needed repair. "Hail, Melpone! Are you here?"

Miriam called again.

Melpone opened a thick curtain across the doorway. "Oh, it's you! You don't really want to come in, do you?"

Miriam was stunned. *Melpone doesn't want me to visit!*

"I was hoping to find you at home. And yes, I want to come in to visit with you unless this is a bad time for that. Can you hold Grace while I step across the open area here? Thanks, Melpone. How are you? You were away from work for three days. I was concerned for you."

Melpone pointed to a small stool. The three legs took Miriam's weight, but she thought it might break if she moved a muscle. She looked around. The walls of the tiny room were streaked, a legacy of water dripping from the roof. There was only one window, and the shutters hung awkwardly. Melpone sat on another stool. Between them was a low, square table. It was clean but wobbly.

Miriam asked about her husband, Phlegon, and if she had heard from him since he left.

"He ran off with Ambrosia to Pergamum you know."

"Yes, you told me that when we talked at the fountain."

"That's what many young men do around here. When they run away, they go to a bigger city. I want to hear from him, but he hasn't contacted me since he left."

They talked for a while about the purple sash at the workshop and then about Melpone's fear of adding purple to the customers' togas. Miriam wanted to say there was little reason to think it would bring the authorities to her doorstep, but she did not want to sound too critical of her new friend.

The room was cut in half by a wall-to-wall curtain hanging across it. It hung from the ceiling by a hook. Obviously, Melpone was keeping something hidden behind the curtain. *What is she keeping unseen back there?*

Miriam heard noises on the other side of the curtain. A man coughed. After a few seconds, an old man peeked around the curtain. Melpone's father was bent over. He had not shaved for days. White whiskers spread out in every direction—on the top of his head, his cheeks, his pointed chin, and his throat and around his nose.

"This is Kiron, my father," said Melpone.

"Pleased to meet you, Kiron. My name is Miriam. Your daughter is a good friend."

Kiron said nothing but simply bobbed his head in recognition.

She heard another noise, a scraping cough. Melpone stepped behind the curtain and started sobbing. After a few moments,

Miriam stood up and walked guardedly to the curtain. It was clean, thin, and made of cheap cotton. *The walls are so dirty, but this curtain is clean. What is happening behind there?*

Miriam put her head between the end of the curtain and the wall. Melpone held a young boy, about six years old, in her arms. Tears dripped off Melpone's cheeks as Miriam stared. The young mother was holding her son, rocking him.

There was something strange about the boy's face. The light was so dim. Melpone's son had been born, well, not normal.

The little boy's face was round like a melon. His eyes didn't focus well, and his mouth and lips were not the same as those found on most children. Miriam wanted to both stare and look away at the same time.

Now everything was clear! Melpone was ashamed to talk about her son. She and her father were struggling with their emotions. Melpone hugged her son, a child who would never speak properly, showering him with love.

Her son hugged her back. His eyes drifted from one place on her face to another, not wholly focusing, not understanding the varied expressions of pride, joy, and fear. The boy tried to speak, but mostly it was meaningless babble given with a broad smile. Miriam smiled back. Holding Grace in one arm, she stepped behind the curtain and sat on the small bed beside Melpone.

"Hello, little boy, can I come and visit you too? Your mama let me come into your house, and now she let me into your bedroom. Perhaps I can be let into your life too?"

Miriam placed her hand on top of the boy's head and rubbed his hair, finishing by tapping the end of his little chin. *Melpone's little boy will never learn well. He's like some of the children in Pergamum, the ones the older children make fun of. He'll need care all his life because he can't go to school. Will he ever work? He just smiles and makes funny sounds. My little girl is twenty months old, and she's learning new words every day.*

"Can you tell me your name, little boy?" Miriam raised her eyes to Melpone's face. Melpone's deepest secret was now shared by another. Someone else could share her burden.

Melpone's lips silently said, "Aulus."

"My...name is...Aulus." The boy stuttered his name with pride. It was hard to understand him, even knowing what he was going to say.

"Aulus, I'm so happy to meet you! What a lovely name, the name of one of the greatest lawyers in Rome! Your daddy and mommy want wonderful things for you. They must have wanted you to be a lawyer too."

The evening with the nine young women came back to her. *Uncle Jonathan invited several young women to his home last week. I wanted to give them a speech called "Real Answers to Real Problems," but now I wonder, what do I actually know about real problems?*

I was going to talk to them about love and trust, respect, and dignity. That's exactly what I see here: love and trust. Melpone loves her little boy, who carries the name of one of the most powerful men in the Senate, and this child can hardly say his own name. Oh, I have so much to learn from Melpone.

"Melpone, thank you for letting me into your home. I could only come into your life after entering your house. In return, I'm going to arrange a special banquet! I'm going to call it the 'Banquet of Purple Honors.' The guild members will celebrate the work that you have completed. If you want to share your deepest secret with the other young women, you can do that. Please, bring Aulus and your father too."

Melpone's eyes filled with tears. No one had ever thought of honoring her or her father.

Miriam walked home with a single thought. *I will recognize Aulus! Until now, his being honored as someone special seemed impossible.*

Chapter 29
The Banquet of Purple Honors

JONATHAN AND REBEKAH'S HOME

Miriam's new friends almost danced on their way to the Ben Shelah home. Only Adelpha had ever received a formal, written invitation before. For the others, this was their first. The invitations showed it was going to be a special event. At the door, Jarib looked official as he examined each small roll of papyrus. "Sunday, November 9: You are invited to a special evening, the Banquet of Purple Honors."

"Please enter," he said, smiling and waving them in.

Miriam kissed each one on both cheeks as they entered. When they had all arrived, she called out, "My new friends from the guild: Adelpha, Dreama, Hesper, Koren, Calandra, Neoma, Celina, and Hypatia! You are so welcome!"

Waiting for them in the large living area were Jonathan and Rebekah. He was at his best with loud laughter and warm greetings.

Hesper said, "We're in the home of Jewish people again. This time it's a big banquet!" They laughed about differences in their customs, such as how they wore tunics, necklaces, and nose rings.

"We are Greek-speaking people, daughters of ancient Lydians," said Adelpha in a very formal tone of voice. "You came to live here. Thank you for taking us into your home."

The meal was about to be served when Melpone, Kiron, and her son arrived. For a moment, there was complete silence. No one had known of Melpone's secret. Within a moment, the boy smiled up at his mother, and then he started to happily babble.

"Did you know Melpone has a son?" Calandra asked under her breath.

Neoma whispered, "No! Did you know she has a son like that? Just imagine...."

Grace spoke continuously to the boy; only a few of her words were understandable. Aulus was encouraged that someone was paying attention to him, and he talked in his own way. People

266

around the room tried to keep their eyes off the children, but this was impossible. Arpoxa's toddler, Saulius, copied Grace, repeating the same actions.

The three children were the center of attention. They tried to catch the puppies and wrapped their arms around their necks, receiving a yelp when they pulled at the ears too hard.

Arte had spent the day in the kitchen and had used his best recipes for this meal. He served roasted meats cut into little pieces with various sauces and both cooked and raw vegetables.

Miriam made sure that Aulus sat close to Grace. For this meal, she had seated them in different combinations with her extended family. Arpoxa reclined with her son, Saulius, at another table. Bani and Serah quickly made friends with the young women. Danila communicated with them more clearly than anyone else.

Miriam placed squares of ginger chicken in Grace's mouth, but she spat it out, took it in her hands, and put it back in, smiling up at her mother. Aulus enjoyed the attention Grace was receiving, so when Melpone fed him some meat the same way, he repeated Grace's movements.

After the meal was complete, a typical banquet would often feature entertainers with slight-of-hand tricks, music, and dances. Miriam didn't want anything like that, so she explained, "Tonight, we'll entertain ourselves. At each of our future dinners, I think we should get to know one another more by having one person tell us her story. I think we should get to know one another better. Does anyone want to tell us about themselves?"

This signal had been agreed to between them, so Melpone stood to tell her story. "You know me as Melpone. This is not my real name. At my birth, I was given a name I later did not want. Did you know that my real name is not Melpone?"

"What's your real name?" Hesper asked.

"My mother, Zephyra, was a priestess at the Temple of Apollo Trimnaios. She had special roles in the dances. Before she married my father, she was in the Greek chorus. She wanted a boy, but she died from medical problems after I was born. Because of all the calamities that were happening, my mother gave me the name Melpomene."

"She named you Tragedy?" Hesper's voice cut like a sharp knife. "Who has heard of a girl other than the muse with that name?"

Dismay showed on the face of each young guest.

"My father and my aunt brought me up. He has been the most tender, caring person. He works when he can, usually in the evenings after I'm back from the workshop. He distributes wood and charcoal. The baths need wood for fires, and charcoal goes to metal workers—the gold, silver, and bronzesmiths.

"My aunt died when I was about eight years old, but she took care of me until then. We were always impoverished. I went to the agora and looked at wealthy women dressed in their finery. In this way, I learned what beautiful clothes looked like. I carried the pictures in my mind, drew them, and transferred them onto a piece of cloth.

"Phlegon, my husband, was older than I was and so handsome and strong! He was a leader in the Young Men's Organization of the Games, so I was taken in by his popularity. He often led the parades honoring Bassos. When he was away so much of the time at the Games in other cities, I started singing. That's what my mother did years before. I'm in the chorus. The present play is a tragedy, and it's being presented next week. And now you can see why I do not like my name.

"I was married at age eighteen. Phlegon had been divorced before, but I did not know that. Father was against our marriage, saying he knew the kind of man Phlegon would be in our home. After three years, I got pregnant. Aulus was born, and then Phlegon mistreated me, beating me a lot. He wanted a healthy, normal baby, not one that would..."

Melpone looked at the floor and did not finish her sentence.

"I met Sibyl one day, and she found out that I liked to sew and work with my hands. She helped me get a job at the guild. Phlegon met Sibyl at the guild. After that, he participated in the festivities at the temples. Our problems didn't get any better. He said bad words to me. Of course, I said bad words back to him."

Everyone leaned forward, intrigued and shocked by her story.

Miriam watched as lines grew deeper on Celina's face.

Melpone's simple words spoke of deep suffering. "He beat me, and I lost my second baby. That's when he left Thyatira, running away with Ambrosia, a woman he met at the temple. I think some of you knew Ambrosia. I've heard that Phlegon now lives in Pergamum.

"I told my story to Miriam. She's heard these details before. I confessed to Miriam, explaining, 'Phlegon says that he will never come back to Thyatira! However, I still love him, and I can't get him out of my mind!'"

Everyone let out their breath slowly, and Neoma broke the silence. "Melpone, we've known you for so long. Really, we never knew the slightest thing about you. Of course we knew what a good seamstress you are but..."

Miriam broke the hush that followed. "Melpone has been deeply hurt by things she had little control over, but she's not the only person like this. Most injuries come from broken relationships. We seek to fill our lives with good things: work, festivals at the temples, and cheering for our athletes. But when we go to bed at night, we think about people who have hurt us or the relationships we would like to have.

"Tonight we are going to do two things. The first is just a little bit unusual, and the second is, well...completely unusual!"

Nervous laughter came from around the circle, and Hesper whispered a little too loudly, "After Melpone's story, what does Miriam mean by 'completely unusual'?"

Miriam took a purple sash out of a small bag. A tiny golden eagle was embroidered on the top end. "In the next few weeks, this sash will be part of a fine linen toga, and in five months, when sailing begins again, it will be sent to Rome. Two others will be made too. Some of you are working on this project."

Melpone took the purple sash from Miriam and stood behind Aulus. With the sash folded in half, she held the top against her son's left shoulder and the bottom end on his right hip. She stood with the boy firmly in front of her so the sash would not fall to the floor.

Grace said some unintelligible sounds and waddled across the room to touch the purple sash displayed against the short white tunic Aulus wore. Saulius joined them from another part of the room. He moved quickly and almost fell, landing on his hands. He got up quickly and ran to touch the purple cloth.

Melpone was so proud of her son, the child who would never walk normally, and she loved him. She laughed as Saulius tried to get close to the purple sash and Grace attempted to push him away. Then both toddlers looked at each other in glee.

"Can she do that? With something destined for the Senate? Can she place it on a child, a child such as...this?" Adelpha's whisper was a little bit too loud.

"Aulus, we honor you for having such a wonderful mother," Miriam declared. "She loves you and takes care of you. She brings you food and everything your family needs."

She asked Melpone's father to stand up. "It's an honor, Kiron, for us to know you and have you here at this banquet. You spend almost all your time with your grandson, caring for him, making meals, and encouraging him. You tell him stories, watch over him, and make sure that he does not fall down those rickety stairs. With any little extra time, you work to earn money. I know you carry heavy loads of wood and sacks of charcoal long distances, coming home late. Friends, Kiron is a father and a grandfather; we invited you here to honor him and his grandson."

She did not say anything more about the condition of their home. "We honor you tonight, Kiron, because God gave you a unique ability: to care for your grandson. We respect you, Kiron, as father and grandfather, staying home day and night and faithfully watching over him.

"Aulus, you are trying to learn to speak; you show a good attitude to all the people you meet. And Melpone, you are faithful in your home and at your job, working hard for the three of you."

Aulus saw everyone smiling, and he responded unexpectedly. He stepped toward Grace and said some words no one could understand. He took Grace's little hand on one side and offered his hand to Saulius on the other. The three of them went to Kiron, rubbed their hands on the soft purple fabric, and started to smile. Then they giggled and laughed. The three children wound their fingers around the purple sash. In the flickering light shed by the oil lamps, the purple shone with beautiful, unusual hues.

The childish gesture, so unexpected, brought giggles from everyone. It was what they needed: relief from the tension of the moment. Adelpha and Hesper glared while the other young women howled with laughter, picking the children up and hugging them.

"Now, the second thing for tonight, before our dessert, which is a lovely almond torte with peach sauce, is something you may not have witnessed before. I want to pray for Melpone. I do not believe her life is a tragedy. 'Tragedy' is not a name. Curses put on people do not have any power when Yeshua Messiah's name comes as a blessing against a curse. His blessings undo the curses people place upon us. His life is more forceful than any condemnation spoken by the most influential person.

"I believe in blessings. Nasty words are sometimes used against us, but they are ineffective when confronted by Yeshua Messiah's power. The Lord's name is Almighty. He calls us to bless one another, especially those going through deep waters."

Complete silence filled the room. Miriam looked around, observing each one. Her declaration went against everything these young women had been taught at home and with friends. They had never heard such a direct confrontation.

For them, Zeus and the gods brought curses and blessings, and they could be manipulated with magic or strange words. For them, sacrifices were made to appease the gods, and magic was something to be feared. They understood a sacrifice to be the means of negotiating with the gods, something important but impersonal.

And Jonathan Ben Shelah's family had never heard the Holy Name uplifted like this before Gentiles, so they were also surprised at what was happening.

Melpone nodded in agreement. "Yes, Miriam, I want a prayer of blessing. I do not want my life to end in heartbreak. I need prayer for Father, Aulus, and me...and for Phlegon."

Miriam explained the reason for her prayer. "The Lord is a God of majesty and might. He is close to those who are broken in spirit. I'm going to pray. Just listen to my words. If you agree with what I'm saying, echo the words in your mind."

She lifted her shawl around her head, covering her hair. She placed her hands before her with the palms upward to the ceiling. Her voice was firm, and she closed her eyes.

"God of our fathers, of Abraham and Isaac and Jacob, the God who delivered us from bondage in Egypt, you created Melpone with love. You made her face beautiful and gave her excellent skills, the abilities of an artist. You enable her to make garments of incredible beauty and value.

"You have strong love for her, but there's much grief in her life, so I bind the dark forces working against Melpone. You gained the victory over all powers, in heaven and on Earth. Yeshua Messiah rose, conquering and defeating our greatest foe, death. He gives us the authority to declare in faith that no power of darkness can overcome this young mother.

"Melpone is a lonely, grieving wife, abandoned because of the calloused heart of her husband, Phlegon. She needs the touch of your Spirit. Use us as your instruments to be good friends to her. Just as needles and thread are used every day to make beautiful pieces of workmanship, things of beauty and honor, use us to create splendor and righteousness in her life. Make her a blessing to many.

"I bless her and all her friends with the understanding of love. Be a husband to her in lonely hours. Teach Aulus to speak, to walk, and to care for himself. Give him a future."

It was the first time Adelpha, Dreama, Hesper, Koren, Calandra, Neoma, Celina, and Hypatia, all descended from Lydian families, had heard a personal prayer. Prayers at temples, honoring Artemis, Demeter, or Athena, were uttered according to strict traditions. Every word had to be repeated correctly.

The women looked at each other while she was praying. Some of them stood to imitate Miriam's posture. Celina covered her hair, folding her shawl the same way Miriam did. Calandra and Hypatia looked at each other, feeling sheepish and not sure what to do.

Miriam did not know how long she had prayed. As she prayed, a current, like a wave of heat, spread up her arms, and her outstretched palms felt hot. It was a healing power, something not of her own doing. With her heart pounding, she extended her right arm around Melpone's shoulder and put her left arm around the boy's waist. She loved this mother, who carried the burden of a boy whose face was not ordinary, who could not speak.

Melpone did not know what to do next. She waited quietly, feeling the warmth at her shoulder. It was unusual, this warmth of acceptance and love. This moment in the Ben Shelah home radiated a feeling of acceptance she had never known. Two weeks earlier, she had been hiding in her house in shame, but tonight her little boy had worn a sash destined for a senator in Rome.

Acceptance, even for one evening, chased away shame.

Miriam closed her eyes and said softly, "Melpone. I want you to have a new name. Instead of Melpomene, or 'Tragedy,' we now understand like this. 'Melpone' can be a combination of three Greek words: *Mello*, I am about; *pempe*, I send; and *agape*, selfless love. We will think of you as *Mel-pon-e*, a new meaning that uplifts you. Think of yourself this way: 'My reason for living is to share love.' Your friends are giving you a new name. It speaks of a high honor.

"Together, we reinterpret your name. Hearing it, we will think of you this way: 'My reason for living is to share love.' Your new name will mean that sweet fruit will come from your life."

272

Melpone opened her eyes while Miriam was praying and saw Celina staring at Miriam, her mouth wide open in wonderment.

For a long moment, Melpone battled three negative emotions. Her name, her station in life, and the living presence of her son all grew from tragedy. Ever since she could remember, she had carried the weight of shame. Now, a new meaning was being created within her name. A new sensation had dawned on Melpone, even as the year was nearing its end.

The words were whispered quietly. "My reason for living is to share love!" She looked around at all the young women with whom she spent much of every day at work.

New thoughts sprouted, much like buds growing on trees in the spring: *That is what I am seeing here tonight. I am accepted as never before. And I think Miriam wants me to keep sending this love on to others. I sensed many new things. Miriam's words were unusual. When she said, "I bless you," I thought, for the first time, I might be forgiven for those bad things I screamed at my husband. I didn't tell Miriam how much I cried aloud after I lost my second baby. Miriam wants my life to be fruitful. She has given me a new name that frees my life from my past!*

A window of redemption opened into her future, casting a brighter light than all the flickering oil lamps set on stands along the wall. Outside was night. Nothing had changed, but the light in the room seemed brighter.

Simultaneously, curiosity and revulsion clashed in the guests' minds, for these words addressed to an unknown deity made them uneasy. They knew that she was blessing and loving them, not criticizing and judging. Each one knew her words were meant to bring healing, but would the temple gods be offended?

Dreama whispered to Adelpha, "Don't say anything! Who knew she was a priestess?"

Hesper was wiping tears from her cheeks. The silence that filled the room was punctuated by several of the young women sniffling. One started to laugh, and then they all joined in nervously.

"Well, that indeed was different!" Adelpha exclaimed softly, but her voice contained a strong current of criticism.

Across the circle, Dreama said, "Another day, would you say a prayer for me too? It would have to be tomorrow of course. I couldn't take anything like that again tonight!"

The guests reluctantly started for home.

Hesper took Calandra's elbow as they left and commented in jest, "I think we should send this purple sash on a fine, new white linen toga with a note: 'This purple sash has graced a boy who can't speak and a poor grandfather who has little work except to take care of the child with untold disabilities. The family says the sash will honor you. They inaugurated it well.' What do you think?"

Calandra's eyes grew big. "Be careful what you say. For the senator who is going to wear it, do you think he would value it more or much less to know the purple had been used at a banquet such as this one?"

Hesper insisted, "Putting a purple sash on this child! Where did Miriam ever get that crazy idea? Is she trying to turn everything upside down?"

"I don't think we know Miriam at all, Hesper." Calandra frowned, trying to think it through. "I don't think she's dangerous. No, Miriam did it intentionally. She is saying something to us, something deep. She knows about mysteries that we do not understand. That's why she honored a poor old man who faithfully cares for his grandchild."

Hesper responded sharply, "How can she dare tell us, even in a symbolic way, that honoring a child with a disability is as worthy as the affairs of state? If that is what she is saying, then she is rebellious! I have many questions after this evening. Is she teaching something against Rome? Is it safe to have a friendship with her, safe to go to her house?"

"Yes, I think so. I want to," Calandra answered. "I think it's safe to form a friendship with someone who asked for that blessing with such passion and devotion."

They chuckled, and Hesper had the last word. "I hope the senator doesn't find out who's already worn his precious treasure. Can you imagine what he would say?"

They were on Acropolis Road when Hesper stopped and firmly gripped her friend's arm. "Say, what do you think the gods are going to do? No one dared to confront Miriam, but she did say that they have no power when opposed by Yeshua!"

Those words would go around in Calandra's mind long after she lay down for the night.

As the guests were leaving, Rebekah kissed each one goodbye.

Then Miriam and Rebekah hugged and burst out laughing as they looked down at the floor. While the guests were leaving, the children had pulled remnants of cloth out of a bag in the corner. Hundreds of tiny, colored odds and ends lay scattered across the mosaic floor. This was a display left by children too young to understand the details of life that bother adults.

Miriam said, "I'm going upstairs to put Grace to sleep. Then I'll come and clean up."

Rebekah looked at the scattered pieces on the floor, wanting to pick them up, but laid back on the couch as her mind wandered into the past. The evening brought back memories of her three oldest boys, all now dead. She was overwhelmed by her thoughts as she gazed at the fragments on the floor.

The fires during the riots in Alexandria, Egypt, had been cruel. Her three little ones' lives had been snuffed out before their time. Fragments of memories came back to her every day.

When Miriam returned after Grace was asleep, she quickly pulled together the scattered cloth pieces and stuffed them back in the bag. Miriam set the bag of scraps on a shelf and returned so that she and Rebekah could sit and talk.

"Last night I wrote a song for you, Aunt Rebekah," she said, as they rested on the couches. She pressed her little finger against her eye against a sudden rush of tears.

"My song is a lament called 'The Remnant.' Auntie, you were talking about the three sons you carry close to your mind's eye, the ones no one can see."

Miriam sang her song for an audience of one.

The words came quickly. She had composed it to sing without a flute, harp, or any other instrument. The lament song joined a fifty-year-old grandmother and her twenty-seven-year-old niece in the common destiny of their people's history.[87]

You thundered:
"Zion will be tramped like a field!
Jerusalem's walls made rubble.
After rejecting me," says God,
"Fire will consume the stubble."

---

[87] The words of this song are taken from Jeremiah 14:19, 22; 15:5, 7, 11; 16:19, 31; 17:7, 14; 18:15; 22:22; 23:17, 20; and 25:34, 36, 38.

But we cried out:
"We've longed for peace, but no good came!
We've abandoned your covenant."
Then we collapsed, wrapped round in shame.
But you still cradled your remnant.

You judged:
"False prophets said that I'd bring peace.
But lightning flashed, and hail poured down.
Now the ferocious storms will cease.
I'll bring you back to rebuild towns."
   So we wept:
   "Heal us, Lord. We need to be healed.
   We looked for peace, but terror came.
   Come, save us! Let us be saved!
   Your safekeeping is all we crave."

You proclaimed:
"Kneel in dust, leaders of the flock!
My fierce, sharp anger has been poured.
No more will all men laugh and mock,
When I send hunger and the sword."
   Then we replied:
   "Our forefathers bowed to false gods.
   So you disciplined us with rods.
   You are our refuge in distress.
   Blessed is the one who trusts the Lord."

You wooed us:
"I know the purpose of my heart.
As rains fall from the skies above,
As I split the Red Sea apart,
I'll show my everlasting love."
   So we respond:
   "We worship you, the mighty One.
   For your name's sake, do not despise.
   Shalom flows from your glorious throne.
   Strengthened in faith and hope, we rise."

Rebekah said nothing. She slowly lowered her head on

Miriam's shoulder. "You understand, my daughter," she whispered

Miriam felt her aunt's tears falling on her shoulder and thought of the many pieces of cloth she had gathered from the floor. *Little remnants...that's all that's left. Families torn apart. God, keep this remnant alive, this tiny family. Without you, what hope do we have? You are eternal, with no beginning and no end. Keep us in your mercy.*

Chapter 30
Seeking Better Understanding

JONATHAN AND REBEKAH'S HOME

Sibyl dropped in at Jonathan's home on Tuesday afternoon. "Hello, Sibyl, may I help you?" asked Miriam.

"I'm here to speak to Rebekah about Chanukah. Is she in?"

"No, Rebekah went to the marketplace to buy food. Do you want to leave a message? Perhaps you want to come in?"

Sibyl looked back at the street and decided to enter. "Certainly. How are you, Miriam? Are you getting used to living in Thyatira?"

"Yes, I am. I'm enjoying it more and more. We've had three good Sunday evenings with guests in our home."

"I heard the young women at the guild speak about it. Dreama told me about your prayer."

"I'm happy she came. She asked good questions."

"She did not appreciate something though."

Miriam's heart pumped hard. "Are you free to tell me?"

"She said, 'Miriam teaches Jewish ideas and puts down Artemis.'"

"I didn't mean to offend Dreama, but if you are asking me about my faith and my declaration of trust in the Lord, then I have to plead guilty." Miriam felt better with the difference between them clearly established.

"Do you intend to cause problems for Jonathan and Rebekah?"

"Why do you ask?"

"Each time I talk with you, I feel something like, well, unfriendliness. You don't respect the beliefs of others at the guild."

"Maybe it's because of the different ways that we understand things."

"Obviously your expectations are different from my mine."

"Sibyl, I don't know what your expectations are, but I want people to know the Lord and his promise. He says, 'I will be your God, and you will be my people.'"

Sibyl sat with her arms folded across her chest, not about to yield. "Too closed-minded, Miriam! I grew up with a Jewish father and a Greek mother, a Gentile. The same words can mean different things.

"My parents stayed together by allowing each other to enjoy their own meaning. I learned to keep peace in the home that way. It was after they insisted on their own way of understanding things that they separated."

"I'm sure you have your reasons for living like that. I grew up in a home with my grandfather, and he followed the covenant whatever the cost."

"What you are saying is this: 'I'll not compromise with anything Sibyl stands for!' Isn't that right, Miriam?"

"I know that the Lord defends the cause of the fatherless and the widow. He loves the alien and them gives food and clothing. We are to love the alien because we were aliens in Egypt.[88] If we are talking about the same God, then we are in fellowship."

"There's quite a bit that you left out, I think," Sibyl said.

"What did I leave out?"

"Life is not so clear cut. I know all the words of Moses. But how do you live the Law of Moses in Thyatira? Not one in ten thousand people accepts your thinking.

"Here, the laws of Rome prevail. People learn about Greek and Roman writers, not Moses. What do you think the boys study at the gymnasium? They become adults, marry, and then raise their children the way they were brought up. Your ideas should take this into account. Simply telling someone that their beliefs are false will shut off all communication with them."

"I understand what you mean, Sibyl. I must hold to my convictions and beliefs and live by them, but I understand that I can't dictate what others must believe. They must be drawn to believe in my Lord. My hope is that what I say and do will make them want to find out more of what I believe."

"I'm glad we each know where we stand with one another," said Sibyl. "That's useful. It helps us to talk more openly with one another. Here comes Rebekah now. Thank you for talking with me."

OLIVE GROVE FARM AT FORTY TREES

With the olive harvest over and most of the fourth-year madder root crop dug up, Nikias felt it was time to take another out-of-town

---

[88] Deuteronomy 10:19–20

visit. The day before, Nikias had asked who wanted to go with him to Stratonike.

Following Anthony's guidelines, he made sure to have at least one of his brothers with him. Nikias invited three of his brothers—Zeno, Alberto, and Lykaios—to go to other villages.

"But whenever we go, you must do all the talking," they said, still feeling fearful of saying anything that might be considered offensive against the gods.

His brother Zeno agreed to go with him; this would be his third visit to one family in Stratonike. Before they left Olive Grove, Nikias said, "I eventually want to see all the towns around and about. I like seeing farms too."

In the back of the cart were two scrolls carefully wrapped in a sack. One was the story of Yeshua as Mark wrote it. The other was a copy of a few psalms.

"It's tough to concentrate on writing," exclaimed Zeno, driving the horses, "with hours of work copying and hardly anything to show for it. Now, when we harvest the olive trees and collect madder root, there's evidence that we did something. It's called 'productive work'!" He was getting tired of the things that seemed so essential to his older brother.

After their return from Stratonike, Nikias continued his longing to visit different villages. In his heart, Nikias wanted to go to Nakrasa and maybe even as far east as Attaleia, a town closer to Thyatira.

He promised himself that when the spring came, he would go as far south as the town where Xenophon lived, the place known for honey. The deaf innkeeper had welcomed him once and requested that he return.

Someday he might even go as far north as Battle Mountain or as far south as Prosperity Village. *I feel all those villages, towns, and farms are calling me.*

At times, before he went to sleep, he told his wife about the small but growing number of followers of the Messiah in Forty Trees and other villages.

HOME OF DELBIN AND DIODOTUS, IN THE CITY OF SARDIS

November 22, in the 12th year of Domitian
From: Diotrephes

To: Mother, Lydia-Naq

Peace. If you are well, then I am well.

It's Saturday again. My messenger went to Smyrna and learned that the suspect there wasn't Anthony. His face had a birthmark whereas Anthony has a scar from war. I have good news though. My messenger says that Anthony and his family are in Thyatira! He learned this from a merchant who goes back and forth between Sardis and Thyatira. There's news in Thyatira: The Ben Shelah family is being talked about due to the arrival of a younger woman and child.

I confirmed it, sending my helper to the Ben Shelah shop here in Sardis. Antipas's brother, Simon, spoke to his steward, saying, 'The last I heard, Anthony went toward Thyatira, but after that, no one seems to know anything.'

Mother, we will have Chrysa in our grasp soon. Getting our baby back from Miriam will not be hard. I'll wait for just the right moment. I hope to give you the good news of the return of my niece within a week.

Chapter 31
Five Shepherds' Village

WHITE HORSE RELAY STATION ON THE INTERIOR ROAD

The trees had lost their leaves, and only a few caravans now braved the roads before the winter snows. Menandro called over his shoulder as he and Omerod rode away. "The harsh winds from Macedonia will come and go before we see the likes of those miserable thieves again!"

They had left to search the ships wintering in the ports along the south shore of the Sea of Marmara. That was three weeks ago, and now the cold wind that he had predicted was blowing.

Anthony felt a sense of anticipation that had not been his for months as he rode around the last bend in the road before White Horse Relay Station. During the previous three weeks, the auxiliaries in Prusa had taught him how to repair wagons. They practiced lifting axles, repeatedly taking wheels off and then putting them back on. He was confident that he could fix any problem that might befall a wagon.

Arriving at the large room at White Horse Relay Station, Anthony, Ateas, Omerod, and Menandro found that the other team members had already arrived and were warming themselves by the brazier.

Light rain fell following a windstorm that had passed by the previous day. A hot drink made with local honey and wild herbs was served by auxiliaries after Ateas and Anthony handed their reins to one of the attendants. Snow glistened on the tops of nearby mountains.

"What's the plan?" asked Sextilius. After the cold wind during the day, he was glad that he would stay put at White Horse Relay Station while Anthony, Omerod, and Menandro took Ateas to visit the shepherds.

Warming their hands in front of the fire, Anthony told them his plans. "Tomorrow we'll take the station's wagon and leave for the village. Hopefully we'll get those shepherds to speak out and tell us what they know. Time is wasting, and the first real storm will soon be here."

"Anthony has a new profession," joked Omerod. "He can take a wagon apart and put it back together. Our wagon has a very squeaky wheel, put that way on purpose. In case he is ever discharged from the army..."

Anthony cut in with "I won't be discharged. Our plan is to arrive at the village entrance, and the wagon will break down there 'by accident.' The event will happen in such a way that the shepherds will not suspect that our purpose is to stay overnight in their village."

The next day, Anthony hitched two horses to a four-wheeled military wagon. A chilly wind blew from the northwest, the sky heavy with dark clouds. As they left the station, the clouds separated; sunlight shone through briefly, and the wind died down. Saying goodbye to Sextilius, Bellinus, and Capito, they pulled onto the road.

In the previous seven days, only five caravans had passed through the station. Anthony, Omerod, Menandro, and Ateas were now the only travelers on the Interior Road. Ateas drew a blanket tightly around himself, afraid the cold would bring on something more severe than the fever he had recently suffered.

Menandro did not see any value in Anthony's strange insistence on taking Ateas. Menandro held the reins and twisted around, yelling over his shoulder, "Glad to know that we need a Scythian to help with Roman security." It was not hard to hear the scorn in his voice.

Anthony would not respond, and Menandro would not let it go. "I can learn more about robbers and bandits than a lame man who can't speak properly," he muttered.

Anthony ignored the comment and leaned toward Omerod. "Before we get to the bridge where the road divides the Postal Road going west and the Interior Road continuing south, I'll have you stop the wagon. We'll lift the front wheels and pretend that we have a problem with the axle. When a shepherd comes to see why we're stopped, we'll ask for help. Until we get some wagon axle grease from the village, we'll just have to live with this squeaky wheel. If they don't have any, I have a jar of it in the back. Whatever they eventually give us, we shall say that it works but use what we brought."

They rounded a bend, turned right, and hugged the side of the hill as they left White Horse. The only noises were from the two horses' hooves, the squeaking left front wheel, and the wind in the bare tree branches. The clouds turned much darker, and light rain started.

"I am out like this one time in Scythia," said Ateas. "No, I am catch by a storm one time. My teeth are start to chatter. When this storm is over, I'm telling you the story."

"Tell me anytime!" said Anthony. His friend's language skills still had far to go.

All Menandro's energy was focused on keeping the horses safely on the road. Cold rainwater dripped off his nose and chin. The wind had picked up, blowing in steady gusts. Soon rain changed to hard pellets. Winds swirled around them.

The horses felt it as well. They tossed their heads and pulled impatiently at the reins.

Before arriving at the canyon, they crossed a little creek. The water had risen due to the recent rains. Soon they would be at the trail leading to the shepherds' village.

They started up a slight hill overlooking the canyon. Below them, rushing to the northeast, the Porsuk River roiled, churned, and made a dash into the second set of double S curves, the shorter, sharper turns. Half a mile farther to the west, the curves were longer. The abandoned building where the merchants had been dumped in the well was hard to see with the snow beginning to fall. The foundations of the old relay station lay beneath two feet of water. Only the walls and some old fenceposts remained visible.

Anthony said, "Now we know why that old station was closed down and moved higher to White Horse Creek. Slow down. There is the path entering Five Shepherds' Village!"

"Rain must have fallen in those mountains two or three days ago to cause that much water in the river," observed Omerod.

The first time Anthony had gazed at the scene was in the summer. The sky had been blue, and the weather was splendid. Now the wind was trying to take his coat into the canyon below. *Seven months ago, we celebrated Eugene and Lyris's marriage in Sardis, and Miriam entertained everyone with her wedding song.*

As rain changed to snow, the other side of the canyon was lost for a moment in a white swirl of twirling flakes. An early winter storm had wrapped them in its grip. Omerod called above the sound of wind gusts, "This kind of storm keeps people indoors for a day or two. I'm afraid our shepherds will not be outside to see us."

Menandro stopped at the side of the road on the path to the village. "It's too cold and wet to do anything about faking the wagon wheel failure," Anthony yelled into the howling wind. "Stay here for a few minutes. Crawl under the wagon for cover. I'm going to ask the head man for hospitality."

He drew his winter cloak around himself and trudged up the gentle slope to the village. His feet were freezing cold as he walked on a thin layer of snow.

Outside the house of the head man who had shown him the village the past summer, Anthony clapped his hands. He stood in the swirling snow, sopping wet, waiting, and clapped his hands again. "Is anyone home?" he yelled. His teeth were chattering.

"What do you want? Who are you?" A shepherd opened his door a notch, looking out. Anthony could not see the man's face, but a dim light told him an oil lamp burned inside.

"It's me, Anthony! You said to come back at any time! Well, we picked the worst time to do so! I have three others with me. We are four strangers, and we need a place to stay!"

"Where are the others?"

"They are close by, at the side of the road. One is lame. The other two are soldiers."

"Hmph! Soldiers! Why would you go anywhere today? Didn't you see the weather turning?" The man shut the door and, a moment later, came out dressed in his winter cloak. They walked quickly, almost running, to where the others were huddled under the wagon but finding little protection from the wind and drifting snow.

They took the wagon to the shepherds' village and unhitched the horses. "Caves are close by, the ones that protect our sheep. We'll take your horses there," yelled the shepherd. He went to another hut and called two shepherds to take the horses to a cave. Omerod and Menandro carried the baggage as the four visitors were led to an empty house belonging to one of the families.

"Why did you leave the safety of White Horse Relay Station? Couldn't you read the signs of the storm coming? I'll get some wood for a fire. You'll need to dry out your clothes. Stay here."

The man disappeared into the dark as the wind, now a gale, blew flecks of snow. He returned with coals in a pot and arranged them in the small fireplace, starting a fire with twigs.

"We rarely get snow so early in the season," observed the shepherd who had first met them. The twigs caught fire, and he carefully arranged the wood over the flames. "This year our weather has been different. Even Pan, the god of shepherds, was confused. Heavy rain one summer day and now snow in early winter."

They laughed as the warmth in the hut gradually lessened the tingling of their cold, wet skin. Later the head man returned with more wood. "We don't have much to share, but we have lots of hospitality! You'll soon have dry clothes. I'm sure you're hungry, so join us at our evening meal. Come to my house in an hour. Explain why you were so stupid as to set out in this kind of weather!"

Anthony whispered in Ateas's ear. "Ateas, tonight we are going to the head man's house. Entertain them with your stories. Don't say a thing about our real reason for being here. Make them laugh, and don't worry about proper sentences at all. Just tell how you traveled on horseback across the steppes, protecting traveling merchants. Tell them about Arpoxa and Saulius. Drag out each story. Include every detail you can think of. Make it last the entire evening. They don't get many outside visitors, and we want to make them feel happy that they took us in."

When the time arrived, they went to the largest hut, and three other shepherds joined them. The five shepherds and four visitors sat on the floor, which was covered with old carpets.

It seldom snowed heavily in this area during the winter. The men who stayed in the village had worked through the summer. They cut and stored feed in the caves to sustain the sheep until spring. The sheep could then be taken to the mountains.

The previous day, as soon as they knew the weather was turning cold, the shepherds had butchered a sheep. The cold weather would keep the meat safe until they had used it all. Tonight they roasted the meat at the fireplace. They sliced it into small pieces for their stew with herbs and two vegetables that Anthony had never seen before.

They then took hot rocks from the fire's coals and placed them in the stew in a large wooden bowl to make the stew hot. A stack of flatbread was laid beside the wooden bowl with a ladle. Each person had a small bowl and scooped the stew into it. They then either slurped it from the edge or picked up the pieces with their fingers and ate it with the bread.

During the meal, the head man of the village did most of the talking. The other shepherds tended to be intimidated by the soldiers and kept quiet. The head man mostly talked about how their supplies during the winter were brought by wagon every few weeks when the weather allowed, and they paid for them with a few sheep.

Anthony looked around. *There's not a single child here and no women. Why? Where are they?*

He said, "That meat dish served with the herbs—it's delicious! We aren't good storytellers, but our friend, Ateas, has a lot of stories. Do you want some good entertainment?"

Ateas felt relaxed after eating his fill and warming up on a cold night. He told many stories about his travels, and his audience appreciated his simple way of talking. Occasionally they interrupted him to ask what a word meant. He spoke for hours. The shepherds had never heard such tales, much less from a Scythian.

After telling about Scythia, he related how he was captured against his will, how he met Arpoxa on the same slave ship, and how they were married in Chalcedon. He and Arpoxa feared that they would be sold and separated, sent to different families. The story of their being bought together by Antipas at the slave auction in Pergamum and then freed and given jobs at Antipas's village brought gasps of surprise.

He acted out how he and his wife had dressed up in Scythian winter clothing in the heat of summer to show Antipas and his workers what they looked like when cold winds blew. He described pointed hats, long jackets lined with fur, decorated trousers, and short boots tied at the ankles to keep their feet dry and warm.

"I'm wanting good Scythian clothes now!" he said to laughter.

His simple way of telling stories won the shepherds over. They had provided a delicious meal, and he returned the favor, giving them one laugh after another. He was more than just a lame man with a story. They had been given a glimpse of the unknown world north of the Black Sea, and they would never forget him.

They had no idea that horses and caravans traveled across vast stretches of the steppes or that merchants far away needed protection from bandits. "Just like we do on the Interior Road," completed the oldest shepherd.

The shepherds made sure their visitors were safe and their

clothing was almost dry. Anthony, Omerod, and Menandro were satisfied after the meal but had no idea what to do the next day.

Worry lines appeared on Anthony's forehead. There was no mention or sign of the runaway slave.

They slept on beds placed around two walls of the hut. When Omerod and Menandro woke up the next morning, Anthony was already awake and peeking through a crack in the door. The ground was covered with snow, and it was falling at a sharp angle.

While the storm hid the Porsuk River and the canyon from view, its turbulent waters created a continuous roar. Winds howled and moaned. The scene could not have been lonelier.

Anthony returned to bed, shivering. The wind gradually died down, and in the early afternoon, a shepherd knocked at the door.

"Come to the cave! Your horses need attention."

The four men left the hut, walking behind the shepherd through the snow. Their toes were soon covered with snow, even though they trod carefully. The wind had died down. The snow drifted down slowly now; large white flakes fell on black woolen cloaks. The shepherd told Omerod and Menandro to enter the cave where their horses had spent the night.

"Stay here to feed and water your horses. Brush them down," the shepherd said. "We may be gone from the village for a long time. There's feed and water in the cave, over there at the back. Anthony and Ateas, you are to come with me to another cave."

Ateas hobbled on his one good leg, balancing himself with his crutches. They walked along the narrow path, passing the sheep caves and going farther than Anthony had gone during his summer visit. Around a sharp bend, looking eastward, they arrived at another shelter cave, larger than the ones closer to the village.

"Go in," directed the shepherd. "I'll come back later."

He left without further explanation, leaving them at the entrance to the cave. Anthony and Ateas looked at each other and shrugged. Half of the entrance had been blocked off with stacked stones to help keep the wind from entering. Anthony could see that a small fire was burning about ten paces into the cave, and smoke drifted upward along the ceiling.

A man at the back of the cave spoke in an unknown tongue. "Who are you?" His tone was soft, urgent, and challenging. "Why have you come?"

"Who's there?" Anthony reached for his short sword, but he had left it in the hut. He peered into the darkness at the back of the cave.

"Are you a friend?"

Ateas replied in his own language. "Yes, we are friends. Who is there?"

A poorly dressed man walked forward slowly. "What is your name? Who are you? Where do you come from?"

Answering in the Pahlavi language, spoken in the city of Bilsk in Scythia, Ateas communicated flawlessly.[89]

"My name is Ateas, and I am the eldest son of Spargapithes, my father.[90] My family is wealthy, and we are owners of horses. My father hired many horsemen, and I rode as a patrol to guard traders traveling to distant places—to Sara, Samara, and Oren. After three months, we arrived at Orsk, where we encountered merchants from Sogdiana.[91] The most valuable merchandise we brought back was silk.

"I was injured when a well caved in and taken as a slave, but now I'm free and serve in the house of Ben Shelah. Most recently, I lived in Sardis. My wife is staying in Thyatira, expecting our second child."

Only silence came from the man in the cave. He stood straight and was taller than average, certainly taller than any of the shepherds. His hair was fair, the color of wheat. His eyes, like those of Ateas, were blue. He looked at Anthony and Ateas, trying to determine whether he could trust these intruders who had found their way into his hiding place. Ateas and the stranger talked for a

---

[89] Bilsk was a large city located in central Ukraine, north of present-day Poltava. Extensive archaeological research examined 45- to 50-foot-high earthen walls (16–17m) that extended 20 miles (33km). They enclosed a city that came to prominence in the 8th–5th centuries BC. Bilsk controlled the north–south trade, which passed from the Black Sea to the interior of present-day Russia.

[90] Spargapithes was a famous king in Scythia about 300 BC.

[91] Scythian horsemen acted as guards for merchants who traveled along the Volga River to townships in Russia. Ateas was a patrol on the journey through Sara, Samara, and Oren. Their trek ended in Orsk. At this point on the Silk Highway, Scythians traded with merchants from Sogdiana, Tajikistan. This narrative about Ateas and Arpoxa is explained with further detail in *Rich Me! A Chronicle of Laodicea, Heartbeats of Courage, Book Five*.

long time.

Anthony could not understand a word. He studied the unknown man. *We have been led to the runaway slave. Does he know anything about the bandits?*

The shepherd returned, bringing food. The four men ate around the fire, squatting to warm their hands and then standing up, turning around, and warming their backsides. Ateas listened as the stranger talked.

Finally, the stranger stopped talking, and Ateas translated his story. "His name Fenius, named for great Scythian king who died long ago. He lived in Olbia, big city, port with many ships. It is city where joining of Hypanis River and Borysthenes River. He knows my uncle's city, Tanais."[92]

As before, his speech was full of errors.

"He has father, he is first fisherman when young, but later his father is metal worker, making bronze statues in shape of leaping dolphins. Then Fenius is going onto many ships as trader. From ships going to other cities. He goes many times for many years. All cities Greek colonies. Roman ships do trading."

Anthony tried to correct Ateas, realizing he could not pass some things by. "You can say, 'He went to Tanais and all the cities on the southern shores of Scythia. They used to be Greek cities. Now they are Roman cities.'"

"Thank you, Anthony. You are good man. You helping me many. Fenius is good cook, and one day he makes food for king. The king of Bosporan Kingdom asks, 'Who made this food?' and after this, he is advancing. Now he is preparing food for palace of king of Bosporan Kingdom.

"One day he is at the Borysthenes docks with his cousin. People are selling things to Roman ships. He is waiting for wheat coming to the king's palace, but those men are loading things onto ships. They are loading furs and wheat and big timbers for ship masts. One Roman sailor man say to him, 'You! Big, strong man! Come and help for one minute!'"

Ateas changed how he was telling the story, now giving a direct translation as if Fenius were speaking. "Next, the sailor man is

---

[92] The cities mentioned are in the south of what is today Crimea and eastern Ukraine. Greek colonies under the control of Miletus were formed several hundred years before Rome dominated the region.

laughing at me. 'You want to be slave? You not want to be slave or no, that's no difference.' He put hand on my mouth and to not scream tell me, but I screaming, 'You can't do this. I work in king's palace. I make bread and foods for many people,' but bad Roman soldier man has hit hard my head. Now I'm not screaming again. Now I waking up and in ship with other slaves. I find my cousin beside me in the ship!

"Now I coming across Black Sea. Like other slaves, I'm sick and vomiting. Now I in other city, Sinop, with slaves. Now I am there for one moon cycle. Again, coming to another city, Chalcedon. Now in Port Daskyleion. Now I with twenty-two slaves in two wagons. I have big rope tying legs."

Ateas had completed the translation and then added, "Anthony, this man is on road where you are traveling and you looking for criminal. He wanting help now many months."

Ateas could not correct the grammar in his storytelling.

Anthony leaned forward, warming his hands over the fire and piecing the details together in his mind. This Scythian slave had been captured by bandits and somehow freed himself. He held important information.

Anthony asked questions using Ateas as a translator. "When did you come here?"

The answers came slowly. "I in wagon with men going to mines. I close to wagon door at back. I coming with slaves when trees have green."

"How long have you been hiding in this cave?"

"I here from when green trees to now snow trees."

There was no doubt that this was the slave they were looking for. The rest of the slave's story gradually emerged.

Fenius had learned to work with bronze from his father but was employed as a master chef in the king's palace. Six months ago, he had been captured as a slave by the rebel legionaries, and his cousin had also been taken.

"When you were in the slave wagon, how did you escape?"

"We leave White Horse place with new soldier. I sitting in wagon and I am tied with rope. Suddenly, when stone walls are high, caravan is stopping.

"We come on road, very crushed. Come into canyon. First, bad man Ota leave slave wagon with two selling people, merchants in first caravan. They go down little hill, cross river on bridge, go into old building.

"My cousin is cutting loose from ropes and cutting door rope. We are climbing over the edge of the road, onto small road, over bridge, but soldier Quintus see us. We run down little hill and cross bridge. No else place to hide. When we are running, Quintus is running after us. We hide behind rock in grass near building. We seeing Ota cut throats of one merchant men.

"Quintus running into building, and we hear big fight. Then Ota come out. I see Ota pushing two dead merchants into well. Too much blood. We make noise like a quiet scream, and new soldier man come to get us. He is going into old building, yelling, 'Two slaves freed! You see them? Where are two slaves?'

"Bad Ota slave man is killing new soldier Quintus and is throwing him in well. Now three men in the well.

"Bad slave man Ota is looking for us. I quick run around building, hiding on roof. Ota come out and see my cousin running, but Ota catching and cut him. Ota bringing cousin back to well and throwing in. I stay hided.

"But Ota didn't find you?"

"No, I am hiding good."

"How did you get from the valley down below to this cave?"

"Ota is looking for me long time; then he is going. After quiet on big road, I go to well and move over cover. My cousin is not drowning because no water in well. Well is not deep. Now I pull cousin out and I sending him to big road. He is to be saying to caravans, 'Please, helping me! Three men in well. All are dead.'"

"I waiting. Hiding in grass across river water. Long time passing. I see many soldiers; men and caravan slaves are coming and helping my cousin. I running away from road. Not wanting to be a slave."

"A shepherd found you. Which shepherd brought you here?"

"Shepherd man bringing you here today. He very kind. He hating those bad mans. Shepherds afraid. They don't want losing children."

"Where are their children?"

"Children are away. Bad soldier men not taking them."

"You are the only one here, the only slave who got away? No one else was cut loose?"

"Yes, I alone for too long time. I sad. Now I am lonely. I wanting help."

"What did you see when you looked into the well?"

"First looking four men. At bottom, two merchants from road coming with us. One soldier man, Quintus, is dead, on top of two merchants. One on top is my cousin. I pulling him out."

"Are you sure they were the merchants?"

"I knowing them. They two caravan owners. We marching many days. Yes, they are dead. Too much bleeding."

"I want to know about the other two merchants. They came in the other caravan. Who were they?"

"Yes, two other men coming to join caravan. Three days more early. Coming at seaport when we go from boat."

"Did you get their names?"

"No names. We all angry and not listening. We planning to cut ropes and go if caravan is stopping on the road. That our good chance. We looking for good chance."

"What happened to the caravan, the animals, and the other slaves? What happened after you got down from the roof? What did you see?"

"Bad men walking around four wagons. Everyone going out of canyon. Soon all slaves, animals are away."

"Those soldiers were criminals—the ones taking you in the slave wagons. Did you ever see them come back to this village?"

"No, I not seeing them more. But shepherds are talking with one bad soldier man."

"Do you know the names used by the soldiers?"

"Ota I knowing at Sinop."

"How long were you in Sinop?"

"In Sinop maybe one moon cycle or more. I not sure."

"How did your cousin get a knife to cut the rope?"

"My cousin is talking to good slave in Chalcedon. That man, good man, giving my cousin knife."

"Why didn't you cut your rope before?"

"All time we have big rope around and cannot free cut."

"You got off in Port Daskyleion?"

"Yes, in Port..." Ateas had trouble pronouncing the name of the little port.

"How many slaves were in your wagon?"

"My wagon too many. We eleven people. We very crushed."

"Tell me step by step what happened that day."

"Good shepherd man is watching sheep while Ota killing. He is seeing many men running into old building and only one walking out. After soldier leave, good shepherd man coming to look. I seeing him. I leave roof. He seeing big blood in many places on stone floor. Then he talking to me but I not understanding. He is afraid and I am afraid. I am walking back at end of day with shepherd man with sheep with much afraid."

Anthony's mind was racing while taking in the information, but he needed time to piece it all together. He wondered about the village with no children.

"The children of the shepherds...where are they?"

"Now I am missing my children. At home seven children, and now I very lonely. I twenty-eight years old and my wife..." The man started to weep. He would not speak anymore.

The evening was coming on. The snow had finished falling, and the slave would not leave the cave, even at the end of the afternoon. Anthony thanked Ateas several times. He had helped, and in his limited way, he had unraveled part of the mystery.

"Ateas, I want you to stay here. Fenius is lonely for his seven children. Even if he is a slave and cannot understand Greek or Latin, he might have heard some words he thought were important. Continue to talk to him. Let me know about anything else you learn. We need to hear a lot more from him. I'll send food and more wood from the village."

The slave's story gave Anthony and his squad much to go on. They had proof that rebel soldiers were illegally bringing slaves to mines and metal shops. They had also dealt with wild animals.

The next morning, Anthony asked the shepherds, "When did you take your wives and children away?"

The shepherd who had taken Anthony and Ateas to the cave replied, "A soldier came four moons ago. It was a very hot day. He was angry. 'You live near the old building in the canyon and sometimes feed your flocks in that area, right? Sometimes bad things happen there. I've heard that ghosts walk those old buildings. If you saw anything happen and report it to the authorities in White Horse or in Aizanoi, those ghosts might come to take your wives and children.'

"We believed him and moved our families to stay with relatives in a village on the Interior Road, one day south by wagon. We took them there right away."

"Did the soldier who spoke to you give his name?"

"Yes, he said, 'My name is Ota, and I have an important message for you. Ghosts might come to take your children.' We lived in fear for more than four moons. They are staying away."

"You'll have your wives and children back very soon. Thank you for giving us shelter during the storm and for bringing us to Fenius. Ateas will stay with him until it's safe to take the slave somewhere. Keep Fenius hidden until your children are back safely."

Just before leaving Five Shepherds' Village, Ateas brought other news. "Fenius is hearing two names. One is in Sinop and other name when getting into ship in Chalcedon. He is hearing names spoken by bad soldiers' men who are guarding them."

"What are the names?" asked Anthony, very much alert.

"He is remembering Craga name in Sinop. In Chalcedon, he is hearing Mithrida name."

"Well done, Ateas!" said Anthony, delighted to have this additional information. The air was cold as the horses pulled the wagon back to White Horse Relay Station.

The route used by the robbers had been confirmed. They brought slaves from Port Borysthenes in the Bosporan Kingdom, sailed around the Black Sea's eastern shores, and let them off at Port Sinop. There, they were trained to work in the homes of Greek-speaking families. After enough time spent in training, ships brought them to Chalcedon at the southern end of the Bosporus, on Marmara's northern shore.

From there, the slaves came by ship to Port Daskyleion.

The soldiers had at least one vessel, perhaps more. Sailors and soldiers, all rebels, were involved. Maybe they now had the name of their general. If not the general, another one of the leaders was named Mithrida. Once again, not a Roman name.

Menandro could not believe that Ateas had played such an important role. Omerod chuckled. "To think you learned so much about wheels and axles and then didn't have to lift a finger to pretend your wagon had an accident!"

Seated around the long table in the White Horse Relay Station, they went over the story once more, step by step. Sextilius listened carefully, taking in every detail. If anyone could put all the pieces together, it would be him.

Omerod was trying to fit together details he was just beginning to understand. "Someone planned all this! This didn't happen overnight!"

Bellinus leaned back, stood up, and then walked around them before he again sat down at the glowing fire. "Following up on all this information means that either our horses will continue to suffer winds, snow, and sleet or we are going to freeze all winter long. Or both! As for me, I want to know what our next assignment is!" As usual, his comments set them laughing.

Sextilius had raised his brow to show puzzlement. "Robberies involve slaves and probably valuable objects. Wild animals were brought as well. To date, we've heard several different names: Craga, Taba, Harpa, Baga, Ota, Spithra, and, lastly, Mithrida. We know that they come from ancient satraps, but what do these names mean, and why do the bandits use them? If we can answer this question, we may have the answer to other riddles. Only one question does not need an answer: Why deal in slaves? We already know that. Slaves bring in lots of money."

Anthony looked around the small circle. "Five days until the end of November. Ground travel will be difficult for several more months. Rains and storms are normal before the next ships sail. For now, we'll take the wagon back to White Horse, and tomorrow let's go back to Aizanoi, if the weather permits. Commander Diogenes Elpis must know these details at once, and he'll inform commanders from Soma to Prusa."

THE MILITARY GARRISON OF AIZANOI

Late in the afternoon, Commander Diogenes Elpis would have been cold had it not been for the brazier. It was filled with glowing charcoal in the center of the room. Standing on a broad base and with a large circumference, it spread heat in every direction. Anthony stood on one side and the commander of the Garrison of Aizanoi on the other as they warmed their hands.

Anthony gave the commander the complete story about the shepherds' cave, the abandoned building where the four murders took place, and the Scythian slave's story.

Then Sextilius spoke. He believed that he had learned something important about the rebels. "At the end of June, I interviewed people in Dascylium-on-the-Lake, as Anthony instructed. It was to determine if centuries-old raider gangs had somehow been reestablished. I had them repeat everything they

296

remembered of the ancient stories of the area and had to keep myself awake.

"Anthony will remember how they went on and on about old customs from the days of Lydian and Persian governors. At one point, they were speaking of the arrival of the Greeks and the rise of Pergamum. In the middle of their rambling, sir, I heard names. I asked them to repeat them. You can't believe how pleased they were to have me interested in their ancient generals and governors.

Diogenes was surprised. "You learned something about rebel bandits simply by listening to those old people who make floor mats for a living? What can they teach us?"

"Older people have more to teach us than we often realize. I just was not paying close enough attention. Tabalus was the first Persian satrap of Sardis after King Croesus lost the battle for the Lydian Empire. I heard that name but didn't think any more about it. I didn't realize what it meant until today."[93]

"What has that to do with bandits?" asked the commander.

"We have been wondering about the names used by the bandits. Listen!" he said, slightly breathless, "One bandit's name was Taba. Doesn't that make the first part of the name Tabalus? Fortunately, I asked them to tell me more about all the satraps one by one. I wrote down all the names. Look at the list. I've been carrying it with me for days."

Commander Diogenes refused to waste time. "Satraps?" he fumed, exasperated with empty talk. "Six centuries ago! People from back then aren't important now? Who's interested in Lydian history and conflicts. Hurry up! What did you learn?"

"You'll see the connection between the gang's names and the satraps' names. I'm convinced that the name of each bandit corresponds with that of one ancient satrap in Lydia. The second satrap was Mazares, a short-lived governor because the Lydians revolted against him. We haven't heard of a 'Maza' yet, but we may in the future if my hunch is correct. The third satrap was Harpagus. He governed for fourteen years. Isn't Harpa the name of another

---

[93] King Croesus (560–546 BC) lost the battle of Sardis in 546 BC. (Some historians, using a slightly different set of dates, place his dates at 595–547 BC). Tabalus (546–545 BC) was the first of many satraps or governors of the Kingdom of Persia. He administered the former Lydian Kingdom for only two years before he was killed.

bandit?

"The next satrap was Bagaeus, the governor in Sardis for only three years. Well, surprise! We've heard about someone with the name Baga. He took the place of one of the murdered merchants. These names and others take us through almost 150 years of Persian domination."

Aizanoi's commanding officer whistled, "So that explains the origins of their nicknames. Each time that a new rebel joined, they gave him the first part of a satrap name. That explains why every name ends in an 'a.' All those Persian names seem to have an 'a' in the middle or at the end."

He understood immediately what Sextilius had discovered and its importance.

"Anthony," said Menandro begrudgingly, "you were right, although I'm ashamed to admit it. We needed the help of both your Scythian friend to find that lost slave and those old storytellers to figure out how these strange names were chosen. Somehow they are using those names for identification." Their chuckling laughter dispelled the stress, although they still had no clue about how to capture the rebels.

Sextilius turned around, warming his backside. "Two names I can't figure out... Craga and Mithrida don't fit the pattern. There was nothing like 'Mithrida' among the satraps."

"None of this name information tells us what to do next," said the commander, slightly annoyed and rising from the supper table later that evening. "Here we are, trying to figure out where the slaves have been taken, and instead, we're dwelling on ancient satraps and names of criminals. We know how they selected their names but not why. How does this help us to capture this bunch of criminals?"

Anthony interjected. "Commander Diogenes, this is a dangerous gang composed of insurgents and deserters from at least one legion, perhaps from more than one. They trust one another and are very well organized. Why are their heroes the satraps of old? What does that tell me? They have considerable interest in the way that ancient Persia governed this area. Are they equally committed to ancient Lydia? Maybe, maybe not.

"There is something about those long-gone Persian lords that they admire. And they understand the army well. They deserted the army in Dacia. Maybe they went to live in Scythia. To me, it has become clear that they operate out of the Black Sea area. Keeping bandits under control has never been an easy task. Now we have other discoveries that may be useful. Bellinus, explain what was found."

Bellinus had spent two weeks comparing recent relay station records to those from the previous year. "We found other evidence, Commander Diogenes. The Roman names of two fake soldiers appeared last year along the roads all the way past Soma. We know they've been working, unknown to us, for two years now.

"That strongly implies that one hundred slaves or more were sold last year by the gang, but we don't know where. There will be some record of their entry into the province, but you can bet they won't show up on tax records. What happened to those slaves? The sale of that many, with each valued at possibly five hundred denarii, would yield a fortune: fifty thousand denarii.

"However, last year we didn't have news of any merchants being killed. Also, last year there was no indication that the gang was dealing in wild animals. That only started in April this year. The animals were all stored at the four villages south of Aizanoi and kept there until they were taken somewhere and sold. Here is what we learned about that event.

"Remember what the men in the four villages told us? The wild animals were taken away about September 27. Well, we traced the path of the bear and boars by checking registration at each station. Here's something to consider. The animals were at Green Waters Relay Station on October 2 and kept there until the Games in Thyatira four days later. Those animals were placed in the hands of a wealthy benefactor, Fabius Bassos. There is no trace of his having bought them. They were just 'delivered.'"

Diogenes whistled. "Are the rebels linked with a benefactor?"

"No sir. There's no indication that he is illegally connected with the rebels. When Bellinus questioned him, he only stated that he bought them from an itinerant salesman shortly before the Games and that the wild animals were a surprise for the Games."

Diogenes kept on. "Did Bassos buy slaves recently?"

"No sir. But he said four old, sick slaves had a chance to earn their freedom. This is not uncommon in Rome and other cities."

They had reached one more dead-end, and nothing else about Fabius Bassos could be learned—for now. But Anthony jumped in with "There are still many other things that we don't know, such as why are they rebelling? What unites them? How are they recruited? Furthermore, we don't know anything about their leaders except that they seem to have been in the army.

"I think they are simply army deserters looking to make fast money by rebelling against Rome's authority and laws. Their military background gives them a natural bond of being 'army brothers.' Using a military-type chain of command gives them internal security."

Diogenes Elpis nodded thoughtfully. "I think your team has learned many things that will lead to the capture of these criminals. Good work, men."

Sextilius added, "I've been thinking. Obviously these men intend to outsmart the authorities. While they are using nicknames among themselves, that doesn't seem to make sense. They would not be using their real names when checking in at the stations. For this reason, they must also be using falsified papers. Here's what I think. They have created a community like a spider's web that's growing bit by bit. That gives them a sense of power to thumb their noses at Rome.

"Could they be related to another rebellion years ago? Some soldiers expected Nero to come from the east and retake his position as emperor. Remember? Under torture, they confessed that they expected Nero to cross the Tigris and Euphrates rivers on dry land to deliver Rome from..."

Out of respect for Emperor Domitian, Sextilius didn't finish his sentence.

Chapter 32
Casting a Long Shadow

FIVE SHEPHERDS' VILLAGE

Near the end of November, the weather had cleared enough for Anthony to lead a team of three military wagons returning to Five Shepherds' Village.

He told the village leader, "You were wise to send your families to safety after those robbers came, but now it's safe for them to return. You were a great help to the army, and we have come with these wagons to bring them back quickly."

The village head man instructed three shepherds to go with the wagons and show them how to get to the other villages. Light-hearted talk made the miles speed by quickly. Ateas was more confident after having told his life story, and he did not mind people laughing at his strange way of talking. He took it as a form of appreciation for having helped to translate the slave's story and unravel the mystery of what took place in the canyon when the murders were committed.

When the wagon arrived at a village, children ran to hug their fathers. The next day, the women and thirty-one children had been returned home, once again sleeping in their own beds.

"Why didn't you tell the authorities about the threats to your families?" Anthony asked.

Everyone had the same answer. "We were afraid! The slave we took in spoke a little bit of Greek, and he said, 'Those are bad men. Killing men. I see them killing people.' We thought they were just bad soldiers. We didn't know they were actually criminals."

As he left Five Shepherds' Village two days later, following a joyful reunion of the men with their wives and children, Anthony took his Scythian friend aside. "Ateas, I want you to stay with these men and their families. Encourage the slave, Fenius. By staying here with him, he won't want to run away. I don't know his future, but for now, I think he'll be much better off to stay here than if he comes with us."

"How long the slave to have to stay here?"

"I don't know."

Ateas looked disappointed. "Long time to stay here?"

"Perhaps."

"When am I seeing Arpoxa again? What happen to slave who helped us here?"

"I don't know. We'll capture the bandits and then figure out what to do with him."

JONATHAN AND REBEKAH'S HOME

Saturday mornings always saw the Ben Shelah family at the Thyatira synagogue. As they walked home after the service, Jonathan asked Rebekah, "Did you notice? Some families avoid talking with us. The elders turned away when I was near."

"Some of us are changing," replied Rebekah. "Those strict guidelines your father put on you as a child hardly matter anymore."

"What do you mean?"

"You spend time at the Temple of Artemis. We have people coming to our house who are members of the Guild of Purple Honors. But the Jewish elders aren't open to change. They live by those strict guidelines I mentioned and will not permit anything new or forbidden."

"Well, Rebekah, some of the things they don't like are good changes. Like tomorrow. We'll start at sunrise with the Holy Meal and end the day with Miriam's friends from the guild learning her songs and dancing!"

THE MILITARY GARRISON OF AIZANOI

The next morning, Commander Diogenes, Anthony, and his five companions cut slices from a cheese round placed in the middle of the table. They folded hot flatbread around the cheese and smeared black olive paste on it. They rolled the bread, holding it so bits and pieces of cheese did not fall onto the floor. The charcoal in the brazier glowed with a dull orange hue as it warmed the room.

"While I was sleeping last night, I realized something!" said Sextilius, arriving late at the table. As usual, he was the last one up, but it wasn't normal for him to be energetic this early. "I know who Mithrida is!"

The others looked at him, amazed.

"And Craga too!"

Omerod rolled his eyes. "You do lots of funny things in your sleep, Sextilius!"

Menandro chimed in, "Another nightmare! Here, some bread and cheese will help."

Capito shook his head. "Tell us another!"

To stop the derisive comments, Sextilius held up his hand. "Mithrida is the general of the robbers' army. Craga leads their fleet or perhaps is the captain of a ship."

"Definitely not dreaming! Sleepwalking? Yes!" added Diogenes, leaning back in his chair. He had been anxious to hear more, but Sextilius was obviously playing a joke on them.

"No, each rebel uses a nickname. Those strange names are taken from significant people in the past, and Mithrida is no different. Answer me this: Who was Rome's greatest foe?"

"Mithridates!" responded the commander. "Mithradates VI! That king! Yes! His home was in the Black Sea area, and he brought about the death of 80,000 Romans in just one day—men, women, and children. By Jove, you are on to something!"

In an instant, Sextilius had their full attention. "Yes, Commander Diogenes. Mithradates VI was Rome's most implacable foe. There's more. What if a rebel leader chose a name with a double reference to both a king and a god? I believe that 'Mithrida' combines two names: Mithradates and Mithras."

The others looked at each other, waiting for a new insight.

"Mithras is an ancient Persian god. He protects, guards the truth, and makes sure oaths are kept. 'Mithrida' is, I believe, a combination name intentionally meant to include both an ancient king and a Persian god. We must find this man and bring him to justice."

Cautious nods greeted his remark.

Sextilius continued, "Remember what they taught us as recruits? The first king of Pontus, Mithradates I, claimed to be descended from both the Persian king Darius *and* the Macedonian conqueror Alexander the Great. When it favored them, this family claimed loyalty to the East. If the political tide swung the other way, those monarchs could identify with Macedonians.

"I woke up in the middle of the night. It hit me suddenly. When the Persians gained control of Sardis, they brought their religion. Even though Alexander the Great later conquered all the land in the south, taking the land back, he could not capture those Persian strongholds along the Black Sea. That was the beginning of a family of kings in Pontus taking that name. For generations, every king called himself by their same heroic family name: 'Mithradates.'"

Diogenes was fully awake. "Yes, the kings of Pontus became friends with King Nicomedes of Bithynia, whose capital was Nicomedia. That region was called Bithynia and Pontus. Mithradates VI briefly succeeded in taking over all of Anatolia."[94]

Sextilius continued, "Mithradates VI carefully planned the 'Day of Purging.' Thousands of Romans were killed on the same day! How did that happen without planning it quietly on a vast scale? An evil monster hated Romans coming into his provinces. And what did Rome do in turn? Our legions fought their fiercest opponent for decades: King Mithradates VI.[95]

"Since these slaves came through Sinop, I think we can conclude that this rebel commander knows the Black Sea region well. Maybe he was born there. And if I'm right, Mithrida wants his followers to think he's both Macedonian and Persian. Anything except a Roman. Smart as a fox."

Anthony wanted more. "If Mithrida is their general, who is Craga?"

Sextilius continued, "Craga has to be his second-in-command. Remember how Mithradates VI supported pirates? Two hundred years ago, rebels were against Rome, complaining about high taxes and injustice. This also came to me last night. Where was the main

---

[94] King Mithradates VI (134–63 BC) controlled the Black Sea region and expanded his kingdom to include large areas of Greece and Asia Minor. This threatened Rome's attempts at eastward expansion. Three wars were fought against him between 88 and 63 BC. At the end of the First War, he killed the Roman general Aquilius on the island of Lesbos by pouring molten gold down his throat. He tortured the prisoner, saying, "So Rome demands taxes? Here! Get a taste of this. It will really make you feel rich!" Countless stories of his cruelty caused great fear to citizens of Roman background in Asia Minor.

[95] The uprising against 80,000 Roman immigrants in Asia Minor took place in 88 BC. The Memmius Memorial in Ephesus commemorates the victory of Cornelius Sulla, the general's grandfather. Sulla won the historic Battle of Orchomenus against Mithradates VI in 85 BC, leading to his being called "The Savior of Asia." This story is described more fully in *An Act of Grace: A Chronicle of Ephesus, Heartbeats of Courage, Book Seven.*

port used by pirates back then? They operated from a harbor called Cragus, near Anti-Cragus, on the southwest shores of Anatolia.[96]

"Like 'Mithrida,' I think 'Craga' is a combination of two other names: Cragus, in a geographical sense, refers to the highest mountain between Patara and Telmissus. But Anti-Cragus, the nearby mountain, is also identified by common folk around there as a dwelling place of Zeus. He is worshiped in celebrations and festivals. So 'Craga' has a religious meaning to the name."

If true, this indicated a display of arrogance and rebellion on a scale they had not imagined.

"So if 'Mithrida' is a combination of two names, that of a Persian god and of a rebel against the armies of Rome, then 'Craga' may combine two meanings. I think his name might include an allusion to a rebel navy and a war. Before defeating Mithradates, Pompey had to defeat pirates based at the foot of Mount Cragus. It took half of Rome's navy to accomplish that mission. One other detail, which could be significant... Who was the hostage being held in Cragus at the time?"

"Why of course!" bellowed Bellinus. "Julius Caesar was the Roman general being held for ransom! Oh! He said he'd be back to crucify those who had held him captive, and he did it too!"

Sextilius added, "If my guess is right, these rebels, Mithrida and Craga, imagine that they can eventually go as far as intercepting shipments of grain to Rome. I suppose that Mithrida uses historical references to motivate his followers. Cragus is 'Craga' in the Cilician language. He must think of himself as a future leader on the seas, perhaps commanding a navy." He stopped, looking intently at the glowing fire in the brazier.

"Keep going," urged Commander Diogenes. "What does this mean for Aizanoi?"

"All right, this may all be just a guess. Robberies have taken

---

[96] Strabo, a famous geographer of antiquity, described two mountains: Cragus, 6,500 feet (2,000m), and Anticragus, 6,000 feet (1,800m). His descriptions fit the present port or resort town of Oludeniz, near Fethiye, Turkey. At the entrance to this bay are ruins of buildings on tiny islands. These may remind visitors of Julius Caesar's war against pirates when about 120,000 soldiers and sailors, 4,000 cavalry, and 270 ships descended on the pirates' cove. Today, gliders jump from the peak of the mountain above luxury homes built against the mountainside.

place using carefully thought-out strategies. We've heard a few names: Taba, Harpa, Baga, Ota, and Tissa. Now, where do these rebels come from? Anthony told us about Legion XXI and said a few legionaries in Upper Germanica were restless. How long ago was that?"

"At the beginning of March, seven years ago," said Anthony.

"Since then, there has been a general disquiet in the province of Moesia. More recently, Domitian suffered the defeat of Legion XXI in Dacia. Soldiers are discontented after fighting barbarians in dense forests. If they are disgruntled with Rome and the emperor, that could explain why they fled."

The commander took a deep breath. "But a rebellion of this type can't stay hidden for long."

"Commander Diogenes, remember that Domitian executed Celsus Vettulenus Civica Ceriales, Governor of the Province of Asia Minor, for 'supporting rebellion.' He executed the governors of Britain and Lower Germanica at the same time. Domitian puts down any form of rebellion ruthlessly."[97]

They stood in a circle, warming themselves around the brazier and pondering what they had heard. Anthony spoke. "An idea came to me while you were talking, Sextilius. Omerod, when will ships begin to arrive at Port Daskyleion?"

"After the middle of February, when the winter weather starts to clear."

"That's when we'll begin capturing them. I have a plan," said Anthony, taking charge. "Sextilius, write up the report to Felicior and Servius. Start on that right away.

"After that is done, we need additional information about those one hundred unaccounted for slaves from last year. At what port were they brought into the province, and where were they sold? Bellinus, Capito, and Sextilius, go *south* from Pergamum to Smyrna and Ephesus. Inspect port entry records and slave market records.

---

[97] Celsus Vettulenus Civica Ceriales was the governor of Asia Minor in AD 87–88 and was executed for rebellion. Domitian also executed other governors: Lucius Mestrius Florus, AD 88–89; Marcus Fulvius Gillo, AD 89–90; Aquillius Regulus, AD 91–92; and Publius Calvisius Ruso, AD 92–93. It appears to have been a time of growing unrest in the Roman Empire. The martyrdom of Antipas and John's exile to Patmos may have taken place during or after this period.

Be back in Soma on January 1 with your findings."

"Omerod and Menandro, see what you can learn by checking slave market records as you go *north* up the coast from Pergamum. Again, you are to be back in Soma on January 1.

"I'll leave for Soma tomorrow so I can go over all the details that we have gathered so far with Commander Servius."

They spent the next hour discussing the details to include in the report Sextilius would compose.

Before leaving in preparation for his journey back to Sardis and Soma, Anthony penned a short summary. It introduced their much longer report, which others would write and attach shortly.

November 30, in the 12th year of Domitian
From: Anthony and Sextilius in Aizanoi
To: Commander Felicior and Commander Servius

Peace. If you are well, then we are well.

This is our report to you, the most complete to date. It summarizes discoveries made during the past four weeks. We hope this information will lead to arrests within the next three months, when the sailing season begins again.

JONATHAN AND REBEKAH'S HOME

Jonathan had sounded cheerful, but Sunday morning, as their guests arrived for the Way of Truth meeting, Miriam watched her uncle.

She knew him well enough to know that he was putting on a brave face to cover something up. *For some reason, he wants to be someone he is not. He can't let anyone see what he is really thinking. He can't admit to having any kind of weakness or conflict and wants to be accepted. He needs to be friends with everyone. Uncle Jonathan can't bring himself to defend the principles that he believes in. He never confronts anyone.*

Miriam put Grace's feet on the floor and led her by the hand; the little girl shrieked with joy as she walked unsteadily. A sense of compassion came over Miriam for her uncle. It reminded her of the feeling in Sardis when she realized she could help other families.

When Sunday evening arrived, the time spent with her new friends from the guild sped by far too quickly. They talked about many subjects: weaving, looms, purple dyes, friendships, dances, the temples, senators in far-off Rome, hairstyles, bronze tweezers for pulling stray hairs, and manicure rasps.

Miriam led them as they again sang some of her previous songs, and then she introduced two new ones and only one quick dance because it was getting late.

When they left, several young women used warm words when thanking her. "Goodbye. You are like an older sister to us," Adelpha said kindly, and the rest agreed.

"Thank you for listening to us like this," said one, warmly accepting Miriam and giving her hostess a hug.

"No one else invites us into their home and gives us such a meaningful good time."

Miriam gave each a warm embrace as they left. "Remember, we have a special day coming soon! Only nine more days until Chanukah! You are going to enjoy it!"

THE MILITARY GARRISON OF SARDIS

On Monday, Commander Felicior opened the seals of the reports received from Anthony. He carefully read about the progress already made, and then he walked to the window overlooking the city of Sardis.

After rereading Anthony's message, he thought, *Excellent work! Anthony has not disappointed me. He's doing what I saw him do a year ago in the forests above Sardis. He's persistent, determined, and alert. These bandits are rebels comparing themselves to the Persian satraps of ancient Sardis.*

After we locate and arrest them, Anthony will come back to Sardis with his wife and child. A real Roman soldier. I think this is adequate proof that he is not the dishonest, conniving person that Diotrephes makes him out to be. When the rebels reappear this spring, Anthony has an excellent chance of capturing them.

OLIVE GROVE FARM AT FORTY TREES

Nikias stopped at the door of his house before going outside to care for his animals. The sky was dark as he pulled his cloak around himself. Wind whipped through the valley. *Always windy here, especially in winter.*

Since becoming a follower of the Way, he began each day with a short prayer. He stopped at the door before going to work and prayed for each person in the five families, including his wife and children. *I should not fear, yet, Lord, I'm afraid for my lifelong sweetheart. She is due to give birth at any time. Protect Penelope!*

Nikias left to feed the horses and cows. While caring for the farm, he had begun to recite Scripture, following Anthony's suggestion. His dog walked behind him, happily wagging its brown tail.

He walked with a determined step, pleased with the better results in copying the story told by Mark. Last week his brothers found the task a bit easier.

As he thought about Anthony, Rebekah, and Miriam and what he had learned from each of them, he realized that he was becoming a better father. His sons were Evander and Hamon, thirteen and eight years old, and his two girls were Rhoda, ten, and Sandra, six. They were the most important people in his life.

Two years before, when he decided to eventually buy a farm, he did not know what to say to his brothers. However, recent trips gave him a better idea of the layout in Thyatira's districts. He decided to keep his plans a secret for a while longer.

Since Penelope was expecting their fifth child, he was debating the name to give to his new little boy. His plans to have his own farm were also going well. *Penelope will deliver safely. God promised it, and he is my shield. He will keep me safe when I go to the villages. I haven't explored all the lands around. That will come next year, and soon I'll have my own farm!*

Won't my brothers be surprised!

THE CITY OF THYATIRA

Four guards from the Acropolis of Sardis arrived in Thyatira on Tuesday morning. Having orders from their commander to find the Ben Shelah house, they asked the way and arrived at Jonathan's door. Two wagons waited outside, and the guards were ready for what might be a tussle with a strong opponent.

"Open up! The Security Guard of the Acropolis of Sardis!"

Arte came to the door, wiping his hands. He was preparing the noon meal and was wet up to his elbows from washing turnips and beans before cooking them. He was alone in the house with Arpoxa and Saulius. Even Grace was away with Miriam. The child had not felt well, so Miriam was buying herbs at the agora to make some medicine. She would boil them in water to make a remedy.

"May I help you?" Arte asked the guards.

"We have instructions to arrest Anthony Suros. Here, read this! We are to take him; his wife, Miriam; and their little child, Chrysa Grace, back to Sardis."

Arte's words had to be forced out. "Who is Anthony Suros?"

"A Roman legionary. He lives here. We were given instructions by the Sardis Acropolis Guard Chief to arrest him. He is living at the home of Jonathan Ben Shelah."

"Yes, this is the home of Jonathan Ben Shelah, but the man you seek does not live here. He has never been here. I have no idea what you are talking about."

"Of course he lives here! Do not try to hide him."

Arte kept the attention of the four guards on Anthony. *I'll not say anything about Miriam and her baby. These are cruel men, and I don't trust a word of what they're saying.*

"What does Anthony Suros look like?"

"He is easy to spot. He has a red scar from his right eye to his chin. Stupid fellow! Almost got his head cut off in a battle."

"Come in and look around. No one here by that name. I swear I've never seen anyone with a scar like that."

Two guards waited outside and two entered, where they saw Arpoxa reclining on a couch. "Who are you?" demanded one of the guards eyeing the woman on the couch.

"My name is Arpoxa. May I help you?"

"Could you help? That's strange! Looks like your baby is coming at any minute! You'll be the one needing help."

"Yes, I'm going to have my baby soon. Why are you here?"

"To arrest the soldier, Anthony Suros. He is wanted in Sardis."

Arpoxa recoiled in fear. Memories flooded back of being dragged away from her home onto a ship in Tanais. Chains had been placed around her twisted feet. She had stood naked in the slave market in Pergamum. The memory of being put up for sale took her breath away. She dreaded being separated from her husband.

Her chest was heaving and her breath came in spurts, but she acted with courage. "I can promise you that no one called Anthony Suros has ever been here. Let me show you around the house. Examine every room. If you find a single piece of armor or sign of a military man living in this house, then you can arrest him. And me as well."

She asked Arte to take Saulius, and she picked up her crutches, a painful way to get around. "Sirs, I'm going to do something I should not do. I'll show you the bedrooms. Look around, but do not take anything."

"We are honest men. We only came for the legionary, his wife, and the child."

She took them to Bani and Serah's room. "A Jewish man and his wife stay here."

They glanced at all the other rooms: Jonathan and Rebekah's, Gil and Danila's, and then hers. She took them to Miriam's and Grace's room.

"This is the last one. A woman stays here with a child, but the child is sick with a breathing problem, and they are out to get medicine." Inspired, she knew how to threaten them. "If you stay in here too long, you might get sick as well."

The men sputtered, snarling. "Are there any other houses on this property?"

"Yes, the stewards' house. Next to the rooms where the slave lives. I will show you." She made as if to walk there, but the guards were impatient.

The young Scythian woman was being kind, honest, and direct, but she moved so slowly. The guards quickly gave up and returned to their wagons.

"No armor, breastplate, helmet, or shield. Nothing resembling an offensive weapon, a sword, or a javelin. There's no soldier here by any name," said one guard. "We searched the house, and what did we find? Nothing! Anthony Suros has never been here."

"I'm glad to be going back emptyhanded," said the youngest guard, "even though our Acropolis Guard Chief will be angry! He'll have to tell the mayor that we failed. He is always at odds with Commander Felicior.

"Ours is such a small jurisdiction—just the small area on top of Sardis Acropolis, nothing more. We came without permission from Commander Felicior, and we would be arresting one of his legionaries, which seems highly irregular! Maybe illegal! I was afraid to arrest Anthony Suros. If it became a problem with the army, the blame would probably fall on us."

The other three laughed at the sensitivities of their younger companion. If they had failed in their assignment, it was not a significant loss. At least they had been to Thyatira, their first time there, and they wanted to enjoy what the city had to offer before riding back the next day.

When Miriam returned home with Grace, Arpoxa and Arte explained everything that had happened when the guards from Sardis came to arrest Anthony.

It was a frightening discussion, mostly since there was no indication of what authority had sent them and whether there was a chance that they would come again.

Miriam immediately wrote an angry description of the whole incident in a letter to Anthony. She wanted Commander Felicior to use his power to ensure there were no more of these raids. If she had been in the house with Grace, the result would have been disastrous.

Chapter 33
Disappointments and Rewards

THE ACROPOLIS IN THE CITY OF SARDIS

The guards sent to arrest Anthony wore miserable expressions as they arrived back in Sardis. The weather had turned cold as they left Thyatira, and they had not been prepared for icy winds. Their exposed skin felt numb. Ascending the steep road up to the top of the Sardian Acropolis, they were shivering and bad-tempered. They reported to Mayor Tymon Tmolus, who was waiting for them.

"Sir, we went to the house, and no one fitting that description has ever been there."

Diotrephes heard the report from the mayor the next day, on Thursday morning. He was furious with the four guards. "Where is he then?" he yelled.

Mayor Tymon had not seen such a display like this before, and the young man's temper surprised him. He was given to understand that the Director of the Department of History was level-headed and disciplined. This fit of rage unnerved the mayor.

Later that afternoon, Diotrephes again confronted the guards. He had finished his classes at the gymnasium and taken the steep walk up to the acropolis. Arriving out of breath, he bellowed, "Why didn't you bring the man we sent you to arrest?"

One of the junior guards said, "He wasn't in the city. We were given access to every room in the house."

"He was in there! I had good information he was staying with the Ben Shelah family."

The senior guard spoke severely. "Diotrephes, we went to the home of Jonathan Ben Shelah. He was not at that home. Only three people were there: a house slave, a crippled woman, and a boy, her toddler. We searched the whole house. She showed us every room. No one had ever seen this man or heard of him."

A cold shiver crept up his back as Diotrephes asked for details about everything in the house. He was especially interested in the lame woman who stayed alone in the house with a child.

"Tell me about the woman. I'm a teacher, and details are important to me."

"From her looks, she is from Scythia, very lame. She has club feet."

It was not the temperate weather that caused a spine-chilling sensation to enter his heart. He saw the acropolis guards look at one another with fear in their eyes.

Hmmm, there can only be one woman like that, crippled in both feet and a Scythian. That is the woman Antipas bought at the slave market. What if my informant made a mistake thinking the Scythian woman and child were Miriam and Chrysa? The guards looked through the bedrooms used for Jonathan's family. What if Miriam and Chrysa stay in one of those rooms? Could she and the baby have been out of the home when the guards arrived?

Where is Anthony? Why does Felicior not tell me the details of Anthony's assignment? I cannot afford another mistake, so I won't pressure Mayor Tymon to send the guards again, but thank Zeus, I think I now know where the child is. I can focus on capturing the child and leave Felicior to worry about Anthony. All I need is a plan. Then my uncle will have his daughter back.

That evening in the comfort and security of Alexina's home, he wrote another letter.

December 4, in the 12th year of Domitian
From: Diotrephes
To: My dear mother, Lydia-Naq

Peace. If you are well, then I am well.

I did not write last week because of special lectures in the Lecture Hall of Karpos. A few people are talking about my speeches, but not many want to attend in the cold weather.

I still have not located Anthony, but that's not important. I think I know where Miriam and the baby live. I used my friendship with Mayor Tymon Tmolus. I requested four guards of the Sardis Acropolis to go to Thyatira. These guards only have the authority to guard the acropolis grounds, nothing else. I think you know that there's bad blood between Commander Felicior and Mayor Tymon.

Four guards from the acropolis were sent to bring Anthony, Miriam, and Chrysa back to Sardis, but they returned emptyhanded.

Commander Felicior was furious when he learned what happened. "Stay out of my jurisdiction! You have no authority over army personnel!" he yelled, and he threatened to arrest me if I interfered with army personnel again.

I'm sure, though, that we know where Miriam and the baby are. I'll wait for the right moment. We'll prevail even though the Ben Shelah family is trying to change our customs. As you know, the motto of the city of Sardis is "Never Enough Gold." The family spreads their teaching through songs and working with poor families. Miriam composed the songs, and as people sing them, they twist the minds of humble people.

Jace is a growing problem for me too because two other teachers complained that I fired him without the process he deserved as a longstanding, popular teacher.

I will not give up despite increasing troubles. Please make a sacrifice to Zeus with a request that I will know how to bring our baby to Pergamum.

Please let Uncle Zoticos read this letter.

JONATHAN AND REBEKAH'S HOME

Chanukah had arrived, and Rebekah and Jonathan's eyes shone with excitement. Miriam invited her new friends from the guild to a meal where Jonathan would explain the importance of this event. Arpoxa hobbled to the table, feeling heavy and expecting her child at any time.

Melpone was present, but her father and son had stayed at home. The young women took off their cloaks and entered chattering, beautifully dressed. Rebekah lit the first candle of Chanukah. The usual menorah had space for seven lamps, but the special Chanukah menorah would be used for eight days.

"Each night, we light one more," said Jonathan, explaining the importance of the event. The women had never heard of the Maccabees. "It's an old tradition that began almost 260 years ago. An enemy captured our city, and he offered a pig as a sacrifice in our temple."

Miriam looked around the crowded room. She sensed that the

presence of young women from the Guild of Purple Honors had an unexpected effect on her uncle, and his voice softened.

Hesper asked, "What does a pig in Jerusalem have to do with lamps in Thyatira?"

"I'll explain. The Jews pushed that evil king out of the city and went to the temple. It had been desecrated; that is, it was made unholy by sacrificing an animal that God does not accept. They had to make the temple clean again, which required eight days of purification. They decided to burn lamps of a special menorah every night for eight nights in a specific sequence. However, special consecrated oil had to be used, and when they started, there wasn't enough for all eight nights.

"The first night they lit one lamp; the second night they lit the first plus one more. On the third night, three lamps shone in the temple. By the eighth night, how many do you think lit up the temple? Yes, all of them! And when the oil was sufficient to light the lamps for all eight days, it was considered a miracle."

Miriam watched the response of each guest.

"Eight lamps! Then it was a miracle!" observed Koren. She closed her eyes.

Adelpha turned from Jonathan to her friends. "You light candles in your house because it's clean? And you eat no pig meat or pig blood? Now I understand why they never serve pork."

"In a way, yes," answered Jonathan, "but there's much more to it."

Calandra felt a thrill. The first lamp lit in this home was linked to a beautiful event in the past. "How did the miracle happen?"

"It was a great moment. God kept the oil burning, even when there was not enough. How it happened, we don't know."

But Adelpha remained skeptical. She thought of festivities celebrated at the guilds. "Is that reason enough for eight nights of feasting? Your custom comes at the time when our temples commemorate the shortest day of the year. I think you just want parties on cold evenings!"

Rebekah looked at Jonathan, and she nodded. He took the hint and explained, "No, the eight nights remind us of the eight days of purification. Also, the lamp is an important symbol: light overcomes darkness. God supplies what we need, sometimes in unusual ways. He always provides."

At the end of the meal, the dishes and tables were cleared away, and Miriam led the women in practicing the songs they had learned at previous meetings. She then introduced them to two new songs that they would further work on at the next meeting. These songs would continue to be heard in the workroom at the guild for several more years.

After the singing practice was complete, most of the young women left. Three stayed behind to talk with Miriam: Calandra, Melpone, and Celina.

Melpone began the conversation, saying, "I have a question. It's something about what my grandmother said when someone asked her, 'How do I get to heaven?'"

"What have you been told?" asked Miriam.

Melpone tossed her head back. "Grandmother told me that to get to heaven, I have to do four things: first, cross a wide chasm on a long path. Second, the path is only the width of a hair or a sharp blade of a two-edged sword. I must not fall off because of the hot flames below. Next, cross the chasm with a lamb in my arms. Finally, find a book with my name in it when I get to the other side. If I do all four, the doors of heaven will open to me. What does all that mean?"

Celina spoke for the first time. "Yes, that's what my grandmother said too."

Miriam gasped. "It's a little bit like a story Yeshua Messiah told!" *Their grandmothers are so near the truth. Close to it and not even aware of it.*

"Yeshua said that his followers must walk a narrow path. He even said he was that path! It's like saying, 'Walk with me,' 'Imitate my life,' or 'Where I go, come along.' In other words, 'Become my followers.' He talked about a wide gate and a narrow gate, and then he said that if we want to be part of the kingdom, we must walk his way and enter through the narrow gate. But I should tell you, being his follower can form chasms with our families."

"I've watched you for months now and how you stand up for what you believe," said Melpone. "Sibyl complained about you one morning at the workshop. She said, 'Miriam is dangerous. Her understanding of life is too narrow, and she does not want to accept the whole truth.'"

"That's what I'm talking about," Miriam added. "Some will object that the narrow road is too restrictive. Melpone, you talked about carrying a lamb across that chasm. Did you know that one of Yeshua Messiah's names is the 'Lamb of God who takes away the sins of the world'? You mentioned a book. The one on the other side is called the 'Book of Life.'"

Melpone responded, "Priests at temples talk about life after death. Gravestones are carved to remember the person who died. On one side, we see the man, his wife, and his child enjoying life, but the side facing where the sun goes down is left blank. No one knows what is over there beyond the sunset. Priests always talk about people leaving this life, but they never ever tell us about what happens after we die."

Miriam told them about the carpenter from Nazareth, who made things out of wood: chairs, tables, and houses. She explained how he healed sick people. They wanted to know more about his life and miracles. All was well until she said that he had been nailed on a cross.

"Then he was a terrible criminal, not a good man!" Calandra interrupted crossly.

"No, he wasn't a criminal; he had never done anything wrong. Romans call it a cross, but we call it a 'tree of sacrifice.' His disciples could not imagine that a small group of women would come to his tomb three days later and find it empty. His being alive again changed everything."

Soon the evening was over, and she kissed each of the three women good night and said goodbye. As she bent toward Melpone's cheeks, she saw tears in the eyes of her new friend.

"I'm glad you invited me," said Celina softly as she put on her cloak.

"Yes, you are a good friend," agreed Calandra.

THE LIBRARY OF PERGAMUM, THE PERGAMUM ACROPOLIS

While Calandra said these words in Thyatira, Zoticos was in Pergamum rereading the letter received from Diotrephes. Zoticos had been the Chief Administrator of the Pergamum Library for two years. After learning that Trifane, the beautiful student in his classes, had borne a daughter, he dreamed of finding the child and bringing her up in his home. He looked at the words in the letter once more, and his heart skipped a beat. *My nephew knows where Chrysa is, and soon I'll have my little daughter with me!*

He paced across his office in the Library of Pergamum and then sat down. Zoticos calculated again. One question kept returning. *Trifane, the woman I loved, gave birth to my daughter in early February. That would mean my daughter is a year and nine months now. Trifane studied with me from October to the end of March...my best student. Then there were those exciting days during the Festival of Zeus...how she loved the theater and tragedies, choirs, and entertainment. She enjoyed the buffoons most of all!*

I lured her here to my office and then to my home. She got pregnant at my house, and now Diotrephes says he'll soon get my daughter back! Bless the gods—an answer to endless offerings. I'll have my daughter in my house, and the Milon family will not die out! The blood of ancient Lydia will flow through our veins for another generation. But how did my daughter come to be in the home of a Roman soldier?

He rose from his chair suddenly, uttering a quiet curse. He could not imagine how Anthony came to have his daughter, Chrysa, in his care. All he knew about Miriam was that she was the granddaughter of that Jew, Antipas, the man who had been appropriately punished.

The memory of the trial in the Roman Theater came back. Every row was filled as more than fifteen thousand people waited for a verdict. There Antipas was, facing the crowd and relating stories about the Jewish carpenter. The short Jew dared to stand up to seven high priests. Each of the most important temples in Pergamum had been represented that night.

He tried to focus on Miriam to see if an image of her face would come to him, but as he closed his eyes, he instead saw the short man raised by a crane and lowered toward the boiling oil. He tried to erase the last words the condemned man spoke. They were loud enough for all to hear. "Praise to God, Adonai, and forgiveness and blessing for the people of Pergamum!"

Zoticos shook his head, ridding himself of those words. He dreamed once again of Trifane in his arms. She was the most wonderful woman he had ever met, although perhaps a bit too young for him.

He longed for her to come to him, to live in his home. *I'm forty-three years old, which means Trifane is twenty-six. I try to imagine her here with Chrysa and me, but it's no use. Anthony and Miriam won't leave my mind. How did they capture my baby?*

Anyway, my nephew, Diotrephes, will be rewarded. He will follow me as Chief Librarian someday, and Trifane will be the mother she was destined to be for my child.

Tired and irritated, Zoticos rolled up the letter. He took a deep breath, thrilled with his thoughts of future satisfaction, and slowly placed the letter down on the center of his desk. He gazed at the scroll for a long time.

JONATHAN AND REBEKAH'S HOME

On Thursday afternoon, Arpoxa felt the first signs of labor. Her water broke, and she called, "Miriam, come quickly!" She sounded weak and fearful. "Call the midwife! My baby! I want Ateas to be here with me!"

Miriam forgot about the formalities of Chanukah and called Rebekah. She walked quickly to the home of the Jewish midwife, who lived close to the synagogue. The two women arrived soon afterward. Arpoxa was in labor for several hours. Rebekah told Arte to prepare simple foods, and the men in the household ate their meal below.

Arpoxa kept crying out, "Ateas, come! Where are you, Ateas?"

Her healthy baby boy was born before dawn, and Arpoxa held him close, admiring his delicate fingers and toes. She rubbed her hand over his head. "Just like his father," she stated with joy.

Saulius woke up crying, not sure why he was sleeping in another room. Miriam took the toddler by the hand. "You have a new baby brother, Saulius! Come. Here is your mommy, and here is your baby brother!"

Rebekah was deeply touched. She had been at the bedside for hours. She said, "Arpoxa, you have a beautiful newborn baby boy, born December 11."

A troubled crease formed on her forehead. *As yet, you have no name. Your father is partially lame and is away on a military assignment. Your mother is completely lame, and here you are, a healthy boy. How will she take care of you plus a two-year-old?*

Rebekah's tears flowed freely, and she wiped them from her cheeks and lips. She tasted her tears. They were salty, and she observed out loud, "Childbirth, the mixture of joy and pain."

OLIVE GROVE FARM AT FORTY TREES

Nikias readied his wagon for another trip. The scrolls inside the bags that he carried to the wagon contained fewer errors.

His brothers were getting better at this challenging work. *We are making fewer mistakes. I like what we copied down last night. "Put your hope in God, for I will yet praise him, my Savior and my God."*[98]

Nikias had prepared for a two-day trip with Zeno, Alberto, and Lykaios. Three small bags containing scrolls were going to be given to families who wanted to know more about Mark's story. He could not wait to see the happy surprise on friends' faces when they opened the bags and found gifts like these!

"We'll be back soon," Nikias told Penelope, speaking tenderly. "We'll be back, and then you can give birth to the new baby. What a joy for us; another healthy baby is on its way soon. Two boys and two girls now, and our third boy will be on his way!"

---

[98] Psalm 42:5

Chapter 34
Songs and Dancing

THE CITY OF THYATIRA

Something about the year's longest night brought both dread and hope to the people in Thyatira. Workshops opened late and closed early, and guild leaders encouraged their workers to congregate at their temples.

Men attended the well-known temples and spoke of profound mysteries. "Hidden things, obscure in their origins, can only be understood if people follow special teachings. Come! Gather in our circle of fellowship so you can fathom it all," they heard.

Among the many mystery religions, four were wildly popular in Thyatira.

Many married women hurried to the Temple of Demeter, recalling Persephone's annual descent into Hades. Everyone longed for green leaves, fresh fruits, blue skies, and warm temperatures. Their offerings guaranteed the return of Persephone.

The largest gathering place for men was the Temple of All Gods, a large temple close to the Fountain of Water Nymphs. Porticos lined three sides of the temple, permitting several different meetings to take place simultaneously.

The coming of the Egyptian merchants had been marked by the arrival of a priest of Isis and Osiris. The Egyptians believed that long ago, Set, the strong son of an Egyptian family, had killed his brother Osiris. Set scattered the remains of Osiris worldwide, causing the days to grow shorter. Life began to die. Isis, the wife of Osiris, started a search with his sister. They found his remains, brought them together, and revived him. Thus, according to the priests of Osiris and Isis, deep magic was theirs alone.

"Osiris deserved to be worshiped," they claimed. "We priests speak of a restored life." This mysterious interpretation brought comfort to a small group during the long nights and short days.

Another group of men, especially those speaking Latin, gathered in a natural cave halfway to the town of Julia Gordus. It was originally carved by a nearby stream at Mount Gordus. With a little work, it had been turned into a temple. Pictures lined the walls of the cave, called the Mithraeum. Mithras ruled worlds that people could only see at night. This Persian god needed four creatures to rule the cosmos: a snake, a raven, a dog, and a scorpion. Pictures on the walls connected little dots copied from the patterns of stars seen in the sky on a clear night. The priests lived by predictions of what was auspicious on which day.

Many men joined the Mithras Cult on December 21, reciting long, secret passages given to them months before. They had sworn secrecy and loyalty to the Mithraeum.

The high priest of Mithras was delighted when so many men recited those verses for the first time. As they sprinkled a pinch of salt into the flame at the altar, the high priest uttered words of initiation. "You have been reborn," he pronounced. "Now the days will grow longer."

The high priest of Mithras stood straight upright, secure in his knowledge of the stars! The constellations of the sky and the signs of the zodiac filled his mind.

Power flowed from the purple and red band decorating his shoulders. He boasted to his assistant, "Never have we had so many men being admitted to our order as this day. Mithras has accepted our homage. Life will sprout again in the fields and on the farms. The number of those coming for initiation is growing each year."

THE MILITARY GARRISON IN SARDIS

While Anthony waited for a more complete report on the sale of slaves in the province of Asia Minor, he spent a day talking with Commander Felicior. He had trained as a scout for battle and was used to tracking enemies through dense forests and then reporting his observations to his commanding officer. Anthony clearly explained the entire sequence of events and what they had learned about the rebels.

After finishing his conference with the garrison commander, he went to the barracks to write a letter.

December 21, in the 12th year of Domitian
From: Anthony
To: Miriam, my wife, who fills my waking moments

Peace be with you and Grace. There are no words to say how much I miss you both. Grace will be learning to talk, saying the phrases only children can put together. I'm missing those moments and can never recover them.

Commander Felicior told me a brief story about Diotrephes and the mayor having the Sardis Acropolis Guard commander send four of his soldiers to arrest me in Thyatira. He said that nothing happened, and he threatened to arrest Diotrephes if he did it again on the grounds of interfering with an official army operation. That should stop whatever Diotrephes is trying to do, but I still do not fully trust that you are safe. Always stay cautious. I'm guessing that you will have told me about it in a letter waiting for me at the farm. I believe that God is watching over and protecting you.

My present assignment began six months ago. Today I gave a lengthy report to Commander Felicior. I'll be here in Sardis until the end of this month and then go to Soma, where the next phase of my assignment will begin. Our progress is slow but very sure. Rome must understand what it's dealing with. Crimes have come to light, some of which we did not know about before.

Two days were spent at Olive Grove. Penelope and Nikias are expecting their fifth child. I experienced hilarity and constant laughter. Can you imagine Nikias training three brothers, barely literate, to copy scrolls? Lykaios is slower than the others, if you know what I mean, and keeps asking Nikias to repeat. When one of them makes another mistake, the others groan. Their wives and children sometimes listen, joining in with comments. They share a great sense of family.

However, visiting them and seeing them act as a family, I feel your absence even more. I watched Nikias and his children. The oldest, Evander, has started helping with farm work. His brother is Hamon, and there are two sisters, Rhoda and Sandra. I love this little family.

One thing still thrills me: understanding how Grandfather Antipas trained followers. He worked through different topics and started explaining his personal thoughts. He talked about shame and guilt, acceptance and forgiveness, honor, mercy, love, and grace. He explained so many things: prayer, solitude, fasting, and helping others. I wish he had given us more training on these and so many other topics.

Nikias has been going to surrounding villages, but I'm worried for him. He is enthusiastic and a bit too overexcited. I fear this might set people against him. Not everyone wants to hear that the gods really do not have power. For this, the authorities called your grandfather "an atheist." I don't want Nikias to suffer.

Tonight, on this shortest day of the year, I say, "Farewell, until the Almighty brings us together again."

I pray it will be soon.

THE CITY OF THYATIRA

Starting on December 23 and lasting all week, parties celebrating Saturnalia filled the streets with noise and activities. Young men and women, and some older ones too, marked the end of the year. They dreamed of the return of spring, of planting, and of harvest time.

Competitions held in the taverns brought together, those who considered themselves excellent judges of wines. Adjudicators tasted each sample.

In other places, men challenged each other. "Who can drink the most and still walk a straight line?"

Previously, clusters of grapes had been cut from the stalk with sharp pruning knives and crushed in vats and the purified juice fermented. Now the new wine made people rejoice in the generosity of Dionysius.

Each night during the last days of the year, the loudest hubbub came from the Temple of Dionysus. The popular god of wine boasted many followers. For a few days, Dionysius was king of the ceremonies.

JONATHAN AND REBEKAH'S HOME

Tuesday evening's special supper at Jonathan's home started off well. However, by the end of the evening, the atmosphere was anything but pleasant. Jonathan welcomed all his guests, happy that Kilan and Orah, his wife, had accepted the invitation. He knew that Kilan wanted to bring the Ben Shelah family firmly into the congregation and distance Sibyl from Jonathan's inner circle.

The conflict began at a table where Sibyl started an argument with Orah.

While Rabbi Hanani was away, Kilan was the temporary president of the synagogue. He reclined at the meal with Orah. Sibyl and Melpone reclined on a couch nearby.

Jonathan heard the first words of a conversation. Wanting to absorb every word, he stopped the comments he was making to another guest.

"Yes, only one God! That's what I believe!" declared Orah, the Jewish woman.

Sibyl's voice held firm. "People in this city, like my mother, believe in many gods."

"The people of Israel have always believed in a God who is righteous and just." Orah bristled. "We would never go back on our belief. We believe in and worship one God."

Sibyl shot back, "Orah, are you saying the God of Israel is superior to the gods respected and worshiped by these people?"

"Let me illustrate this," said Orah. "Do you remember the ancient story of Aqhat?"

"Of course I know that story! We all do," Sibyl answered. A puzzled look on her face suggested that she wondered why an important woman in the synagogue would speak about a Persian myth.

Orah continued, "Sibyl, I'm telling you this myth to show you this. In your stories, gods fight among themselves. Pagan gods are capricious, vindictive, and jealous. They have nothing to offer us!"

Jonathan leaned forward, wanting to step in and hoping to avoid a controversy. He could see that Sibyl was going to reject Orah's logic. He opened his mouth to say something, but no words came. *I want to add something here, but my heart is empty. I can't respond to either Orah or Sibyl.*

He heard Sibyl disagree. "No, not at all! They show that people want to live forever. It's this yearning, a legitimate one, that causes conflicts."

Orah, unable to control herself, shouted in Jonathan's house, "Pagan gods are petty and jealous! They bring violence, and fights break out between them. Do you believe those gods control your life, Sibyl? Your sister, Hulda, has been sick for months. If the gods caused it, why don't they heal her? How many sacrifices have you made for her?" It was the first time that Orah had confronted Sibyl, something she had wanted to do for months.

Sibyl did not say a word. She chafed at the implication that the gods were powerless.

Jonathan closed his eyes, a pained look on his face. He went back to many experiences in his life. *I want to explain what I believe. I used to be able to do it with ease. Orah speaks her mind so clearly. But since I started spending so much time in the Temples of Apollo and Artemis, I've lost an essential part of who I used to be.*

OLIVE GROVE FARM AT FORTY TREES

Penelope's fifth child was born on Tuesday, just after midnight. The midwife, who had been called from Forty Trees, cut the cord and gently placed the newborn in her father's strong arms.

"Dear Penelope has given you another child. Two boys and now three girls! Your next one will be a boy, so your family will always end up balanced, boys and girls, a beautiful family!"

"I don't feel beautiful right now," Penelope said, sighing, taking the baby, and feeling the warmth and love. She was grateful for another safe delivery.

"You helped us with five babies. Thank you so much," Nikias said to the midwife. "You must be both happy and tired because it's late. It's a good thing that you came when you did; she delivered so quickly, not like last time. Stay overnight. I'll take you back to Forty Trees in the wagon after the sun comes up."

To his children, he said, "God answered our prayers. He gave us another healthy child. Your mother is fine. Now we need to think of a name for your sister."

He started to sing for joy and burst out, "You are our little girl, Melody! This will be your name! We love you, Melody!""

JONATHAN AND REBEKAH'S HOME

On the last night of the year, the Ben Shelah family offered Miriam's new friends a special meal. Miriam planned her topic with care.

"Tonight I would like the group to discuss something interesting," she began. "Can we talk about high priests? We Jews do not have one now, as you know. Since the destruction of our temple twenty-two years ago, there has been no priesthood. Let's hear about high priests. Who will start us off?"

The women attending Greek temples had endless stories about high priests, many of them humorous. Dreama and Hesper warmed to the subject with stories of when they were children.

Neoma told stories, bringing much laughter. She was a born actress and imitated the mannerisms, showing how priests held their hands. She exaggerated her actions, and the young women loved her warmth and humor.

Miriam observed, "You told us many stories, but I didn't hear words about mercy or warmth. Compassion...yes, that's the word I'm looking for. How do priests care for your people?"

Suddenly the laughter changed to silence. The topic was close to home. Everyone had lost someone from their wider circle of friends in the last twelve months, but they could not think of when a priest of any temple had provided any sort of comfort for their pain or sorrow.

"Let me tell you about my personal high priest," Miriam began. "Yeshua Messiah came from heaven to experience death—what a strange assignment!"

She quoted from a letter she had recently read. "'The children of the earth are made of flesh and blood, and he became human to share in their humanity. This was so that by his death he might destroy him who holds the power of death, the devil. He came to free those who all their lives were held in slavery by the fear of dying. He had to be made like us in every way for this reason: to become a merciful and faithful high priest in service to God. He also came to make atonement for the sins of all people. Because he himself suffered when he was tempted, he can help those who are being tempted.'[99] Have you ever heard about this high priest?"

Dreama said, "I haven't. Your high priest came down from heaven? Where did he live?"

"He is making people like us into his temple, a dwelling place," said Miriam simply.

"I never heard of that kind of a temple!" said Dreama.

Hesper added, "You mean to say your high priest destroyed our god, Hades? If he did, then why do babies still die? I don't understand. Explain it again please."

"Yes, babies still die. But we have a living hope and a promise that we'll live with him in heaven forever after we die."

Calandra looked far away. "I would love to know one who is merciful and kind, not a priest who acts distant from us and who

---

[99] Based on Hebrews 2:14–18

kills animals and makes sacrifices." She sounded dissatisfied with something.

Miriam looked around the circle and stopped when she saw Celina. "My high priest…" Celina started to say, and then she half-whispered the words for the first time. "Did you say, '*He is able to help those who are being tempted*'? *He can help me?*"

"Yes, that's the story of Yeshua, our Messiah," Miriam agreed, having heard the words spoken quietly. "Before he came, we Jews believed his purpose was to free us from the Romans. That sounds funny since my husband is a Roman and a legionary!"

She was met with a laugh, a much needed moment of humor.

"Instead, Yeshua brought a better deliverance. He came to free us from the fear we all carry, that of death. Our high priest understands us."

She paused. Everyone was leaning forward, even Adelpha and Sibyl. It was the moment she was waiting for, even though she had imagined it would take a lot longer to come to the point where she would sing the song she had composed for tonight.

The new song had begun to form in her mind as she walked home several days ago. She hated to think of Grace climbing and falling over the patio railing as had happened to the little boy, Attalay Tantalus, who fell to his death over the edge of a cliff in Pergamum.

For an instant, thinking about the little aristocratic boy's death, she pictured Grace falling and being unable to help her.

She would have to care for Grace in so many ways before she became an adult. She felt the responsibility of motherhood and the dread of a child dying. Mothers carried fears of their own death and that of their children.

The enormity of raising a child and losing one… *How can anyone bring comfort to a mourning mother? How can the hope of the resurrection be more than just a wish? How can I comfort anyone completely unless I have been there first?*

"I have a new song for this group that I think fits what we have been talking about. I called this song 'Children of the Resurrection.' This song uses a mournful tune I heard in Thyatira. I asked my new relative, Danila, to play the flute. Melpone agreed to accompany me with the tambourine, and Shiri plays the harp. They will play an interlude between the last two verses.

"I'll sing it twice, and then we can sing it together. That way, you'll have the words in mind when you go home."

One baby smiles and laughs, such great hope,
Friends bring gifts. What a joy for everyone!
A second mother wonders how she'll cope.
"We've no money, but my boy's so handsome!"
One hugs a daughter, another a son.

All mothers fear when the baby is ill.
The father's heart is full of trepidation.
"Is this a cold? Is it worse? Or will it kill?
Must death always be our portion?"
Fathers long for resurrection.

Mothers flee from situations dire:
Floods, flames, family enmity.
Some parents talk of war and fire.
Death creeps in, robbing posterity.
Mothers wish for resurrection.

Danila played the chorus tune on the flute. Melpone tapped her tambourine, and Shiri repeated the melody on a harp before the last two verses.

Bathsheba watched as her son's health waned.
King David had no other choice.
"Can I bring our child back again?"
Across the years, we still hear his voice:
"Soon, we'll all find resurrection."

Our high priest knows our feeble frame:
Faithful, merciful, kind kinsman.
"He destroyed death's power!" we exclaim.
"No one needs to stay an orphan.
We're children of the resurrection!"

The subject of hope after a child's death brought a shaft of the light in the fading hours of the year. Each one had a different response.

Before leaving the house, Sibyl leaned close to Miriam. "That's a topic we have to talk about some more. I'm not sure I believe in Yeshua in quite the same way."

Next, Melpone embraced her friend and did not want to let go. "As you sang, I thought of the contrast between your music and the recent Greek play I attended. The drama in the theater left people drowning in pain, but your song, even though it is set to a mournful tune, has words that lift me out of death and misfortune."

She gave Miriam an embrace, whispering, "No one ever told me about all this! I would never have understood about resurrection if you had not taught me. Thank you!"

Calandra and Celina came together and went to the door. Calandra wanted to know more but was skeptical. She shrugged and left without much comment, but Celina said, "I have something important to talk about with you when we have time."

As Miriam watched an involuntary shudder shake the young woman's shoulders, she thought, *Celina is now ready to talk about the deep things of her heart.*

Adelpha, Dreama, Hesper, Koren, and Neoma thanked Rebekah and Miriam for the party but said nothing about the conversation and not a word about her song.

Hypatia was the last to leave, and she grasped Miriam by the shoulders. "You know," she said, "if what you are singing is true, then it makes all the difference. It would make all the difference...."

She left it at that without finishing her thoughts. On the last night of the year, her questions were hard to express in words.

Purple Honors

Part 3
Slaves and Captors

January
AD 93

Chapter 34
Marks of Loyalty

THE MILITARY GARRISON IN SOMA

Cold gusts blew through Soma on the first day of the new year. Anthony and the members of his squad stood at attention. Standing before his company, Commander Servius addressed the thirty-six regulars who stood in formation, nine wide and four deep. "Across the Roman Empire today, legionaries swear the Solemn Oath. Soldiers, sailors, and auxiliaries all declare allegiance. At least 375,000 trained men protect the empire.

"To the east, legions guard the Euphrates River. Persian troops threaten us there. To the north, we face barbarians. From the Lower Rhine in the west, along the Danube River and along the Black Sea, more than half of Caesar's legions secure our frontiers against unruly enemies.[100]

"While we stand at attention here, we are joined with the twenty-five legions across the empire, from Britain to Persia and the Black Sea to northern Africa.

"Dedicated, experienced in battle, and successful in conquests—this is our glory. We are honored to be in the most powerful army the world has seen. Legion XXI, the Predators, is no more, and Dacia remains our enemy, but Rome will soon govern there.

"Asia Minor, where we live, is a peaceful province. The Soma Garrison is only a small division. Here, regulars guard the Postal Road between Pergamum and Thyatira. We welcome the new squad members from the Sardis garrison. Now declare the Solemn Oath!" he barked. "Caesar is lord and god!"

Their reply came back instantly. "Caesar is lord and god!"

---

[100] Many Roman authors wrote about the military. Cassius Dio, *History;* Frontinus, wrote *Strategemata;* Florus, *Epitome;* and Vitruvius, *De Architectura.* Polybius wrote *Histories.* He was a Greek historian and a close friend of Scipio, an important Roman general who described details of military life. These five classical authors described various aspects of the military organization, weapons, war strategy, history of battles, defense against missiles and other weapons, and the navy.

Commander Servius had placed Anthony in the front row, in front of the Golden Eagle. He watched Anthony closely, and afterward, calling him to his office, Servius spoke severely. "Soldier, you did not declare the Solemn Oath."

"Sir, I have repeated the oath thousands of times."

"You said, 'Caesar is lord.' The full declaration is 'Caesar is lord and god.' You know this!"

Anthony stood tall. "Sir, for more than one hundred years, soldiers pronounced three words: 'Caesar is lord.' That was all that was demanded. They affirmed complete loyalty to Rome even before Augustus became emperor. When I began military service under Domitian's father, Emperor Vespasian, I declared these three words: 'Caesar is lord.' After Vespasian's death, his son Titus became our emperor, and the oath continued the same: 'Caesar is lord.' Only in recent days was this changed. Domitian added two words: 'and god.' I am repeating what I was taught and what millions of soldiers have declared."

"We are no longer under Vespasian or Titus," Servius snarled. He spoke one word at a time. "Do you respect your emperor?" A threat underlay each pause.

"Sir, my face carries the price of my allegiance to Caesar. I almost died protecting Rome from barbarians, the ones you mentioned in your discourse just now."

Servius finally had the opportunity to pursue each detail he wanted to know. *This is the time to learn about Anthony's wound.*

"Commander Felicior assigned you this task of eradicating these bandits, did he not?"

"Yes sir."

"What is your status right now?"

"I'm a reservist on special assignment. In five years, I hope to retire in Philippi."

"And before Felicior, who was your commander?"

"Commander Cassius in Pergamum. I was an instructor, beginning four years ago."

"And before that, who was your commanding officer?"

"I was under General Celsus Vettulenus Civica Ceriales in Upper Germanica."

"Where did you join Legion XXI, the Predators? How old were you?"

"In Rome, at age 17, I said my first oath to Emperor Vespasian in his third year."[101]

"And your assignments?"

"Legion XXI was capturing large pieces of territory in Upper Germanica. I was sent to observe barbarians in villages before the army made an attack. We conquered an important area in the first month of Domitian's reign, the city of Vic Portos. That's in the Black Forest. With that city in our hands, our legion marched to the Neckar River."

"Your legion marched to the Neckar River and laid down roads in that area?"

"Yes, ten years after I became a legionary, Alisinensium was controlled by the Legion.[102] Later, a bridge was put across the Neckar River."

"What led to your being wounded?"

"I learned that three officers had rebellious tendencies. I overheard them speaking against the emperor, questioning his military and political decisions. Even after Vespasian was crowned emperor, a small group of legionaries resisted his authority."

Servius snarled, sharp lines forming around his mouth. "Resisted his authority? Is that possible?"

"Yes sir, and the army's highest officials know it. The loyalties of a few soldiers remained with General Vitellius, even after he was killed by Vespasian."

"Suros! It's dangerous to speak of political intrigue in the army!"

"Yes, and I know that you are aware of the events of Legion XXI six years ago."

"I know about that minor rebellion. Celsus Vettulenus Civica Ceriales became the governor of Asia Minor. He was executed for rebellion.' So were two other governors. Suros, you will submit to Domitian! Or do you want to face the wrath of the army? I want no more of your warped thinking. No more of it! You are dismissed."

Servius stood in front of his desk and watched Anthony turn and leave the office. *I could declare Suros a rebel and send him to*

---

[101] Anthony joined the army on January 1, AD 73.

[102] The city of Portos in southwestern Germany, today called Pforzheim, was conquered about AD 81. About two years later, the village of Alisinensium, today known as Bad Wimpfen, became the strategic point at which a wooden bridge was constructed to cross the Neckar River.

Smyrna for a court martial. That would give me increased visibility by my superiors because they would see my zeal for maintaining discipline and order within the army ranks. But it would end the search for the criminals when we are getting close to arresting the whole gang. In that case, a significant task would fail, and it would reflect poorly on how my leadership at the Garrison of Soma is judged.

No. I'll have to wait until this operation is successfully completed before I declare his disloyalty to the emperor and send him to trial. I will be known for clearing the roads of pirates and then eliminating a rebel.

THE SYNAGOGUE OF THYATIRA

A week later, on Saturday, an important gathering took place in the synagogue portico. Sibyl was explaining her new prophetic visions. She had written a list on a papyrus scroll, titled it "My New Prophecies for This Year," and showed it to any who would listen.

People spread the news quickly. "Come learn about your future!" Everyone wanted to know what lay ahead. However, when the elders of the congregation heard what Sibyl had done, their voices indicated astonishment.

They demanded time with Jonathan and Rebekah. "Something must be done," one man said. "I know our rabbi is away deciding important matters, but we have to act. Sibyl, the woman with the Jewish father and Greek mother, claims to have a gift of prophecy. People point to things she said. Sibyl claims to have predicted the rain in the summer last year and many other things, too, that have not been exactly accurate.

"She is a special friend of your family, isn't that right? It's well known that she spends more time at the Temple of Artemis than at the synagogue. For that matter, how can you permit her to come to your house?"

The meeting ended without a satisfactory resolution. No one wanted to be responsible for asking Sibyl to leave the fellowship after she declared that her father had been a well-known elder in the Synagogue of Rome.

The elders left with a demanding comment. "Jonathan, she is your friend, and for now, we are requiring that you put a stop to her declaring her prophecies on the grounds of the synagogue. The elders will be meeting to talk about what else we must do to keep this from misleading anyone in the congregation."

THE PORT OF SINOP, THE BLACK SEA

Craga sat with eight of his trusted friends in a small house he had rented for the winter on the southern shore of the Black Sea. He breathed deeply, enjoying the fresh air of Sinop's port. In a few hours, they would return to the tavern, enjoy wine, and brag about future accomplishments. For the time being, they were away from eavesdroppers. This was an ideal place to lay out their plans for the new season. On the shore below, yesterday's storm still sent waves and spray high into the air.

Gray clouds rushed along, darkening the horizon and giving the choppy waves a menacing look. However, in an unusual moment for late January, the sun shone through the clouds.

Craga looked at each of his friends and began to outline his plans for the coming year. He now used the title "tribune" for each of them, a term taken from the army.

"Last year, I promised a surprise. I've worked out how we're going to expand our maneuvers. Here are the plans for March through August. Our ship will be sailing from Sinop and through Chalcedon. This year, all slaves will go to the mines. That's where we got our greatest profits over the last two years."

The nine tribunes celebrated, punching their fists into the air. "More money!" beamed Maza. The space between his two front teeth gave him a crazed, menacing look.

"The first shipment leaves Sinop in March and will arrive in Port Daskyleion in early April. Ota, Tissa, Spithra, and Baga, you'll conduct our merchandise—forty slaves—to the mines. I'm assigning ten of our 'auxiliaries' to go with you. When necessary, one of the auxiliaries will act as a merchant at the check stations and will be provided with false identification. Since we own all these slaves, we won't have any outside merchants going with us.

"Arta, you'll meet up with Tira in Chalcedon as soon as it is safe for the ship to travel. He stayed there over the winter, working to bring more recruits into our growing army. I want you to plan out how we will be training and using the new people.

"A month later, in late April, Arta and Tira, you and five auxiliaries will take another twenty slaves from Sinop to arrive in May. We'll repeat it, with twenty more arriving in June, the same in

July, and twenty again in August. Altogether, that means one hundred slaves! We'll be sharing as much as 50,000 denarii, minus the expenses."

Cheers came from the eight rebels. They were delighted when Craga said, "Remember, our next meeting will be on May 10 after the May delivery to the mines! Then, to prosperity!"

Later, at the Sinop Tavern, under the shadow of the Fortress of Sinop, Craga raised a cup of wine and made a toast: "To prosperity!"

They didn't say why they were so happy, but other man at the tavern also raised their tankards. All joined in the New Year's cheer. The sense of goodwill was contagious, and even the owner of the bar joined in: "To prosperity!"

OLIVE GROVE FARM AT FORTY TREES

Arriving home, three of the brothers jumped down from the wagon, delighted to be back at the farm. What they hoped would be only a short visit to Gelembe, a village west of Stratonike, had caused them to question the risks of their brother's trips.

"Nikias! Never again!" they called out loudly, exasperated by the experience. "Don't count on us to go again!"

Zeno explained to his family what had happened. Naian was almost sick with worry as she hugged him. Three days had passed without seeing her husband. He said, "A storm struck when we got close to the village, and we had to stay there for two nights. Fortunately, the Gelembe inn owner took us in, or we might have perished!"

And then, turning to his older brother, he swore, "I'm not going with you again on any more expeditions! This trip almost left my wife a widow!"

Nikias interrupted, getting emotional. "No, you have it all wrong! Look how happy the Gelembe innkeeper's family was to have us stay there. Listen, everyone! This trip was a blessing because..." But he was outnumbered.

His notions were not acceptable to his brothers or their wives. And even more painful, Penelope now agreed with them. She said, "Nikias, please stop your travels around the countryside. What are you trying to accomplish?"

Chapter 36
Conflict in the Synagogue

THE SYNAGOGUE OF THYATIRA

As Nikias and Zeno were having their disagreement, another heated conversation was taking place. Today the elders' meeting at the Thyatira synagogue erupted with angry words. For years, the congregation's elders had given Jonathan permission to gather his friends from the Way of Truth at the portico.

On Friday nights, non-Jews were encouraged to sit quietly in the portico. Here, they learned about Adonai through teaching, prayers, and preaching. Usually the same privilege was extended for Saturday morning worship.

This agreement had brought harmony between Jews and non-Jews. The elders had some control over those meetings, but they had none over what Jonathan did in his own home.

"We must make a decision," Kilan declared, looking around the room. "We know that many things taught by Jonathan Ben Shelah and his friends are diverging from our beliefs and practices. Take the name of their Sunday morning meeting. It's called a 'love feast.' They say, 'We are remembering Yeshua Messiah.' They are taking in people who are ignorant of our history and many of those know nothing of the truth. Worse, his influence is spreading."

The concern this morning was how to reprimand Jonathan. He was a loyal financial supporter, one of the most generous members. They did not know how to stop him from extending his influence outside the Jewish families without bringing an end to his charitable contributions.

Kilan called Jonathan aside on the last Sabbath of January. "Jonathan, we want to talk with you in the coming week. What is the best day for us to meet?"

Jonathan knew what the meeting was about: either Sibyl or the teaching at the Way of Truth or both. He preferred a slight delay, hoping that hard feelings would mellow over the next week. "Please come to my home a few days from now, on the second Sunday afternoon in February."

341

JONATHAN AND REBEKAH'S HOME

Kilan and the elders came to the Ben Shelah home mid-afternoon, fully resolved to settle the issue. "Jonathan, thank you for inviting us to your home. I'm sure you understand our concerns. Getting to the point quickly, we want your friendships with 'God-fearers' to be more Jewish, not less."

"And what if I cannot follow every detail of your request?"

"We have spent many days pondering this question. Our reply is that the synagogue will not continue friendship and communion with a Jewish family that does not respect Jewish traditions."

Jonathan had faced many difficulties during his years in Thyatira, but this was a new crisis.

Can I accept the position of the Synagogue Council? They want me to discard the scrolls in Greek, the ones I brought from Egypt, and use only our original language, Hebrew. Their demand is that we must teach only about Adonai and leave Yeshua Messiah aside. Can I do that?

They only accept Hebrew names. My son is married to Danila, which is a very Phrygian name. Do they want me to send her back to Laodicea? What about my business interests with the guilds?

"Will you grant me a delay?" Jonathan asked, struggling to buy time. "A big decision like this involves my wife too. We are a close-knit household."

The elders already knew that Jonathan would request a delay.

Kilan looked sad but resolved. "No. We will not be put off any longer. Do not try to put us off! We are serious. We want a purified congregation, one without errors! Your Way of Truth, as a group, is banned from the synagogue grounds. You may attend, but neither you nor anyone in your family is permitted to speak."

The elders left without a satisfactory answer, but they knew they had made their position clear.

Miriam walked into Jonathan's home before the Jewish elders left, having come from a meeting with Celina. She asked them, "Won't you please stay for my daughter's second birthday celebration?"

"Maybe we'll stay another day," Kilan answered, "but we won't right now."

As Miriam entered, Grace ran into her arms. "Mommy! Come

342

home! Mommy! Come home!" The little girl ran as fast as her balance would permit.

The elders heard Miriam comment, "Such a big girl now! Two years old today, and what a wonderful little girl you are! Happy birthday, my precious one. February 8 is your special day!"

Miriam leaned Grace's head against her shoulder, and the child stayed that way for a second. Then she squirmed out of her mother's arms, saying, "No! Grace run, Mommy! Grace run!"

After the elders left the house, Jonathan and Rebekah went to talk privately in his library. He sat heavily into his chair and sighed deeply.

"I wish life didn't involve difficult decisions! You know my dilemma. Guild members attend the functions of the temple, the social side of my life. On the other hand, my home life revolves around Jewish traditions, customs, and special days. How can I leave either one of these parts of my life?"

He stood up and walked around the room. "The Jewish men at the synagogue have their own form of a guild. They loan money and arrange for merchandise to be sold and transported. In this way, not a single elder is involved in a guild. I don't know…maybe we should move away from Thyatira and start all over again!"

"Hush, my husband," said Rebekah. "We've faced difficulties before. We'll get through this together. Learn to lower your voice! Some things are private, you know! I suggest we postpone worrying about this for now. After all, this is Grace's second birthday. Cheer up! We are blessed to have small children around us. For them, life is simple. Get down to their level, and most of your problems will disappear."

Grace ran to Saulius. Arpoxa's little boy pushed Grace over, and tears flowed. Then Grace raced around the room, stumbled, and bruised her knee. She fell, sobbing, and for a moment refused to be comforted.

Watching, Miriam thought about what she had just seen.

This is what I do. Grace cried over something little, a scratch on her knee. After Anthony's last letter, I'm afraid of something. Is his commander giving him a more difficult task? Is Diotrephes going to try another kidnapping? He doesn't say that, but I can read between the lines. I'm nervous for him and me.

The children played with newborn brown puppies, laughing and running to catch up to them. On the other side of the room, Bani, Gil, Jarib, and Gedalya sat with their heads close together, talking in soft voices.

It was not the right moment to speak with them. Miriam felt alone and wanted privacy. Jonathan and Rebekah were still talking in the library.

At the evening meal, Grace was given the special honor for her birthday: being the first to be served the tasty food. Afterward, Rebekah told Miriam what had happened in the meeting with the elders.

Miriam explained in detail the similar events that occurred to Antipas in Pergamum and Simon in Sardis. They had refused to comply with the synagogue's demands and were expelled. Antipas was eventually removed from their Book of Life. Now Jonathan could face the same fate.

Miriam took Grace to her room and hummed a lullaby. As soon as she set Grace on the bed, she fell asleep. Miriam traced the outline of the little fingers as she prayed for her uncle.

Jonathan has arrived at a crucial moment. What path will he follow? That's his decision. My life is not easy either, although Jonathan cannot imagine what I'm feeling. When will I have my own baby? Arpoxa has two children, and I've never even been pregnant! Arpoxa can't look after one child properly. Why doesn't the Almighty let me have my own child?

Miriam asked herself the same questions again. She laid back on the bed, her arms stretched out. Then she folded her arms across her chest and took a deep breath.

The more she thought about it, the more distressed she became. She wanted Anthony back, safe with her, where he belonged. She longed to feel his arms around her and wanted his advice on many things.

She didn't want to be anxious, so she began to pray. She recalled each of the people living in the thirty-eight houses in Antipas's village in Pergamum, and she was soon asleep. As she prayed for others, concern for her problems melted away.

In the morning, she woke up with a tune going through her mind. As she sang the song, joining words to the melody, she thought about the last day and its events.

Sleep is gone. In the dark, I toss and turn.
No one hears me as with tears I mourn.
Again, I hear the screams, see buildings burn.
Mommy's hurt. Daddy's dead. Inside I am torn.

But in the dark, my hands to you I raise.
A light! Upon your majesty I gaze.
I'll worship you with joy through all my days.
Your covenant forever leads me to praise.

Oh, fickle me! I tremble in my dreams.
I dread the darkness, frightened to extremes.
Disgrace, rejection: free me from such schemes.
Accepting grace, I hope. Your mercy gleams.

As in the dark, my hands to you I raise.
Such light! Upon your majesty I gaze.
I'll worship you with joy through all my days.
Your covenant forever causes me to praise.

Grace fell and cried because she hurt her knee.
Imaginations of the worst degree,
Awful, appalling feelings conquered me.
Why fear? Lord, in you, I have been set free.

So in the dark, my hands to you I raise.
Your light! Upon your majesty I gaze.
I'll worship you with joy through all my days.
Your covenant forever inspires praise.

Chapter 37
News from the Mines

THE MILITARY GARRISON IN SOMA

Anthony reread the letter delivered to him by the military postal carrier. He tried to understand what Felicior was thinking about when he wrote the note.

February 24, in the 12th year of Domitian
From: Commander Felicior Priscus in Sardis
To: Scout Instructor Anthony Suros in Soma

> *If you are well, then I am well.*
> *Before you travel again, send me a report on slaves sold to the mines.*
> *A rumor says that I will be assigned to the Garrison of Philadelphia starting July 1, the expected military duty transfer date.*
> *If this happens, I suspect that my task will be to keep the Southern Road between Philadelphia and Laodicea free of bandits. Handle this information wisely.*

Anthony walked back and forth across the room. *Felicior transferred from Sardis? Someone else will be appointed as the commander of the garrison in Sardis. Not good news for me. Few men have Felicior's patience and insight. Only Commander Felicior seems to tolerate why I do not say the Solemn Oath as Domitian demands. What is he really saying? He wants me to "handle this information wisely." What does he mean by that?*

Gathering his team together for planning, Anthony showed them the letter just received from Felicior and waited for their responses. The six sat in a circle on three-legged stools around the table.

Menandro had finally found an opportunity to vent his

346

frustrations about Anthony's leadership. He glanced around at the others before speaking. "Obviously Commander Felicior has concerns. He wonders about your loyalty and effectiveness because you still haven't captured all the rebels. You could be less confident of yourself; you are too bold sometimes."

Anthony listened without responding. "Go on," he said.

Omerod observed, "Overall, this letter is positive. He wants our report."

Anthony paused, aware that he was becoming more patient, less apt to judge others. *When I act confidently like this, others sometimes take it as pride.*

"I'm worried," Anthony explained. "We do not know if Felicior is being singled out or not. Personally, I think it's a demotion. Philadelphia is a smaller city than Sardis. Obviously what I'm going to tell you now is confidential.

"Commander Felicior Priscus is a cousin to one of the three senators executed by Domitian. A few years ago, Helvetius Priscus the Younger provoked Domitian. The emperor had just announced his 'Law of Majestas,' controlling manners, actions, and games. Any perceived offense against the empire or the emperor warrants either banishment or execution. Domitian wanted this law to be applied against senators, but lawyer Helvetius Priscus resisted. You know that Domitian's guard assassinated the senator.

"Now, here is where this gets interesting. Helvetius Priscus the Younger had his seat in the Senate because he was the heir of Helvetius Priscus the Elder. And who executed the elder Priscus, the older lawyer? Domitian's father, Emperor Vespasian.

"Two emperors from the same family. A twelve-year gap between the two assassinations. Fathers and sons, both philosophers, both emperors. Both senators argued that laws are to be formulated and approved by the Senate, not by the emperor.

"Commander Felicior knows why his cousin and his cousin's father were eliminated, so is it possible that he may be demoted because of his family relationship with the senators? Or is something going on in Philadelphia that would require a commander with Felicior's excellent credentials?"

Menandro cleared his throat before saying, "I think I speak for all of us here. We appreciate the trust you placed in us. You made yourself vulnerable, first, by showing us the letter. Next, you opened a small window for us into Rome's complicated relationship with the senatorial province of Asia Minor."

Catching his breath, Anthony thought, *We are becoming a team. That's important if we are to work together to catch these criminals.* He blinked several times and said, "Now give me the information that we are going to send to Servius and Felicior. What did you find out about the legal and illegal sales of slaves, and where did the missing one hundred slaves go?"

Sextilius, Bellinus, and Capito, having traveled south, summarized their records on slave auctions in Smyrna and Ephesus. They had found nothing suspicious. Even information from smaller towns and cities indicated nothing amiss.

However, Omerod and Menandro, after going north on the Coastal Road, had found ample evidence of the rebels' actions.

Menandro began, "We started in Kisthene. It's half a day's ride from there to Adramyttium. Once there, we stayed in the garrison while carrying out our work. The city is a port facing the Aegean Sea, and a winter storm came up. We couldn't do anything while rain pounded the city. Ships inside the harbor were safe of course. Still, for two days, everyone in Adramyttium was working to keep the vessels secured against the blustery winds.

"On the third day, we tried to find the slave market's master. Apparently he had learned that soldiers were asking questions about slaves. When we went to visit him, he had just left! His house slaves didn't know if he had gone north to Alexandria Troas or Assos or southward to Pergamum and Smyrna.

"But we came away with crucial information. Of the 322 slaves having come through the harbor last year, 222 are accounted for by the tax office. They were sold legally, and we traced the taxes paid for them. We didn't try to follow up on those 222 because it would have been an endless task. They are toiling on roads, public buildings, workshops, farms, homes, and marketplaces.

"But for the other one hundred slaves, well, no taxes were paid. Nor could we find the men! Harbor records show them coming through the Black Sea to Chalcedon. But there is no indication of them being sold. No taxes were collected, and no receipts were made for their sale in Adramyttium. The master of the slave market simply did not record their existence. We kept the discrepancy to ourselves lest it become a warning to someone that may be party to the crime.

"We visited a home where a family had one woman as a house

slave. She told us, 'I think I know why you are asking questions. I've been a slave for thirty years. I'm only forty-six years old but look at me! I look like I'm seventy-two!' And yes, she did look old!

"She continued, 'I know what it is to be a slave, what good conditions are, and how bad conditions bring suffering. We house slaves all know what happens to the illegals. You must look in the mines. That's where they usually wind up.'

"What a perceptive woman! Scythians can never escape, even if they do get free. They stand out. They're too obvious. But in the mines, who can trace them with their fair skin and blue eyes? We asked the commander of the Garrison of Adramyttium for permission to go to the mines, and we rode toward the mountains a few miles to a mining town called Andeira.[103]

"We needed to talk to the mine supervisor, but how would we approach him if we suspected that he was part of a crime ring?

"Omerod made up a story to start a conversation with the supervisor. We went there pretending to be the gang's soldiers. He explained, 'Thyatira has been getting all the money for metal production for generations. Now I have friends who want to start making bronze products in Sardis, but they need metal ore from your mines. Would a request like this change your operations?'

"The mine supervisor didn't act suspicious at all. 'What you are asking for is impossible. Our ore has always been sent to Thyatira.'

"Omerod replied, 'If additional money is required, then that would not be a problem. What would you need if we wanted shipments of ore to start making bronze products in Sardis?' Right away, we saw denarii dancing around behind his eyes. If Thyatira and Sardis were both vying for ore, the price might go up."

"An excellent way to get the mine supervisor to talk," Anthony agreed.

Omerod picked up the story. "I said, 'You would need to dig out more ore. That means more workers. Listen, we can get you many more slaves once the next sailing season begins. They don't speak

---

[103] The ancient ruins of Andeira, near Asurtepe, inland from Ayvalik and Edremit, are rarely visited. Little archaeological research has been carried out. These mines were referred to by the historian Strabo. "There is a stone near Andeira which when calcined becomes iron; then when heated in a furnace with a certain earth, it yields zinc," which at that time was called "false silver."

either Greek or Latin, so they are not the kind to ever run away.' It was a clue, hinting that we knew about Scythians.

"After that, he launched into a speech, believing us to be part of the rebel gang. He said, 'I'm pleased with the new slaves you brought. We are excavating more ore: copper from one of the mines and tin from this one. False silver comes from that one.'"[104]

"He said, 'Do you want to see the slaves?' and I answered, 'No, simply make sure you have space for one hundred more. Mithrida wants to know if last year's agreement is still in place for the coming season,' and then he said, 'Yes, the same agreement.' He didn't bat an eyelid at the mention of Mithrida.

"I asked, 'What did you do with the wounded slaves?' He said, 'What we agreed on. I sent four to Thyatira for the Games. They were worthless. Of course the agreement stands! I can take in another one hundred slaves this year, the same amount as last year. The officials in town won't take bribes for more than that—too dangerous.' He then got suspicious. 'Say! You didn't come to change our agreement, did you?'

"I said, 'No, nothing of the kind. We wanted to confirm that you can take one hundred more slaves this year.' He looked at me suddenly, and the expression on his face changed. His mouth fell, and there was fear in his eyes. 'You weren't here last year! I don't remember your faces. Who are you? What are your names? Where are you from?'"

Menandro took his turn at telling the story. "On the spur of the moment, Omerod answered, 'Of course! We didn't introduce ourselves properly! Sorry, I'm Oma, and this is Muna.'

"Then the supervisor looked nervous. 'Last year Ota was the leader. Who is yours?' Again Omerod saved us with another quick answer. 'Our leader is Antha.' Afterward, we realized the irony of it all fitting together. You are our leader, 'Antha,' or Anthony!

"Omerod made up this story to calm the supervisor's suspicions. 'Antha is short for Marcus Antonius, the greatest general Caesar Augustus faced. Absolutely true—Antha's wife comes from Alexandria, Egypt, just as the original Antonius took

---

[104] This region in Turkey is rich in metals and minerals: gold, silver, iron, copper, lead, zinc, manganese, sulphur, lignite, alum, sulphate of iron, salt, and gypsum. Some sites include galleries, writing on mine walls, ruins of fortresses nearby, and fortification walls.

Cleopatra, queen of Egypt.'

"At that, I almost giggled. We didn't dare look at one another. Later, down the road, I almost fell off my horse laughing."

Anthony chuckled. "So now I've got a bandit's name. Thanks to you, I'm following the marriage customs of Marcus Antonius! And you recruited our whole team as bandits with that gang?"

Omerod spoke, "I thought, why not capture the rebels and send them to the mine to learn what a life sentence is like! Poor souls, those slaves working in mines, digging in the dark and using flaming rags set on poles for light. Their life expectancy is only five or ten years, perhaps more. The work? Grueling labor. The mine superintendent had no idea we were not part of the gang. I asked if there were any problems with the master of the slave market in town, and the supervisor said, 'The master was satisfied with the payments.'

"We know both are in on the crooked activity. I told the supervisor to calm the slave market master who had evaded us and tell him we were part of the gang, checking that he was still in the operation. I think we minimized suspicions by doing that."

"Very well," said Anthony. "The supervisor would talk to the next rebels delivering slaves to the mines. He'll tell them that soldiers with these the names of Muna and Oma stopped by and that their leader is Antha. That will alert them, maybe letting them know we are onto their scheme. It's time to prepare for their first delivery of slaves this year. We'll need to capture them before they hear those names."

Sextilius got the point. "Let's not arrest them when they arrive at Port Daskyleion but as they deliver their next lot of slaves. This will dismantle their operation, including the crooks at the slave market and at the mine."

Anthony nodded in agreement. "I've been thinking about when the murders occurred last year, and there seems to be a pattern there. If we take those dates and back up to when the slaves probably arrived at Port Daskyleion, it is approximately the first of each month. Sailing season starts in a few weeks, and if I'm right, we can expect the next ship to arrive in Port Daskyleion between March 27 and April 4. We have about one month to prepare."

"How do you know all that?" asked Capito.

"Tell me you spent the last month consulting the stars for dates," laughed Omerod.

Anthony shook his head. "That guess at the ship's arrival is based on the few event dates that this team has gathered at the check stations.

"This is what we know: The mines in Andeira are expecting deliveries totaling one hundred slaves this summer. We are sure they will come in at Port Daskyleion, the same as the last forty-two slaves delivered in the previous year. Until we know different, let's assume a delivery is coming to the port between March 27 and April 4. Those slaves will be delivered to the mines at Andeira using the Interior and Postal Roads through Aizanoi.

"Here are our next steps: Sextilius and Bellinus, I want you to go to Port Daskyleion. Ride fast. Tell the garrison what we have learned. Be ready for rebels in case they dock their ship earlier than I calculated.

"Omerod and Menandro, starting at Aizanoi and heading north, stop at each relay station, inn, and military post. Explain our plan to each officer. Explain what we know and how we learned it. Do this all the way along to Prusa and then join Sextilius and Bellinus at Port Daskyleion. Tell them that we will be sending through a caravan of illegal slaves and fake soldiers. We will send a rider to all stations alerting them to pass it through with no questions.

"Capito and I will do the same for the southern stations from Sardis to Aizanoi and all the way to the mines. We'll instruct every relay station and military post of our plans. We'll meet you at Port Daskyleion in mid-March. That is the earliest we could expect a ship from Sinop. Let's hope they keep the same schedule as last year, a shipload each month."

They nodded. The time had now come to confront the criminals.

OLIVE GROVE FARM AT FORTY TREES

By the second Sunday in March, Nikias dreamed of returning to the family he had visited in Gelembe, where he and his brothers found protection during the winter storm. Spring was here, and it was time to plant vegetables and care for newborn lambs. Nikias asked his brothers if they would go with him for a day, but they refused.

"Nikias, you are too attached to those old scrolls! Not everything in them is meant for us, and our wives don't want us to go," complained Alberto. "Besides, our brother Kozma is adamant and says it's wrong to go to these towns. Yesterday he swore a prophetic oath, saying, 'Nikias will be punished for not making sacrifices to Artemis.'"

Nikias wondered how to get around these objections. *I want to obey Anthony, but my brothers won't cooperate with me. However, I might be able to travel faster on my own. Maybe that is what I should do.*

"Jonathan's workers have one day a week off from farm work," he said to Penelope. "I'll only be gone for one day."

He left on a Sunday morning, going much faster by horse than he would by wagon. He reached the family with five children by noon. He spent an hour explaining to all seven what he had learned and then left, planning to be home by nightfall.

"We never heard anything like this before," said the innkeeper. "Please spend more time with us. Come again soon and stay for a while."

On the way back home, his spirit soared. He imagined himself gliding like a bird, higher than Mount Tarhala. As his horse trotted through Soma, he looked up at the mountain peak. His whole life had been lived within sight of Mount Tarhala.

Nikias was home before dark. "See, I promised I would be back with you tonight," he said to his anxious wife.

JONATHAN AND REBEKAH'S HOME

March 11, in the 12th year of Domitian
From: Miriam
To: My beloved

Peace and joy; if you are well, then I also am well.

Time moves slowly, and I think of you all the time. I never know where you are. Nikias comes to the city and talks with Uncle Jonathan and Jarib. He told me that he went to a village west of Olive Grove two weeks ago. A family of seven received copies of Grandpa Antipas's scrolls, and they want further teaching.

Grace is growing so quickly. She is talking more now. She wants to do everything for herself and insists on putting her little tunic on by herself, even when she gets all caught up in it. I wish you were here to see it. She keeps saying, "Da-da coming? Da-da coming?" and I reply, "Yes, Daddy is coming soon."

Aunt Rebekah opened up about her feelings against the people who murdered her three small boys during the Alexandrian riots. She says there's only one thing that can take away the desire for revenge. Auntie said, "I fell into despair. For a year, I could only think of my little boys. Then I remembered the scripture where God says, 'Those who honor me I will honor, but those who despise me will be disdained.'"[105]

Confusion in the synagogue has not died down. Kilan says, "Jonathan, you and the people in your assembly are more dedicated to following the customs of Thyatira and the teachings of that carpenter than to following Jewish customs." Non-Jews can still come to the portico to listen to the sanctuary service, but they may not teach. They have not yet forbidden his teaching at the home assembly, but the lines have hardened, and I think they will do that. We haven't gone there for worship with the congregation in three weeks.

Please hurry back. I can't stand the waiting.

OLIVE GROVE FARM AT FORTY TREES

Sensing the time had come to confront Nikias, the three brothers invited him to Zeno's house to discuss his travels away from the farm. The house smelled of the fresh flowers picked off shrubs planted around the house, and Zeno's wife put out some fresh bread and honey for the occasion.

"Nikias, we need to talk to you about all these trips you've been making. You're neglecting your family. What about your responsibilities here at the farm? We know you like to meet people, to see where other people live, but Jonathan doesn't pay you to take time away from Olive Grove."

Nikias bit his lower lip and leaned forward, his heart beating rapidly. He had almost decided on which farm he wanted to buy. "All right, but I need to make just one more trip. I stayed in a little town about a year ago. An old couple takes care of the Apollonius Inn there. There's one little village beyond there that I want to check out, Prosperity Village. Then I will come back. Who will come

---

[105] 1 Samuel 2:30

with me?"

They were solidly against Nikias going away from Olive Grove to other towns and villages. Zeno passed Nikias some raisins and then walked back and forth as he made his point. "Nikias, think about it. We all have work to do, and you spend many days each year going back and forth to Thyatira as it is, taking products into the city."

"Here's an idea," Nikias said hopefully. "I'll go alone and be away for only three days: one day to go there, one day to talk to the old couple, and a day to return. The old man is a specialist in fixing axles and mending wagons. I'll be all right."

They disagreed. "You are obstinate, Nikias!"

Nikias smiled. He had a sneaky plan that would soon give him three days away from home. "All right, I'm putting this trip off for a while. Only one more trip…later."

JONATHAN AND REBEKAH'S HOME

Miriam dragged her feet. She had little energy, even when playing with Grace and Saulius or talking with Arpoxa. Scary thoughts flashed through her mind, and she worried that Anthony might fall off a horse or that he would be targeted by bandits.

Afraid of the worst, she had worked herself into a state of fear. *What if I don't see him again? What would happen to me? I'll be twenty-eight in less than a month. If I were a widow… No, I won't think about that. But if I hadn't married Anthony or we hadn't adopted Chrysa Grace…I couldn't imagine life without her. Dear God! It's a sacrifice to be married to an army man. He's never home!*

Sibyl makes sacrifices at the temple. She pours out a cup of wine when she prays, but I won't make a sacrifice like that. My life will be a libation! I'll let my life be poured out. I want to serve others, people like Melpone and her friends, even if some of them don't accept me. Lord, it hurts to be rejected. It's like dying inside.

She counted the months since their marriage. In April, it would be two years. Of that time, Anthony had been working with Felicior for how many months? Was it really twenty-two months ago when he was assigned to the garrison in Sardis? *Oh, Lord. I love him so much. And I miss Grandpa Antipas so much.*

Miriam slowly slipped onto her knees, staying there and enjoying the floral scents of her uncle's home. Grace came into the room, walked to her mother, and put her hand on her mother's face.

She felt teardrops.

"Mama cry?" she asked. "Mama cry?"

"Come to me, my darling. I love you so much. Oh! I never want to lose you," said Miriam, pulling Grace tight against her bosom. She whispered, "I love you. Oh, I love you so much."

Passover had arrived. Jonathan and Rebekah had the whole household gathered for the Seder meal. The seating was arranged so that the eldest sat at one end. The youngest person was at the other end of a long table. Miriam was almost in the middle. Shiri sat to the right of Miriam, and Serah sat to her left. Jarib and all his family members were present as well.

Grace and Saulius played on the floor at the end of the table. Arte felt self-conscious and stood apart, insisting he could not sit or recline in their presence. He thought how ironic it was of them to be so introspective of their own past slavery in Egypt and still hold him as a slave.

It was a holy moment, and two candles were lit. Rebekah sat down after making sure the candles would continue burning.

Jonathan looked around. "During the past days, this house was cleansed of leaven. Thank you, Rebekah and Miriam! Let us also ask God to remove leaven from our hearts."

Before they could eat, they had to wash their hands. Jonathan washed Rebekah's hands. She took the jug to wash Miriam's hands, and thus the jar was passed down the table, each person pouring a little water over the next person's hands. A small towel was used to dry the hands.

After a towel had been passed to the last person, Jonathan asked, "Who may ascend the hill of the Lord?"[106] Next he took a sprig of parsley, dipped it into a small bowl of salt water, and tasted it. He said, "It is bitter. The Israelites groaned in their slavery. They cried out, and their cry for help because of their slavery went up to God."[107]

As Danila heard the whole story, Miriam observed the lines on her face reflected contrasting emotions: puzzlement, fear, relief, and mystery. This was her first Passover.

Jonathan said, "Hear, O Israel: The Lord our God, the Lord is

---

[106] Psalm 24:3
[107] Exodus 2:23

one. Love the Lord your God with all your heart and with all your soul and with all your strength. These commandments that I give you today are to be upon your hearts. Impress them on your children. Talk about them when you sit at home and when you walk along the road, when you lie down and when you get up."[108]

Rebekah quoted her passage. "We remember, 'I will bring you out from under the yoke of the Egyptians.'[109] This is the Cup of Sanctification."

After Jonathan spoke briefly about the *matzah* bread, noting that it looked like someone's back after it had been hit and broken, Serah said, "'I will free you from being slaves.'[110]... This is the Cup of Deliverance."

Bitter herbs, called *maror*, were passed around to be eaten with the matzah, reminding each one of their painful lives as slaves in Egypt. The vegetables were dipped twice, and Shiri said, "'I will redeem you with an outstretched arm and with mighty acts of judgment.'[111] This is the Cup of Redemption."

Arte brought in a delicious dinner of lamb, worth the long wait. Passover meant joy, and wine stimulated laughter because this ceremony spoke of liberty. The sweet taste of the roasted meat, the scents from several vegetables, and a perfect blend of sauces produced a sense of harmony and well-being. All were satisfied, and the entire Passover meal was complete, except for the final cup.

After the meal, Miriam completed the fourth "I will." She paused before quoting the well-known words. "'I will take you as my own people, and I will be your God. I will bring you to the land I gave to Abraham, Isaac, and Jacob, and I will give it to you as a possession.'[112] This is the Cup of Restoration."

Jonathan explained, "By the tradition set by our Messiah, we'll not drink the fourth cup. Rather, we will postpone that for when the kingdom is complete and we are in the presence of the Messiah. Let's hear a song that Miriam composed two nights ago."

Miriam had practiced her song with Danila, Gil, and Bani, and they reached for their instruments. She explained how she

---

[108] Deuteronomy 6:4–7
[109] Exodus 6:6
[110] Ibid.
[111] Ibid.
[112] Exodus 6:7

continued to struggle with the loss of her mother. In her heart, an emptiness would not go away. "I felt let down these past months," she started. "I find it hard to be in your home at times. Don't get me wrong please! It's not about you. It's because I'm a long way from my husband. Or perhaps I should say, Anthony is a long way from me. I constantly miss my grandfather too."

Miriam was honest about her feelings and struggles, and the songs she had written were sincere. The family laughed and relaxed, and her tears were close to the surface when Antipas's name was mentioned.

"When I don't feel like singing because my feelings point me another way, the Spirit seems to turn me around. I sense healing when I obey the Spirit's leading to sing. It's because I'm going beyond feeling sorry for myself and beginning to think of others."

The musicians started playing the melody for the song. She closed her eyes, trying to imagine herself as a slave and then being delivered, but all she could see in her mind was a slave she had seen at work in the Bronzesmiths' Guild.

She remembered the strong scent of stale sweat, the smoke, and the roar of the fire in the furnace. Perspiration dripped from the slave's face. His strong arms endlessly pounded and shaped red-hot metal. She wondered if he felt resentment over his lot in life.

The longing to be free overwhelmed her. "I'm going to sing about Egypt," she said.

Loud whips cracked, lashing bleeding backs.
How long had we been waiting to be free?
Freedom came, we quickly left, but then we faced the Sea!
We fled Egyptian soldiers, fearing their attacks.
Men made slaves by Pharaoh's proclamation
Packed their belongings, believing God would win.
Liberty had stirred their hearts from deep within.
    Drink with me the Cup of Our Sanctification.

Pharaoh's army ruled severely.
Burdens multiplied—constant heavy loads.
Flies buzzed 'round; locusts flew. Watch out for those toads!
The firstborn's dead! His parents loved him dearly.
Blood splashed on doorposts gave assurance.

Then freedom came. Countless lambs were sacrificed.
Our lives resembled herbs: bitter, cut, and diced.
    Drink with me the Cup of Our Deliverance.

Sorcerers raged! Moses brought signs!
"Our God told us, 'Prepare! It's time to move.'"
Pharaoh shrieked and raged, "I do not approve!"
Could his threats overpower God's designs?
Liberty's road lay hidden, hard to find.
Freedom came to slaves who suffered cruel affliction.
God declared, "These chains will no longer bind."
    Drink with me the Cup of Our Redemption.

Memories were bleak, stark, foreboding.
The men thrash slaves, reducing human worth.
Slave masters' oppression diminished joy and mirth.
Our injured souls felt happiness eroding.
But hark! A voice! "I am your King and God.
You're mine!" Overwhelmed, we sing! We are awed.
Now, through Yeshua's living exaltation,
    We are forgiven!
    Lift with me the Cup of Restoration.

Chapter 38
Port Daskyleion

PORT DASKYLEION ON THE SEA OF MARMARA

Wildflowers bent in the breeze, bobbing their heads in the early spring. The six soldiers waiting on the low hill overlooking the entrance to Port Daskyleion harbor were confident they were closing in on the marauders. The last days of March had brought blue skies and steady winds, ideal for ships coming south from the Bosporus.

"Beautiful...if we could just enjoy it more," stated Bellinus.

"It's gorgeous, a gift of Artemis even while we wait for the crooks," Menandro agreed.

They had taken their position on a small cliff overlooking the village. Nature had not bestowed a natural shelter on the port, but it received a helping hand because many slaves had placed massive stone blocks in the shape of a long fishhook to create a secure harbor. The bay faced west, so it needed protection from winds whipping across the extensive stretch of water from the Macedonian side of the Sea of Marmara.

Several ships were sailing into the harbor. Anthony and his team walked from the clifftop into the town to see if they were legitimate vessels. They arrived at the point where the stone pier jutted out into the bay. Calm water in the inner harbor reflected each ship's image. Ships arrived and were moored with their stern to the dock.

The smells of the sea and fresh fish enchanted Anthony and his friends. For eight days, the six soldiers had waited. They had wandered the shore during that time and were now on a first-name basis with bakers, town workers, and smiths.

Merchants arrived from the Black Sea, unloading their wares: animal skins, pottery, jewelry, charms, and slaves. Products found their way to Asia Minor and the eastern provinces through this port. Captains barked orders at crew members as they put out from port, sailing north with their goods: dried figs, nuts, wine, and items made of copper, iron, and bronze.

One ship sailed for Scythia, the most northerly shores of the Black Sea. A merchant was related to families there, and he accompanied his merchandise. His products were highly sought after: amber beads, Egyptian scarfs made of gold- and blue-colored material, yellow and blue glass bottles for perfume, and terra cotta figurines. All were carefully packed in boxes stowed in the ship's cargo hold. He had made this trip many times.

Iron spearheads and a gold diadem wrapped in a small purple bag were being taken to Scythia's governor. The merchant had packed an additional special gift: a little bronze lion to hold scrolls open. It was an amber color, almost gold-like, the finest that Thyatira produced.

By midmorning, small waves began to form whitecaps. Another ship left port, and experienced crew members steered the boat out of the harbor. White seagulls dipped and rose on air currents. Children waved as the vessel caught the open sea breezes and bucked the waves. Farther away, little local fishing boats bobbed on dark blue waters.

A bireme warship edged away from the harbor. The rowers propelled the massive ship to open water. Waves broke against the prow, flowing over its bronze beak formerly used to ram enemy vessels. The ship's painted black eyes scanned the waters ahead for hidden dangers. As the vessel encountered whitecaps, the sailors raised a large rectangular sail. With the brisk winds, the ship would cross the Sea of Marmara and reach Nicomedia less than ten hours later.

A newly arrived ship edged into the harbor. Sailors lowered the sail, and oarsmen slowed the vessel and turned the stern toward the dock. A line was thrown, and several minutes later, the ship was in position with the stern against the pier. Men shouted as they dropped an anchor at the prow and continued to moor the boat safely. Slaves emerged from the hold, squinting in the bright light.

Each slave had blond hair and light skin. Sextilius counted twenty slaves standing shackled close to the ship. They were guarded by two soldiers. Two others were still on the ship, watching cargo being unloaded.

Anthony's heart skipped a beat. *Four soldiers and twenty slaves!*

Menandro and Capito, dressed in military gear, walked up to the two soldiers on the boat, their red capes hanging over their backs and looking like they were expected. Each was fully armed, as were other soldiers on duty.

"Looks like we have two caravans ready to march," commented Menandro out loud as he approached the soldiers. "We have not met yet. I'm Muna, and this is Capta. Our leader, Antha, wants to talk with you in the office over there before you see anyone else."

"We weren't expecting to be met, but I'm glad you're here. It makes me feel safer. I'm Ota, and this is Tissa. Spithra and Baga are still on board."

"We'll talk with your friends later," said Menandro. "Come to Commander Antha's office. He's in charge now. Our movement in this area is growing much stronger." Nodding toward the slaves, he said, "You'll be able to take them to the mines without any interference. We've completed all arrangements there."

Menandro's comments brought a look of concern to Ota at first. Still, as he continued confidently, Tissa and Ota smiled at each other.

They were ushered into the garrison office close to the fishing docks. "I'm Antha," said Anthony, standing and smiling broadly. "This is my aide, Sexta. Okay, Muna and Capta, I want you both to wait outside the office. Make sure no one comes in to interrupt us while we are doing our 'paperwork.'"

Anthony had previously instructed the other soldiers to interrupt if needed. Security details had been worked out with the garrison commander. Commander Felicior's orders were clear. Anthony had the authority to do whatever was necessary to apprehend the gangsters. For this, he needed his whole team to be part of the ruse. If his setup failed, he would need extra soldiers to help subdue the bandits.

"I'm Ota, and this is Tissa," said the taller one, greeting Anthony. He took his helmet off and held it under his left arm.

Tissa had not expected a welcoming party. "We were not told about you."

Anthony's grin was genuine. "We joined the operation over the winter months. I chose my name, or to be more precise, it was chosen for me, just as yours were. My ancestor fought hard against the greatest emperor of them all, Augustus."

"Are you named for Marcos Antonius, Octavian's enemy?" asked Tissa. In his opinion, Marcos Antonius led the sharpest opposition to Octavian in the Eastern Mediterranean. Like all soldiers, Tissa had studied the Battle of Actium, and he wanted to impress Antha.

"Ah! Antonius, the ideal rebel! He started in the East and led half of Rome's legions from Egypt to Macedonia. Antonius lost the naval Battle of Actium but slipped through the naval blockade, sailing with Cleopatra back to Egypt. In those days, insurgents really knew how to resist Rome!"

Seeing the satisfaction of reminiscing on battles and naval encounters, Anthony risked a comment. "Tissa, you enjoy strategy and confrontation, don't you?"

"Yes, I do," Tissa responded enthusiastically.

Details of the famous battle 124 years before served as a common reference point for soldiers. Anthony painted a picture of rebels losing when confronted by Rome.

"With Tissa talking like this, I think of Cleopatra sailing through the gap provided by her ships fighting on each flank. I hate to imagine all those soldiers burning in the galleys, flaming arrows killing thousands of soldiers, just as Marcus Antonius slipped through Octavian's blockade. Oh! Men on fire! And all those ships sinking beneath the waves!"

Anthony had confidently slipped into "bandit talk." *If only the robbers could understand what I just said! I have reminded these revolutionaries that rebellion always ends with brutal pain. Conflicts against Domitian will only end one way: with another victory for the empire.*

Tissa also needed to show that he understood how Octavian won. "Marcus Antonius lost his lines of communication. The supply line was also lost." He sighed. "Marcus Antonius would have made a good emperor. Never mind...we'll have a better one soon!"

While the thieves were absorbing the conversation rooted in history, he decided to draw them out. "I know that Craga goes over those sea battles. Did he draw lessons for you from that conflict?" They nodded.

He continued, "I imagine he uses that skirmish to say that we are going to gain more victories, right? See this scar? I, too, carry the marks of rebellion on me. I fought in Upper Germanica. I faced treachery, but I lived to tell the tale. Where did you fight?"

By now, Ota was convinced that Anthony and his team were part of their gang. His initial reservations were laid to rest because Anthony seemed to know so much about them.

He said, "I fought with Legion V, Macedonia."

Anthony directed a question to Tissa. "What about you? Where did you fight?"

"I was part of Legion IV, Flavia Felix. When we moved into Moesia, ready to fight Dacia, we occupied the area where Legion VII, Claudia, had been. There was growing discontent in the legion. Food was scarce. Like Ota, poorly run battles in Dacia and the disorderly conduct last year pushed me across the line.

"I'm convinced that Rome will continue to fight Dacia and continue to fail. Support for Domitian is weakening after several reversals. The defeat of Legion XXI last summer brought our organization many new recruits because deserters ended up north of the Black Sea. Our ranks are increasing. We, 'The Faithful,' will continue to grow in strength."

Anthony had all the information he wanted. The name of their army, "The Faithful," had also fallen into his lap. These rebels possessed many details about the growing insurgence.

"Well, I'm here to make sure you deliver the slaves to the mines without the loss of one single man. Not a single slave will be lost this year, not like last year! Craga learned about your mistake, Ota. Two slaves escaped. Tissa, you should have been more observant! Be more careful! Never let slaves cut themselves loose again!"

Ota's eyes opened and closed rapidly. He shifted his weight and looked down, placing his feet firmly on the floor, and then he stood at attention, as straight as a javelin.

All that happened at the rear of a slave train. How could a stranger in this small port know about it? I'm convinced that no one revealed what had transpired, so how did Antha learn about it? And how did Craga find out? Who else knew? I believe Craga worked behind my back, bringing Antha into place to put a watch on me. I will follow all that Antha was told to do.

"He's all right, Tissa," said Ota, nodding his head. "No need to worry. Antha knows. He's one of us."

Anthony watched Ota's reaction. He was convinced now that they had penetrated the brigand's secrets. Every gang member had two dreads: the fear of being found out and the anxiety of being accused of inferior performance.

Anthony had gained instant respect, and he surprised them again. "It's not what *I* know that's important. It's what *Craga* knows and, above him, *Mithrida* too."

364

Ota and Tissa looked at one another. Anthony had passed the first obstacle of being aware of their activities. Now he showed that he was familiar with their chain of command.

Ota and Tissa needed assurance that passage to the mines was safe, so Anthony instructed, "The former commander of this garrison informed me that you had rented two slave wagons in the city. Your auxiliaries will have to bring them here for loading.

"Take your normal course of action. Make sure the slaves get lots of food. Tell them to eat as much as they want. I have arranged this all along the way. Slaves won't work in the mines well if they have been starved before getting there. We want a reputation of providing the best slaves."

Ota and Tissa laughed nervously. "Hear that? Antha wants to give the best slaves for the mines!"

Anthony ignored the laughter. He needed to know how the slaves were going to be placed on the wagons. "Who is going to travel with the slave wagons?"

Tissa answered, "Our trusted auxiliaries. Two wagons, ten slaves in each, plus ten auxiliaries to make sure no one escapes—our usual plan. We usually have five auxiliaries, but on this trip, we are training five new recruits."

Other pieces of the puzzle were falling into place. Anthony took charge, "Except last year. You carried eleven in each of the two wagons. That's when things went badly, and you had to rearrange the slaves before leaving Porsuk Canyon.

"You are free to begin your march right away. At White Horse Relay Station, and every other one too, you will not have to insist that your caravan be the first one to leave each morning. You have no merchants to deal with. No more killing! That is an order! Not even the shepherds downstream from the canyon will give you problems!"

Ota grinned. "So you know about the shepherds too!"

"Yes, I do. I know many other things too. Ota, you, Tissa, Spithra, and Baga will stay with the twenty men to be sold in Adramyttium. Once you arrive, immediately take the slaves to the master of the slave market. Act like you have registered them. Then go to the mine superintendent at Andeira. He'll be waiting for you. After that, you can return to Adramyttium for a swim in the wonderful warm water."

Everything confirmed their belief. Craga had recruited Antha and Sexta. "Now, one last thing, Ota. When does the ship return to this port? Craga told us it would be about the end of next month, but he couldn't be exact."

"Yes, Arta and Tira are due on or about the twenty-eighth of April."

Anthony said, "You are dismissed. We have talked enough."

The bandits, fearing nothing, saluted mockingly.

After they were gone, Anthony asked Omerod, Menandro, Bellinus, and Capito to join him and Sextilius. The garrison commander listened while Anthony gave instructions.

"Omerod and Menandro, leave today. Make good time! Take fresh horses all along the way. Tell every officer to let this caravan pass unimpeded. Tell them, 'The bandits and their accomplices will be arrested, caught in the act of handing the slaves over to mines in Andeira. When caught red-handed, the mines' superintendent will confess that he bought slaves from these bandits last year.' It's better than arresting them now. In case of difficulties, inform Commander Servius and Commander Felicior."

Their plan to introduce themselves to the criminals had worked perfectly. Anthony turned to Sextilius, Bellinus, and Capito. "The four of us will all stay here for the next several weeks. When we greet the next incoming ship, we'll try to do the same things we did this time. If they respond to us as this group did, that will be perfect.

"Remember, our chief aim is to find the leaders, Mithrida and Craga. We need more information, but we can't be so inquisitive that the fake soldier slave drivers or ship crews suspect us. Any questions?"

Anthony told the garrison commander to prepare for another ship with illegal slaves arriving around April 28. Sextilius remarked, "If we get lucky and also have Mithrida and Craga arriving on the ship, we'll be with you to give them a warm welcome." He grinned. "But I don't think we could fool them!"

THE NEW FORUM, THE CITY OF PERGAMUM

While all this was happening in Port Daskyleion, Marcos, the Ben Shelah family lawyer, was in Pergamum. This morning, his first task was to make his way through the agora to the bank with several documents. It was time to send another installment of Eliab Ben Shelah's estate to Miriam and her uncles.

Walking into the New Forum, the largest of the three market squares, he stopped on the white marble stone pavement known as the Slave Market. In two more weeks, during the Festival of Zeus, the market would be filled with wealthy men. Potential buyers would be poking, prodding, and examining the naked human cargo before the auction. Marcos remembered the day, four years before, when Antipas had redeemed Ateas and Arpoxa. They were the last two slaves auctioned that day.

Marcos waited to talk with a young clerk at the bank. They went over the newly assigned payment documents to be sent to banks in other cities. The clerk frowned. "This is a new assignment for me," he said. "Please explain to me what I am to do for you."

"I'm the executor of Eliab Ben Shelah's will, and I have been the family's lawyer for several years," Marcos explained. "These are approval documents from courts in Ephesus and Pergamum. Every six months, I assign payments to each of the heirs. These will show you how this was done before your predecessor died.

"This is the third of ten payments," he continued. "A wealthy Egyptian died and left his estate to six brothers in Asia Minor and three heirs in Alexandria. Similar payments were made last year. Each installment is to be paid out six months apart.

"Amos Ben Shelah is the eldest son, so he receives a double share from the estate. Send the money to his bank in Philadelphia. Each of the others gets a single portion. Prepare the documents so that funds are available in the respective banks on May 1. The next payment is to be made so it arrives on November 1.

"Here are the names in the order of birth and their cities. The previous correspondence is correct, so just copy what was done before. One of the heirs, Antipas Ben Shelah, has died, and his granddaughter, Miriam Bat Johanan, receives his share. She is in Thyatira now. Send her portion to Jonathan Ben Shelah in Thyatira. He is acting on her behalf and will have the funds given to her."

JONATHAN AND REBEKAH'S HOME

Arpoxa was downstairs early, sitting in the kitchen and humming a tune. She had a twinkle in her eye as she greeted Miriam.

Arte's arms were covered with flour as he prepared flatbread for the day's meals. Saulius and Grace began to argue over kitchen utensils; they loved the sound of clanging pots. Arpoxa interrupted her song, "Not now, Saulius! Quiet please!" as she nursed her baby.

"Arpoxa! You're singing so early in the morning?" Miriam asked.

"Yes, Miriam. I'm thrilled. Remember what today is?"

"Certainly, today is my birthday!" exclaimed Miriam.

"And my redemption day too! Four years ago, when I was eighteen, your grandfather kindly redeemed me at the slave market. I was so upset, a helpless slave and tied to Ateas. A rope held our feet together. As if either of us could have run away! Oh, Miriam, I was so afraid that Ateas and I would be separated forever. But even so, your Grandfather Antipas chose to buy both of us. He said, 'I saw the way that young man looked at you and the look of love and concern in your face and thought, 'Those two love each other. Those two cripples are coming home with me.'"

"Yes, I remember Grandpa telling that story many times."

"We were pushed into the market area, like animals or pieces of clothing. The slave master made me put my clothes on the wooden platform. Next I opened my eyes and saw all those men walking around, looking and poking at me. That was so humiliating. But you know, this year, since I have this new little baby, I don't think about it so often."

"It was terrible," agreed Miriam. "I was watching from under the awnings, close to the shops in the Pergamum agora."

"It all happened so fast. I didn't understand anything that was taking place. I had just been taken from my native land, and I didn't know a word of your language."

"And now look at you, Arpoxa! You speak Greek with hardly any accent, and you speak without mistakes most of the time. Well, I still have to teach you a few more things."

"And I'm rapidly learning Latin too. If I'm going to be a free woman in Roman society, I need to speak Latin. But do you think I'll ever be useful, to others, I mean?"

Miriam looked at Arpoxa's twisted feet. "You are a wonderful mother. Soon Ateas will come back from his work with Anthony. Your husband will see his new little child. Now it's not only your redemption day, Arpoxa, or my birthday. We have another reason to celebrate! Come, Grace! It's your adoption day too! We need a huge party."

Arpoxa had learned to read as well as speak and sing. "I read something yesterday," she said, "and I understand something new.

I have been redeemed two times."

"How is that?" asked Miriam.

Arpoxa was beaming. "Antipas took us to the house he had built for us. We thought we would be slaves, but a few days later, Antipas gave us our redemption papers. The scroll you were reading yesterday says that another price was paid, that Yeshua Messiah died. Through his sacrifice, I have another redemption: freedom because of Messiah's punishment and shame. Two times redemptions."

Arpoxa tried to stand up. "Oh, some things in Greek I find so hard to rightly say. I wish I could stand up properly and dance. That's how happy I am. What a happy day, your birthday twenty-eight times, my redemption day four times, and Grace's adoption day two times."

Miriam smiled. "Observe the grammar details carefully. The event follows the number, and numbers are described like this: 'It's your twenty-eighth birthday, my fourth redemption day, and Grace's second adoption day.' You have to switch numbers around this way when you go from Scythian to Greek."

"Oh, there's so much to remember to truly speaking!" groaned Arpoxa, forgetting another detail Miriam had explained to her.

Chapter 39
Successes and Failures

PORT DASKYLEION ON THE SEA OF MARMARA

During April, ships docked every day at Port Daskyleion. The wind blew steadily from the west or northwest. Still, sailors needed to be watchful because changing winds were dangerous. Unexpected wind gusts could blow them against rocky shores.

Omerod and Menandro had returned from Adramyttium, bringing back the two slave wagons used by the gang. Omerod told them what happened.

"Our friendly 'slave traders' made it through the relay stations easily and quickly. In the end, they delivered the shipment of slaves to the mine's manager. We heard them say, 'Antha was right when he said that he had managed to infiltrate every relay station along the way. He got all the officers to cooperate! We never imagined that so many people would come over to Craga and Mithrida's side! Many more have joined the Faithful.' They had no idea what was coming next."

Sextilius asked, "Can you describe the expression on their faces as they were arrested?"

Menandro spoke. "Oh, when they realized they were under arrest! It was swearing and cursing like you never heard in your life! We planned it all with the Garrison of Adramyttium taking charge. The rebels had no idea that a trap had been set. All were taken in: four rebels 'soldiers,' their ten auxiliaries, the master of the slave market, and the mine's superintendent. In all, sixteen insurgents. We had to hurry back to be here."

Bellinus asked, "What about the slaves? What is happening to them?"

"All twenty are being held at the Garrison of Adramyttium. This case will go to the governor in Ephesus. A decision could be delayed since many questions need to be answered. I requested that the slaves not go to the mines."

Anthony and his small group kept watching for the return of the ship linked to the bandits. On Tuesday morning, April 28, Menandro spotted the vessel. "There! Isn't that the same ship? The sail is mended in the same place! Yes, this is the one! They're back, everyone!"

The squad hurried down the small hill along the cobbled streets and arrived at the harbor. As before, slaves were unloaded and stood on the dock, bound together with ropes. Capito counted twenty slaves being lined up on the wharf. They were being watched by five auxiliaries.

A forward section of the hull had been damaged, perhaps during a windstorm on the Black Sea. Its repairs were obvious. A new timber replaced an old one on the prow. Planks that had been changed were a slightly lighter-colored wood at mid-ships above the waterline. The repair at the stern also indicated previous damage to the vessel.

Menandro and Capito approached the two in charge. "Hail! We are here to meet you, a special welcome by the Faithful! I'm Muna, and this is Capta," Menandro cheerfully explained.

"I'm Arta; he is Tira," replied one of the bandits.

"We want to talk with you before you meet the commander of the garrison," said Capta. "Commander Antha and his aide Sexta will give you some good news."

The man whose name was Tira frowned. He leaned over to Arta, who was shorter. The two men exchanged a few words. They instructed their auxiliaries to watch the slaves. "We'll be back soon to take the slaves to the slave wagons," said Tira,

They walked into the garrison, close to the dock. Anthony and Sextilius waited for them in the office. "This is our new commander, Commander Antha," said Sextilius, "and I'm Sexta."

Simple furnishings met their gaze, and the rebels glanced around furtively. They seemed uncomfortable. A small brown military table was positioned in the center of the room with four chairs around it.

Anthony began, "New officers are serving at relay stations all the way to the mines, and this will make our work easier, more secure from prying eyes. Just yesterday, we received news that last month's shipment of slaves arrived at the mines. The two slave wagons have been returned here for your trip to Adramyttium. Please be seated."

"We'll stay standing, Antha," stated Tira. Then, with a growl, he asked, "Who are you? I've never seen you before."

"No," replied Anthony patiently, again beckoning to the chairs with his hand, "you haven't met me before. I'm a new recruit. As Craga and Mithrida instructed, I recruited five others."

"Who recruited you?" Tira stood with his head cocked back, looking through narrowed eyelids. His hand was on his sword. One foot was positioned ahead of the other as if he were waiting for an attack from Anthony. "I don't remember Craga telling me about you."

Anthony's heart was pounding, but he took a deep breath and let it out very slowly. "No, you would not remember us. You've been in Chalcedon and points farther north. We came from the south. How would you have had the chance to hear from Craga?"

"I don't believe you are one of us," said Tira. "Who are you?"

"I met with Ota and Tissa when they arrived on the last day of March. They led the first two wagons. Spithra and Baga went with them. Ten auxiliaries, five being trained on their first trip, and two slave wagons. They delivered the wagons to the mines, as I've just mentioned. Before they left on the Interior Road, I gave them the same information I want to give to both of you."

"But they..." Tira left his sentence unfinished.

"I made sure the roads are safe. Relay stations are successfully infiltrated all the way from here to the mines." Anthony wondered how specific to be. He did not want to cause further doubts. "Craga's instructions were that we have to infiltrate."

"Antha is short for what?" Tira persisted with his questions.

"Marcus Antonius rebelled against Octavian. In fact, I did not choose the name. It was chosen for me. Truth be told, Anthony is my real name. Antha became my name for being part of the Faithful."

A heavy silence filled the garrison office while Tira listened, perhaps weighing the details he had just heard against the risks involved in his work as a rebel.

"I might accept that your name was chosen by Craga. He is the only one who can choose our names. But you," Tira said, looking at Sextilius, "are a fake! An imposter! I don't have to look at you twice to know it! You're not part of the Faithful, and you never will be."

Sextilius blinked several times. "That's a harsh denunciation when we are here to help you. You'll get through every relay station, arrive safely in Adramyttium, and deliver these slaves to the mines in Andeira. It's not like last year, when four unnecessary murders were committed by Ota in Porsuk Canyon."

Sextilius studied Arta's face as if to read his emotions. The mention of the four murders brought an instant reaction. His lips dropped down at the corners, and his face took on a dark color. "All right, so you know our plans and what happened last summer. Who told you?"

Anthony answered, "I can safely tell you that I learned it from one of the cleverest men I ever met. He described the entire operation to me, step by step. Now let's put everything about Porsuk Canyon and last summer behind us because Sexta has been to every location where you intend to go. I can assure you that the road is completely safe, all the way."

Arte's eyes were mere slits as he hissed, "I don't believe you know every detail about Porsuk Canyon. How is that possible?"

"Well, for my part, I know about the two slaves who escaped last year. Perhaps you did not know that one of the escapees got away. He hid from Ota. I found him in a cave, hiding at Five Shepherds Village. I know that two of twenty-two slaves escaped that day, yet twenty-two slaves were still sold in Aizanoi. I just don't know where the extra two 'new' slaves came from. But I do know about the shepherds' children being taken away with the mothers to a place that none could find. That was Ota's work."

This last detail was new to Tira, and his shoulders sagged. Arta spoke up. "Tira, don't be so suspicious! Can't you see? They do know everything, the whole scheme, from where the slaves come from to where they end up." He turned to Anthony. "Yes, you are right. Two slaves did escape, but we had to have the numbers matching for the next relay station records. So two old slaves were purchased before entering Aizanoi, and their owners were happy to be rid of them. When we realized how badly Ota had upset our plans by the murder of that extra soldier, we almost disowned him!"

Anthony prodded gently, "And that's why you used your alternative identity papers from Aizanoi to the coast."

"Yes." Arta turned to Tira. "I think we need to listen to what Antha and Sexta have to say. You are satisfied, aren't you?" He appeared to be ready to trust Anthony and Sextilius.

However, Arta's question gave Tira a moment to reflect. "No, actually, Arte, I'm not satisfied. Not at all! They are impostors. They know about our actions, what happened last year, and our plans for this year as well. Since Craga didn't give you all this information, who did?" He repeatedly swore as he addressed Sextilius.

Arta was pressed between loyalty to his fellow bandit and these two strangers, who seemed to know everything. "Tira, sit down! Let's get the full story from them!"

"No, quite the opposite. Arta, I never did trust Spithra. It had to be him! I think Spithra has turned these unknown men into our enemies. They are not part of the Faithful, and they are a threat to us."

Anthony spoke slowly, "Tira, sit down and let us explain why what I have to tell you that is so important. Craga doesn't know everything that happened. Last year, two caravan merchants 'disappeared.' Did you know that their bodies were discovered and that the military became suspicious? I intervened on your behalf. You won't have problems from here all the way to the mines. Your caravan can leave today if you want...."

Tira would not be put off. He was like a dog gnawing on a bone. "No, I'm not one bit satisfied! Your name is Sexta, right?" He had latched onto this detail and would not let go. Tira went back to the day he was initiated by Craga and Mithrida.

"Arta, do you remember what Craga said when we were initiated? 'For protection, each one of you is matched against one of our ancestors, Persian satraps, or Persian nobles. Two members of the Faithful may not use the same name.' Was that not the agreement?"

"Yes. Craga told us, 'Two of you will never have the same name.'"

"Agreed. Our names provide immediate security, preventing anyone from infiltrating. There cannot be two members with the name 'Sexta.' The Sexta we know works with Mithrida, bringing the best young men from the north...." He realized he had to be careful to not give away too much.

"Today we arrived in Port Daskyleion, and here is a second 'Sexta.' Something is wrong, and it's not my memory. These men know everything, yet they are not part of us."

Tira turned from Arta and glared at Anthony. "You aren't really one of us. I'll prove it with only four questions. Where did Craga meet you? What was the oath you made to become one of the

Faithful? What was the first commission given to you? What did you have to declare to break your oath to the emperor?"

He waited while Anthony and Sextilius tried to turn the conversation back to the delivery of slaves to the mines.

"You can't answer these questions or another hundred I could put to you!" Tira's challenge hung in the air like bad smells in crowded cities, and Anthony refused to answer.

Snarling like a trapped animal, Tira growled, "Arta, prepare to fight your way out of this office. This was a trap; I knew it right away. They're imposters, and they've taken similar names to trick us. This 'Sexta' is a fake! Note how different their names are. Antha, Muna, and Capta have nothing in common with Persian names."

Saying this, Tira readied his short sword. Arta did the same.

Anthony and Sextilius reached behind their shoulders and slowly undid their red capes. "Don't be silly, Tira. Be patient," Anthony said. "We'll help you march from Port Daskyleion this afternoon or tomorrow morning. You are free to go. I can promise you that no one will stop you from here all the way to the mines, more than two weeks. All the details are in place."

Tira was not finished with his questions. "Tell us this then. Where were the wild animals taken?"

"I know the names of the four villages near Aizanoi. The animals were sold to the benefactor of Thyatira, a man by the name of Bassos."

Arta was increasingly persuaded by Anthony. Hearing the prompt answer, he remarked, "See, Tira? These fellows know everything! The only way to have all this information would be that they have been in touch with Craga. Maybe Craga did give this man the name 'Sexta.'"

Arta slowly lifted his hand from his short sword, put his hands on the table, and began to sit down. He was willing to talk.

Tira, however, was not finished. "So you know where the animals were kept and where they delivered the cargo. But, Antha, you are an actor. Tell me, which legion did Craga serve in? And Mithrida, where did he come from? What can you tell us about the Faithful?"

Knowing that a wrong answer would totally alert Tira, Anthony placed his sword on the table in front of him, still unwilling to fight. He walked to the door without saying a word. Anthony's action of laying his sword on the table and walking away from it was a gesture to disarm suspicion. He opened the door and walked back into the center of the room.

"Relax. The door is open. My sword is on the table. Why would I do that if I were not part of the Faithful? The door is open if you want to go."

He smiled and turned so his back was almost facing the rebels. Further words were not going to convince the robbers.

"As I said, the door is open, and you are safe here. Let's talk about Craga and about Mithrida and the legion they served in. I want to help you get our merchandise to market."

"The door is open" was a signal to alert Menandro and Capito to be ready for trouble. Several soldiers were gathered at the end of the corridor. The phrase "I want to help you" was their signal to enter the office with swords at the ready.

Tira's sword collided against Omerod's, the sharp sound of metal against metal, but Tira was also facing Bellinus. Capito slipped behind, pushing Tira forward and pulling the rebel's foot backward at the same moment. Off balance, Tira stumbled and fell face down on the hard marble floor. The point of Omerod's sword at Tira's neck discouraged further resistance.

"I knew you were imposters!" Tira yelled.

Arta continued battling and cursing in a steady stream as he was backed against a wall. He was a better fighter than Tira, an excellent swordsman, and he kept three soldiers at bay for several minutes. A deep, bleeding slash on his right shoulder forced him to submit.

Tira's language was foul, and he refused to cooperate. "You'll rot in hell! You'll never find Craga! He's expecting us to meet him."

"Shut up!" screamed Arta. "Not another word! Nothing to use against us!"

"Where is Craga? Where is Mithrida? Where will we find them?" Omerod demanded.

Twisting arms and pressing swords against their necks, they threatened the two rebels. "Under the shadow of the fortress Klazomenai Oenaeum," Tira gave in reluctantly.

Arta's eyes were blazing, and he repeatedly shouted, "Prosperity will be Craga's lot while you rot in hades!"

"What do these expressions mean? Where will Craga be? What kind of prosperity are you talking about?" roared Anthony.

"We don't know" came the repeated answers. "We were to find

out from the others only after we delivered these slaves to the mines. Everything about prosperity and the future was communicated in code. I think Craga is going to tell us about our future prosperity."

Screaming loudly like an infuriated beast cornered and about to be killed, Tira struggled against the cords being tied around his wrists and ankles.

As he was being dragged away, he shouted, "Craga knows how many slaves are being delivered. When they don't arrive, he'll know. You'll never find him."

Arta bellowed, "Shut up, Tira. Just shut up! Control yourself!"

Both Arta and Tira cursed the bindings around their wrists and ankles. The slaves were brought to a prison building. Because the five auxiliaries working with Arta and Tira were unarmed, they offered little resistance and soon were rounded up.

Anthony asked to speak with the garrison commander, who called a meeting to include all the local soldiers. From the start, the officer demanded that he get the credit for capturing the rebels.

A question started a prolonged discussion when Menandro asked, "What should be done with these two bandit-soldiers? The slaves captured at the mines are being taken to Ephesus for the governor to decide their fate. However, we are in Bithynia and Pontus, a different province."

Bellinus answered, "An investigation combined with torture might take place in Prusa just to get important information quickly. These rebels will certainly be executed. When we started this project, Servius said he wanted the bandits brought to Soma in chains. Let's see if the Prusa Garrison commander is willing to honor that demand."

Almost three hours passed, including their noon meal, before a full description of events was completed, questions from the local legionaries were answered, and plans were made for bringing the criminals to justice.

The awkward moment came when the commander and the master of the port contended that the captured slaves and the seven criminals remain in their custody. However, Anthony and Sextilius told them that they were under orders from Soma and Sardis, so the discussion that ensued regarded the rights of the two provinces involved, Asia Minor and Bithynia.

Finally the commander agreed to have them all taken to Prusa, but he insisted that his name and the master of the port be listed as responsible when reports on the event were being finalized. Anthony agreed to this request.

As they were preparing to celebrate, a soldier went outside and then rushed back into the office. "Their ship has cast off! It sailed out of the harbor!"

Sextilius yelled, "While we were fighting and tying up these men, their ship left! Tira's screams must have been a signal to the crew. Remember how one of his crew stood outside the officer's office. Their ship must have quickly sailed away at the first sign of a disturbance. Soldiers, we are not the only ones who were prepared for problems. Insurgents also think ahead."

Anthony frowned. "This is an unforeseen complication. Those sailors will inform their superiors, and 'The Faithful' will not send slaves through this port again. They won't give up! They'll find another way, but it will be difficult to anticipate their next move. Servius will not be pleased."

Sextilius continued, "We have intercepted forty slaves. Four 'tribunes' were arrested a month ago and another two today. That's six key leaders. They had the help of fifteen auxiliaries. Adding them up would indicate that Craga will be expecting twenty-one 'Faithful' members to meet him. When and where? We don't know. If he's in Chalcedon or Sinop, the sailors will alert him. Otherwise, he may not find out what happened until later."

Anthony pounded his fist on the table, frustrated that he had not immediately gone to the harbor to secure the ship. Now nothing could be done about that but to guess the result.

Anthony sat down and wrote out the report for Commander Servius and Commander Felicior. Completing it, he read it to the garrison commander, Sextilius, Menandro, and Capito. The soldiers and officers working in the port came to the evening meal table celebrating their good fortune in capturing the rebels.

As they discussed the earlier conversations with the rebels, Anthony commented, "I'm totally mystified by the phrase that Tira yelled: 'Under the shadow of the fortress Klazomenai Oenaeum.' What does it mean?"

Sextilius answered, "I know of the places but haven't got a clue what the phrase means. Oenaeum is a small port on the Black Sea. Hardly anyone goes there, but there is a small fortress about three miles inland.

"Klazomenai isn't a port. It's a small olive-producing village on the Bay of Smyrna. Both places have military watchtowers close by. We know they are not speaking nonsense; it makes sense to them. It must be code for something. I think we should ask the army to investigate those two places."

Capito repeated the phrase as if repetition might make things more understandable. "Under the shadow of the fortress Klazomenai Oenaeum."

Anthony held his breath and let it out slowly. "Sextilius and I must leave for Soma in the morning. We'll stop briefly in Sardis. Servius and Felicior need to learn right away what happened."

Sextilius held up his hand. "Anthony, there's one more detail you need to take care of."

"What is that?"

"When you and I are on the way to Soma, we should ask the commander at White Horse Relay Station to have his men pick up Ateas at Five Shepherds' Village and take him to the Prusa Garrison. He should be a translator for this last group of slaves. His way of talking is strange, but his help is invaluable. He may learn more about how the gang operates. That lame Scythian man! He is useful."

"Good idea, Sextilius. Capito and Bellinus, as you are traveling, stop along the way at every relay station, inn, and garrison. Give officers a brief report. Help them understand what happened. I want you in Soma by May 10.

"Omerod and Menandro, deliver Tira, Arta, and the slaves to the Garrison of Prusa. Ateas will be sent up from White Horse to question the slaves. Take good notes. When that's done, arrange for Ateas to be taken to Thyatira by military wagon. He'll not be able to ride horseback at the speed you'll have to travel, and normal couriers also ride too fast. He must take the slower way back. I also want you to join us in Soma by May 10."

Sextilius had finished his meal and thought out loud, "We've captured six rebels. However, five eluded us: Mithrida, Craga, Taba, Harpa, and one other. We now know his name—Sexta."

JONATHAN AND REBEKAH'S HOME

While Anthony and Sextilius were starting their return trip to Soma, Miriam wrote another letter. She was worried because she had not heard from Anthony for weeks. Also, the last time Nikias came to the city, he did not speak to Miriam.

April 28, in the 12th year of Domitian
From: Miriam
To: My wonderful husband

> *Peace and greetings. If you are well, I am also well.*
>
> *This is the most extended silence since you started your assignment. I decided not to be upset this time, unlike the way I felt almost a year ago.*
>
> *We had a special feast day at our house while the Festival of Zeus was going on. Women from the Guild of Purple Honors came to hear Arpoxa's story. Her Greek is much better now. She told what it was like to be a slave and how Grandpa Antipas bought her at the slave market. None of the women could imagine the change in her life from slavery to freedom.*
>
> *My birthday was the same day. We feasted again, something Uncle Jonathan loves to do. The feast lasted until late in the evening. It was also the second anniversary of Grace's adoption day.*
>
> *Sibyl didn't arrive until late. She had expected Melpone and the young women to go with her to the Temple of Artemis. Sibyl was disappointed to go alone. When she came to the house, her words had an angry tone. Sibyl made another prophecy, and then Melpone confronted her: "I wonder if you realize this, Sibyl. We prefer the blessings of Miriam to the scary things you say."*
>
> *Hurry home! Oh, you should hear the sweet things Grace is learning to say.*

Chapter 40
Prosperity

OLIVE GROVE FARM AT FORTY TREES

After a sharp disagreement between Nikias and his four brothers, all five households were on edge. Nikias thought that he, as the oldest, should be able to lead. His brothers should willingly obey.

He attempted to explain several times. "Look! Jonathan made me his steward. He said we have free days for rest and to use as we want. And this is what I want us to do."

Lykaios countered, "Nikias! Do the work Jonathan wants you to do, and give up on these trips to other towns. Be satisfied with staying at home. You are driving us too hard. You haven't given us a rest day for three weeks. During the festival, what did everyone else do in Forty Trees? They sang and danced. They were drinking and going to the temple! And us? You made us work hard for Jonathan Ben Shelah."

"Listen, my older brother! We went with you several times last year, taking scrolls to towns and villages in the Lycus Valley. You took us to villages north, west, and east. But we've decided we are not going to go with you anymore."

Zeno added his piece. "You're always going somewhere. You go to Thyatira and Sardis. You transport items for Jonathan's shop. That's enough! Stay at home! Your baby daughter needs you."

Nikias replied, "Listen, my brothers! This will be my last trip for many months. I promise. I'm going to go to some small villages south of us, and I will be back on the third day."

Zeno stood with Naian, his wife. Alberto had his arm around Thyra's shoulders. Between them, Lykaios and Zenia stepped in, and then Kozma completed the circle. Nikias found his entire family standing up to him, and he would not have a brother to accompany him on his next trip.

Even Penelope, his wife, agreed with them.

Kozma rebuked his brother. "Nikias, you are our oldest brother and I'm the youngest, but I must tell you this: You have abandoned the beliefs our mother taught us. Your teachings about Yeshua Messiah generate conflict. I figured out why you had us working so hard. While workers on nearby farms went to the festival, you wanted to keep us away from wine and dancing. Isn't that right? Now you want to make up for backbreaking labor these last two weeks by taking three days away from work and asking us to go with you."

Nikias showed his annoyance with a deep frown. "Please, Kozma! I want to see other farms and learn how other people keep their orchards."

They argued, and in the end, it was clear he would have to go alone. His brothers would stay at home at Olive Grove.

Nikias remembered Anthony's instruction, but his memory was dimmed by other thoughts. *I want a farm of my own. That's the secret I haven't explained, but I will tell them my plans after this next trip.*

Anthony instructed, *"Never go alone! Always go with one or two others."* *Nothing happened to me when I went off by myself a few times. How can I obey Anthony if no one will travel with me? After this next trip, I'll tell them about my plans. They'll be surprised.*

Nikias left early in the morning with a horse pulling a small wagon. The second Saturday morning in May promised to be a perfect spring day. He drank in the sounds of birds in the trees and watched them flying and swooping down. He held his breath, enjoying the scent of spring in full bloom. Young colts danced and ran across enclosed pastures.

At the Inn of Apollonius, Nikias thanked the elderly Greek man, Xenophon, for his fine hospitality. Alysia, his wife, served Nikias hot flat bread with honey and cheese. Being interested in all the towns and villages, he asked about villages on the lower slopes of Mount Aspordenon.

"On the way, you'll come to several small villages," explained Alysia. "My relatives live close by. Tell them that I sent you! Go along the base of Mount Aspordenon. I have many relatives there and in Prosperity Village."

Nikias patted his horse on the nose and rubbed its neck affectionately before leaving. He climbed onto the wagon, determined to go as far as Mount Aspordenon. He would work his way back, arriving in Olive Grove Farm on Monday night.

Before telling Penelope of his decision to buy a farm, he would scout out the lower lands on the mountain's eastern skirt. Perhaps one of the farms in this region would be better for her and his growing family. Better than the others he had seen.

"Thank you, Xenophon and Alysia, for your hospitality," he called. He took the reins and clicked his tongue at the horse. Calling back, he reminded them, "Read the scroll! You'll enjoy the story by Mark!"

Thrilled by dreams of owning his own farm and feeling a little guilty, he left the city of honey gatherers.[113]

Nikias knew his brothers were irritated by his going away like this. *I won't do it again. The next time I go to Thyatira, I will talk to Jonathan. I'm sure he'll help me, perhaps giving me a loan to get started.*

THE MILITARY GARRISON IN SOMA

The sun was setting on May 7 under a clear red sky.

Anthony and Sextilius rode through Forty Trees and changed horses at the relay station for the last time. The light was almost gone when they arrived at the garrison at Soma. It had been a long ride in hot weather, and both were grateful to have another day before they met with Commander Servius. On Sunday afternoon, the other four team members arrived.

Even though they were tired, the six legionaries gathered to discuss the information they would report on their activities. Commander Servius wanted the latest details, and he asked many questions, seeking clarification.

"We've pieced it together slowly how they organize themselves. Some of it was guesswork," explained Sextilius, "but always it was a waiting game."

Servius leaned forward expectantly. "I want every detail."

Anthony explained how the first ship in March came into Port Daskyleion. The rebels were sent on to the mines at Andeira to be captured along with the mine supervisor.

Sextilius added, "After the first group of twenty slaves, ten

---

[113] The distance between Prosperity Village and Apollonius is 11 miles (17km).

auxiliaries, and four rebels were captured, a month went by. Just as we anticipated, their ship returned.

"Tira is intelligent, rebellious, and clearheaded. We could not convince him that we were actual members of the Faithful. But after a short struggle, we had Arta and Tira in chains. Five rebellious auxiliaries arrived with them. They brought twenty more slaves. So this summer, we captured six of their leaders and fifteen auxiliaries. The commander in Prusa is waiting for your order to get them here. As you instructed us, you will have all the rebels here in chains.

"What's more important, we came to this conclusion: There are another five commanders in the Faithful. We know their fake army names."

"Where are their leaders?" demanded Servius. Anthony saw a new intensity in the commander's eyes.

"We don't know," Anthony answered, "but we intend to catch them, sir."

"How will you do that, Suros?"

"On our way here, we left reports at each relay station. Our next objective is to find the five remaining leaders. We have a clue, but it doesn't make sense...yet."

They talked for a few more minutes. Once all the facts had been communicated, Servius dismissed the team members. Anthony turned to go, but Servius added, "Suros, I want to talk to you privately first thing in the morning."

"Certainly," responded Anthony.

On Monday, chirping birds and noisy roosters woke all the soldiers at the Garrison of Soma. Trees and bushes, birds, and wildflowers presented a picture of peace. It was a dawn with the promise of a calm, clear spring day.

Anthony stood before Commander Servius, who requested him to sit down. "The time has arrived for promotions. Commander Felicior is being transferred to Philadelphia. I am being promoted as Commander of the Sardis Garrison, taking over his position."

Anthony kept his face blank, but worrisome thoughts flashed through his mind. *Servius can't control his sense of pleasure and triumph. That means that when our squad returns to Sardis, he will persecute me for my beliefs in the Jewish Messiah. I will no longer have Felicior's protection. Not good news.*

"Is that all, sir?" asked Anthony.

"No. Commander Felicior takes up his new duties early. The change is due to the ailing health of the commander in Miletus. On June 1, I will assume my new assignment as Commander of the Sardis Garrison. In three weeks, I will be your commander.

"Now, before assuming my command, I must talk with you about a few matters. I learned that you received a farm, normally given only to retired legionaries. Your property is just outside Philippi in Macedonia, is it not? And it's rented out?"

"Sir, the land documents are in my name. As I told you previously, I was awarded the farm but then recovered from my wound. I was given reservist status, and the Philippi Garrison commander allowed me to rent out the farm.

"I received rent for two years, but all of that money was deposited with the commander of the Philippi Garrison. At present, a retired army man is living there, and I will not personally be receiving the money. When I reach retirement, I can return to Philippi and claim my farm back, but all of the rent will belong to the Philippi Garrison."

"You became a legionary at age seventeen. You are now a reservist, and in five years, you will complete your military service. Is it not irregular to have received land for retirement and then have it rented out before you actually retire?"

Anthony answered, "Sir, the authorities in Rome awarded me the property. At that time, it looked as if I could never serve in the army again. I was in a weakened state. Everything was done regularly. I was sent to Philippi under the assumption that I could not carry on.

"Sir, I can assure you that army authorities did not request that I return the land. Quite the opposite. Because of the circumstances in Upper Germanica, they assigned me to be a scout instructor to Pergamum."

"Anthony," said Servius, striding back and forth in his office, "several interesting 'facts' capture my attention. First, farming land is only given to retired legionaries, yet you did not stay retired. Second, you have received rent for several years. Third, you continue to refuse to say the Solemn Oath properly. You remember our previous conversation?"

"Yes, sir, I remember it clearly." *The army officials know about my farm and the rent situation. Servius has a point against me about the Solemn Oath, but Commander Felicior knows my thinking on that.*

"Fourth, the training you gave to recruits who were sent to Legion XXI, the Predators, was 'below standard.' Your legion was defeated, and an inquiry is underway. It's being said that the scouts didn't do their job correctly."

Anthony squirmed, anxious to respond to this unjust charge.

Ridiculous! The authorities in Philippi know all about it. I declare the Solemn Oath as it ought to be said. And about the scouts "not being prepared for war," I trained them well. Could I be responsible for a legion's defeat?

"Fifth, I think you essentially confirmed in our meeting that your incompetence in Port Daskyleion resulted in Arta and Tira being apprehended earlier than planned. Our agreement was to catch them in the act. They should have been arrested as they delivered the slaves to mine owners."

Anthony forced himself to keep from speaking.

How were we to know that Tira wouldn't believe us? We could not know that Craga had already designated another rebel as Sexta. And we don't know where Craga is. From what we heard, I think he is somewhere close by, about to meet his fellow criminals.

"Sixth, you were sent to capture the leaders of these rebels. However, they are still looters, free, able to come and go at will."

"We intend to catch the leaders, sir!"

Servius paused. His next words were menacing. "I know that you are a reservist, but I intend to find out if you are hiding irregularities, things the army doesn't know about. I did not expect such low achievements from a legionary. On Wednesday morning, you will return to Sardis. Report to Commander Felicior. Don't go anywhere else. You will respond to me about all these concerns in a few days. You are dismissed."

OLIVE GROVE FARM AT FORTY TREES

"Let's go for a visit to Olive Grove," said Anthony to Sextilius. Before midmorning, they had covered the eight miles and were arriving at the farm. Four farmers welcomed them to the farm; they looked discouraged and miserable.

"What's the matter?" Anthony asked, dismounting. "How can you be gloomy on such a beautiful spring day?"

"Nikias is gone and said he'd be away for three or four days."

"When did he leave, and where did he go?"

"He wanted to go alone. Said he was going to villages he had never visited before."

"He went alone? To which villages?" Anthony's voice rose higher than usual.

"The first night was to be in Apollonius with the deaf innkeeper. Then he said he was going as far as Prosperity. He said it's a pretty village with a high hill behind it. We expect him back at the end of the fourth day, tomorrow."

Sextilius picked up on the detail. "Did you say Prosperity?"

"Yes. It's a tiny village hidden in the fold of a mountain pass."

"Anthony, remember, Tira was shouting, 'Prosperity will be Craga's lot while you rot in hades!' He repeated it many times. We thought 'prosperity' was a condition in life, but what if it's the name of a village where bandits are hiding? What if it was also a signal to the ship's crew? What if he was talking about a place?

Anthony yelled, "Yes, the other expression indicated places too—Klazomenai-Oenaeum. We know Oenaeum is far to the north. Klazomenai is a village to the west of Smyrna. Prosperity...could it be a place too? Maybe we misunderstood! Could that village be their meeting place? If so, Arta and Tira were probably lying about not knowing where Craga was waiting. Nikias could be in danger!"

They galloped back to Soma, found Servius, and told him what they had just learned. "Sir! We may have a lead on the bandits!"

Anthony explained the possible connection to the rebel's use of the term Prosperity. "We need all the regulars you can muster, sir!" Anthony saw a gleam in the officer's eyes as if he understood the arrival of a unique opportunity. "Sir, there are twenty in your garrison right now."

"Right. I'll need to keep two here with me to man the garrison. I'll send two men ahead of your detachment to advise the three relay stations to have all their horses saddled and ready. That means I'll send sixteen with you, Suros. You are responsible for them and the other five in your squad."

Anthony calculated. "Altogether, we have captured twenty-one persons. If their leaders are waiting to meet them at Prosperity Village, we should arrive as if we are the rebels they expect to meet. We'll be twenty-two coming on horses, arriving in a cloud of dust. That's about the right number.

"We'll look like a detachment from a distance if that's what they are hoping for. Some regulars must look like auxiliaries, the others like legionaries with armor. This could be dangerous. If Craga is not meeting his rebels, we'll soon know and we'll come back."

Instantly, the garrison came alive. Two riders sprinted off on Soma's fastest horses. They would make sure fresh mounts were ready to leave as soon as the group arrived at the relay stations. They would change horses three times.

Twenty-two horses were saddled for the detachment as men ran for their weapons. Anthony told them they would first go to Apollonius to make sure Nikias was not at the inn.

They rode quickly. The sun had passed its highest point when Anthony and the detachment arrived at the small town's inn. The town's innkeeper and his wife were finishing their noon meal.

Xenophon and Alysia confirmed that Nikias had stayed at their inn the previous night. "He intended to stay tonight with my relative in Prosperity Village," said Alysia, trying to be helpful.

"Why would he go there? Did he show a particular interest in that village?" Sextilius asked.

"I told him it's the prettiest place around. Prosperity Village is where the morning's first sun rays hit, lighting up a giant cliff. It was a lookout point for generations of soldiers," answered Alysia. "Sometimes the villagers call it 'the village of light.' He was determined to see all the villages along the bottom of the mountain. He said, 'Someday I'm going to be a farmer and own my own land.' He's a pleasant man, and I wish him well."

"Well, we need to find him," said Anthony.

"I do hope he is not in trouble!" Alysia exclaimed.

"No, he's not in trouble with us!" Anthony called out as they left in a gallop.

They dashed the eleven miles across the valley. As they passed through small villages, children stood waving at the side of the road. The sound of horses passing in a hurry brought men and women rushing to line the route.

By midafternoon, after pushing their horses, they were approaching the base of Mount Aspordenon. Anthony held up his hand and stopped the troops for a short rest and some instructions. "These are dangerous men!" shouted Anthony. "They'll have a lookout. To the rebels, a detachment coming may put them at ease because that's what they expect. When we get to the village, spread out.

"Ask about the children. First, make sure they are safe. I know their tactics. Rebels instill fear to control others. If this is where they are hiding, the villagers will see us as friends, not enemies. If Craga or any of the rebels are here, their men will be expecting his 'soldiers.'

"However, they'll very quickly know something is wrong. A single noise, a scream, swearing, anything could warn the criminals."

They started again, taking the left at a fork in the road following Xenophon's directions. Arriving at the village, they went up a shallow rise. The narrow lane gradually curved back on itself, but the closer they came to the houses, the steeper it became.

They approached the entrance to the village and slowed down. The horses were tired, and spittle foamed around the bits in their mouths.

Prosperity Village was not an appropriate name. Its houses, single-level dwellings with flat roofs, were shabby. Flies flew in swarms everywhere. Pigs scurried about, picking through garbage. Old dogs lay asleep on the ground.

Anthony, riding with Sextilius, declared, "Such a filthy place. Imagine! Calling this place 'Prosperity'! What a violation, not only of the Greek language but of future hopes as well!"

"Additional reinforcements for Craga and Mithrida send greetings to you," called Anthony to the guard at the entrance of the village. He jumped down from his sweaty horse.

The guard had been waiting for the correct code word. However, the names "Craga and Mithrida" satisfied him. "Good, we need you. We have been short of good, strong arms, and I'm glad to see our soldiers," said the guard. "What's your name?"

"My name is Antha," said Anthony, "one of Mithrida's newest friends. How long have you been waiting for us?"

"We expected you yesterday or the day before. What caused the delay?"

"We came as quickly as we could," said Anthony. He beckoned to the others. "I want you to meet these new additions to your village."

While some formed a circle around the guard, who did not know anything was amiss, Sextilius stood behind him. If someone watched from the high cliff behind them or from any of the homes around the village entrance, what happened next would not be noticed.

In a second, Sextilius had his dagger against the guard's throat, "Scream and you die. If you don't scream, you'll live longer...your choice. That's a good decision. You want to live. Walk naturally with me to that house, where you'll be bound and gagged, but you will live. A guard will watch over you. Remember, one shout, and you die."

One of the soldiers took the guard's place at the village entrance. The others scattered across the road through the center of the town. There were no other guards to be found.

A typical village would have had dozens of children leaving their houses and lining the narrow streets if they heard horses thundering up the road to their village. Nevertheless, here in Prosperity Village, there was not a child in sight.

Sextilius whispered in the guard's ear, "Which house belongs to the village leader?" The guard pointed to a house close by.

"Where is Nikias, the farmer who came yesterday?" The man pointed to a house farther up the road. Above that house rose the cliff.

Anthony approached the village chief's house, knowing that he would have observed their arrival. He stood at the door, speaking quietly. "Don't be afraid. We know that robbers have taken your children. We are soldiers who are here to rescue your children. Where are they?"

The village chief, a father of five children, cautiously opened the door and pointed the way. "Our children are being kept in those two houses over there, along the road."

Anthony sent five regulars up the narrow lane, two more on each side of the building, and the same number went to the second house.

Anthony rapped on the front door and called, "Sorry to be late. We're here to take over!" Two of Craga's men guarding the children opened the door, relieved that their shift had ended.

It was difficult work watching over so many young rascals, and the raiders had been expecting backups. They had been promised assistance and were fretting because reinforcements had not arrived. "Finally! I was beginning to get worried. Wasn't the agreement that we would meet you here yesterday?"

"We are here now!" said Anthony. "Do you have any weapons

here?"

"No, we don't want children getting hurt. We left the swords and daggers in the house under the cliff. We don't want anyone getting poked or wounded."

In an instant, the rebels were gagged and tied by their hands and feet. The village leader's face was red as he sneered down at the two helpless criminals. "You terrorized our village! I said you would regret keeping our children as hostages. Now it's your turn to be afraid!"

The children were liberated but told to keep quiet. "Stay quiet for another hour. If you make any noise, you will bring the troublemakers' leader, and he will hurt you. Do you want that?"

They all shook their heads and said, "No!"

The same surprise met the guards in the second house. The children there were also released, and two soldiers from Soma were assigned to watch the children. The children knew Craga was a cruel man, and they were delighted to be freed.

Sextilius spoke to the village elder again. "Where are Craga and his men staying?"

"Just below the cliff. That's the house up there, half a mile from here. From the village, walk toward the cliff through the olive and fruit trees. After the orchard, you'll find a large house. It's my father's old home. From the front, it looks like two floors but just the top story if you come in from the back. That's because it's built against the side of the hill. I think some of your soldiers should attack from the rear. Remember, the roof is flat with steps going down in the middle into the largest room."

The afternoon sun had begun to cast its first shadows. Two villagers led them up a narrow, winding trail through an orchard. They stood under olive trees at the base of a cliff as they examined the two-story house that butted up against the bottom of the rock face.

Anthony counted three rope ladders attached at the top of the vertical wall of stone. Where one of the ladders disappeared at the top, they made out the figures of four men. One of the four waved. Anthony walked out into the open and waved back.

Sextilius said in a low tone, "The lookouts! Everything looks normal to them. They're expecting their fellow gang members to show up. Well, here we are!"

Anthony added, "It won't take too long for them to realize

something is wrong. Circle the building."

He waved his hand in a circle as a signal, sending several to attack by entering the top of the house. "Remember, Commander Servius wants them taken alive. We'll need to question those men to discover their future plans. Look for Nikias! He may be in the house."

Walking up to the house and standing outside an open window, they heard angry voices. "One more time—where is your so-called 'friend'?"

The sharp crack of a whip was followed by a swift kick. A man groaned loudly, muttering between clenched teeth, "I've told you everything I know! How many times do I have to tell you? Anthony Suros is a legionary. He's keeping the Postal Road safe. That's all I know."

The sting of a whip brought another scream of pain. "You know more than that!" came another shrill voice.

Eight legionaries walked up the hill behind the house, and Anthony assigned six to enter the house from the front. A guard sitting on the flat roof above the building looked up from his game of dice, and for the first time, he realized he did not recognize any of the approaching soldiers.

He shouted, looking up at the top of the cliff, "We have company but not the kind that we want!"

The loud call alerted everyone. The robber who was whipping the man inside the house heard the shout and was puzzled by the expression "We have company" and didn't know what to do: to continue beating or prepare to fight.

Anthony and Sextilius crashed through the front door, and they took in the scene. Nikias lay on the floor. Bound hand and foot, his back was bloodied. Six rebels stood over the body, but none had a sword. One man held down the prisoner's head, another held his feet, and the third readied a bloody whip to scourge their hostage. Three others stood at the bottom of the stairs.

Shouting, "Secure them! I want them alive!" Anthony and several soldiers seized the robbers.

Sextilius's booming voice filled the room. "You are under arrest for crimes against the laws of Rome! Down on the floor, face down. Now!"

One screamed, "We are not proper soldiers! Have mercy! We are auxiliaries recruited by Craga!"

In a moment, all six were bound and lying on their stomachs.

While Sextilius and Anthony seized and bound the rebels in the large room, their companions on the roof were also quickly subdued in the surprise attack. They had been playing a game of dice, and a single dagger was useless against skilled Roman warriors.

Bellinus, Capito, and Omerod marched their two prisoners down the stairs at their swords' points. They were tied up and added to the other prisoners on the floor.

Anthony was concerned about the condition of his badly beaten friend, Nikias. "Menandro, attend to him while we interrogate the prisoners. Stop the blood loss as much as possible."

Anthony took over the questioning of the rebel who had alerted the rest to their arrival. "Quickly, who bought the wild animals?"

No answer was forthcoming. Anthony pushed the blade a little deeper. "Who was buying the wild animals last year?" A drop of blood appeared at the base of his neck. More would come unless there was an answer.

"Some big benefactor called Fabius Bassos bought them."

"Who sold him those wild animals, and why was he interested in them?"

Each answer came only after receiving a further pointed prod from Sextilius. "Tira sold them to Bassos to entertain the city during the games in Thyatira."

"Where are Craga and the others?"

"Outside on the cliff. They've been up there for more than an hour."

"How did they come to Asia Minor?"

"Through Klazomenai and Smyrna. Craga got off the ship at the village of Klazomenai."

"How were Tira and Arta supposed to know where to go?"

"The mine supervisor and master of the slave market were instructed to tell them to come here."

"All of them have been arrested."

On the other side of the room, Sextilius was speaking to the youngest prisoner. Fright showed in his eyes as he glanced back and forth, trying to decide how much he should say.

"What do you know about the slaves? Do you know where they

are being taken?"

"Yes, they are taken to work in the mines, but Craga is upset. He is waiting for six other leaders. They were supposed to be here by now: Ota and Tissa, Spithra and Baga, and Tira and Arta. Craga has been swearing at us because forty slaves and fifteen auxiliaries disappeared. He knows something went wrong but hasn't been able to discover what it was."

Sextilius pressed the point of his dagger against the auxiliary's neck. "Where is Craga? Is he here somewhere?"

The man fell on his knees, his head bent down to the floor. He looked up at the ceiling and said, "He's keeping watch. He's on the top of the cliff."

"Who else is with Craga?

"Three others: Harpa, Maza, and Taba."

"Why are they up there keeping watch and not you?"

"They were nervous because it was taking too long for reinforcements to come."

Sextilius looked across the room at Anthony. He bellowed, "Capture Craga! He's here at the top of the cliff!" They rushed to the top of the house and looked up.

Four rebels were standing close together on the rocky ledge, peering down, trying to understand what was happening inside the building.

Anthony looked closely, examining the features of each one. Then he recognized one of them.

Craga! I know you!

Oh! And your full name too! Claudius Carshena Datis. You're the scout who attacked me! Descended from Persian noblemen—you often bragged about your character and relationship to Datis, the ancient Median admiral. He destroyed the Greek navy! And if you wanted to be like him, you've failed. We are going to apprehend you.

I remember now, and it's easy to understand! You were the centurion who came to talk with the two tribunes planning political moves for Legion XXI, the Predators. And you were assigned to protect the eastern bank of the Neckar River from Germanic tribesmen. You followed me under the bridge that day. You insisted on being behind me on that scouting duty. It was you at the end of the line, coming behind me!

Anthony yelled, looking at the four figures on the top of the cliff. "I know you," he cried in a loud voice. "You're Claudius! You walked behind me when we went under the bridge to find those so-called 'barbarian invaders'!"

Details came together as a pattern, thoughts tumbling over one another. *Yes, it's coming back. After talking to the guards on the river's eastern side, Claudius came behind me as we went below those bridge supports. He was ordered into my detachment that morning by... Who had the authority to assign Claudius to my squad that day?*

Yes, Tribune Flavius Memucan Parshandatha, one of the two tribunes I reported to the general. Could Flavius be the 'General' of the Faithful? Could Flavius be Mithrida?

Yes, Flavius and Claudius often had their heads together in the officers' tent. And as I fell, I thrust my sword, reaching out to slash his leg. And I think I know who the other 'Sexta' is. He must be the second tribune I reported. Those three deserted the army and set up the Faithful, a gang capturing slaves and selling wild animals in the province of Asia Minor!

Anthony and Sextilius looked up, their faces clouded in dismay as Taba, Maza, and Harpa cut the three rope ladders. They slithered down, hitting the ground with a smack. The rebels were isolated at the top of the sheer cliff.

There was no quick way up the two-hundred-foot ledge. Anthony sent regulars along the sloping rock face to the far right, the only other way up, which would take many minutes. He watched, exasperated because their element of surprise had vanished. His attempt to capture the leaders had failed.

In frustration, he hollered, "You'll be hunted and killed, Craga! We'll find you!"

"You are a loser. You always were, Anthony Suros!"

"We'll arrest you and bring you to justice. You are Claudius Carshena Datis!"

"From up here, you look pathetic, Scar Face! How did you ever survive that episode?"

Sextilius shouted to the soldiers moving slowly up the right side of the cliff, "When you reach the top, go left along the rocks."

Craga and the three others threw large rocks at the climbers. One struck a soldier, wounding his shoulder, and he screamed in pain and fell to his knees, his arm dangling lifelessly.

While the soldiers continued clambering up the lower cliff's side, Anthony kept Craga in conversation. He thundered, "The two legions were separated, even though you didn't want it, Craga!

Rebellion always fails. You don't stand a chance. We know you sell slaves and wild animals. Better yet, six cowards in your gang will be executed: Ota, Tissa, Spithra, Baga, Arta, and Tira.

"The mine superintendent will be treated as a criminal, and his actions against Rome will result in execution! All the slaves you sent to the mines have been collected and returned to Scythia because they were brought here illegally. Everything you've done, including trying to kill me, ended in failure."

Craga shrieked in frustration, "You're wrong! Legion XXI is destroyed, Scar Face! Wait for other legions to also meet their fate! All Rome's forces will be shattered by the Faithful!"

Anthony's voice was still loud but calmer after realizing that the purpose of the gang's rebellion had emerged. "You don't really believe that! Your rebellion is failing like that of every oppressor!"

Two soldiers climbed along the narrow and steep trail to the top. They now kept out of the range of the rebels who had been throwing stones at them. In a few minutes, they would reach a narrow shelf, and from there, they could move to the highest point of the stone face.

Realizing the danger, Craga walked painfully away from the edge. The man was limping!

Anthony could hardly believe his eyes. *I wounded him even as he tried to kill me. It's his left leg! That's where my sword hit him. Where are they going? If there's a clear path down the mountain on the other side, they may be able to escape. They may have planned for that too.*

Several minutes later, the soldiers from Soma arrived at the highest point of the cliff. Craga, Taba, Maza, and Harpa had been standing there, but now they were nowhere to be seen. The rebels had disappeared into the dense forest behind the cliff. The sun's rays were growing longer, and the forest was full of dark shadows.

"Suros, the four rebel leaders escaped! There's no sign of them now!" one soldier called.

It was getting dark when Anthony and the soldiers returned to the large house at the cliff's base. They found Capito and Bellinus pouring water on a back bloody from whipping. Nikias had sustained deep wounds and had trouble breathing. Every breath brought him further pain.

Seeing Nikias in this condition, Anthony was livid, angry for the torture inflicted on him, and exasperated that he had traveled alone, disobeying the instructions given to him.

Nikias groaned as he talked. Pain was overtaking him. Describing his ordeal took several minutes, and Anthony and his men listened without interrupting.

"I came to the village...guard met me...asked, 'Who are you?' I told him...Nikias...father of five children. Their guard asked, 'Where are you from?' I said, 'Olive Grove, near Forty Trees...'

"He demanded, 'Does anyone know...you came to Prosperity Village?' I answered, 'Yes, my brothers know...'"

"'Do you know any soldiers...ever talked with soldiers?'

"'Yes.'

"The man...was angry. 'Who?'

"'Anthony Suros...knows I like to travel to farms...' The guard said, 'What does your friend do?'

"'He...keeps the Postal Road...safe.'

"That...made them...terribly angry...brought me...whipped me...kicking my ribs...hurts to breathe.

"The guard said, 'Where is this soldier?'

"'I don't know...where he is.' Didn't believe...kicked me... whipped me."

Anthony wondered what to do. The sun had set, and to take Nikias back at night on the narrow road along the mountain's base was dangerous, probably impossible. Would he last until morning? He sent Omerod and Menandro to ready the wagon from Forty Trees Farm. He decided to leave at dawn and shuddered as he thought about the next day.

We've taken in six bandits, but four others—Craga, Taba, Maza, and Harpa—fled. Commander Servius will go berserk.

He tried to sleep, but too much was on his mind.

Early in the morning, the farm wagon was ready with its horse hitched for the journey. "What's the fastest route from here to Soma?"

The village chief suggested, "The road beside the mountain hasn't been repaired after the winter runoff...lots of potholes. Just go back the way you came. You'll get to Soma quickest."

Anthony explained his plan to the village leader. "Sextilius and I will take Nikias to his family. I am leaving the soldiers here. Some will guard the prisoners. The others will search the forest above the village and back along the gorge. I'll have them search the entrance to the valley where the forest meets the open plain. I want those thugs captured! Servius will have the prisoners taken to Soma in slave wagons, which should be here by tomorrow afternoon."

Parents and children waved goodbye as the wagon left, carrying Nikias. The village chief called to Anthony, "Thank you! Thank you! Our children are safe now! They slept in their own homes again last night. No harm was done, but they are badly shaken. Thank you for helping us."

"I must leave quickly and get Nikias to his family. Goodbye."

Chapter 41
Nikias

ON THE PLAINS OF THYATIRA

Anthony and Sextilius traveled as quickly as possible, passing through four small villages before arriving at Apollonius. There they transferred Nikias to a sturdier wagon. The military relay station would provide fresh horses for a faster arrival. Ointments and clean rags covered his wounds, but Nikias groaned repeatedly.

They hurried as best they could, but the wagon made slow progress, and Nikias moaned in pain at every bump in the road. The afternoon sun was getting low in the sky when they arrived at Forty Trees. Shadows from the mountain blocked out the sun's rays. At the check station, Sextilius signed for a horse and rode on to the Garrison of Soma, taking the news to Commander Servius and requesting two slave wagons to transport all the prisoners back from Prosperity Village. Anthony continued in the wagon taking Nikias to the farm.

The unexpected arrival of their brother at Olive Grove Farm caused an outcry. One of the brothers, Alberto, saw them arriving, ran to the wagon, and shouted, "Nikias is back!"

And then "Oh no! He's hurt! Come! Quickly everyone!"

Seeing his brother bloodied and unconscious, he called in a quivering voice, "Penelope, come! You have to see this."

Nikias had been so alive, so confident on Saturday morning, whistling and singing aloud. Now, on Wednesday evening, he was bruised, beaten, and barely conscious. The four brothers carefully lifted him off the wagon and took him to his house.

Penelope knelt beside him and wept, crying loudly while pouring oil on her husband's face and ribs. Blood had dried on one side of his head. She winced as she examined the bruises on his chest. His rib cage was worse.

When Alberto turned Nikias over, Penelope almost fainted. His back was bloodied. She poured oil on his wounds, moaning and crying out, "Dear God, don't let him die! I need him! How would I raise five little ones alone?" Tears flowed down her face.

Anthony told them to pray and he lifted his hands up as he had seen Antipas do, but he felt heavy and tired. The quick dash to find Nikias in Prosperity Village had been exhausting, and Anthony had hardly slept last night. The desperately slow ride back to Olive Grove had drained his energy from him, and he was afraid he was going to lose his friend, the cheerful farmer.

Later that evening, Nikias opened his eyes a few times and then closed them. "I love you, Pen," he said.

He was on his stomach, and he looked sideways at his wife and started to cry. "I should have...listened to you. I disappointed...Anthony. I disobeyed...I should have waited...I wanted it for you...."

Saying that, he fell unconscious.

The dim light in the house hid their long faces. Nikias was sleeping, his face pale and his breathing shallow. Dried blood and marks on his back resembled wagon ruts on worn-out marble pavement along Roman roads. Old pavement stones could be replaced, but the farmer's life was hanging by a thread. No doctor could be found to attend to him.

OLIVE GROVE FARM AT FORTY TREES
May 14, in the 12th year of Domitian
From: Anthony
To: Miriam

Peace. If you are well, then I am also well.

You will receive this letter through Alberto, the second of the five brothers on Jonathan's olive grove. This letter brings sad news because Nikias died from wounds yesterday morning.

Nikias spent evenings as your grandfather did, reading scrolls aloud while three brothers copied them. Later, he took these new scrolls to small villages. His outgoing nature made him friends everywhere.

Earlier, I instructed him, "Always travel with another person." His brothers didn't like being away from home and recently told him they would not go with him. Kozma, the youngest, is a devotee of Artemis, and he actively resisted.

Nikias went to Apollonius. After talking to the old couple in the inn, he left for Prosperity Village. He did not know that was the bandits' temporary hideout.

On Monday, I left Soma with a detachment. That same day, we found him at Prosperity Village. Strangely, Nikias led us to the criminals we have been hunting.

We brought Nikias down to Apollonius, where we changed to a larger wagon. Along the way, he muttered a few words. I told Penelope what he said on this trip to their home.

Penelope had her five children around her when he died: Evander, Rhoda, Hamon, Sandra, and little Melody. The oldest boy is almost fourteen, and the baby girl isn't even six months old. Penelope wept uncontrollably, holding her baby girl with one hand and stroking her dead husband's head with the other. The other four women in Olive Grove—Naian, Thyra, Zenia, and Leta—have been kind, providing food; Penelope's children needed comforting.

They asked me to speak about Nikias before they laid him in the ground.

I said, "Nikias was a good friend, the only one who ever asked me to tell every detail of my life! He listened well and was not satisfied with simple explanations. He wanted to know everything: why I became a legionary; what my mother thought of the army; how my training took place; how I learned to use swords, bows, and arrows; and what daily life in the army was like. He asked good questions and was not content with superficial thoughts."

They were crying as I said, "When I met him, Nikias was afraid of death. The thought of dying frightened him terribly. Miriam sang a song as he drove my family on a wagon through the Cemetery of the Kings of Sardis. That song made all the difference to him. For him, death began to lose its sting. He sang that song over and over.

"We all wish he had been more careful. It was his idea to travel to new places. In Prosperity Village, we found a note in his belongings, supposed to be a surprise on his arrival back home. He wrote, 'My dear Penelope, this is my last trip. On my next trip to Thyatira, I'm going to ask Jonathan Ben Shelah for a loan. After looking at towns and land all around, I have found a farm to call our own. It is close to Olive Grove, close to my brothers. I love them and never want to disappoint

them....' It did not finish what he had intended to say.

"He leaves a huge hole, one that can't be filled by anyone else. Penelope told me about his love for his children, the affection he showed her, and his constant, unbridled optimism. He worked hard, even during the Festival of Artemis. He wanted a loan from Jonathan and was preparing to ask him for it."

Penelope had him figured out. She interrupted my little speech. "All this was not a surprise. I knew he wanted a farm. The idea grew during this past year. I didn't let on that I knew his secret. Of course, he couldn't keep a secret from anyone, least of all from me!"

I continued talking. "Now his questions are answered. He has found everlasting prosperity. This dear, simple man loved his Lord. He insisted on visiting every nearby village, wanting folk to know his faith and to share his joy.

"These were his last words to me as we put him in the wagon to bring him home: 'Tell Penelope I want my own farm. Prosperity Village sounded good until I saw it. It's a miserable place. I'm going to buy a farm near Stratonike.'"

I said many other things. They laughed and cried at the same time when I told stories of how Nikias commented on everything. The brothers were astonished. None of the four brothers knew that he wanted his own farm and orchard. This explained, in a small way, why he wanted to travel to other places. Partly he wanted to share his enthusiasm about the Messiah, and partly he wanted to become a landowner.

We buried him at the edge of Olive Grove, overlooking the river.

Does this mean my assignment is complete now? Unfortunately no. We've captured many robbers, but regrettably, four leaders escaped.

I hope Felicior will let you and Grace return to Sardis, the only way I can think of being with you. Often I am faint with longing for you. It has been almost a year since I held you in my arms. Every memory of you is precious.

THE MILITARY GARRISON IN SOMA

On Friday, after the prisoners were jailed in Soma, Servius called the detachment together. "I want a full written report. One copy goes to Commander Felicior and another copy to Ephesus."

Anthony described how their unexpected arrival permitted a successful raid against all the rebels except the four leaders, who had escaped in the late afternoon. At that, Servius exploded. "Four leaders escaped? Such incompetence! You had them in your hand! They will continue wreaking havoc. Didn't you know enough to arrest them when you saw them?"

"Yes sir, but they were two hundred feet above our men on a mountain cliff. We know who they are, and I believe we'll capture them."

Servius swore colorfully; his face was the hue of dull red coals at the ironsmith's. "Capturing underlings is not a triumph. You failed me again. Poor leadership!"

"Not completely, sir. I know who Craga is. He was in Legion XXI, the Predators."

"You know this Craga?"

"He was a centurion, and he led a cohort. His title and name were Centurion Claudius Carshena Datis. He was 'First Javelin,' meaning he was the most highly regarded of Legion XXI's centurions. He is 'Craga,' the one we have been looking for. His ancestor was Datis, the famous Persian naval officer who battled Greece. This will all be included in the army's report.

"On March 15, nine years ago, I was in Upper Germanica and brought information to my tribune at the officers' table. They met in the large officer's tent. Barbarians were resisting us, and we knew that villagers were planning a strike.

"As I left, I overheard Datis speaking at the officers' table. Our legion had won several battles during the wintertime, and it was time for bragging. Datis said, 'My ancestor led the naval invasion against Greece. He cleverly destroyed the Greek fleet. Hundreds of ships were burned.' He also said some things that bordered on treason. Of course, over the next four weeks, I found reason to return to the officers' tent. Finally, I was convinced that a rebellion was being formed.

"On April 10 of that year, I asked for a conference with General Celsus Vettulenus Civica Ceriales. Five days later, I met with him and said, 'Sir, it's not normal for a scout to speak with the general, but this is of interest. I believe three officers—two tribunes and one centurion—are involved in political discussions. Isn't it against army regulations?'

"Five weeks later, I was wounded in an ambush and didn't learn what happened to the officers who were plotting rebellion." Anthony rubbed his hand on his scar.

"This information will also be written in the report. Their leader was Tribune Flavius Memucan Parshandatha. We believe that he is 'Mithrida.' You'll notice that Claudius and Flavius have Roman personal names and Persian family names: Datis and Parshandatha! Their families go back to princes who lived here five hundred years ago when Persia ruled this region."

"Yes, this is important. How did you deduce this?"

"I didn't figure it out. It was the investigation Sextilius carried out and the conclusions he reached earlier. If he is right, then we may have discovered what binds these rebels together. It might be a strong affiliation with Persia's lost empire. He believes that they are trying to bring back Persian influence or use it as a pretext to bring others with Persian roots into their gang."

"How certain are you of this?"

"Completely convinced."

"You talked with Craga but not with Mithrida."

"Right. When I saw Craga—Claudius Datis—up on the cliff, this is what came back to me. I remembered the scene with the three officers around the table. The officers took meals in the large army tent, and one was Tribune Flavius Memucan Parshandatha. He boasted of being born in Trapezus on the Black Sea, which Persia once controlled. He often crowed about his family. At one evening meal, he said that his ancestor was Mithredath, the treasurer of the king of Persia.[114] He was gloating about ancestry, nobility, lands, and fruit gardens near Susa. Living in Trapezus, he probably was attached to the memory of Mithradates VI. His religion is Persian.

"Sir, Sextilius is convinced that Persian history and religion are mixed up in this rebellion. We know that he is right because all the robbers we caught use names linked to satraps who governed Sardis. Persian kings appointed them to govern the people in this region."

Servius paced back and forth along the wall of his office, mulling over the strange theory. He assumed an austere tone. "What do these rebels want? For the Persian Empire to return? We'll soon learn. As I said previously, the Miletus Garrison

---

[114] Ezra 1:8

commander is gravely sick, so our command transfers are to take place a month early. The commander in Philadelphia is going to Miletus, and Commander Felicior is being transferred to Philadelphia earlier than expected.

"This squad of yours will be based at the Sardis Garrison, and in two weeks, all of you will answer to me. Suros, once Commander Felicior goes to Philadelphia, you will continue as leader of the other five soldiers. This report will go to my superiors in Smyrna, with a copy to Ephesus. Now I'm beginning an inquiry into the reason that those four leaders are still free."

Chapter 42
First Fruits of Harvest

JONATHAN AND REBEKAH'S HOME,

Disagreements between Kilan and Jonathan had turned increasingly sour, and they came to a head in the first two weeks of May. Several elders in the Thyatira synagogue agreed that the God-fearers group had wandered too far from their original purpose. The original intent was to teach Jewish beliefs, customs, and traditions to non-Jews. No matter that their rabbi was far away or that they had decided to restate their position. Jonathan's home had become a forum where others had started to teach their own beliefs. This was a danger to the Jewish community.

Kilan summarized their sentiments when he met with Jonathan late in the afternoon on the day before Pentecost. "The Synagogue Council has decided that the portico will be closed to members of the Way of Truth. However, we can't stop those 'God-fearer' people from coming to your house.

"You may continue to welcome these people into your home, but let me warn you: They are like leaven, a silent, contaminating influence. Regarding worship for your family and our congregation, you will no longer light the Sabbath lamps, declare the Shema, read the Torah to the congregation, or participate at the front. This is for as long as you continue to collaborate with those people. You may observe only as part of the congregation, and you must not speak of that Jewish carpenter."

Jonathan tried to speak but could not. *I continue to be cut off but not completely. I can keep friends in both camps. My generosity runs freely in their direction and my hospitality in the other. My position and worth in the congregation are greatly diminished—a terrible blow.*

Sitting down to the meal at home that evening, Jonathan announced that Kilan had confirmed the elders' decision to bar the Way of Truth from meeting in the portico.

He continued, "As a family, we'll continue meeting early on

Sunday mornings to remember Yeshua Messiah's resurrection. No one may hold meetings on the portico. Furthermore, they may not attend the synagogue services or participate in fellowship. Those are Kilan's orders. However, our non-Jewish friends are welcome at this house."

The enormity of Kilan's decision reminded Miriam of what had happened twice before, first in Pergamum against Antipas and then last year against her uncle Simon in Sardis. Previously, the relationship of Jewish leaders with God-fearers was cordial, but patience had worn thin. To the elders, the many false ideas and pagan myths of the non-Jewish attendees were intolerable. They had to be eliminated from the synagogue grounds.

On Sunday morning, the day of Pentecost, Jonathan welcomed his friends. He had explained the significance of the festival being celebrated. The Holy Meal was observed, and at the end of the service, he spoke. "My dear friends, I explained to you the counting of the *omer* and what we have done these past fifty days. We've had fasting and prayer on many days. However, I must also tell you something disappointing. Here is what Kilan, the Synagogue Council leader, told me yesterday afternoon: Only Jews are welcomed at Sabbath worship. Non-Jews may stay in the portico if they remain silent."

A hush fell over all who were sitting in Jonathan's great room. Some who valued the growing bonds of fellowship with Jewish families wept as they realized that some relationships must come to an end. Jonathan, for the first time in many days, had no words. He nodded toward Miriam and raised his eyebrows as if to say, "Do you have a song for us this morning?"

Miriam was standing with the group of young women from the Guild of Purple Honors. They stood embracing, tears flowing down their cheeks, not ashamed of the deep emotions churning within them. *What can I sing to close a meeting like this? Today is a festival day, a time of joy. Pentecost is our Feast Day of First Fruits. I don't have a new song to sing for this occasion.*

She felt joy during sadness and thought of the words from Isaiah she had treasured for years, which she had set to a tune while in Sardis. She moved to be in front of the gathering.

"I have words of encouragement for you from the ancient writings," she said. "A disagreement has arisen, and we must accept the decision given to Uncle Jonathan. We must not rebel with a spirit of self-righteousness. Adonai promises guidance for those who have lost their path and comfort for the brokenhearted."

She sang words Grandfather Antipas had taught her years ago.

Build up! Build up! Prepare the road. Prepare the land,
Remove the obstacles out of the way for my people,
For this is what the high and lofty One says,
He who lives forever, whose name is holy:
"I live in a high and holy place, but also
With him who is contrite and lowly in spirit."

He says, "I will revive the spirit of the lowly and the contrite.
I will not accuse forever.
Nor will I always be angry,
For then, the spirit of the man would grow faint before me.
I was enraged by his sinful greed,
I punished him and hid my face in anger.

"I have seen his ways, but I will heal him.
I will guide him.
And I will restore comfort to him,
Creating praise on the lips of the mourners in Israel.
Peace, peace to those far and near,
And I will heal them."[115]

As she sang the lines, her own heart ached. *Lord, I am hurt and lost and in mourning. How much longer until Commander Felicior allows Anthony to come to me? Why is Felicior keeping my husband away from me? Today is exactly one year since I saw him.*

Miriam looked at each person individually, those sitting on the floor and those standing next to the walls.

A man called out, "Please, Miriam, sing it again." She repeated it, and after singing it several times, each person knew Isaiah's words by heart.

She was not ashamed of the message: hope, healing, and restoration. The way that this Pentecost service happened in the Ben Shelah home could not have been planned. It was indeed a

---

[115] Based on Isaiah 57:14–18

gathering of first fruits.

She smiled at each of the young women from the Guild of Purple Honors who were present.

Miriam sang the song once more. Danila came to sing beside Miriam. Celina stood up and came to her other side. Friends wrapped an arm around Miriam's shoulders as they sang.

Celina whispered, "I never understood about all this before you came. How would I have known about Adonai if you hadn't come to us? I still have so much to learn. I need to tell you about my home and my life." She looked away and then whispered some more. "I want to be a believer as well."

Danila took Miriam's hand. "I have heard it over and over living in this house, being married to Bani. I heard the message with my ears. Today, though, I understood with my heart. Include me too when you teach Celina, will you?"

"I have questions too," said Calandra, drawing close. She had joined the small circle around Miriam. Hypatia came to stand between Calandra and Danila. "Is there room for anyone else in this circle?"

They laughed together, and the circle opened a little wider.

THE MILITARY GARRISON IN SARDIS

Although Commander Felicior preferred to stay at the Sardis Garrison rather than moving to Philadelphia, he had no choice in the matter. Decisions for assignments at the beginning of July had already been made in Ephesus, the provincial capital. News had come that the health condition of the garrison commander in Miletus had worsened.

Two days later, all the regulars in Miletus mourned the passing of their commander.

Two orders went out from Ephesus. The first was to the Philadelphia Garrison commander, who was instructed to make a hasty move to Miletus. The other was sent to Commander Felicior Priscus: "Take command of the Garrison of Philadelphia immediately."

Felicior would leave Sardis on Tuesday morning and arrive in Philadelphia the same day, five days before the end of the month. He decided to send a short, more informal message by military courier to Anthony and his selected men in the special squad. One outstanding matter demanded attention: He wanted to clarify the authority lines until the month's end.

May 26, in the 12th year of Domitian
From: Commander Felicior
To: Anthony, Omerod, Menandro, Sextilius, Bellinus, and Capito

> *Greetings. If you are well, then I am well.*
> *The report from Commander Servius came, and I read it carefully: most of the gang captured, the illegal slaves in the mines retrieved, and four leaders escaped.*
> *My new commission as Commander of the Philadelphia Garrison begins today. I leave Sardis this morning and take over the command at that garrison tomorrow morning. This will be my last letter from Sardis. As of June 1, Monday, next week, Commander Servius will be your commander. However, until June 1, you will continue under my authority.*
> *I wish you all well. Your services rendered to the empire are impressive and commendable. Thank you for making the Postal Road safe once more.*

THE MILITARY GARRISON IN PHILADELPHIA

As part of taking up his new post, Felicior was briefed Wednesday morning by the existing garrison commander on his new assignment's exceptional difficulties. It was the reason he had been selected as the commander for this smaller city. In Ephesus, his leadership in the rounding up of the criminals selling slaves had received favorable notice.

Merchants often travelled from the low-lying Cogamis River Valley near Philadelphia, along an elevated region up to a mountain pass called the Gate, and then down again to the Lycus and Meander Rivers in the southern valleys.

Thieves had frequently operated along this series of rolling hills. Highwaymen had pounced on merchants and then disappeared into nearby forests with stolen merchandise. To reduce the security problem, a special patrol called the Regiment of the Gate had been created to keep constant watch. Local civil unrest had recently required using this special patrol to quell local riots.

Now the Military Command of Asia Minor needed someone

with Felicior's ability to keep the Gate open and free from bandits.

His first day at his new post was the previous commander's last day. During the transition of responsibility, the news was anything but good.

"As I leave for Miletus, I leave you an unwelcome situation. Unrest has been growing for five months. Domitian ordered for half of the local vineyards to be cut down. Wheat has been planted in the new fields for local consumption and some to be sent to Rome. However, protests broke out two months ago. Peasants and villagers discovered that they lack knowledge and equipment for wheat farming. There is little wheat available in the area until harvest, so the grain prices remain high, and since employment is down due to the reduced vineyards, few can afford to buy what grain there is.

"The protest movement began in Sasorta, and it is growing. The people are demanding we open the city emergency grain storage. Consequently, I transferred legionaries from the Regiment of the Gate to control the protests, leaving fewer guards on the road. A robbery at 'The Gate' was reported this morning!"

Felicior had not expected a significant event on his first day in Philadelphia, certainly not another crisis. "And obviously, that bigger problem, the robbery, is one that will fall into my lap?" he asked.

"Yes, I'm sorry to say. A long camel caravan was attacked. The owner, a famous merchant of Hierapolis, is on his way to Rome again. As a result, this is going to become a political matter.

"Titus Flavius Zeuxis, the wealthiest merchant in the Lycus Valley, demands safe passage from Hierapolis through Philadelphia to Sardis and to Smyrna at the coast. He has never been assaulted in all his trips to Rome. Now this happens, close to his home city! He says a formal complaint will be lodged in Ephesus over this matter. I suggest you are going to need reinforcements quickly."

Felicior slumped in his chair and glumly looked at the ceiling. "All this on my first morning here! A riot in Sasorta and a major political problem stemming from a robbery. Perhaps this chaos was caused by four robbers who recently escaped arrest. I've been pursuing them for a year, supervising six soldiers in a squad that I formed. We have captured most of the rebel gang, but those four rogues may be the ones who assaulted Titus Flavius Zeuxis."

"Commander Felicior, since you have been hunting that bandit gang, why not bring in the soldiers who helped you, the squad you mentioned? I believe an order for transfer issued to your detachment will be valid to the last day in May. You have the authority to assign them to me here in Philadelphia. I can accept the transfer, and when I leave tomorrow, they will be yours to command. Commander Servius may have some say over giving you all the team members since that would reduce his manpower in Sardis. You'll need to have their pay transferred here also."

Felicior acted immediately. "I need a scribe to write some letters." One hour later, he said, "Have these letters delivered to the Garrison of Soma immediately. I want my men here in Philadelphia! Fast!"

THE MILITARY GARRISON IN SOMA

Late Thursday morning, May 28, two scrolls were delivered by military courier to the Garrison of Soma. Commander Servius read the orders and frowned. Because they carried the signatures of both commanders, the outgoing and incoming officers, he would have to comply.

As they gathered for the noon meal, Servius came to the table where Anthony and his squad sat. "I have news and new orders. First, the slave who was discovered hiding in the cave will be sent back to his family. He helped us find out who the leaders of the gang were, and he suffered needlessly. He'll be home after a year away from his family. The army is also returning the other captives of the gang to Scythia. They were brought here illegally.

"Second, Commander Felicior sent a message. He wants his squad in Philadelphia immediately. There is a shortage of farm work in the Philadelphia area, resulting in riots and protests. Additionally, an outbreak of banditry on the road to Laodicea means Anthony, Omerod, and Bellinus are needed there. Felicior thinks that this may be related to Craga and his gang."

"Capito and Menandro, I need you to help keep order in Sardis. You will not be going to Philadelphia.

"Sextilius, I congratulate you on completing twenty-five years in the army. I wish you well as you go back to Syracuse, Sicily, to manage your father's holdings. "

"Soldier, I need to see you in private," Servius said, calling Anthony aside. "A personal letter also came, addressed to you. I'm sorry you will not serve under my command, but, Legionary

Anthony Suros, you leave me just as I'm following up on several concerns relating to your character. My investigation into your past is not finished. Remember that."

His dark gaze and tightly pursed lips said more than his words.

After taking the letter from Servius a little too quickly, Anthony broke the seal and read it, trying not to smile. Then he made a request. "Sir, for my move to Philadelphia, I request a military wagon to pick up some belongings at Olive Grove Farm. I wish to meet my family in Thyatira before leaving for Philadelphia. I haven't had a day's rest for weeks.

"I request four days to arrive in Philadelphia instead of the normal two days for such a move. That will allow one day of rest, a day for packing, and two days for the wagon trip. As written here, Commander Felicior indicates that my wife and child are to move there also."

"Permission granted. Felicior mentioned you would be requesting a military wagon. Tomorrow, Friday, you'll start your transition to Philadelphia." Anthony immediately started a letter to be sent to Miriam.

Servius turned to attend to other issues. He was sending the prisoners captured in Prosperity Village to the courts in Smyrna. There they would face Roman justice.

After that, he needed to prepare for his own move to take over the Sardis Garrison.

JONATHAN AND REBEKAH'S HOME

On Friday morning, horses' hooves were heard clattering down the street. The city patrol had directed a courier to Jonathan Ben Shelah's house. As Jonathan's family was reclining at breakfast, the letter arrived for Miriam.

Arte called to Jonathan, "A message! For Miriam!"

She opened the seals, and an instant later, she shrieked, holding the letter to her chest. "Anthony is coming today! He'll be here before midafternoon. He has been transferred to Philadelphia!"

She picked Grace up, dancing in small steps with her, and the house was in an uproar, questions popping up faster than mushrooms in Jonathan's garden in the spring.

"Is he going to stay here? How long? Will we be able to talk with him about his work?"

"Is he still a soldier?" Danila asked.

Gil leaned forward. "Why is he coming today? What's happened?"

Rebekah was puzzled. "What do you mean, transferred?"

She said, "I don't know!" to each question, turned, and rushed away, not bothering to tell them the details contained in the letter. Anthony had written it quickly as a note.

My dear, this is not a proper letter, only a quick note. Pack up and be ready to leave Sunday morning. Commander Felicior wants me in Philadelphia for a new assignment. He says to bring you with me, but he didn't say where you would stay. I'll be staying in the barracks. Can you arrange to stay with your Uncle Amos and Aunt Abigail? Commander Felicior has given me the use of a military wagon to move our things. You, Grace, and I will go together. This is not a temporary assignment, because there is social unrest in and around Philadelphia. I'll tell you more when I see you. I hope to be with you tomorrow by midafternoon, earlier if possible. Two of the soldiers in my squad, Omerod and Bellinus, are going on ahead to Philadelphia. Sextilius is going back to his home in Sicily for retirement. Capito and Menandro are needed in Sardis to help with the social unrest there. I hope Ateas and Arpoxa will come to Philadelphia with us. They can be returned to Sardis if they prefer that. Ateas will be returned from Prusa soon.

Miriam ran up the stairs, singing and laughing. She placed Grace on the bed, held the little girl's hands, and danced, singing softly in a sing-song voice so no one else could hear.

"Daddy is coming! Daddy is coming! We are going to Philadelphia. He is coming today. We are going to live as a family again! Tomorrow we'll have him all to ourselves!"

Chapter 43
Saying Good-Bye

OLIVE GROVE FARM AT FORTY TREES

Having left Soma early Friday morning, Anthony arrived at Forty Trees. Many memories returned as he turned onto the narrow lane leading to Olive Grove Farm. He had borrowed a horse and a pack pony with a carry-frame from the relay station to move his gear and the things he would retrieve from storage at the farm. The brothers were surprised to see Anthony again so soon. He asked to see Antipas's scrolls, selected all but the business-related scrolls, and tied them in bags onto the pack pony frame for the trip to Thyatira.

Zeno was now in charge. Anthony said farewell to Naian, Alberto and Thyra, Lykaios and Zenia, and Kozma and Leta.

He spent time with Penelope, again feeling the recent loss of Nikias. Anthony wondered how Penelope would manage with five young children. While praying with her, he tried to imagine the pangs of widowhood. She was crying as he left, her face tucked against Melody's black hair.

As he left, he wondered, *Will Evander be able to support the family? Can an almost-fourteen-year-old do the work of his father? How will Penelope manage raising five children by herself? Thank goodness for the community of the other families and all their cousins.*

Midafternoon found Anthony entering the city gate of Thyatira. The city guards escorted him to Jonathan's home, where the whole family was waiting. He almost fell over as Miriam hugged him. One arm encircled Grace, and the other hugged Miriam. Rebekah came in on the hug, and then the whole family came forward.

As they entered the home, everyone had questions; he could not finish one sentence before someone else began talking. Arpoxa sat on one of the couches, holding her new son in her hands.

"Hello, Anthony! Welcome, but can you tell me where my husband is?"

"Yes, I certainly can! Ateas is on his way here from Prusa. I had to have him returned here on a military wagon for his safety. It's a long trip. Your family can live with us in Philadelphia if you want to. You can also return to Sardis if you would prefer that. Commander Felicior says he knows Ateas is returning here. He'll send a wagon from Philadelphia to bring your family there next week unless I tell him that you would rather go back to Uncle Simon's. He would arrange for that. Ateas was a great help in tracking down the rebels. We could not have done it without him. I hope you will come to Philadelphia, but you must do what is best for both of you. Let Jonathan know, and he'll contact us."

Anthony picked up Arpoxa's new baby boy and did a little dance. Arpoxa began to cry; she longed for Ateas as much as Miriam had been missing Anthony.

The remaining afternoon passed quickly with questions and introductions. Anthony met Miriam's friends, and as the big room filled up, she introduced many more people.

The mood was festive, and a feast was being prepared. "I received many letters from Miriam, so I think I know each of you very well!" he said good-naturedly.

They asked him about his assignment, and he said, "For a year, we have been searching for bandits. We captured most of them, but a few escaped, and now my commander wants me in Philadelphia."

He had never had such a welcome! Melpone brought Kiron and Aulus. Everyone remarked on how much the seven-year-old was now talking. He had had a birthday and was being accepted by everyone. The little boy wanted to touch Anthony's armor, and then he reached up to run his fingers along the scar on the soldier's face.

More of Miriam's friends arrived: Dreama, Celina, Hypatia, Neoma, Koren, and Calandra. Sibyl came shortly afterward and so did both overseers at the workshop. Adelpha came with Hesper and a few other friends who did not see eye to eye with Miriam. They all wanted to see this Roman soldier. Anthony tried to remember everyone's names but got mixed up trying to match names, work, and relationships.

Jonathan and Rebekah agreed a feast was the only way to celebrate Miriam's leaving for Philadelphia. His voice expressed shock. "Leaving so soon! We'll greatly miss you."

That evening, so many came to the feast that the couches were not sufficient for all the small groups. Instead, people stood around the house or sat on rugs. At the hastily prepared banquet, Jonathan, Rebekah, and Bani reclined on one couch. Anthony, Miriam, and Arpoxa, with their children, were placed to their right. Everyone was surprised that Melpone, Kiron, and Aulus sat at the table as honored guests.

Miriam overheard Sibyl's quiet, nasty comment. "Why should a little boy who can't speak properly, who can't even think, and who can never go to school get a place at the most important table?"

After the dinner, Anthony said, "I've come from Soma to take my lovely wife and daughter away! Sorry, but that's the life of a legionary!" His comments and effortless style brought laughter. Everyone was relaxed and looking forward to hearing from Miriam's husband.

Feeling more at home, he said, "There's only time to tell you a little bit of my story. The whole story would keep you here far too long. As you can see from my face," he stopped to turn his face so all could see, "I carry scars. Those came from my time as a legionary in Upper Germanica. A soldier is not supposed to talk about them, but I believe many of us also carry scars people can't see."

He described Germanic tribes, their villages, and hilly lands, dark forests, and high-peaked mountains divided by wide rivers. Then he spoke about the bandits. "We've stopped their destructive activities, at least for a while. I'm not permitted to describe these men in detail, but we cleared the roads, making those safe again. A few evil men still try to have an easy life by stealing from others, and well, that's why I'm being sent to Philadelphia!"

People cheered and clapped.

When he had finished, the people applauded once more. Others called out, "We've just started to hear from you. Tell us stories from your time in the legion!" Two men raised their hands. "Tell us what you think of Dacia. Why did we lose the war?"

Anthony waved his hands. "Too many questions! I can't begin to answer them all."

Miriam spoke for a few minutes. "This is a big change for me. Yesterday I woke up and it was like any other day. As the breakfast meal was ending, I received a message, a short letter to say Anthony was coming. He's taking me to Philadelphia. Soldiers have to obey their officers, so I either go with my husband or stay here!"

Several called out. "Sorry, Anthony, we're not letting her go!"

"Don't go with him! Stay here, Miriam!"

"There's not even a choice! She has to go. He is her husband!"

Aulus whispered, "I wish you...stay with me, Miriam." Leaning toward him, Miriam gave him a hug.

She spoke. "A year ago, I came to Thyatira saying, 'This is a noisy, hardworking city that I'll never get used to, and I'll never have friends here.' But I was wrong! I learned to love many people, and I've seen selfless 'agape love' at work. I also found how many struggles, hurts, injuries, disappointments, and lost dreams fill this city. I think that's why God gives me songs—to cheer my spirit and to share love with others."

Shiri said, "Oh! We *must* sing some songs while we're still together," and she ran to Jonathan's library, where the instruments were kept.

She took the flute and gave Danila a harp. Gil and Bani brought tambourines. Miriam started to sing, one song after another. People stood up and formed a long line. Singing, swaying, and dancing slowly, the line made a circle moving around the room. It was a time of celebration and merriment, both poignant and cheerful. The person they had grown to love was leaving them. She had brought them joy and hope.

As every song was sung, Anthony became more surprised. Miriam shrugged, looked at Anthony, and whispered, "I didn't tell you about the songs. Sing along! I'll teach them to you later."

Finally the singing stopped, and people sat on the carpets once again. Jonathan said, "I think it's appropriate that we ask Melpone to thank Miriam on our behalf."

"I didn't know Jonathan would ask me to say goodbye to my best friend," Melpone said slowly. "It's hard to say farewell. I remember the first day I met Miriam. She was outside the Temple of Artemis and introduced herself. Later, she came to the workshop where I was making purple treasures! She was always friendly. I saw the joy in her eyes, a happiness I did not have. I always looked away from people because, well, life was hard."

Suddenly, she became more confident. "I'm one of the people Anthony talked about. I carry many scars inside. My name, given to me at birth, meant 'catastrophe, disappointment, tragedy.' I changed it because I did not want my life to turn out like that. I prayed over and over to Artemis, Apollo, and Demeter: 'Please change my life!'

"How and why it happened, I do not know, but Miriam came to

my house. We are needy, and I must work while my father stays with Aulus, my son. She came not just once. Each time she brought healing words, songs, and good thoughts.

"Not everyone agrees with her beliefs, but I found with her a sense of community that's different than anything else in Thyatira."

People clapped and cheered, agreeing with her.

"One day I was able to understand these words: 'I will be your God, and you will be my people.' I realized that Miriam wanted a new kind of community for all of us. That day I started to believe. Her songs acknowledge our pain and our scars, but she lifted us beyond ourselves. She taught me about Yeshua Messiah and how he cares for us. He was resurrected, he hears our prayers, and he gives us hope. She said to me, 'Your sins are forgiven in Yeshua Messiah's name. You are a child of the light, not of the darkness; you are called to be a light to the world.'. Then she gave me a new name. Well, not a new name but an interpretation of my name. She taught me the meaning of my name: 'My reason for living is to share love.' That's what my name means now."

This time there was no cheering. Melpone's words caused deep reflection.

"You know, I have two good abilities. One is my eyesight, and the other is my nimble fingers. I can sew, so I was chosen to work on special sashes to be used by senators. Friends started visiting my son and other children too. They also have disabilities. Together, we are teaching our children.

"I saw the difference that 'agape love' makes. I was stitching togas for senators one day when I realized this: Threads woven into a fabric create new patterns. That's like my life. I'm learning new habits and new ways to think about myself and others."

Melpone had never made such a long speech. "Sorry for talking so much," she said.

"No, please keep on talking!" "Keep on!" "Don't stop now!" All were captured by her words.

She picked up her thoughts again. "I talked to Miriam about the traumas of my life and not having a mother to teach me. That was disturbing, not having a normal childhood. But Miriam faced loss too; her mother died fleeing Jerusalem. She taught me how to face up to traumas that come our way. My husband went away. I have a son who needs someone with him all the time. I'm poor. I lived in fear."

She walked around the small, square table to hug her friend, "Miriam, you'll never know what it has meant to me that you came to visit and to stay in Thyatira. I would never have known what you believe. My son would never have been able to speak like he can now if you and your friends, my friends at the workshop, hadn't spent time with us. Aulus has improved so much. We can't even give you a meal, but I can tell you we love you. Thank you for agape love. You'll always be in our hearts."

As Melpone said this, she looked behind her. Aulus had risen from his place on the couch, from his place of honor at the head table, and he took Miriam's hand.

Aulus made the first speech of his life. "I feel I...special. Miriam came to...house...was kind...talked us...sang us...stories to us. She said...come to her house...I love her. She...me feel special...said I...sing too. She...me feel special and others too."

People applauded and shouted.

Then they stood on their feet for him. His grandfather had never heard him say so much. The first time he came to the Ben Shelah house, Aulus could barely say his name. All this encouragement brought a broad smile to his pudgy face.

As others gave words of appreciation, Anthony saw the outstanding bonds of affection.

He took Jonathan aside. "Uncle Jonathan, we really do need to notify Uncle Amos in Philadelphia that we are coming rather than have it come as a complete surprise. Please send a note by pigeon to him and Aunt Abigail that Miriam and I and the baby will be arriving in three days by wagon.

"Ateas is on his way here to be with Arpoxa, but how will they feel staying in Thyatira without many friends? I told Arpoxa that they may return to Sardis, where they have friends and work, or come to Philadelphia. We can work out something for them there also. The army will provide transportation either way. I'm sure they would not be happy here, even if Arpoxa can help with embroidery work. Neither of them would have enough close friends.

"Please request lodging for Miriam and me. They may be unwilling or unable to take us in, and I would have to find other arrangements for us, but at least they will know that we're coming. We'll have to pray that Ateas and Arpoxa will be happy with whatever they want to do. Miriam is Arpoxa's best friend."

The next day, Anthony and Miriam would get to sleep late, pack their belongings, and prepare some food for the trip to Philadelphia. These people would not see her again for a long time, so it was past midnight when the last person left.

Arte left the doorway where he had been standing, watching everything. "I'm just a slave," he said, "but I'll have something special to remember you by. I'll be the last one to say goodbye to you, and this will stay in my memory all my life."

Anthony turned on the stairs to wait for Miriam as Arte spoke to her, and then they went upstairs. Grace was already sleeping. He shut the door.

"We are together again, my wife," he said tenderly. "I dreamed of you every night."

"I did too," she said, placing her arms around his shoulders, "except I dreamed of you during the day as well. And occasionally, I had a nightmare. I thought bad things might be happening to you."

"Well, nothing bad is going to happen tonight," he said. "Quite the opposite. I've been away from you far too long."

He took her in his arms. The warmth of his kisses expressed the passion he had felt for her during the past year.

"I've been faithful to you all these days," he said as Miriam lay down on their bed. "Many people tonight said how much they loved you. Now let me show you how much I love you."

DIODOTUS AND DELBIN'S HOME IN THE CITY OF SARDIS

May 30, in the 12th year of Domitian
From: Diotrephes
To: Mother and Uncle Zoticos

Greetings. If you are well, then I am well.

It's very early in the morning as I write, but I slept only a little last night. I must tell you the latest news. Commander Felicior now serves in Philadelphia, and Commander Servius is here in Sardis. I learned yesterday of the new officer's arrival and immediately introduced myself to him.

I told him that we teachers at the gymnasium are concerned about the recent disruptions in the valley. With many vineyards around Philadelphia being replaced with other crops, small farmers, peasants, laborers, and slaves are in an uproar.

I know you'll be interested in my conversation. I asked Servius, "Have you heard anything about my old friend Anthony Suros and his wife, Miriam?" I added, "He's not that good of a friend, but I want to talk with him again."

Servius said, "Yes, he, his wife, and his daughter were transferred to Philadelphia at the request of Commander Felicior."

I asked, "Will he stay in his new assignment for a long time?"

He answered, "He's going to be there for quite some time I believe. It's not easy hunting down this gang of rebels. I don't envy him this new task because it's a nasty job finding mutineers. He'll be on the road most of the time. Also, imagine trying to control all those rioting peasants who've lost their jobs and income!"

I almost jumped for joy because we know where our little Chrysa is going to be. Anthony will be away for days on end. With Miriam and the baby in Philadelphia, this will give me a chance to finally take her from Miriam.

I will give Servius information about people and events in Sardis so that he'll learn to trust me. Along the way, I plan to continue making accusations against Anthony, creating difficulties for him in the army.

I forgot to mention that a year ago, I gave Cleon a recommendation that secured him a job in Philadelphia. He works at the Inn of the Open Door, recently purchased by Amos Ben Shelah, so he'll be useful as eyes and ears for my plan to bring Chrysa back to you.

Soon Chrysa will be in our home; we are going to be a family. I will write you as other events show that the gods smile upon us.

ON THE POSTAL ROAD FROM THYATIRA TO SARDIS

Early on Sunday, a military auxiliary in Soma prepared a four-wheeled wagon and harnessed the horses for the two-day wagon ride to Philadelphia. He later returned to Forty Trees Relay Station with Anthony's borrowed horse and pack pony.

Anthony and Arte loaded the families' baggage and some food for the trip, and with many hugs and words of farewell, they were ready to leave. Jonathan's family and friends walked beside the wagon to the city entrance and then stood beside the gate as it left the city. The young women from the guild gathered, many standing with their fathers and mothers too. A large crowd waved and blew kisses. Miriam and Anthony waved back.

Grace said, "That's goodbye, Mommy?" She wore a little bonnet to keep the early summer sun out of her eyes.

"Yes, my dear, we won't see them for a long time. We are going to a new house."

They were silent for a long time after they lost sight of their family and friends waving goodbye. Miriam turned around to wave one last time. She couldn't imagine it—tears were coming to her eyes! A year ago, the last thing she would have expected was sadness at saying goodbye to anybody in Thyatira.

As they rode, Anthony explained what had happened. "Today is the second day Servius is acting as the new commander of the Garrison of Sardis. He wanted me to return to Sardis, which would have meant I would be serving under his control. However, last Thursday, I received orders from Commander Felicior. A difficult assignment awaits me in Philadelphia. I'll not be under the heavy thumb I felt on me every day, whether I was with Servius in his office or on the road."

He held on as the wagon bounced. *I won't tell Miriam about Servius. He is upset by my not saying, "Caesar is lord and god." Nor all the other things he said against me. That would just cause worry for her.*

"What kind of a thumb? A thick one with callouses?"

"You don't want to know about him," Anthony replied. "Let's talk about you."

"Well, my dear, I had my twenty-eighth birthday without you and our second anniversary too." Miriam sighed. "There's so much to tell you. First, there was a wedding. I didn't like the way my cousin got married—but I'll tell you about that later. Two babies were born. You didn't meet Hulda, a woman who is sick in bed. Always tired and despondent, all we heard about her was this: 'She is never improving.' If you had been there, you would have witnessed people constantly coming and going from Uncle Jonathan's house. I have many long stories. So much has happened! And now I'm upset about Nikias dying at Uncle Jonathan's farm."

"We have lots of time for every detail! What about the Thyatira synagogue?"

"The Jews at the synagogue couldn't decide on how to treat Uncle Jonathan, but because of Sibyl's detrimental influence, they said the Way of Truth Assembly can't meet at the portico anymore! Can you believe that Sibyl calls herself a prophetess? A few things she said did come true, but most don't! I'm afraid she's led more than just a few people on immoral paths. Uncle Jonathan was stopped from participating in services at the synagogue, and he has pretty much stopped going to worship times."

"That's a big story! And not a pleasant one, I can tell."

"The happenings in the synagogue and in Uncle Jonathan's house... I tried to write it all in my letters but couldn't begin to tell you everything."

"Me too," he said. "I can't wait to tell you about the villages all around Thyatira!" Anthony described his future assignment. "Now we're supposed to keep the roads safe all the way to Laodicea. There are some bad situations, and that puts pressure on the road security soldiers. That will now be my team and me."

Grace bounced up and down, pointing at dozens of horses grazing at the relay station they were passing. She said, "Horses, horses, Mommy?"

"Yes, dear," she said, pointing to them, "horses, nice horses."

"Tracking the bandits has been tricky. They have a clever leader. He got away from us just when we had caught up to him."

Miriam asked a question that had been on her mind since she received Anthony's letter. "Felicior called you to catch bandits in Philadelphia. Why?"

"Felicior believes they may be the leaders of the band I was chasing, Craga and three others. He thinks they are behind the latest road robbery. Plus, there are riots and demonstrations by farmers in the area that require more soldiers to control them than he had available."

Grace wanted to sit in Anthony's lap, so he rubbed his nose against her cheek and said, "Little Chrysa Grace, your daddy missed you so much. My, you grew up so much in one year!"

Turning to Miriam, he added, "Do you remember what I said two years ago? We were coming from Pergamum, and I said, 'It's amazing what your grandfather did despite constant persecution.' I told Nikias about Antipas and how he trained people. Then Nikias got into Antipas's notes and became very enthusiastic. He wanted to imitate Antipas, even without the full cooperation of his brothers. Friday I collected all of Antipas's scrolls, letters, and diaries when I passed through Olive Grove. Look how full this cart is! Clothes? Hardly any, but I'm bringing almost everything from your grandfather's library! I left the business scrolls at the farm. How did I become part of such a family, where books and scrolls are more important than clothing and jewelry?"

She poked him good-naturedly in the ribs.

Neither said anything for a while. They were enthralled by colorful scenes of village people bent over working the land and weeding the crops. Women worked in large groups. On their left, Mount Gordus touched the sky.

Miriam came back to his earlier comments. "Yes, God's power in Grandpa's life was very evident. He used his time well. He kept two shops in Pergamum, trained people, and cared for widows. For eighteen years, he led worship; built businesses; taught, baptized, and trained new leaders; helped the poor; and taught men to make copies of scrolls. He loaned money without interest and never stopped training scribes or sending people to preach to the cities north of Pergamum. He led an establishment with almost forty houses built for the workers. Yes, it was amazing."

Anthony asked, already knowing the answer, "And you still miss him?"

"Oh yes, I miss him so much. At first I thought of him every day and cried for what they did to him. Now when I think of him, I'm proud of him as well as sad. I think my feelings have changed. I see how much he did, and I'm thankful to have been part of his home."

Anthony added, "For me, it was an atmosphere of love, care, and devotion, not just in his house with you but in the assembly that met there."

"Well, it was my home, so it was natural," she said. "However, after having lived in Sardis and then in Thyatira, I know an atmosphere like that doesn't just happen. It's hard to foster love between people. People feel anxious about so many things. Grandpa Antipas was patient you know. I still wonder that he never cursed his enemies. He was able to bless them, even with his dying breath.

"I'm sad he didn't die a natural death. But Pergamum's temples and priests couldn't crush his spirit. He would not yield to their pressures, even if doing so would have saved his life."

They were close to Green Valley Inn and had been continuously talking. "Well, from what I've read from your letters and from what I saw at dinner last night, you take after Antipas a lot! You took the story of God's covenant, his wisdom, and the life of Yeshua Messiah to the workers in a Thyatira guild. I heard someone say that the Guild of Purple Honors is one of the three most important social groups there."

Miriam beamed while holding their little girl. Grace made funny noises when the wagon jostled on the uneven roadway stones as they went down a small hill. From there, the road ran close to the mountain. During a moment of quiet, words for a song came together in her mind.

Anthony pursuing thieves, riding north and south.
Chasing dishonest crooks who assumed strange names.
Letters could not express the words that filled my mouth.
Outlaws captured; slaves set free: This has gained you fame.

Yearning for friends, my face was darkened with a frown.
I often felt alone; then a poor boy needed love.
His mother changed. Fear no longer holds her down.
Friends learned to praise the Lord, to sing of God above.

Leaving feelings of being sad alone, I joyfully bend my knee.
I gained power through praises as hardships came to me.

Anthony interrupted her thoughts. "I heard two fathers of the young women talking last night. One said, 'These people really love one another. Look at the difference it makes! Did you ever hear of anyone coming to the insulae to teach handicapped children?' Miriam, you'll have to tell me how you taught all those people about acceptance and forgiveness."

She laughed, playing with Grace's little hands. "Yes, there's so much to talk about!"

On the lower slopes of the mountain, olive trees grew in large orchards planted in straight lines. Villagers pruned the trees, clearing out the least unproductive branches in preparation for summer growth.

"Look, Grace," he said, pointing toward the mountain. "See

those people cutting the branches? You won't understand, but a tree has to be pruned until it looks bare. Then, after a year, branches grow out again. They produce good olives again. Miriam, I think the Lord is cutting branches out of my life."

Miriam looked at him with a question on her face. "What's being cut out?"

Anthony responded quickly. "He took you away from me for a year! Now, what does a man's life look like when he has been pruned? If I'm cutting an olive tree, that means harvest time is just ahead."

Grace echoed, "Cutting trees? Daddy cutting trees?"

"No, Gracie," he said, laughing. "It's taken me two years to discover that during suffering, I communicate more with God. I don't get to write the end of my story. He is writing the book of our lives. That's too much for you to understand now, but someday I'll explain it all to you."

Miriam loved having him by her side talking about everything and anything. However, there was something in his voice, in his meaning, she didn't understand. "Anthony, are we safe now? Are you safe with Commander Felicior? I think you're worried about something."

He looked straight ahead. *Miriam will be afraid if I say anything about the threats Servius served up as if they were portions of meat ready to chew on. Are they real threats, or is he bluffing? I don't yet understand the new risks regarding 'The Gate.' I've never been to Philadelphia!*

He avoided her questions. "Do you want to hear something funny? My new military name is Antha, short for Anthony." He told her how they had learned about the robbers' names. "Omerod, in a flash of imagination, gave himself a new name, 'Oma.' Menandro became 'Muna.' Sextilius, who was the sixth child born in his family, got a new name too: 'Sexta.'"

"Who gave you the name 'Antha'?"

"Omerod did that. He said, 'The newest leader in our fake gang is Antha, named after the greatest foe Augustus Caesar ever had to battle.' That was me of course. Then he added, 'Antha has a wife from Alexandria, Egypt, just like the original Anthony took Queen Cleopatra.' Amazingly, that reassured the supervisor buying the slaves at the mine."

"What! What did Omerod say my name was?"

"He said, 'Antha married Cleopatra.' Brilliant!"

"Your right-hand man calls me 'Cleopatra'?"

"Yes, but don't worry. He is a good-natured fellow, and you'll enjoy meeting him."

Miriam became serious. "Anthony, about living with Amos and Abigail, I want to talk about a serious issue. Although Uncle Jonathan sent a notice of our arrival, I'm not sure they will take us in. Abigail was deeply stricken by the loss of her children during the siege of Jerusalem. Marcos probably told Amos that you are a soldier...."

Anthony went back to a prayer he first made in Sardis many months before. *Lord, let me see Abigail face to face. I want to say the words she needs to hear. You gave me a special message when we lived in Sardis. Abigail is wounded. She lost six of her seven children. Miriam said Abigail still lives with trauma after the siege. Let me speak to her!*

He put his arm around Miriam and spoke softly. "I want to speak with Abigail, to tell her my feelings of loss for the deaths of her children during the siege of Jerusalem. Here we are, going to Philadelphia, named for 'The Brothers Who Loved Each Other'! The memory of two brothers lives forever because others witnessed their love. Do you think brotherly love is so rare that a city has to be named for it once it happens? Do you believe that agape love can overcome deep sorrows? Even the sorrows from the terrible loss that Abigail came to know?

"We also have to pray that something works out for Ateas and Arpoxa. Sardis will be no problem if they want to return there, and I'm sure you would like to have Arpoxa in Philadelphia as a friend. I think they would be very lonely in Thyatira. They are both good workers but restricted in what they can work on."

He pulled her closer. "Miriam, Philadelphia will be our city of love. Your uncle and aunt, your cousin live there. This will become our city. I'll stay there, working with Felicior. You'll have our babies there. Afterward, we can retire in Philippi on my farm."

The wagon bumped along the stone-paved road. They passed a caravan of camels moving slowly. Their horses felt the heat of summer, and sweat shone on strong dark brown necks. Grace intently watched a flock of sheep. The animals were bunched up together, ambling from one pasture to another.

Miriam looked up at him and said contentedly, "Anthony, this journey is too short for me to tell you everything that happened. I learned that nothing is as simple as it appears at the first glance. Fame and fortune, position, and prestige—those are what people want, but when you look closer, the truth is different. Melpone's name meant tragedy, yet her life is a blessing to many. People in the city thought that Bassos was their hero, yet Arte told me the latest gossip going around the slaves' grapevine. It's reported that Bassos, the richest, most honored man in Thyatira, won't be charged for breaking the law. He is known as the benefactor. He'll find a way to avoid any criminal accusation."

Anthony already was on top of that choice bit of news. *During questioning by Servius, Bassos claimed he bought the animals and prizes from some unknown stranger. He claims that he had no idea that a criminal gang was involved.*

"Yes, things like that happen. Imagine a wealthy man using disreputable means to stay wealthy or just to seek being honored! Now, do you remember the everyday phrase used in Sardis? Never enough gold. Probably they use it in other cities too. You gave me an alternate phrase, and it has been with me every day this past year: Never enough love. Take your time as you tell me each story, my love. My stories of army experiences don't involve honor and fame. No, they are about deceit and corruption. I'd rather hear your stories. Start from the very first day and tell me everything, in the order that it happened, so that I can understand it all. Don't leave out the details. Agreed?"

She snuggled up close to him. "Yes, agreed."

They turned right onto the pathway leading to Green Valley Inn, where they would stay for the night. "That phrase gave me hope," she said. "That's what I thought of so many times when I was lonely during the past months: Never enough love."

She looked up at him, pulled him close, and then whispered, "Your love has changed me in so many ways, and being with you is the greatest honor I could ever have. Yes, your love is the best honor of all."

MAKING SENSE OF THE NOVEL AND THINKING ABOUT
PURPLE HONORS: A CHRONICLE OF THYATIRA

The following questions will help the reader to consider how each character in the novel fits within the overall story. Some characters will continue throughout the set of seven books. It is helpful to consider the motives and experiences that drive them.

1. Anthony and Miriam, the two principal persons in this novel, are reunited after one year of being separated. Although Anthony's challenges come from his duties in the army and Miriam's from living in the city of Thyatira, both show themselves to be leaders. What aspects of their characters make them successful in such diverse situations? Think about your life: Can you describe your responses to conditions that made you successful at various points in your life?

2. Considering Miriam's relationships in Thyatira, how does she develop friendship with each person in the Ben Shelah household? Consider:
> Jonathan and Rebekah
> Bani and Serah
> Gil and Danila
> Arte

What approach do you take toward the various personalities in your family circle?

3. Becoming friends with Melpone and the young women at the Guild of Purple Workers took time and effort. How did Miriam develop her relationship with each person? Consider:
> Melpone, Aulus, and Kiron
> Adelpha, Dreama, Hesper, Koren, Calandra, Neoma, Celina, and
> Hypatia, the women workers in the guild

How do you develop new relationships?

4. Miriam's most challenging relationship in Thyatira was with Sibyl. What was the basis for the conflict between them, and why did others not have the same degree of tension with Sibyl?
How do you manage conflicts with people who have different

attitudes toward life?

5. In this novel, we find several approaches toward wealth, status, and popularity. Consider:
>   Mayor Aurelius Tatianos
>   Fabius Bassos, the Benefactor
>   Kilan, the leader of the synagogue
>   Jonathan Ben Shelah, the head of a family
>   Miriam, a guest in a large manufacturing city

What kind of emphasis do you place on these three facets of life?

6. The Roman military was charged with keeping peace in the provinces. Each of the three commanding officers had his own personality. What were the main motivations of each person? How do personal motives influence the outcome of a story? Consider:
>   Commander Servius Callistratus in Soma
>   Commander Felicior Priscus in Sardis
>   Commander Diogenes Elpis in Aizanoi

7. A large part of the novel deals with gaining information and insights. How are skills and knowledge passed on and received in these groups?
>   In the army, think about Anthony.
>   In the criminals' gang, consider Craga.
>   In Thyatira, consider Miriam.
>   In Olive Grove, consider Nikias.

How do you gather information, and what difference does it make in your life or the lives of others?

8. Nikias is an essential person in the novel. Think about him and show how he enters the story at each point of his life. What are his strengths, and what are his weaknesses?

What are your strengths and weaknesses? How do they affect those people with whom you interact every day?

9. Success and failure are significant themes in the book. Commander Servius Callistratus in Soma and Commander Felicior Priscus in Sardis both demand success. How do they differ in their understanding of a victorious soldier? To what extent is Miriam a success or a failure as a guest in Thyatira?

10. How was the gospel about the Jewish Messiah made clear to various individuals?
    Jonathan and Rebekah
    Gil and Danila
    Melpone and her father
    Ateas and Arpoxa
    Sibyl Sambathe and her sister, Hulda

If you enjoyed this book,
please consider ranking it on Amazon or another book site
and posting a brief review.
You can also mention it on social media.
Please contact the author at:

Century One Chronicles,
PO Box 25013, Morningside Avenue PO
255 Morningside Avenue,
Toronto, ON M1E 0A7 Canada

If you would like a Zoom visit to your book club
or an interview for your blog:

centuryonechronicles@gmail.com

Website:

https://sites.google.com/thechroniclesofcourage.com/chroniclesofcourage/home

THYATIRA, GAIUS, AND DIOTREPHES IN THE BIBLE

Revelation 2:18–29

To the Angel of the church in Thyatira, write:

These are the words of the Son of God, whose eyes are like blazing fire and whose feet are like burnished bronze. I know your deeds, your love and faith, your service and perseverance, and that you are now doing more than you did at first.

Nevertheless, I have this against you. You tolerate that woman Jezebel, who calls herself a prophetess. By her teaching she misleads my servants into sexual immorality and the eating of food sacrificed to idols. I have given her time to repent of her immorality, but she is unwilling. So I will cast her on a bed of suffering, and I will make those who commit adultery with her suffer intensely, unless they repent of her ways. I will strike her children dead. Then all the churches will know that I am he who searches hearts and minds, and I will repay each of you according to your deeds. Now I say to the rest of you in Thyatira, to you who do not hold to her teaching and have not learned Satan's so-called deep secrets (I will not impose any other burden on you): Only hold on to what you have until I come.

To him who overcomes and does my will to the end, I will give authority over the nations—He will rule them with an iron scepter, he will dash them to pieces like pottery—just as I have received authority from my Father. I will also give him the morning star. He who has an ear, let him hear what the Spirit says to the churches.

3 John 1–13

The elder,

To my dear friend, Gaius, whom I love in the truth.

Dear friend, I pray that you may enjoy good health and that all may go well with you, even as your soul is getting along well. It gave me great joy to have some brothers come and tell me about your faithfulness to the truth and how you continue to walk in the truth. I have no greater joy than to hear that my children are walking in the truth.

Dear friend, you are faithful in what you are doing for the brothers, even though they are strangers to you. They have told the church about your love. You will do well to send them on their way in a manner worthy of God. It was for the sake of the Name that they went out, receiving no help from the pagans. We ought therefore to show hospitality to such men so that we may work together for the truth.

I wrote to the church, but **Diotrephes**, *who loves to be first, will have nothing to do with us. So if I come, I will call attention to what he is doing, gossiping maliciously about us. Not satisfied with that, he refuses to welcome the brothers. He also stops those who want to do so and puts them out of the church.*

Dear friend, do not imitate what is evil but what is good. Anyone who does what is good is from God. Anyone who does what is evil has not seen God. Demetrius is well spoken of by everyone— and even by the truth itself. We also speak well of him, and you know that our testimony is true.

I have much to write to you, but I do not want to do so with pen and ink. I hope to see you soon, and we will talk face to face.

Peace to you. The friends here send their greetings. Greet the friends there by name.

HEARTBEATS OF COURAGE

Book Four

Inn of the Open Door
A Chronicle of Philadelphia

Chapter 1
Disturbance at the Gates

THE TOWN OF SASTORA, ASIA MINOR

Thelma placed her foot firmly against the rough pavement, pushing back as hard as she could. Still the angry, noisy mob behind her kept shoving her forward toward the soldiers. Beside her stood a stout man who was trying to protect her.

"Now I'm sorry that I brought you to the demonstration!" Rastus yelled, but it was hard to hear him, even with his mouth close to the young woman's ear. He was the town's baker, and like everyone else in Sasorta, he had run out of wheat.

Ordinary people from Sasorta shouted for the storehouses to be opened but were not prepared to push against soldiers holding lances and swords. Between the crowd and the grain storehouses behind the civic buildings were a dozen soldiers ordered to keep them out.

Shoved from behind, Rastus stepped on Thelma's foot, but in the clamor, no one heard her sharp cry of pain.

"Sorry," he shouted, "I didn't mean to hurt you, but I hoped they might give us access to the grain today. The situation is worse here in Sasorta than the town where you came from." His voice was drowned out by constant commotion. Irate men kept elbowing toward the guards, preventing access to the town's grain storage facility.

Thelma was facing one of the soldiers guarding the gate. Sweat poured down his forehead under a bright, shiny helmet. He rode a black horse, and his knuckles were white as he gripped his sword, hoping he would not have to use it on unshaven men and chanting women who demanded access to the grain bins. He kicked the horse's ribs with his heels, keeping it faced toward the incensed throng.

Fear was in Thelma's eyes as she loosened her grip on Rastus's arm. She wanted him to hear her thoughts, but the shouting of the crowd was too raucous. *Why did he bring me here? Can't he see that the guards will keep everyone away from the storehouses? What can a few hundred farmers do against a dozen armed soldiers?*

A man pushed Thelma forward, and she lost her balance, falling badly. Standing up, she bumped into a man holding a sharpened stick. Starving villagers waved farm tools and table knives. A councilman barged past Thelma, shoving her backward and yelling at the soldiers. "I'm one of the businessmen who make decisions here in Sasorta, and our children have nothing to eat!"

The soldier with red feathers on his legionary's helmet snarled, "Keep back, councilman, or a sword will slit your throat! No one gets into the emergency food storage area until the mayor of Philadelphia gives the order, and that will not come today!"

People turned around as they heard a horse rushing toward the soldiers. Thelma looked at the rider's face, stifled a scream, and grabbed at Rastus. The young man on a horse plowed through the crowd, and the mob parted to let him pass.

"Let us go to the grain bins!" he screamed. Clad in a workman's light brown tunic, his eyes bulging and one hand sweeping the air, he threatened the guards. "You're bluffing, and you won't keep us out!"

The young rider was no more than twenty years of age. His pale brown horse approached the line of guards, its nostrils quivering. As the horse reared up, unable to go on, the young man slid backward, falling heavily to the ground. Shouts and yelling resounded in the town square. The horse, off-balance, saw the point of a lance, tried to turn backward, and landed heavily on the young man's chest. The animal struggled to its feet, turned to one side, and trotted off, its ears twitching and tail swishing.

Thelma ran toward the young man. "No!" Her long scream was a shrill cry for help. Few heard her above the uproar. She sobbed, begging anyone to help the limp figure lying on the polished marble pavement. "Come help him! He's injured." Blood started seeped from his mouth, a sign of internal injuries. His chest had been crushed, and he was unconscious.

Men screamed, "We want food! We demand work!"

However, they would not be satisfied today. Rome always held the upper hand.

An hour passed before the crowd thinned out. Thelma, with tears streaming down her face, began to scream. Then she whimpered, crying mournfully as the man lying on the pavement stopped breathing. Her urgent cries for help were of no use.

"Rastus," she gasped, "look! My husband! He's dead!" She gazed at the lifeless body on the ground. "Oh, my dear husband! Why did you do that?"

THE ENTRANCE TO PHILADELPHIA, ASIA MINOR

Miriam closed her eyes, flinching as the scene flashed by again in her mind. Earlier, when Anthony, Miriam, and Grace had reached Sasorta, they had heard wild cries. The raucous mob was gathered in front of the civic buildings. The screams still echoed in her mind. She had not seen the woman crying beside the man who got crushed, but Anthony told her about the accident when he got back onto the wagon.

Later, as they arrived in Philadelphia, they passed the homes of thousands of families who lived outside the city walls. Squalor was everywhere. Two- and three-storied humble apartment buildings known as *insulae* were crowded close together, leaving little breathing space. Children played near stinking open sewers. Grace, who was two years old, cringed as she pointed to hungry dogs slinking along the walls.

As they entered the city, the Valley Gate guards examined the wagon. "We come from Thyatira," said Anthony. "I'm an army soldier assigned to the Philadelphia Garrison. I'm moving my family from Thyatira. This document is Commander Felicior's order for the transfer. This is my wife, Miriam, and the little girl is our daughter. This wagon contains our clothing and a collection of scrolls. Our first stop in the city will be the garrison."

The guards were satisfied and let the wagon pass into the city.

Hundreds, perhaps thousands, of people were walking along the streets of Philadelphia. Sellers hawked their wares, hoping for a few more sales at the end of the day. Donkeys brayed, and merchants cursed their camels, telling them to move more quickly. The Avenue of Philadelphia was crowded, full of people, animals, pedestrians, and four-wheeled carts. Farmers sold vegetables and fruit, shouting and raising their voices until they clinched a favorable price. Then, shaking hands with their customer as they sealed a favorable deal, they smiled broadly.

Two merchants had just finished the long, three-day walk from Laodicea and Hierapolis. They laughed, slapping each other on the shoulder as they sat drinking beer outside a tavern. Miriam watched their camels, which had lined up for fresh mountain water after a long walk over the Messogis mountain pass. Slaves owned by the merchants stood beside the camels. Their animals knelt awkwardly, descending first to their front knees and then throwing their weight toward the rear and onto their back legs and knees. The merchants had passed through "The Door." It was a tricky section where the road from Laodicea twisted and turned on its way through a high mountain pass and then down into the Cogamis Valley.

Many buildings that had collapsed during earthquakes decades ago still lay in awkward, broken piles. The people remembered the scores of deaths that resulted and were reluctant to clear the land and rebuild. Miriam stared at one of the ruins. The buckled roof seemed ready to cave in, so no one lived in it. It had been elegant at one time. Robust and thick stone walls suggested a wealthy family had lived there, but now it was vacant and neglected.[116]

When they reached the garrison compound, they were admitted after Anthony presented his documents to the guard. They were directed toward Commander Felicior's office. "Miriam, I will check in with Felicior and find out when he may want me to start work. Hopefully I will be right back, and we can continue on to Uncle Amos's home."

THE MILITARY GARRISON IN PHILADELPHIA

Commander Felicior Priscus turned from the window in his office to talk with Anthony Suros. The officer had thick, dark eyebrows, and his attentive eyes took in every detail. Like all officers in the army, Felicior was clean-shaven. His polished breastplate shone with two eagles in flight above two horses. This breastplate belonged to the Garrison of Philadelphia, and it had a special meaning. The Philadelphia Garrison had a specific task: to keep the Southern Road open and secure for merchants, farmers, and random travelers.

In the past, far too many robberies had taken place on the steep road connecting Philadelphia with Laodicea and Hierapolis as well

---

[116] The earthquake of AD 17, which struck Philadelphia and Sardis, made a profound mark on the contemporary world around the province of Asia and as far away as Rome. Citizens of Philadelphia were afraid to re-enter their homes long afterward because of aftershocks. Many lived outside the city walls for years. Further destruction took place in an earthquake centred near Laodicea in AD 60. Rebuilding was slow to begin.

as other cities farther east.

Felicior glanced out the window. He admired the plain to the east and taking in the first hint of the end of the day. The valley's bright green was dulled. He had two hours before dusk.

A square military table stood between them with three documents on it. The largest, a map held open with four lead weights, showed six small towns around Philadelphia. The most ornate scroll was an order from Emperor Domitian that was issued the previous summer:

"Half of the province's vineyards are to be torn out and replaced by grain crops to increase supply of food needs to Rome and Asia Minor."

The third was a scroll written only three days earlier by Commander Servius Callistratus. He had recently moved to Sardis to take control of the Sardis Garrison.

"Suros, I'm glad to see you've arrived! I wasn't expecting you until tomorrow morning. The other two members of your team, Bellinus and Omerod, came in on Saturday."

Felicior's sharp gaze held those he addressed. His low, raspy voice added to his sense of authority. "I'm glad you came in a little early. We need all the help we can get." He held up the letter from Sardis. "Commander Servius is not satisfied with your previous mission, Suros." Felicior stood erect behind his desk, waiting for a reply.

AFTERWORD

How did a tiny group of followers of Yeshua Messiah not only survive persecution in the Roman Empire but continue to grow in number despite pain and suffering? How did their faith in a Jewish Messiah spread, reaching both rich and poor, men and women, Jews and non-Jews, slaves and free?

Such thoughts intrigued me while living in Turkey, with its 5,600 archaeological sites. My teenage interest in the Roman Empire as a boy in Kenya, Africa, returned. Later I was blessed with other teachers who made history come alive.

Turkey's unique geographical features are enhanced with the lasting beauty of changing seasons. The visual attractiveness of the land is deeply satisfying. The country is famously known for millions of tourists who arrive each year. Seeing this opportunity, I joined others in promoting faith tourism, which is important to the country. Tourist groups I hosted wanted to spend time at the sites of seven ancient cities.

At the end of each day, we relaxed and often engaged in questions and discussions. Having explored Troy one time as a tour group, we sat down for a fish dinner. We searched our imaginations to describe people who might have lived there three thousand years ago. What were their professions? What happened at the port every day, and who built the buildings?

Out of those conversations came a strong impulse to go beyond the stones strewn over the ground and imagine an ancient city throbbing with all sorts of people. From this came the idea of Antipas being the central character of a novel.

I wanted readers to travel in their imaginations, walk up and down steep streets, and learn to shop in crowded markets. What was it like to receive an invitation for a tasty meal in ancient homes? It was essential to meet living, breathing people. What were their hopes and fears, their politics, and their religious beliefs? I wanted to understand their conflicts and difficulties, their victories, and their defeats.

At first, I thought a single book would do. I had plans to describe each city, but it became clear that a single novel would not do justice to the geography, history, and civic functions. To examine the nature of Roman government and Greek culture would demand more than one book.

Three years passed before the story spanning seven novels had jelled in my mind. The seven books would weave elements of the seven letters of Revelation into the cultural background. Unlike the seven churches' order as they appear in the first chapters of the Book of Revelation, the narrative in this saga begins in Pergamum and ends in Ephesus.

At the conclusion of the story in the last book, *An Act of Grace: A Chronicle of Ephesus*, many characters from the earlier novels are brought face to face for a climactic ending.

If you have enjoyed this book, I hope you will take the time to post your thoughts in a customer review on Amazon.com and mention it on social media. Besides telling your friends about it, this is an effective way to spread the word about a book you enjoyed.

ACKNOWLEDGEMENTS

For years, my wife Cathie and I were privileged to live in Turkey. We learned to appreciate the commitment of present-day believers to Jesus Christ. We have friends who live in the same region as these seven novels. Our Turkish friends encouraged me in ways they will never know.

During those years in Turkey, many Turkish citizens offered us friendship and hospitality. They not only helped me to enjoy their country but they made us feel safe. My thanks to them for helping us to learn about their way of life. Frequently, we switched to topics that helped us understand the history of their land.

Archaeologists continue to excavate numerous ancient cities in Turkey. These researchers' findings supplied dates, names, and details for cities and towns mentioned in these seven novels.

Museum staff were delighted to have interested visitors examine their displays. They passed on much helpful information. I am grateful to the countless scores of people who enriched my life in the locations mentioned in these novels. Without their help, none of this would have been written.

During my high school years, I was blessed by capable history teachers at Rift Valley Academy, Kenya. Dr. Ian Rennie at Regent College, University of British Columbia, guided me in historical research at a critical time in my life. He demanded accuracy, which was character-forming.

Several friends provided the impetus for creating the storyline and bringing it to a conclusion. Blair Clark worked with me for several years, especially in coordinating faith tourism. Raye Han, a Turkish tour guide of boundless enthusiasm, taught us about her country, giving endless details and sharing a spiritual passion. Visitors to Turkey were amazed at her professionalism as well as that of other tour guides.

Friends at the City of David Messianic Synagogue in Toronto,

Canada, contributed much to the Jewish aspect. I am thankful to each one in this Messianic congregation. Through them, I became aware of various aspects of Jewish life and thought, and they helped to build me up in my faith.

Without the help of Jerry Whittaker as an editor, these books would not have made it to the press. No one could wish for a more capable and discerning friend. His creative suggestions and analysis improved the storyline and character development at each stage.

Friends and family members enriched the story through their comments. Robert, Elizabeth, Samuel, and Aimee Lumkes offered unique inter-generational feedback. Pearl Thomas, Anne Clark, Magdalena Smith, John Forrester, Susan and Max Debeeson, George Bristow, Noreen Wilson, Frank Martin, Ken Wakefield, Lou Mulligan, George Jakeway, and Michael Thoss provided helpful opinions as early readers.

Other support came from friends and churches; their names are found in the Book of Life, and my appreciation extends to each one.

Daphne Parsekian graciously became my final editor, and I am grateful for her careful reading and her willing spirit in going through the final steps before sending this manuscript to the printers. She helped me immensely.

Finally, my wife Cathie has been patient with me through the many ups and downs while working on these manuscripts. No words can fully express my appreciation for her unending encouragement.

Appendix
Thyatira: 300 BC – 1923

BC

300   The town was known as Pelopia, a small town under the control of Lysimachus.

290   King Seleucid I Nicator, from Antioch, captured the town and renamed it Thyatira, meaning "Daughter" (or perhaps this was an ancient Lydian name).

262   Thyatira came under the control of the Kingdom of Pergamum as an outpost against the Seleucid Kingdom when King Eumenes I defeated King Antiochus I near Sardis.

262–190 Thyatira suffered constant reverses in the struggle between the Kingdom of Pergamum and the Seleucid Kingdom, probably changing hands several times.

133   War between Prusa (modern-day city of Bursa, Turkey) and General Sulla from Rome

26   With the arrival of *Pax Romana* under Caesar Augustus, Thyatira grew as a manufacturing and marketing center. Inscriptions mention these guilds: bronzesmiths, bakers, leatherworkers, tanners, woolworkers, linen-workers, potters, dyers, and outer garments.

AD

46   Lydia, from Thyatira and a seller of purple, accepted the Christian message in Philippi.

50–60 Growth of a Christian congregation

95   A letter to Thyatira is written in the Apocalypse

100–200 Growth of the city as a major manufacturing and marketing center. Historically, a Christian fellowship in Thyatira was important enough to be listed among those addressed by Jesus Christ in John's Revelation. Pergamum experienced persecution periodically until the year AD 313. After the rule of Constantine, this church became the center of an active bishopric. Several bishops from the city are known through the history of the Greek Orthodox Church.

366   Roman Emperor Valens defeated Procopius, a pretender
        to the Empire, near Thyatira
1453   The city gradually decreased in power and influence, long
        before the fall of Constantinople. Under the Ottomans, the
        population was entirely Muslim.
1919   Under Turkish Ottomans, Thyatira was changed to
        Akhisar or White Castle.
1922   The Greek Orthodox Church appointed an Exarch for
        Thyatira

Present Day: The city's population is 100,000, about the same as
at the end of the first century.

Excavations of Ancient Thyatira

Only a tiny section of Thyatira has been excavated. Many visitors
find it to be the least satisfying ruins of the Seven Cities. A
government agency permits entrance into the open-air museum.
The walls of an ancient basilica, built about AD 500, can be
examined. Also, a portion of the agora, or marketplace, is
identifiable. Remains of the Triple Arch at the center of the city
have been reassembled on its ancient site. These ruins are visible
at the center of the main thoroughfare through the modern city.

Made in United States
North Haven, CT
22 October 2022

25775736R00246